P9-CEU-080

The most exciting things to happen in Dullsville in my lifetime, in chronological order:

1. The 3:10 train jumped its tracks, spilling boxes of Tootsie Rolls, which we devoured.

2. A senior flushed a cherry bomb down the toilet, exploding the sewage line, closing school for a week.

3. On my sixteenth birthday a family rumored to be vampires moved into the haunted Mansion on top of Benson Hill!

PRAISE FOR

Vampire Kisses

An ALA Quick Pick for Young Adult Readers
A New York Public Library Book for the Teen Age

"All in all, a good read for those who want a vampire love story without the gore." —*School Library Journal*

"As in her *Teenage Mermaid*, Schreiber adds some refreshing twists to genre archetypes and modern-day stereotypes."
—*Publishers Weekly*

"Horror hooks such as a haunted mansion, a romantic teenage vampire, and a dark heroine who wins against the golden guys make this a title that readers will bite into with Goth gusto." —*The Bulletin of the Center for Children's Books*

"Schreiber uses a careful balance of humor, irony, pathos, and romance as she develops a plot that introduces the possibility of a real vampire." —ALA *Booklist*

Kissing Coffins
Vampire Kisses 2

"Raven is exactly the kind of girl a Goth can look up to."
—*Morbid Outlook* magazine

"Readers will love this funny novel with bite!"
—*Wow* magazine

Vampireville
Vampire Kisses 3

"A fun, fast read for vampire fans."—*School Library Journal*

Dance with a Vampire
Vampire Kisses 4

"This novel, like the first three, is never short on laughs and shudders. Alexander is as romantic as ever, and Raven is still delightfully earthy. Schreiber again concocts a lively and suspenseful story that ends on a tantalizing cliffhanger. Fans of the series will be anxious to find out whether Raven's relationship with Alexander will survive."
—*VOYA*

"A good choice for Goth lovers and fans of romantic vampire stories."
—*School Library Journal*

Also by Ellen Schreiber

VAMPIRE KISSES 4: DANCE WITH A VAMPIRE

VAMPIRE KISSES 5: THE COFFIN CLUB

VAMPIRE KISSES 6: ROYAL BLOOD

TEENAGE MERMAID

COMEDY GIRL

VAMPIRE KISSES: BLOOD RELATIVES

Ellen Schreiber

Vampire Kisses: The Beginning

Vampire Kisses

◆

Vampire Kisses 2: Kissing Coffins

◆

Vampire Kisses 3: Vampireville

KATHERINE TEGEN BOOKS
An Imprint of HarperCollins Publishers

Katherine Tegen Books is an imprint of HarperCollins Publishers.

Vampire Kisses: The Beginning
Copyright © 2009 by Ellen Schreiber
All rights reserved. Printed in the United States of America.
No part of this book may be used or reproduced in any manner whatsoever without
written permission except in the case of brief quotations embodied in critical articles
and reviews. For information address HarperCollins Children's Books, a division of
HarperCollins Publishers, 10 East 53rd Street, New York, NY 10022.
www.harperteen.com
Originally published in separate volumes as *Vampire Kisses* (2003),
Vampire Kisses 2: Kissing Coffins (2005), and *Vampire Kisses 3: Vampireville* (2006).

Library of Congress Cataloging-in-Publication Data is available.
ISBN 978-0-06-177894-0

Typography by Sasha Illingworth
09 10 11 12 13 LP/RRDH 10 9 8 7 6 5 4 3 2
❖
First Edition

CONTENTS

To my father, Gary Schreiber,
with all my love;
for giving me the wings to fly.

"I want a relationship
I can finally sink my teeth into."
—Alexander Sterling

B.L.4.1
Pts 6

It first happened when I was five.

I had just finished coloring in *My Kindergarten Book*. It was filled with Picasso-like drawings of my mom and dad, an Elmer's-glued, tissue-papered collage, and the answers to questions (favorite color, pets, best friend, etc.) written down by our hundred-year-old teacher, Mrs. Peevish.

My classmates and I were sitting in a semicircle on the floor in the reading area. "Bradley, what do you want to be when you grow up?" Mrs. Peevish asked after all the other questions had been answered.

"A fire fighter!" he shouted.

"Cindi?"

"Uh . . . a nurse," Cindi Warren whispered meekly.

Mrs. Peevish went through the rest of the class. Police officers. Astronauts. Football players. Finally it was my turn.

"Raven, what do you want to be when you grow up?" Mrs. Peevish asked, her green eyes staring through me.

I said nothing.

"An actress?"

I shook my head.

"A doctor?"

"Nuh, uh," I said.

"A flight attendant?"

"Yuck!" I replied.

"Then what?" she asked, annoyed.

I thought for a moment. "I want to be . . ."

"Yes?"

"I want to be . . . a vampire!" I shouted, to the shock and amazement of Mrs. Peevish and my classmates. For a moment I thought she started to laugh; maybe she really did. The children sitting next to me inched away.

I spent most of my childhood watching others inch away.

I was conceived on my dad's water bed—or on the rooftop of my mom's college dorm under twinkling stars—depending on which one of my parents is telling the story. They were soul mates that couldn't part with the seventies: true love mixed with drugs, some raspberry incense, and the music of the Grateful Dead. A beaded-jeweled, halter-topped, cutoff blue-jeaned, barefooted girl, intertwined with a long-haired, unshaven, Elton John–spectacled, suntanned, leather-vested, bell-bottomed-and-sandaled guy. I think they're lucky I wasn't more eccentric. I could have wanted to be a beaded-haired hippie werewolf! But somehow I became obsessed with vampires.

Sarah and Paul Madison became more responsible after my entrance into this world—or I'll rephrase it and say my parents were "less glassy eyed." They sold the Volkswagen flower power van that they were living in and actually started renting property. Our hippie apartment was decorated with 3-D glow-in-the-dark flower posters and orange tubes with a Play-Doh substance that moved on its own—lava lamps—that you could stare at forever. It was the best time ever. The three of us laughed and played Chutes and Ladders, and squeezed Twinkies between our teeth. We stayed up late, watching Dracula movies, *Dark Shadows* with the infamous Barnabas Collins, and *Batman* on a black-and-white TV we'd received when we opened a bank account. I felt secure under the blanket of midnight, rubbing Mom's growing belly, which made noises like the orange lava lamps. I figured she was going to give birth to more moving Play-Doh.

Everything changed when she gave birth to the playdough—only it wasn't Play-Doh. She gave birth to Nerd Boy! How could she? How could she destroy all the Twinkie nights? Now she went to bed early, and that creation that my parents called "Billy" cried and fussed all night. I was suddenly alone. It was Dracula—the Dracula on TV—that kept me company while Mom slept, Nerd Boy wailed, and Dad changed smelly diapers in the darkness.

And if that wasn't bad enough, suddenly they sent me to a place that wasn't my apartment, that didn't have wild 3-D flower posters on the walls, but boring collages of kids' handprints. *Who decorates around here?* I wondered. It was overcrowded with Sears catalog girls in frilly dresses and Sears catalog boys in tapered pants and perfectly combed hair. Mom and Dad called it "kindergarten."

"They'll be your friends," my mom reassured me, as I clung to her side for dear life. She waved good-bye and blew me kisses as I stood alone beside the matronly Mrs. Peevish, which was as alone as one can get. I watched my mom walk away with Nerd Boy on her hip as she took him back to the place filled with glow-in-the-dark posters, monster movies, and Twinkies.

Somehow I made it through the day. Cutting and gluing black paper on black paper, finger painting Barbie's lips black, and telling the assistant teacher ghost stories, while the Sears catalog kids ran around like they were all cousins at an all-American family picnic. I was even happy to see Nerd Boy when Mom finally came to pick me up.

That night she found me with my lips pressed against the TV screen, trying to kiss Christopher Lee in *Horror of Dracula*.

"Raven! What are you doing up so late? You have school tomorrow!"

"What?" I said. The Hostess cherry pie that I had been eating fell to the floor, and my heart fell with it.

"But I thought it was just the one time?" I said, panicked.

"Sweet Raven. You have to go every day!"

Every day? The words echoed inside my head. It was a life sentence!

That night Nerd Boy couldn't hope to compete with my dramatic wailing and crying. As I lay alone in my bed, I prayed for eternal darkness and a sun that never rose.

Unfortunately the next day I awoke to a blinding light, and a monster headache.

I longed to be around at least one person that I could connect with. But I couldn't find any, at home or school. At home the lava lamps were replaced with Tiffany-style floor lamps, the glow-in-the-dark posters were covered with Laura Ashley wallpaper, and our grainy black-and-white TV was upgraded to a twenty-five-inch color model.

At school instead of singing the songs of *Mary Poppins*, I whistled the theme to *The Exorcist*.

Halfway through kindergarten I tried to become a vampire. Trevor Mitchell, a perfectly combed blond with sparkling green eyes, was my nemesis from the moment I stared him down when he tried to cut in front of me on the slide. He hated me, because I was the only kid who wasn't afraid of him. The kids and teachers kissed up to him, because his father owned most of the land their houses sat on. Trevor was in a biting phase, not because he wanted to be a vampire like me, but just because he was mean. He had taken pieces of flesh out of everyone but me. And I was starting to get ticked off!

We were on the playground, standing by the basketball hoop, when I pinched the skin of his puny little arm so hard I thought blood would squirt out. His face turned beet red. I stood motionless and waited. Trevor's body trembled with anger, and his eyes swelled with vengeance as I mischievously smiled back. Then he left his dental impressions in my expectant hand. Mrs. Peevish was forced to sit him against the school wall, and I happily danced around the playground, waiting to transform into a vampire bat.

"That Raven is an odd one," I overheard Mrs. Peevish saying to another teacher as I skipped past the crying Trevor, who was now throwing a fit against the hard black-top. I blew him a grateful kiss with my bitten hand.

I wore my wound proudly as I got on the school swing. I could fly now, right? But I'd need something to take me into warp speed. The seat went as high as the top of the fence, but I was aiming for the puffy clouds. The rusty swing started to buckle when I jumped off. I planned to fly across the playground—all the way to a startled Trevor. Instead I plummeted to the muddy earth, doing further damage to my tooth-marked hand. I cried more from the fact that I didn't possess super-natural powers like my heroes on TV than because of my throbbing flesh.

With my bite trapped under ice, Mrs. Peevish sat me against the wall to rest while the spoiled snot-nosed Trevor was now free to play. He blew me a teasing kiss and said, "Thank you." I stuck out my tongue and called him a name I had heard a mobster say in *The Godfather*. Mrs. Peevish immediately sent me inside. I was sent inside a lot during my childhood recesses. I was destined to take a recess from recess.

The official welcome sign to my town should read, "Welcome to Dullsville—bigger than a cave, but small enough to feel claustrophobic!"

A population of 8,000 look-alikes, a weather forecast that's perfectly miserable all year round—sunny—fenced in cookie-cutter houses, and sprawling farmland—that's Dullsville. The 8:10 freight train that runs through town separates the wrong side of the tracks from the right side, the cornfields from the golf course, the tractors from the golf carts. I think the town has it backward. How can land that grows corn and wheat be worth less than land filled with sand traps?

The hundred-year-old courthouse sits on the town square. I haven't gotten into enough trouble to be dragged there—yet. Boutiques, a travel agent, a computer store, a florist, and a second-run movie theater all sit happily around the square.

I wish our house could lie on the railroad tracks, on wheels, and carry us out of town, but we're on the right side near the country club. Dullsville. The only exciting place is an abandoned mansion an exiled baroness built on top of Benson Hill, where she died in isolation.

I have only one friend in Dullsville—a farm girl, Becky Miller, who is more unpopular than I am. I was in third grade when I officially met her. Sitting on the school steps waiting for my mom to pick me up (late as usual) now that she was trying to be a Corporate Cathy, I noticed an impish girl cowering at the bottom of the steps, crying like a baby. She didn't have any friends, since she was shy and lived on the east side of the tracks. She was one of the few farm girls in our school and sat two rows behind me in class.

"What's wrong?" I asked, feeling sorry for her.

"My mom forgot me!" she hollered, her hands covering her pathetic, wet face.

"No, she didn't," I consoled.

"She's never this late!" she cried.

"Maybe she's stuck in traffic."

"You think so?"

"Sure! Or maybe she got a call from one of those nosey sales people that always asks, 'Is your mother home?' "

"Really?"

"Happens all the time. Or maybe she had to stop for snacks, and there was a long line at 7-Eleven."

"Would she do that?"

"Why not, you have to eat, don't you? So never fear. She'll be here."

And sure enough, a blue pickup drove up with one apologetic mother and a friendly, fluffy sheepdog.

"My mom says you can come over Saturday if it's okay with your parents," Becky said, running back to me.

No one had ever invited me to their house before. I wasn't shy like Becky but I was just as unpopular. I was always late for school because I overslept; I wore sunglasses in class and I had opinions, atypical in Dullsville.

Becky had a backyard as big as Transylvania—a great place to hide and play monsters and eat all the fresh apples a growling third-grade stomach could hold. I was the only kid in our class who didn't beat her up, exclude her, or call her names, and I even kicked anyone who tried. She was my three-dimensional shadow. I was her best friend and her bodyguard. And still am.

When I wasn't playing with Becky, I spent my time applying black lipstick and nail polish, scuffing my already-worn combat boots, and burying my head behind Anne Rice novels. I was eleven when our family went to New Orleans for vacation. Mom and Dad wanted to play blackjack on the Flamingo riverboat casino. Nerd Boy wanted to go to the aquarium. But I knew where I was going: I wanted to visit the house of Anne Rice's birth, the historical homes she had restored, and the mansion she now called home.

I stood mesmerized outside its iron gate, a Gothic mega-mansion, my mom (my uninvited chaperone) by my side. I could sense ravens flying overhead, even though there probably weren't any. It was a shame I hadn't come at night—it would have been that much more beautiful. Several girls who looked just like me stood across the street, taking pictures. I wanted to rush over and say, "Be my friends. We can tour the cemeteries together!" It was the first time in my life I felt like I belonged. I was in the city where they stack coffins on top of one another so you can see them, instead of burying them deep within the earth. There were college guys with two-toned spiky blond hair. Funky people were everywhere, except on Bourbon Street, where the tourists looked like they'd flown in from Dullsville. Suddenly a limousine pulled around the corner. The blackest limo I had ever seen. The driver, complete with black chauffeur's hat, opened the door, and she stepped out!

I freaked and watched motionless, like time was standing still. Right before my eyes was my idol of all living idols, Anne Rice!

She glowed like a movie star, a Gothic angel, a heavenly creature. Her long black hair flowed over her shoulders and glistened; she wore a golden headband, a long, flowing silky skirt, and a fabulous vampirish, dark cloak. I was speechless. I thought I might go into shock.

Fortunately my mom's never speechless.

"Could my daughter please have your autograph?"

"Sure," the queen of nocturnal adventures sweetly replied.

I walked toward her, as if my marshmallow legs would melt under the sun at any moment.

After she signed a yellow Post-it note my mom found in her purse, the Gothic starlet and I were standing beside each other, smiling, her arm around my waist.

Anne Rice had agreed to take a picture with me!

I had never smiled like that in my life. She probably smiled like she'd smiled a million times before. A moment she'll never remember, a moment I'll never forget.

Why didn't I tell her I loved her books? Why didn't I tell her how much she meant to me? That I thought she had a handle on things like no one else did?

I screamed with excitement for the rest of the day, reenacting the scene over and over for my dad and Nerd Boy at our antique-filled, pastel pink bed-and-breakfast. It was our first day in New Orleans, and I was ready to go home. Who cared about a stupid aquarium, the French Quarter, blues bands and Mardi Gras beads when I'd just seen a vampire angel?

I waited all day to get the film developed, only to find that the picture of me and Anne Rice didn't come out. Sullen, I retreated back to the hotel with my mother. Despite the fact she and I had appeared in photographs separately, could it be possible that the combination of the two vampire-lovers couldn't be captured on film? Or rather it was just a reminder that she was a brilliant best-selling writer, and I was a screamy, dreamy child going through a dark phase. Or maybe it was that my mom was a lousy photographer.

3

My Sweet Sixteenth birthday. Shouldn't all birthdays be sweet? Why should sixteen be any sweeter? It seemed like a lot of hype to me!

In Dullsville, they celebrate today, my sixteenth birthday, as any other day.

It all started with Nerd Boy's shouting at me. "Get up, Raven. You don't want to be late. It's time for school!"

How could two kids come from the same parents and be so different? Maybe there is something to that theory about the mailman. But in Nerd Boy's case my mother must have had an affair with the librarian.

I dragged myself out of bed and put on a black, cotton sleeveless dress and black hiking boots, and outlined my full lips with black lipstick.

Two white-flowered cakes, one in the shape of a 1 and

the other in the shape of a 6, awaited me on the kitchen table.

I grazed the 6 cake with my index finger and licked the icing off.

"Happy birthday!" my mom said, kissing me. "That's for tonight, but you can have this now," she said handing me a package.

"Happy birthday, Rave," my dad said, also giving me a kiss on the cheek.

"I bet you have no idea what you're giving me," I teased my dad as I held the package.

"No. But I'm sure it cost a lot."

I shook the light package in my hand and heard a rattle. I stared at the Happy Birthday wrapping paper. It could be the keys to a car—my very own Batmobile! After all, it was my sixteenth birthday.

"I wanted to buy you something special," my mom said, smiling.

I ripped the package open excitedly and lifted the jewelry box lid. A string of shiny white pearls stared back at me.

"Every girl should have a pearl necklace for special occasions." My mom gleamed.

This was my mom's corporate version of hippie love beads. I forced a crooked smile as I tried to hide my disappointment. "Thanks," I said, hugging them both. I began to put the necklace back in the box, but my parents glared at me, so I reluctantly modeled it for them.

"It looks gorgeous on you." My mom glowed.

"I'll save them for something really special," I replied, putting them back in the box.

The doorbell rang and Becky came in with a small black gift bag.

"Happy birthday!" she shouted as we went into the living room.

"Thanks. You didn't have to get me anything."

"You say that every year," she teased and handed me the bag. "By the way, I saw a moving van last night outside the Mansion!" she whispered.

"No way! Someone finally moved in?"

"Guess so. But all I saw were the movers carrying in oak desks, grandfather clocks, and huge crates marked 'Soil.' And they have a teenage son."

"He was probably born wearing khaki pants. And I'm sure his parents are some boring Ivy Leaguers," I replied. "I hope they don't remodel it and chase out all the spiders."

"Yeah. And tear down the gate and put up a white picket fence."

"And a plastic goose on the front lawn."

We both giggled like mad as I stuck my hand into the bag.

"I wanted to buy you something special, since you're sixteen."

I pulled out a black leather necklace with a pewter charm. The charm was a bat!

"I love it!" I screamed, putting it on.

My mom leered at me from the kitchen.

"Next time we'll give her money," I heard her tell my father.

"Pearls!" I whispered to Becky as we left the house.

I was in gym class wearing a black shirt, shorts, and combat boots instead of the required white-on-white and gym shoes. *Really, what's the point?* I thought. Does a white ensemble make a student a better athlete?

"Raven, I don't feel like sending you to the office today. Why don't you just give me a break for once and wear what you're supposed to wear?" Mr. Harris, the gym teacher, whined.

"It's my birthday. Maybe you could give *me* a break this once!"

He stared at me, not knowing what to say. "Just today," he finally agreed. "And not because it's your birthday, but because I'm not in the mood to send you to the office."

Becky and I giggled as we went off toward the bleachers where the class was waiting.

Trevor Mitchell, my kindergarten nemesis, and his shuffling sidekick, Matt Wells, followed us. They were perfectly combed, conservative, rich soccer snobs. They knew they were great looking, and it made me sick that they were so cocky.

"Sweet sixteen!" Trevor said, obviously having overheard my chat with Mr. Harris. "How lovely! Just ripe for love, don't you think, Matt?" They were close on our heels.

"Yeah, dude," Matt agreed.

"But maybe there's a reason she doesn't wear white—

white is for virgins, right, Raven?"

He was gorgeous, no doubt about it. His green eyes were beautiful, and his hair looked as perfect as a model's. He had a girl for every day of the week. He was a bad boy, but he was a rich bad boy, which made him very boring.

"Hey, I'm not the one wearing white underwear, am I?" I asked. "You're right—there's a reason I wear black. Maybe you're the one who oughta get out more. "

Becky and I sat on the far end of the bleachers, leaving Trevor and Matt standing on the track.

"So how are you spending your birthday?" Trevor shouted, sitting with the rest of the class, loud enough for everyone to hear. "You and farmer Becky sitting home on a Friday night, watching *Friday the Thirteenth*? Maybe placing some personal ads? 'Sixteen-year-old single white monster girl seeks mate to bond with for eternity.'"

The whole class laughed.

I didn't like it when Trevor teased me, but I liked it even less when he teased Becky.

"No, we were thinking of crashing Matt's party tonight. Otherwise there won't be anyone interesting there."

Everyone was shocked, and Becky rolled her eyes, as if to say, *What are you dragging me into now?* We had never been to one of Matt's highly publicized parties. We were never invited, and we wouldn't have gone if we were. At least I wouldn't.

The whole class waited for Trevor's reaction.

"Sure, you and Igor can come . . . but remember, we

drink beer, not blood!" The whole class laughed again, and Trevor high-fived Matt.

Just then Mr. Harris blew his whistle, signaling us to hightail it off the bleachers and run like greyhounds around the track.

But Becky and I walked, indifferent to our sweating classmates.

"We can't go to Matt's party," Becky said. "Who knows what they'll do to us?"

"We'll see what they do. Or what we'll do. It's my Sweet Sixteenth, remember? A birthday to never forget!"

4

T he most exciting things to happen in Dullsville in my lifetime, in chronological order:

1. The 3:10 train jumped its tracks, spilling boxes of Tootsie Rolls, which we devoured.
2. A senior flushed a cherry bomb down the toilet, exploding the sewage line, closing school for a week.
3. On my sixteenth birthday a family rumored to be vampires moved into the haunted Mansion on top of Benson Hill!

The legend of the Mansion went like this: It was built by a Romanian baroness who fled her country after a peasant revolt in which her husband and most of his family were killed. The baroness built her new home on Benson Hill to resemble her European estate in every detail, except for the corpses.

She lived with her servants in complete isolation, terrified of strangers and crowds. I was a small child at the time of her death and never met her, although I used to play by her solitary monument in the cemetery. Folks said she would sit by the upstairs window in the evenings staring at the moon, and that even now, when the moon is full, if you look from just the right angle, you can see her ghost sitting in that same window gazing at the sky.

But I never saw her.

The Mansion has been boarded up ever since. Rumor had it there was a witchlike Romanian daughter interested in black magic. In any case, she wasn't interested in Dullsville (smart lady!) and never claimed the place.

The Mansion on Benson Hill was quite gorgeous to me in its Gothic way, but an eyesore to everyone else. It was the biggest house in town—and the emptiest. My dad says that's because it's in probate. Becky says it's because it's haunted. I think it's because women in this town are afraid of dust.

The Mansion, of course, had always fascinated me. It was my Barbie Dream House, and I climbed the hill many nights hoping to spot a ghost. But I actually went inside only once, when I was twelve. I was hoping I could fix it up and make it my playhouse. I was going to put up a sign that said, NO NERD BOYS ALLOWED. One night I climbed the wrought iron gate and scurried up the winding driveway.

The Mansion was truly magnificent, with vines dripping down its sides like falling tears, chipped paint, shattered roof tiles, and a spooky attic window. The wooden door stood like Godzilla, tall and powerful—and locked. I snuck around the back. All the windows were boarded up with long nails, but I noticed some loose boards hanging over the basement window. I was trying to pull them loose when I heard voices.

I crouched behind some bushes as a gang of high-school seniors stumbled near. Most were drunk and one was scared.

"C'mon, Jack, we've all done it," they lied, pushing a guy wearing a baseball cap toward the Mansion. "Go in and get us a shrunken head!"

I could see Jack Patterson was nervous. He was a handsome crush-worthy guy, the kind who should be spending his time shooting hoops or making girls swoon, not sneaking into haunted houses to win friends.

It was like Jack had already seen a ghost as he approached the Mansion. Suddenly he looked behind the bushes where I was hiding. I gasped and he screamed. I thought we were both going to have a heart attack. I crouched back down, because I heard the gang approaching.

"He's screaming like a little girl and he's not even in yet!" one of them teased.

"Get outta here!" Jack said to the guys. "I'm supposed to do this alone, right?"

He waited for the others to retreat and then nodded to me that it was clear.

"Damn, girl, you scared me! What are you doing here?"

"I live here and lost my keys. I'm just trying to get back in," I joked.

He caught his breath and smiled. "Who are you?"

"Raven. I already know who you are. You're Jack Patterson. Your father owns the department store where my mom buys her swank purses. I've seen you working the cash register."

"Yeah, I thought you looked familiar."

"So why are you here?"

"It's a dare. My friends think the place is haunted, and I'm supposed to sneak inside and get a souvenir."

"Like an old couch?"

He smiled that same smile. "Yeah, goofball. But it doesn't matter. There's no way—"

"Yes, there is!" And I showed him the loose boards at the basement window.

"You go in first," he said, prodding me forward with trembling hands. "You're smaller."

I slithered easily through the window.

Inside, it was really dark, even for me. I could barely make out the cobwebs. I loved it! There were stacks of cardboard boxes everywhere, and it smelled like a basement that had been there since the beginning of time.

"C'mon already!" I said.

"I can't move! I'm stuck."

"You have to move. Do you want them to find you with your backside hanging out?"

I yanked and pushed and pulled. Finally Jack came through, to my relief, but not his.

I led the terrified senior through the moldy basement. He held on to my hand so tight I thought he would break my fingers.

But it was nice to hold his hand. It was big and strong and masculine. Not like Nerd Boy's, whose tiny hand always felt squishy and smarmy.

"Where are we going?" he whispered in a terrified voice. "I can't see a thing!"

I could make out the shapes of massive chairs and sofas, covered with dusty white cloth, probably once belonging to the old woman who stared at the moon.

"I see some stairs," I said. "Just follow me."

"I'm not going any further! Are you crazy?"

"How about a full-length mirror?" I teased, peeking behind a cloth.

"I'll take one of these empty boxes!"

"That's no good. Your friends will kill you. You'll be a laughingstock the rest of your life. Believe me, I know how it is."

I looked back at him and saw the terror on his face. I wasn't sure if he was scared of his friends outside or of the basement steps that might cave in at the slightest pressure. Or maybe he was afraid of ghosts.

"Okay," I said. "You wait here."

"Like I could go anywhere? I have no idea how to get back!"

"But first . . . "

"What?"

"Let go of my hand!"

"Oh, yeah."

He let me go. "Raven—"

"What?"

"Be careful!"

I paused. "Jack, do you believe in ghosts?"

"No, of course not!"

"So you don't think there is a ghost here? Of that old woman?"

"Shhh! Don't talk so loud!"

I smiled with expectation. But then I remembered his gang's dare and grabbed his baseball cap. He screamed again.

"Relax, it's just me, not one of those spooky ghosts you don't believe in."

I carefully ascended the creaky steps and bumped into a closed door at the top. But it opened when I turned the knob. I was in a wide hallway. Moonlight was shining through cracks in the boarded windows. The Mansion seemed even bigger on the inside. I caressed the walls as I walked, the dust softly caking my hands. I turned a corner and stumbled upon a grand staircase. What treasures lay at the top of it? Is that where the ghosts of the baroness appeared?

I tiptoed up the stairs, as mouselike as I could in my heavy combat boots.

The first door was locked, as was the second and third. I leaned my ear to the fourth door, and I heard the sound of faint crying from the other side. A cold chill ran through me. I was in heaven. As I listened closer, I realized it was only the wind whistling through the boarded windows. I opened a closet, which creaked like an old coffin. Maybe I'd find a skeleton! The only thing I discovered, however, were several old hangers sporting cobwebs instead of clothes. I wondered where the ghosts were. I peered into the library. An open book lay on a small table, as if the woman who stared at the moon had been reading it when she died.

I grabbed *Romanian Castles* off the shelf, hoping it would open a secret passageway into a spook-filled dungeon. Nothing moved except a hairy brown spider that scooted across the dusty shelf.

But the next moment, I heard a loud sound and nearly jumped through the roof—it was the honking of a horn! Startled, I dropped the book. I had totally forgotten about Jack's gang and my new mission.

I ran back down the grand staircase, leaping over the last steps. A bright light was beaming through the boarded-up windows in the living room. I climbed onto the bay window and peered out, safely hidden behind the boards. I could see the seniors sitting on the hood of their car, the headlights shining up through the gate of the Mansion.

One of them was looking in my direction, so I pushed Jack's cap out through an opening between the boards and waved it like I had just landed on the moon. I felt triumphant. The seniors gave the thumbs up in reply.

I found Jack in a sweat, sitting in a corner of the basement on top of some wooden crates. He must have been thinking about rats as well as ghosts.

He grabbed me like a child grabs his mother. "What took you so long?"

I replaced the cap on his head. "You'll need this."

"What did you do with it?"

"I let them know you made it in okay. Ready?"

"Ready!" And he pulled me back through the window like the place was on fire. I noticed he didn't get stuck this time.

We shoved the board back in place. It looked as if we had never been there. "We don't want this to be easy for anyone else," I said.

He stared back like he didn't know what to make of me, or how to thank me.

"Wait! I didn't get a souvenir!" he realized.

"I'll go back in."

"No way!" he said, grabbing my arm.

I thought for a moment.

"Here, take this." I gave him my necklace. A black leather band with an onyx medallion. "It only cost three dollars, but it looks like it was owned by a baroness. Just don't let anyone appraise it."

"But you did all the work, and I'll get all the credit."

"Take it before I change my mind."

"Thanks!"

He weighed the necklace in his hand and gave me a warm kiss on my cheek. I hid behind the crumbling gazebo as he ran back down to his buddies, dangling the necklace in front of their faces, getting high fives. They adored him now and so did I. I held my filthy hand against my freshly kissed cheek.

After that day Jack hung out with the cool club and even became class president. From time to time, I'd see him around the town square, and he'd always have a huge smile for me.

I didn't have a chance to return to my Barbie Dream House. Word spread that Jack had snuck into the Mansion. Fearful that more kids might break in, police patrolled the area at night. It would be years till I visited the Mansion again.

Still sweaty from gym class, Becky and I passed the Mansion on our way home. I noticed something I had never seen before, a light in the window. Windows—they weren't boarded up anymore!

"Becky, look!" I screamed with excitement. This was the best birthday present of all! There was a figure standing in the attic window, staring up at the stars.

"Oh, no! It's true, Raven. There are ghosts!" she screamed, clutching onto my arm.

"Well, this ghost drives a black Mercedes!" I said, pointing to the snazzy car parked in the driveway.

"Let's go," she pleaded.

Suddenly the attic light went out.

We both gasped at the same time. Becky's nails dug into my thrift-store sweater. We waited, wide-eyed and speechless.

"C'mon, let's go!" Becky said.

I didn't move.

"Raven, I'm already late for dinner! We'll be doubly late for Matt's party."

"You've got the hots for ol' Mattie?" I teased, my eyes glued to the Mansion.

But when she didn't reply, I turned to face her. Becky's cheeks were flushed.

"You do!" I said with a gasp. "And you think *I*'m weird!" I declared, shaking my head.

"Raven, I've got to go!"

I would have waited till morning, but whoever was inside wasn't coming out.

The light in the attic window had lit a fire in my soul.

"I saw a Mercedes parked at the Mansion!" I informed my family at dinner. I was late as usual, this time for my own birthday dinner.

"I heard they looked like the Addams Family," Nerd Boy said.

"Maybe they have a daughter your age. Someone who doesn't like to get into trouble," my mother added.

"Then I'd have no use for her."

"Maybe she has a father I can play tennis with," my father said hopefully.

"Whoever it is will need to get rid of all those old mirrors and crates," I added, not realizing what I had said.

They all looked at me. "What crates?" my mom asked. "Don't tell me you've snuck into that house!"

"It's just something I heard."

"Raven!" my mother said in that disapproving mother tone.

It seemed no one in Dullsville had seen the new owners. It was wonderful to have a mystery in this town for a change. Everyone already knew most everything that happened in Dullsville, and most of it wasn't worth knowing.

Matt Wells lived on the good side of town, at the edge of Oakley Woods. Becky and I arrived late and entered the party like we were movie stars entering a premiere. Or rather I did. Poor Becky hung tightly to my side like she was visiting the dentist.

"It'll be okay," I reassured her. "It's a party!"

But I knew why she was nervous. We were subjecting ourselves to ridicule when we could have been safely at home watching TV like Trevor said. But why should the snobs have all the fun? Just because Matt's bedroom was the size of my living room? Just because we didn't wear clothes that were "in"? So that meant I should sit home on my sixteenth birthday?

I felt like Moses parting the Red Sea, as a crowd of snobs dispersed from the hallway upon our entry. Our classmates eyeballed me, decked out in my usual Gothic garb. Too bad Tommy Hilfiger wasn't there. He'd have been flattered. Everyone was wearing his clothes like a school uniform. The sound of Aerosmith rocked throughout Matt's living room. A thick layer of smoke hung above the couches, and the smell of beer permeated the air like cheap incense. Couples who weren't staring disapprovingly at us were staring adoringly at each other. It was going to be useless to try to talk to anyone.

"I can't believe you showed up," Matt said, spotting us in the hallway. "I'd take a picture, but I don't know if you'd be visible!" Yet despite his bark, Matt wasn't as cruel as Trevor. "Beers are out back," he then said. "Want me to show you the way?"

Becky was in awe of Matt. She shook her head and locked herself in the hallway bathroom. Matt laughed and headed for the kitchen. I waited in the living room by a concert-sized speaker, perusing the CDs. Michael Bolton, Celine Dion, and a bunch of show tunes. I wasn't surprised.

I went back to check on Becky and found the bathroom door open. She wasn't in the hallway, so I walked through the crowd of hammered classmates to the kitchen. A group of hundred-dollar-hairstyle girls glared at me and left, leaving me alone. Or so I thought.

"Hey, sexy Monster Chick," a voice said behind me. It was Trevor.

He was leaning against the wall next to me, a can of Budweiser dangling from his hand.

"Does that line work for you at every party?"

He smiled a seductive smile. "I've never kissed a girl with black lips before."

"You've never kissed a girl before," I said and walked past him.

He grabbed my arm and pulled me back to him. He

looked at me with his blue eyes and kissed me on the mouth! I have to admit, he was a great kisser, and it didn't hurt that he was gorgeous.

Trevor Mitchell had never even touched me, much less kissed me, except when he bit me in kindergarten. The most I ever got was a thump on the head when I walked too close to him. He had to be drunk. Maybe it was a joke—maybe he was just trying to mess me up. But the way his lips felt against mine, it seemed like we were both enjoying it. I didn't know what to think as he pulled me out the back door, past an inebriated couple mashing on the steps, past garbage cans and the fountain, under tall trees and darkness.

"Are you scared of the dark, Monster Girl?" The woods let so little light in, it was hard to make out the red stripes on his sweater.

"No, I quite like it."

He pushed me up against a tree and started kissing me for real. His hands were everywhere—on me, on the tree.

"I've always wanted to kiss a vampire!" he said, coming up for air.

"I've always wanted to kiss a Neanderthal."

He laughed and went on kissing me.

"So does this mean we're going together?" I asked. Now I was the one coming up for air.

"What?"

"Like when we go to school? We'll hold hands in the halls and hang out together at lunch? See movies on the weekends?"

"Yeah, whatever."

"Then we're going together?"

"Yeah." He laughed. "You can watch me play soccer and I can watch you turn into a bat." He began softly biting me on the neck. "I bet you like it like this, don't you, Monster Girl?"

My heart sank. Of course, I didn't really want to be Trevor's girlfriend. It's not like he was Mars and I was Venus—we weren't even from the same universe! And I didn't even like him, really. I knew why he'd brought me out here, I knew what he wanted to do, and I knew who he was going to tell. And at the end of it all, he might win ten dollars from all his betting buddies for "getting the Goth Chick." I had hoped he was going to prove me wrong. Instead, he was proving me right.

It was time to get down to business. "Wanna see why I don't wear white? Wanna fly with me?"

"Yeah." He smiled, sort of startled, but very eager. "I bet you fly like Supergirl!"

I urged him over the picket fence into the woods. I could obviously see better than he. My nocturnal habits had always made me a great observer in the dark. Not as good as a cat, but close. I felt safe and secure, with the beautiful moon now guiding me. I looked up and saw several bats fluttering over the trees. I'd never seen bats in Dullsville. But I didn't go to that many parties, either.

"I can't see," Trevor said, removing a branch from his hair.

As we walked on, he flailed his arms like he was going

to hit something. Some people are violent drunks; some are slobbering drunks. But Trevor was a terrified drunk. He was really becoming quite unattractive.

"Let's stop here," he said.

"No, just a little bit further," I said, following the bats as they flew into the woods. "It's my sixteenth birthday. I want this to be a night I'll never forget! We need total privacy."

"This is plenty private," he said, groping around and trying to kiss me.

"We're almost there," I said, tugging him on. The lights from the house could no longer be seen, and we couldn't walk five steps without hitting a tree.

"This is perfect!" I finally said.

He squeezed me hard, not because he loved me, but because he was afraid. It was pathetic.

There was a gentle wind blowing through the trees, and the smell of autumn leaves. I heard bats chirping high overhead. The full moon illuminated their wings. It would have been romantic, if only I had had a real boyfriend with me.

Trevor was completely blind in the darkness, feeling everything with his hands and lips. He kissed me all over my face and touched the small of my back. Even blind, it didn't take him long to find the buttons on my shirt.

"No, you first," I told him.

I lifted off his sweater, as unclumsily as I could. I had never done this before. He was wearing a V-neck T-shirt underneath and an undershirt underneath that. *This is going to take forever*, I thought.

I felt his naked chest. Why not? It was right in front of me. It was soft and smooth and muscular.

He pulled me closer, my lacy, black rayon shirt touching his naked torso.

"Now you, baby. I want you so bad," he said, straight out of some skin flick on cable.

"Me too, baby." I sighed, rolling my eyes.

I leaned him down slowly on the damp earth. I slid off his loafers and socks. He eagerly took off the rest.

He lay propped up on his arms, completely naked. I stared down at him in the faint moonlight, savoring the moment. How many girls had Mr. Gorgeous laid out by a tree, only to cast them aside the next day? I wasn't the first and I wasn't going to be the last. I was just going to be different.

"Hurry up—come over here," he said. "I'm cold!"

"I'll just be a minute. I don't want you to see me undress."

"I can't see you! I can't even see my own hands!"

"Well, just hang on."

I had Trevor Mitchell's clothes in my arms. His sweater, V-neck, undershirt, khakis, socks, loafers, and underwear. I had his power. His mask. I had his whole life. What was a girl to do?

This girl ran. I ran so hard, like I had never run before. Like I had been training every day in phys ed class. If Mr. Harris could have seen me then, he surely would have put me on the track team.

The bats flew off, too, as if they were in sync with my

movements. I quickly reached the house, Trevor's ensemble wadded in my arms. The snobs drinking on the back porch were too busy talking about their shallow lives to notice me emptying a trash bag half filled with beer cans and stuffing in Trevor's clothes.

I carried the bag into the house and grabbed a startled Becky by the arm. She was delivering beer to a table of poker players.

"Where were you?" she screamed. "I couldn't find you anywhere! I was forced to wait on these creeps! Back and forth—beer, chips, beer, chips. And now cigars! Raven, where am I supposed to get cigars?"

"Forget about cigars! We've gotta run!"

"Hey, toots, where are those pretzels?" a drunken jock demanded.

"The bar is closed!" I said in his face. "Great service demands a great tip!" I grabbed his poker earnings and stuffed them into Becky's purse. "Time to go!" I said, pulling her away.

"What's in the bag?" she asked.

"Trash, what else?"

I pushed her out the front door. The nice thing about not having friends was there was no one to say good-bye to. "What happened?" she kept asking as I pulled her across the front yard. Her ten-year-old pickup truck sat at the end of the street, waiting for us like home base. "Where were you, Raven? You have leaves in your hair."

I waited until we were halfway home before I turned

to her with a huge grin and shouted, "I screwed Trevor Mitchell!"

"You did what?" she shouted back, almost swerving off the road. "With who?"

"I screwed Trevor Mitchell."

"You didn't! You couldn't! You wouldn't!"

"No, I mean figuratively. I screwed him so bad, Becky, and I have the clothes to prove it!" And I pulled them out of the trash bag one by one.

We laughed and shrieked as Becky turned a corner near Benson Hill.

Somehow Trevor would find his way out of the darkness. But he wouldn't have his rich threads to mask himself. He'd be naked, cold, alone. Exposed for who he really was.

I would remember my Sweet Sixteenth birthday for the rest of my life, and now Trevor Mitchell would, too.

As we drove along the desolate country road that twisted around Benson Hill, the headlights shone against the creepy trees. Moths attacked the windshield as if warning us to choose another way.

"The Mansion's totally dark," I said as we approached it. "Wanna stop for a look-see?"

"Your birthday's over," Becky said in an exhausted voice, keeping her foot on the gas pedal. "We'll go next year."

Suddenly the headlights illuminated a figure standing in the middle of the road.

"Watch out!" I yelled.

A guy with moonlight-white skin and long black hair, clothed in a black coat, black jeans, and black Doc Martens, quickly raised his arm to shield his eyes—seemingly from the glare of the headlights rather than the imminent impact of Becky's pickup.

Becky slammed her brakes. We heard a *thud*.

"Are you okay?" she cried.

"Yes. Are you?"

"Did I hit him?" she yelled, panicking.

"I don't know."

"I can't look," she said, hiding her head on the steering wheel. "I can't!" She started to cry.

I jumped out of the truck and anxiously peered around the front, afraid of what I might find lying in the road.

But I saw nothing.

I checked underneath the truck and looked for dents. On closer inspection, I noticed blood splattered on the fender.

"Are you okay?" I called out.

But there was no response.

I grabbed a flashlight from Becky's glove compartment.

"What are you doing?" she asked, worried.

"Searching."

"For what?"

"There was some blood—"

"Blood?" Becky cried. "I've killed someone!"

"Calm down. It could have been a deer."

"A deer doesn't wear black jeans! I'm calling nine-one-one."

"Go ahead—but where's the body?" I reasoned. "You weren't going fast enough to catapult him into the woods."

"Maybe he's under the truck!"

"I already looked. You probably just bumped him and he took off. But I want to make sure."

Becky grabbed my arm, digging her nails into my flesh. "Raven, don't go! Let's get out of here! I'm calling nine-one-one!"

"Lock the door if you have to," I said, tearing myself free. "But keep the engine and the lights on."

"Raven, tell me this . . . " Becky exclaimed breathlessly, gazing at me with terrified eyes. "What normal guy would be walking in the middle of a pitch-black road? Do you think he might be a—?"

I felt the pleasant tingle of goosebumps on my arms.

"Becky, don't get my hopes up!"

I combed the bushes that went down to the creek. Then I headed for the hillside leading up toward the Mansion.

I let out a shriek.

"What is it?" Becky cried, rolling down the window.

Blood! Thick puddles in the grass! But there was no body! I followed the bloodstains, afraid bits of his corpse were strewn everywhere. And then I tripped over something hard. I looked down, anticipating a severed head. I apprehensively shone my flashlight on it. It was a dented paint bucket.

"Is he dead?" Becky gasped as I returned to the truck.

"No, but I think you may have killed his can," I said, dangling the bucket in front of her. "What was he doing painting in the middle of the night? And where was he going?"

"It was just paint!" Becky said with a gasp of relief, hanging up her cell phone and revving the engine. "Let's get out of here!"

"What was that jerk doing walking in the middle of the road at night?" I wondered out loud. "Maybe he was going to paint some graffiti or something."

"Where did he come from? Where could he have gone so fast?" she mumbled back at me.

In the rearview mirror I caught the reflection of the darkened Mansion just in time to see a light go on in the attic window.

6

Exposed

The story of Naked Trevor spread immediately through Dullsville High. Some students said he stumbled into Matt's house in a trash-bag diaper; others said he was found passed out naked on the back lawn. No one had a clue I was involved. Only Trevor Boy knew the real story. Apparently he tried to pass it off to his buddies as an encounter with a cheerleader. Either way, everyone got a laugh.

Trevor left me alone. He wouldn't even make eye contact with me. Gothic Girl had finally gotten the goods on the popular Soccer Snob. But I didn't want him to accuse me of theft. I had to give his clothes back, right?

First there was the shoe. I think it was the left. I strung it on the outside of my locker. At first no one seemed to notice the hanging loafer. Those who finally did looked at it and walked on. But the next morning it was gone. One person had noticed it. Now it was time for others to take notice besides good ol' Trevor.

The right brown loafer was strung up in the same fashion. But next to it was a sign: MISSING SOMETHING, TREVOR?

This time I heard giggles as students passed. They didn't realize whose locker it was. But they'd soon be catching on.

Each day a sock would hang out, or a T-shirt. I started noticing Snob Girls who would never talk to me suddenly looking over in algebra with smiling approval. They had been Trevor Tree Girls, promised everything, with nothing to show for it. Well, I had plenty to show.

By the time his khaki pants were hung out, complete with grass stains and dirt, everyone knew whose locker it was. Now kids in the hall were grinning at me. Guys weren't exactly asking me out, but I was suddenly popular—in a quiet kind of way.

Except, of course, with Trevor. But I felt safe. Now that everyone knew whose locker it was, he would be the prime suspect if anything happened to me.

But he did make the odd threat.

"I'll kick your ass, Monster," he said one day. He grabbed my jaw in his hands when Becky and I were starting to walk home.

"Combat boots hurt more than loafers, Neanderthal," I shot back. My face was pressed between his hands.

"Let her go," Matt said, pulling him away. I could see even Matt had enjoyed my prank. I'm sure he got tired of the Trevor attitude sometimes. After all, he was stuck being Trevor's best friend.

"You'll never be anything more than a freak!" Trevor shouted. Fortunately Matt pulled him away again. I didn't feel like going to battle after a long day at school.

"You just wait! You just wait!" he called back to me.

"Talk to my lawyer!" I yelled, secretly hoping I wasn't going to need a plastic surgeon instead.

Time for the grand finale. Lots of students were gathered around my locker. I even saw a freshman taking pictures.

It was the climax everyone had been waiting for: Trevor's white Calvin Klein underwear hot-glued to my locker. The sign underneath read: WHITE IS FOR VIRGINS, RIGHT TREVOR?

It would be up there for a while. Everyone saw it. I mean everyone!

"Raven, you defaced school property," Principal Smith scolded me later that day. I had been in Principal Smith's office so many times, it was like seeing an old friend.

"Those lockers have been here forever, Frank," I replied. "Maybe it's time you tell the school board we need new ones."

"I don't think you see the seriousness involved here, Raven. You ruined a locker and embarrassed an honors student."

"What honor? Ask your straight-A cheerleaders and half the drill team how many times he's embarrassed them!"

Principal Smith rattled his pencil in frustration.

"We need to get you involved in something, Raven. Some club you can belong to, something that will help you make friends."

"The chess club have any openings? Or how about the math club?" I asked sarcastically.

"There are other activities."

"Can you guarantee me a spot on the cheerleading squad? Of course, I'd have to wear a black pleated skirt."

"That's one you have to try out for. But I bet you'd be great."

"Obviously honors students, like Trevor, really respect cheerleaders."

"Raven, high school is hard for most kids. That's just the way it is. Even the people who look as though they belong usually don't feel they belong. But you have so much going for you. You're imaginative. You're smart. You'll figure it out. Just don't damage any more lockers while you're trying to find the answers."

"Sure, Frank," I said, taking the detention slip. "See you soon."

"Not too soon, okay, Raven?"

"I'll try not to work you too hard," I said and closed the door.

The next day I noticed something on my locker that I hadn't put up. In black paint was written: RAVEN IS A HORROR!

I smiled. Very clever, Trevor. Very clever. I felt warm inside. It was the first time he had ever complimented me.

7

Happy Halloween

Halloween. My favorite day of the year. The one day of the year that I fit in. It's the only day everyone accepts and compliments me, and I even get rewarded for it by generous neighbors who don't think I'm too old to celebrate—or are more likely too afraid of what my tricks would be.

But this year I decided I really wanted to wear a costume. I shopped in stores I usually never went to and borrowed things from my mom. I strangled my hair into a ponytail and pink barrettes and wore a lusciously soft white cashmere sweater with a pink tennis skirt. I gave myself a healthy glow with some of my mom's base and blush and wore a soft plum lipstick. I even carried my dad's tennis racket. I went around the house saying things like, "Mummy dear, I'll be home after my tennis lesson!"

Nerd Boy didn't recognize me as I passed him in the kitchen. Then his mouth dropped open when he realized it was me and not a neighbor's kid dropping over for sugar.

"I've never seen you look so . . . good," he said, dressed as a baseball player. I thought I was going to be sick right there and then.

My parents wanted to take pictures. Go figure. They were acting as if I was going to the prom. I let them take just one. I figured my dad should finally have a picture of me he could proudly hang at the office.

Becky and I were eating lunch in the cafeteria later that day. Everyone looked at me like I was the new girl. Really, no one recognized me. It was fun at first, then a bit annoying. I got stares when I dressed in black. I got stares when I dressed in white. I couldn't win! Then Trevor came into the cafeteria dressed as Dracula. His hair was slicked back, and he was sporting a black cape. He had plastic fangs and red-hot lips.

He stood with Matt as he glanced all around to find me. He wanted to rub his new look in my face. Matt finally pointed to me and Trevor did a double take. He stared at me long and hard, looked me up and down. I had never seen him gaze at me like that before. It was as if he was in major Crushville, as he checked out my preppy white sweater and healthy glow.

I thought for sure he'd come over and say something stupid, but instead he sat at the opposite side of the cafeteria with his back to me. He even left before I did.

I was free of him! But I was wrong. I should have known our truce wouldn't last.

My little pumpkin basket was almost filled with Smarties, Snickers, Mary Janes, Jolly Ranchers, Dubble Bubble gum, and lots of other tasty treats. And most importantly— spider rings and temporary tattoos. Becky and I had walked all over town and now wondered what awaited us at the front door of the mysterious Mansion. We were saving the best house for last. Apparently so was everyone else.

There was actually a line to the front door. It was like we were at Disney World. Ghouls, punks, bums, Mickey Mouse, Fred Flintstone, and Homer Simpson were all eagerly waiting their turn. And a bunch of coiffed parents who showed up to steal a peek inside. The circus was in town, and everyone had come to look at the freaks.

"He's really creepy," a twelve-year-old Frankenstein remarked to a pint-sized werewolf as they passed us.

Nerd Boy spotted me and Becky as he walked down the driveway.

"It's well worth the wait, Raven. You'll love it! This is my sister!" he proudly said to his geekoid Batman friend, who looked at me with junior crush-boy eyes.

"Did you see any shrunken heads? Or monsters with fangs?" I asked.

"No."

"Then maybe we're wasting our time."

"That old man is really freaky. He looks scary and he isn't even wearing a costume!"

I could see Nerd Boy was trying to bond with me, since this was the first time he could actually show me off to his friend. But I could also see Nerdo was expecting a verbal body slam.

"Thanks for the info."

"Thanks? Uh . . . yeah . . . of course, Sis."

"I'll see you at home, if you want to trade any candy bars."

Nerd Boy nodded willingly. He smiled and left like he had finally met his long lost sister.

Becky and I eagerly waited our turn. We were last in line, and as Charlie Brown and a witch who were in front of us stepped away with their goods, the door closed. I looked at the S-shaped knocker and wondered if it was the initial of the new owner. When I peered closer, I saw it was a serpent with emerald eyes. I rapped it gently, hoping the Gothic guy would answer. I wanted to ask him if he was the one in the road the other night, and if so, what he had been doing? Most people got their exercise at the gym, not on spooky country roads in the dead of night. But no one answered.

"Let's go," Becky suggested nervously.

"No, we waited forever for this! I'm not turning back until I get some candy. He owes us!"

"I'm tired. We've been out all night. It's probably just some creepy old guy who wants to go to bed. And I do, too."

"We can't leave now."

"I'm going home, Raven."

"I can't believe you're so chicken. C'mon, I thought we were best friends."

"We are. But it's late."

"Okay, okay. I'll call you tomorrow and tell you all about Mister Creepy."

There were enough treaters walking around that I wasn't afraid for mousy Becky. She'd get home safe. But would I?

I stared at the serpent knocker and wondered what stood behind the huge wooden door. Maybe the new owner would pull me inside and hold me captive in his haunted mansion. I could only hope!

I knocked again and waited. And waited.

I knocked again. I banged and banged and banged. My hand was starting to hurt. I dashed around to the side, then I heard the locks coming unlatched and the creaky door open. I quickly ran back up the front steps. And there he was, standing before me: Creepy Man.

He was tall and skinny, his face and hands pale as snow, in sharp contrast to his dark butler's uniform. He had no hair, not like he'd lost it, but like he'd never had any, and bulging green monster eyes. He looked like he had been alive for centuries. I loved him.

"We have no more candy, miss," he said in a deep foreign accent as he peered down at me.

"Really? But you must have something. Some peanut-butter twists? A piece of toast?"

He opened the door, no further than necessary. I couldn't see anything behind him. What did the place look like inside? How had it changed since I had snuck in four years before? And who were "we," and did they look creepy, too? We could all be friends. I felt someone watching, looming, and I tried to step past the doorway.

"Who else lives here?" I asked boldly. "Do you have a son?"

"I don't have any children, miss. And I'm sorry, but we don't have a crumb left." He started to shut the door.

"Wait!" I blurted out and blocked the door open with my shoe. I reached into my pumpkin basket and pulled out a Snickers and a spider ring. "I'd like to welcome you to the neighborhood. This is my favorite candy and my favorite Halloween treat. I hope you like them, too."

He almost didn't smile. But then as I placed the treats in his spidery snow-white fingers, he smiled a creaky, crackly, skinny-toothed smile. Even his bulging eyes seemed to twinkle.

"See you!" I said, dancing down the steps.

I had met the creepy man! Everyone in town could say they had gotten candy from him, but who else could say they had given him a treat?

I spun around on the front lawn and looked back at the grand Mansion. I saw a shadowy figure watching from the attic window. Was it Gothic Guy? I quickly stopped spinning and stared back, but there wasn't anyone there, just the ruffle of a dark curtain.

I had just passed through the iron gate when a ghoulish vampire in a red Camaro drove up to the curb.

"Want a ride, little girl?" Trevor asked. Matt the

Farmer sat comfortably behind the wheel.

"My mother told me not to talk to strangers," I said, taking a difficult bite of a Mary Jane. I was not in the mood for a Trevor confrontation.

"I'm not a stranger, babe. Aren't you too old to be trick-or-treating?"

"Aren't you too old to be toilet-papering the town?"

Trevor got out of the car and came over to me. He looked particularly sexy. Of course, I find all vampires sexy, even fake ones.

"What are you supposed to be?" he asked.

"I'm dressed up as a freak, can't you tell?"

He was trying to be cool but was stepping on himself. I was the only girl that had said no to him. The only girl in town he could never have. I had always been a mystery because of the way I dressed and behaved, and now I was standing before him dressed as his perfect dream girl.

"So you're visiting Amityville by yourself?" He stared up at the Mansion. "You're a wicked chick, aren't you?" He glanced down, sending chills through me—he was gorgeous in his Dracula cape.

I said nothing.

"I bet you've never kissed a vampire before," he said, his plastic teeth shining in the moonlight.

"Well, when you see one, let me know," I said, and started to walk away.

He grabbed my arm.

"Give it a rest, Trevor!"

He pulled me in closer. "Well, I've never kissed a

tennis player," he joked.

I laughed, it was such a corny line. He kissed me full on the mouth, his plastic teeth getting in the way. And I let him. Maybe I was still dizzy from spinning on the lawn.

He finally came up for air.

"Well, now you have!" I said, pulling away. "I think Farmer Matt is waiting for you!"

"I didn't get any candy!" he said, fingering my pumpkin basket. He pulled out a Snickers bar.

"Hey, that's my favorite! Take a peanut-butter twist."

He gobbled up the Snickers with his vampire teeth, which came loose and fell on the ground, dripping with chocolate and caramel. I quickly reached for them, but he grabbed my arm, spilling my candy everywhere.

"Look what you've done!" I shouted.

He grabbed handfuls of candy and stuffed them into his jeans. I watched as my remaining treats were strewn across the lawn. The only candy I could salvage were some boring Smarties and a smashed Mars Bar.

"Still want to be an item?" he asked, his pockets stuffed full with my night's work as he pulled me close. "Still want to be my girlfriend?"

Suddenly he let me go and started toward the Mansion. "Now I'll get some real candy."

I grabbed his arm this time. Who knew what Trevor would do if he reached the door?

"Miss me already?" he asked, startled that I hadn't run away.

"They're out of candy."

"Well, I'll just see about that!"

"Their lights are off. They went to sleep."

"This'll wake them up." He pulled out a can of spray paint from underneath his cape. "They definitely need someone who knows how to decorate!"

He walked on toward the Mansion. I ran after him.

"No, Trevor. Don't!"

He pushed past me. He was going to vandalize the one thing in this town that was truly beautiful.

"No!" I cried.

He popped the lid and shook the can.

I tried to pull his arm away, but he threw me down.

"Let's see . . . how about 'Welcome to the neighborhood!'?"

"Don't, Trevor, don't!"

"Or 'Vampires love company!' I'll sign your name."

Not only was he going to deface their property, he was going to frame me for it. He shook the can once more. And began to spray the Mansion.

I rushed to my feet and pulled back my tennis racket. I used to play with my father, and no game was more important to win than this one. I locked my eyes on the aluminum paint-filled cylinder as if it were a ball, and smacked it as hard as I could. The can spun off into the distance, and, like my usual game, I lost my grip and the racket went flying after it. Trevor let out a yell so loud I thought the whole world would hear. I guess I had hit more than the can.

Suddenly the front door light came on, and I heard the

jingle of locks being unlatched.

"We gotta get out of here!" I yelled to Trevor, who was crouching down, holding his wounded hand.

I was ready to make my escape when I felt something I had never felt before: a presence. I turned around and let out a soundless gasp, because fear had taken my breath away. I stood frozen.

There he was. Not Creepy Man. Not Mr. or Mrs. Mansion Family. But Gothic Guy, Gothic Mate, Gothic Prince. He stood before me, like a knight of night!

His long black hair lay heavy on his shoulders. His eyes were dark, deep, lovely, lonely, adoringly intelligent, dreamy. A gateway into his dark soul. He, too, stood motionless, breathing me in. His face was pale like mine and his tight black T-shirt was tucked into his black jeans, which were tucked into monster-chic punk-rock combat boots.

Normally fear is something I feel only when I know my mom's hosting a Mary Kay party and wants to use me as a model. But we were on private property, and my curiosity to meet this strange creature was overwhelmed by my terror of being caught.

The tennis shoes really were a good choice tonight. I could hear Trevor yelling at me as he followed me in flight, "You monster! You broke my hand!"

I raced through the open gate and climbed into the waiting Camaro.

"Drive me home!" I screamed. "Now!"

Matt was startled by his unexpected passenger. He just

stared at me, in silent denial.

"Drive me now! Or I'll tell the police you were involved!"

"The police?" he blurted out. "What's Trevor got us into now?"

I could see the angry Count Trevor running down the driveway, his cape flowing in the wind. He was almost at the gate. Gothic Guy hadn't moved but continued to stare straight at me.

"Drive! Just drive the freakin' car!" I screamed at the top of my lungs.

The motor started and we peeled away until the Mansion and its unusual occupants were out of view. I turned around and looked out the back window at a shouting Dracula Trevor chasing after us.

"Happy Halloween," I said to Matt as I let out a sigh of relief.

I was making my way to history class when I spotted Trevor walking ahead of me. I noticed something unusual about his indoor ensemble—he was wearing a golf glove on his right hand.

"Making a fashion statement?" I teased, catching up to him. "I guess it's a good thing you don't play soccer with your hands!"

He ignored my comments and continued to walk to class.

"Guess you'll have to miss a few sessions of graffiti club," I joked. "Since your trigger finger is out of commission."

He stopped and stared at me coldly. But he thought better of speaking and walked on.

Ouch! I guess I hurt more than his hand.

"I see you made it home safely," I continued, pursuing

him. "Matt took great care of me. He's a perfect gentle-man!"

But then I realized everything. I had taken away Trevor's pride, his girlfriends, and now had forced his best friend to betray him and side with the enemy. I felt sorry for him . . . almost.

Trevor paused, staring down at me like he was going to explode. But I was distracted by a strange figure talking to the secretary in the principal's office. It was Creepy Man! Standing pale in the bright fluorescent light, his long gray overcoat shrouding his skinny body. And hanging from his pale, bony hand was my dad's tennis racket.

I pulled a fuming Trevor to the wall, where we could safely overhear the conversation.

"What are you doing?" Trevor asked, trying to wriggle away.

"Shhh! That's the butler from the Mansion!" I whispered, pointing.

"So what?"

"He's looking for us!"

"How can he be looking for us? It was dark, stupid!"

"That guy saw us! He probably found the spray cans on the lawn and whatever stuff you sprayed on the wall as proof! And he has my dad's tennis racket!"

"Damn, freak, if you hadn't hit me none of this would have happened."

"If you hadn't been born, none of this would have happened, you creep. Shhh, already!"

"Sir, you can leave the racket with us and we can make

an announcement," I heard Mrs. Gerber reply. "What did you say the girl was wearing?"

"A tennis outfit, miss."

"For Halloween?" She laughed and reached for the racket.

But Creepy Man drew back. "I'd prefer to keep it in my possession for now. If you find the owner, she knows where she can claim it. Good day," he said and bowed to a charmed Mrs. Gerber.

I freaked and pulled Trevor behind a statue of Teddy Roosevelt. "It's a trap," I said, squeezing Trevor's gloved hand. "I'll show up and the police will be waiting with handcuffs!"

Students stared at Creepy Man as he walked creepily toward the front doors, glancing around as he left. He was looking for us.

"He's taking the evidence with him, and that evidence is worth two hundred dollars," I whispered to Trevor.

"Yeah, the evidence," he said. "Against you!"

"Me? Your fingerprints were all over it. That guy saw you, too."

"He only saw me running. He could have been after you. You were mad he ran out of candy, so you sprayed his house until he heard you making noise, then you dropped your candy and tennis racket when the lights came on," Trevor said, like he was Sherlock Holmes solving the Case of the Missing Tennis Racket.

"You're going to pin this on me? I can't believe you!"

"Don't worry, I don't think you'll go to jail over this,

babe. You'll just get a major spanking by that crazy butler."

I had gotten in enough trouble for things I had done; I didn't want to be punished for things I hadn't done.

Trevor started walking to class.

I caught up to him. "I'll drag you down so bad if anything happens!"

"Who will they believe, freak—an honors student who is a star soccer player or a two-bit gothic chick with one friend, who spends more time in the principal's office than in class?"

"You owe me a tennis racket!" I shouted helplessly as Trevor sauntered off.

I admit it, Trevor had avenged himself for the Naked Woods Night. Because of him I'd lost my dad's fancy-schmancy racket. And more importantly, he'd made me the enemy in the eyes of the only people in town who might understand me and be my friends. They were my freedom from Dullsville and my connection to humanity, but now because of Trevor, the Mansion would be harder to get into than when it was boarded up.

Y ou what?" my father yelled during dinner after I told
him I lost his racket.

"Well, it's not exactly lost. I just don't have it."

"Then get it back if you know where it is."

"That would be impossible right now."

"But I have a game tomorrow!"

"I know, Dad, but you have other rackets." I tried to
deflate the power of that one particular racket. Big mistake!

"Others? It's that easy for you? Just go buy another
Prince Precision OS racket?"

"I didn't mean that—"

"It's bad enough you deface property at school!"

"I'm sorry, but—"

"Sorry's not good enough this time. Sorry's not going
to win me my game tomorrow. My racket is. I can't believe

I let you take it out of here in the first place!"

"But, Dad, I'm sure you made mistakes when you were a hippie teenager!"

"And I paid for them! Like you're going to pay for my racket."

My bank account had about five dollars in it, the remains of my Sweet Sixteenth birthday money. And I still owed Premiere Video twenty-five dollars in late fees. I quickly did the math in my head. Dad was going to have to keep my allowance until I was thirty.

Then he said the three words that reverberated in my head and made me go dizzy with fury. As he said them I thought I was going to explode into a million unhappy pieces.

"Get a job!" he proclaimed. "It's about time, too. Maybe that'll teach you some responsibility!"

"Can't you just spank me? Or ground me? Or not speak to me for years like parents do on those talk shows? Please, Dad!"

"It's final! End of story! I'll help you find a job if you can't on your own. But you'll have to do the work yourself."

I ran to my room, wailing like baby Nerd Boy, screaming at the top of my lungs, "You people just don't understand the pressure of being a teenager in my generation!"

As I cried on my bed, I fantasized about sneaking into the Mansion like I did with Jack Patterson when I was twelve, and retrieving the racket.

But I also knew I was a little bigger in the hips now

and that the window we'd used had been replaced. I'm sure the new owners also had a security system and, in any case, where would I look for the racket with so many rooms and closets? And while I was searching frantically, I was sure to be caught by Creepy Man wielding a gun or some medieval torture device. A part-time job was a less menacing scenario, but not by much.

At this point I really wished I were a vampire—I'd never heard of Dracula's having a job.

Connections. They'd be wonderful if my dad knew Steven Spielberg or the Queen of England, but Janice Armstrong of Armstrong Travel just doesn't cut it for me.

Far worse than having to show up there after school three days a week, answering phones in a perky voice, photocopying tickets with that hideous blinding flash in my eyes, and talking to yuppies going to Europe for the fourth time was the totally conservative dress code.

"I'm sorry, but you won't be able to wear those . . . " Janice began, staring at my shoes. "What do you kids call them?"

"Combat boots."

"We aren't the army. And it's okay to wear lipstick, but it should be red."

"Red?"

"But you can pick any shade."

Very generous, Janice! "How about pink?"

"Pink would be great. And you'll need to wear skirts. But not too short."

"Red skirts?" I asked.

"No, they don't have to be red. They can be green or blue."

"I can pick any shade?" If she was going to make me feel like an idiot, I was going to act like one.

"Certainly. And hose—"

"Not black?"

"Not ripped."

"And the nail polish," she began, staring at my fingertips.

"Not black, but any shade of red. Or pink would be great," I recited.

"Very good," she said with a big smile. "You're fitting in already!"

"Thanks, I guess," I said as I got up to leave. I checked my watch. The interview had taken fifteen minutes, but it felt like an hour. This job was going to be complete torture.

"I'll see you tomorrow, at four o'clock then, Raven. Any questions?"

"Do I get paid for the interview?"

"You're father said you were bright, but he didn't mention your wonderful sense of humor. We'll get along great. Who knows, you may want to be a travel agent when you get older."

Mrs. Peevish, my infamous kindergarten teacher, would have been proud.

"I already know what I want to be," I replied. I wanted to say a vampire, just for old time's sake. But I knew she wouldn't get it.

"What do you want to be?"

"A professional tennis player. They get free rackets!"

My mother bought me some horrible brightly colored Corporate Cathy gear so I could fit neatly into the package of Dullsville's business world. I pulled them out of the shopping bags and freaked when I saw the price tags.

"Yikes! These outfits cost more than the tennis racket. Just keep them and we'll be even."

"That's not the point!"

"This doesn't make sense."

I reluctantly modeled a white blouse and blue knee-length skirt. My mother looked at me like I was the daughter she always wanted.

"Don't you remember wearing halter tops, braids, and bell-bottoms?" I asked. "What I wear isn't that much different for my generation."

"I'm not that little girl anymore, Raven. And besides, I never wore lipstick. I went *au naturel*."

"Ugh," I said, and rolled my eyes.

"Being a teenager is hard, I know. But you'll eventually find out who you really are."

"I know who I am! And working at a travel agency and wearing a white blouse and hose isn't going to make me find the 'inner me.'"

"Oh, sweetie." She tried to hug me. "When you're a teenager, you think that no one understands you and the whole world is against you."

"No, it's just this town that's against me. I'd go crazy,

Mom, if I thought the whole world was against me!"

She hugged me hard and this time I let her. "I love you, Raven," she said, like only a smooshy mom can. "You're beautiful in black, but you're smashing in red!"

"Quit it, Mom, you're wrinkling my new blouse."

"I thought you'd never say that!" she said, and squeezed me even tighter.

The part-time after-school gig had to go. How could I get the scoop on the Mansion family if I was going to be at work all afternoon? I had to drag all those dry-clean-only clothes with me to school and keep them neatly in my locker until school was over. My new afternoon punishment tore me up inside.

"Why doesn't that guy go to school?" I asked Becky as I was getting dressed.

"Maybe he isn't registered yet."

"If I didn't have this stupid job, we could go investigate right now. Ugh!"

I was envious of Becky, because she got to go home to the land of cable TV and microwave popcorn, while I went from a school desk to a reception desk.

After parting ways with Becky, I snuck into the restroom and wiped off my black lipstick with a wet paper towel and replaced it with some ultra-flashy shade of red. I truly looked like a ghost with my pale complexion. I reluctantly put on my bright red rayon-and-cotton blends. "I'll miss you, but we'll be back together in a few hours," I said to my black dress and combat boots, placing them in my backpack.

I gave myself a once over—this was one time I really thought being a vampire would come in handy. Maybe I'd look in the mirror and see nothing. Instead I saw a miserable girl standing awkwardly in her red rayon outfit.

I slithered out of the restroom looking right and left like I was crossing the street and made my escape safely out the front door. Or so I thought.

Trevor was standing on the front steps.

I freaked when I saw him but tried to ignore his presence and move on. I wanted to run, but I wasn't used to skinny heels.

"Hey, Halloween's over!" he shouted, following me. "Where's your tennis skirt? Going to some costume party as Suzie Secretary?"

I continued to ignore him, but he grabbed my arm.

I couldn't let him know that I was working, or where I was working, and, most of all, that I was working because I had to pay my father back for the tennis racket Trevor had made me lose. It would have brought him too much joy.

He looked me over, that same look he had given me when he first saw me in my tennis outfit. This time I was his corporate dream girl.

"So, where are you going?"

"None of your business!"

"Really? I didn't think we kept secrets from each other."

"Get lost already."

"I'll just walk with you then."

I stopped. "You will not walk with me! You will not go anywhere with me! You will leave me alone! For good. Forever!"

"You don't seem your usual loving self," he said, laughing. "Having a bad hair day? You should be used to that by now."

"Trevor, it's over. Your games and mine! You don't have to harass me anymore. We're even. We're even for all of eternity. Okay? So just get out of my face!"

He ran after me when I stormed off.

"Are we breaking up? I didn't know we were going together, baby. Please don't leave me," he begged, jokingly.

I walked quickly past the school fence and scurried down the sidewalk. I had five minutes to get to Armstrong Travel.

"I can't live without you!" he said sarcastically, catching up. "Are you mad because I never gave you black roses? I'll make it up to you. I'll get you new clothes—from the graveyard." He howled with laughter. "Just don't leave me, babe!"

"Cut it out!" I was fuming. He probably had two hundred dollars in his back pocket and I'd have to work for eons in a place I hated because of his stupid antics.

"Just tell me where you're going?"

"Trevor, quit it! Get out of here! I'll get a restraining order if I have to!"

"Do you have a date?" He wasn't going to give up.

"Go away!"

"You're meeting someone?"

"Buzz off!"

"Do you have an interview? An interview . . . with the vampire?"

"Get out of my face!"

"Are you going to . . . work?"

I stopped. "No! Are you totally crazy? That's so lame!"

"You are! You've got a job!" He danced around. "I'm so proud of you, my little gothic baby has found herself a job!"

I was fuming inside.

"Trying to better your life? Or are you paying Daddy back for that fancy little tennis racket?"

I was ready to hit him, and this time send his head flying off into the distance instead of a can of spray paint.

Just then Matt pulled up. "Trevor, dude. You said you'd be on the steps. I don't have time to drive all over town trying to find you. We have to go."

"Good, your baby-sitter found you," I said.

"I'd offer you a ride to work, but we have places to be," Trevor teased.

As the Camaro whizzed off I looked at my watch. Great! My first day of work and I was late.

Big Ben, the Eiffel Tower, and a Hawaiian sunset loomed behind the reception desk at Armstrong Travel, a constant reminder that there was life outside Dullsville, and that excitement was very far away.

The only thing exciting about working at Armstrong's was the gossip. Under normal circumstances, I found the scandals of the town quite boring—the mayor seen cavorting with a Vegas showgirl, a local TV reporter from WGYS faking an alien abduction story, a Brownie leader embezzling earnings from the cookie bake-off.

But now life was different—there have been Mansion family sightings!

Ruby, the perky partner, filled me in on all the latest. She's like a walking *National Enquirer*.

"It's still a mystery what the husband does—" referring to the Mansion family—"but he's obviously wealthy.

The butler does the grocery shopping at Wexley's on Saturday at exactly eight o'clock P.M. and picks up the dry cleaning on Tuesdays—all dark suits and cloaks. The wife is a tall pale woman in her mid-forties with long dark hair and she always wears dark sunglasses."

"It's like they're vampires," Ruby concluded, not knowing about my fascination. "They've only been seen at night; they look so ghoulish, dark, and brooding, like they're straight out of a B-movie horror flick. And no visitors have been inside that house. Not one. Do you think they're hiding something?"

I was hanging on Ruby's every word.

"They've lived there for over a month," she continued, "and haven't painted the place, or even cut the grass! They've probably even added creaky doors!"

Janice laughed out loud and ignored her ringing phone. "Marcy Jacobs was saying the same thing," Janice added. "Can you imagine? Not mowing your lawn or planting flowers. Don't they wonder what the neighbors think?"

"Maybe they don't care what the neighbors think. Maybe they like it that way," I interjected.

They both looked at me in horror.

"But get this," Ruby said. "I heard that the wife was at Georgio's Italian Bistro and ordered Henry's special antipasto . . . without garlic! That's what Natalie Mitchell says her son said."

So? I thought. *I like a full moon. Does that make me a were-wolf? Big deal. And who can trust Trevor and his family?* The buzzing of the front door brought the gossip session to a complete halt. And the new customer made us all buzz.

It was Creepy Man!

"I have to finish something in the back!" I whispered to Ruby, whose eyes were riveted to the bony man.

I scurried as fast as I could, not looking back until I was safely standing behind the Xerox machine. Yet I yearned to run to good ol' Creepy, squeeze his fragile body and tell him I was sorry for the Trevor Halloween paint job. I wanted to listen to all he had to say about the world as he knew it, his adventures and travels. But I couldn't, so I cowered behind the copy machine, and copied my hand.

"I'd like two tickets to Bucharest," I heard him say, taking a seat at Ruby's desk.

I craned my neck to see him.

"Bucharest?" Ruby asked.

"Yes, Bucharest, Romania."

"And when would you be going?"

"I'm not going, madam. The tickets are for Mr. and Mrs. Sterling. They would like to depart on November first, for three months."

Ruby fiddled with her computer. "Two seats . . . in economy?"

"No, first-class please. Just as long as the flight attendants serve them some bloody wine, the Sterlings are always happy!" he said in his thick accent, laughing.

Ruby laughed back awkwardly and I chuckled inside.

She went over the itinerary and handed him a copy.

"It's like giving blood, the cost of tickets these days!"

Creepy Man laughed, signing.

This was getting good!

Ruby swiped his credit card. "And you're not going, sir?" she asked, as he signed his name, trying to pull more info out of him. Way to go, Rubes!

"No, the boy and I will stay behind."

Boy? Was he referring to Gothic Guy? Or did the Sterlings have a child I could baby-sit? I could play hide-and-seek with him in the Mansion.

"The Sterlings have a boy?" Ruby asked.

"He doesn't get out much. Stays in his room listening to loud music. That's what they do at seventeen."

Seventeen? Did I hear him right? Seventeen? He was talking about Gothic Guy. But why wasn't he in school?

"He's always had a tutor. Or as you say in this country, he's been home-schooled," Creepy Man answered, as if he had read my mind. Or he should have said, Mansion schooled! No one was home-schooled in Dullsville.

"Seventeen?" Ruby repeated, trying to pump more information from his brittle bones.

"Yes, seventeen . . . going on one hundred."

"I know how that is," Ruby interjected. "My girl just turned thirteen, and she thinks she knows everything!"

"He acts like he's lived before, if you know what I mean, with all his grand opinions about the world." Creepy Man laughed a maniacal laugh that sent him into a coughing frenzy.

"Can I get you anything else?"

"I'd like a town map."

"Our town?" she asked, with a laugh. "I'm not sure we even have them."

She turned to Janice, who just shook her head.

"There's the main square and the cornfields," Ruby said, rifling through her desk. "Are you sure you don't want a map of somewhere more exciting?" she asked, offering him a map of Greece.

"This is all the excitement a man of my age can handle, thank you," he said with a grin. "The square reminds me of my village in Europe. It's been centuries since I've seen it."

"Centuries?" Ruby asked, curiously. "Then you hide your age well," she teased.

If anyone could get info on the walking dead, it was Ruby. She could flirt with the best of them.

Creepy Man's face turned from a white wine to a bright burgundy.

"You are so kind, dear," he said, tapping his bald head with a red silk handkerchief. "Thank you for your time," he said, preparing to leave. "It's been lovely, and you have been lovely, too." He grabbed her hand in his bony fingers and smiled a crackling smile.

As he stood up, he looked directly at me and through me like he knew he had seen me before. I could feel his cold stare as I frantically turned around, quickly gathering together the thirteen copies of my hand.

I didn't dare turn back around until I heard the door close. I peered out as he walked past the front window— and he glanced back like he was looking straight through me. I felt a chill go through my body. I loved it.

The rest of the day whizzed by. I hardly noticed it was after six.

I slung my black bag over my shoulder.

"Wow, we'll have to pay you for overtime!" Ruby said, as I got up from the reception desk.

If I couldn't be Elvira or the Bride of Dracula, I'd be Ruby. She was the complete opposite of me in her white-on-white—white go-go boots with a tight white vinyl dress, or a smart white pants suit with white heels. She wore bob-length white-blond hair and always touched up her make-up with a white compact that bore an R made of red rhinestones. She even had a white poodle that she sometimes brought to the agency. She always had boyfriends coming in to visit. They knew she was major class.

I approached her desk, which was covered with white crystals, white angel ornaments, and a smiling thirteen-year-old girl framed in white Lucite.

"Ruby?" I asked as she fiddled with her white leather purse.

"What, honey?"

"I was just wondering?" I said, twisting my purse strap. "Do you . . ."

"What is it, dear? Sit down." She grabbed Janice's chair and wheeled it next to hers.

"About today . . . I know this sounds crazy, but do you . . . well . . . do you believe in . . . vampires?"

"Do I ?" She laughed, fingering her crystal necklace. "I

believe in a lot of things, honey."

"But do you believe in vampires?"

"No!"

"Oh." I tried not to show my disappointment.

"But what do I know?" she chuckled. "My sister, Kate, swears she saw the ghost of an old farmer in a cornfield when we were kids. And I dated this guy who saw something silver shoot straight up in the sky, and my best friend, Evelyn, swears numerology helped her find a husband, and my chiropractor heals people by putting magnets on their joints. What's fantasy for some is reality for others."

I hung on her every word.

"So do I believe in vampires?" she continued. "No. But I also didn't believe Rock Hudson was gay. So what do I know?" She smiled a sparkling white smile.

I laughed as I walked to the door.

"Raven?"

"Yes?"

"What do you believe in?"

"I believe in—finding out!"

I'm on a mission!" I screamed to Becky, who was already waiting on the swings in Evans Park. I had told her to meet me at seven P.M. "You'll never believe what's happening!"

"You have another pair of Trevor's underwear?"

"Trevor who? No, this is way beyond him! Way beyond the city limits. This is totally out of this world!"

"What gives?"

"I have all the dirt on the Mansion family!"

"Oh, the vampires?"

"You know?"

"It's all over town. Some say it's the way they dress. Some say they're just weird. Mr. Mitchell told my father they must be inhuman since they ate at Georgio's and held the garlic."

"But that's the Mitchells. Still, I may have to add that to my journal. Every bit of info is crucial!"

"Is this why we're meeting?"

"Becky, do you . . . believe in vampires?"

"No."

"No?"

"No!"

"That's it? You're not even going to think about it?"

"You could have asked me that on the phone. I cut out early on a second helping of macaroni and cheese!"

"This is of major importance!"

"Are you mad? Do you want me to believe in vampires?"

"Well . . ."

"Raven, do you believe in them?"

"I've wanted to for years. But who knows? I didn't believe Rock Hudson was gay."

"Who's Rock Hudson?"

I rolled my eyes. "Never mind. I asked you to meet me here to help me out on my mission. See, the answers lie not in rumors, but in truths, and the truth lies in that Mansion. And every Saturday night Creepy Butler Man goes to Wexley's for an hour of grocery shopping. I drove by the Mansion, and they don't seem to have a security system. And if I play my cards right, Gothic Guy will be keeping to himself in his attic room of blaring Marilyn Manson angst. He'll never hear me."

"He'll never hear you doing what?"

"Finding the truth."

"This sounds so way out."

"Thank you."

"So you need me to be at my house waiting by the phone, so when you get safely home, you can call me and share all the details?"

I stared at her hard.

"No, I need you to be my lookout."

"You know this is trespassing? Like *really* trespassing? Like breaking and entering?"

"Well, if I can find an open window, then I won't be breaking. I'll only be entering. And if it all goes as planned, no one will be the wiser and so then I won't even be entering. I won't even get in trouble for exiting!"

"I shouldn't . . ."

"You should."

"I can't."

"You can."

"I won't."

"You will!"

The conversation stopped. "You will!" I said, this time sternly. I hated to be bossy, but it had to be done. I got up from my swing. "I won't steal anything. You'll be an accomplice to nothing. But if I do find out something major, colossal, spectacular, totally out of this world, then we can both share the Nobel Prize."

"We have till Saturday, right?"

"Yes. Which gives me plenty of time to gather more

info and comb the Mansion grounds. And you have plenty of time to—"

"Think of excuses?"

I smiled. "No, to finish your macaroni and cheese."

It was better than graduation day: the day my part-time job was over. I had safely cleared $200 after taxes. Enough for dear old dad to buy a sparkling new tennis racket and a new can of bright neon-yellow tennis balls.

I felt a little tinge of melancholy as I picked up my sweater to leave Armstrong Travel, my check safely in my purse. Ruby gave me a huge hug, a real hug, not like Janice's porcelain baby-doll hug.

I waved good-bye to Big Ben, the Eiffel Tower, and the Hawaiian sunset.

"Feel free to come back anytime!" Ruby said. "I'm really going to miss you. You're one of a kind, Raven."

"You are, too!"

She really was, and it was nice to have finally bonded with someone who was different from the average Dullsvillian.

"Some day you'll find a one-of-a-kind guy who is just like you!"

"Thanks, Ruby!"

It was the most tender thing anyone had ever said to me.

Just then Kyle Garrison, Dullsville's golf pro, came in to flirt with Ruby. She had found a lot of one-of-a-kinds for herself. But she deserved it.

I placed my paycheck on my night table, and I curled up in bed, happy that my prison sentence was over and that I could cash the check tomorrow and proudly hand all my earnings over to Dad. But of course I couldn't sleep. I lay awake all night, wondering what my one-of-a-kind guy would look like. I prayed he didn't wear plaid pants like Kyle the golf pro.

Then I thought about the guy at the Mansion. And wondered if I'd already met my one-of-a-kind.

"What are you so smiley about?" Trevor asked me the next day after lunch. I couldn't help but smile, even to Trevor. I was that happy.

"I'm retired." I beamed. "Now I can just live off the interest!"

"Really? Congratulations. But I got so used to seeing you in your cute secretary outfits. You can wear them just for me now," he said, leaning in close.

"Get off," I yelled, pushing him away. "You're not going to spoil my day!"

"I won't spoil your day," he said, standing back. "I'm

proud of you." He smiled a gorgeous smile, but it was mixed with underlying evil. "Now you should have enough money to take me out. I like horror films."

"But they're too scary for children like you. I'll call you in a couple years."

I laughed and walked on. This time he didn't stop me. I guess he really wasn't going to spoil my day after all.

Eighth period was finally over. I quickly went to meet Becky at my locker for an after-school ice cream and Mansion plan update. There was a crowd of students standing around my locker. Becky tried to lead me away, but I pushed past her, through the gawking students.

As I approached, the gawking students stepped back.

I looked at my locker, and my heart fell to the floor. Hanging by rope attached to silver duct tape was my father's Prince tennis racket and a sign that read, GAME OVER! I WIN!

My head started to spin like in *The Exorcist*. Trevor Mitchell had kept the racket the whole time. Could he have somehow gotten it the day Creepy Man came to school?

My body shook with fury. All those ringing phone lines, all those angry customers, all the boring faxes, the sickening taste of envelopes. Watching people fly, drive, and ski their way out of Dullsville as I handed them their tickets to freedom. All because Trevor had been waiting for the right moment to return the racket.

I let out a scream that started in my boots and ended echoing off the walls.

Several startled teachers ran out to see what had happened.

"Raven, are you okay?" Ms. Lenny asked.

I didn't know if the crowd had dispersed or was still hanging on; I only saw the tennis racket. I couldn't breathe, much less speak.

"What happened?" Mr. Burns shouted.

"Are you choking? Do you have asthma?" Ms. Lenny asked.

"Trevor Mitchell—" I began through gritted teeth.

"Yes?"

"He's been beaten up. He's in the hospital!"

"What? How?"

"Where? When?" the panicked teachers inquired alternately.

I took a deep breath. "I don't know how or where!" I turned to them, my body fuming and my head ready to explode. "But I'll tell you this—it'll be soon!"

The puzzled teachers stared back.

I grabbed the tennis racket with all my might, yanking it so hard the duct tape ripped off a band of green paint from my already grungy locker.

I bolted out of school, thirsting for blood.

Students were scattered on the front lawn, waiting for rides. When I didn't find Trevor, I marched around the back.

I spotted him at the bottom of the hill on the soccer field. Waiting for me. He was surrounded by the entire soccer team.

Trevor had planned this. He had patiently waited for this day as I impatiently worked. He knew I'd come after him. He knew I'd be fuming. He knew I'd want to fight. And now he could prove to his buddies that he was king again, that he had gotten Gothic Girl, if not by the tree, then by the racket. And he wanted all his buddies to witness it.

I moved quickly, charged with a bloodthirsty rage. I stormed down the hill to the soccer field, thirteen jocks and one proud antagonist staring at me. Everyone waiting for me to get the bait, and the bait was Trevor.

I pushed past the soccer snobs and walked up to Trevor, clutching my dad's racket, ready for the kill.

"I had it the whole time," he confessed. "I chased that freaky butler dude down that day after school. He wanted to give the racket back himself, but I told him I was your boyfriend. He seemed disappointed."

"You told him you were my boyfriend? Gross!"

"It's grosser for me, babe. You'd be going out with a soccer player. I'd be going out with a freak show!"

I pulled back the racket to take a swing.

"I was going to return it sooner, but you looked so happy going to work."

"You're going to have to wear more than a golf glove when I get through with you this time!"

I swung at him and he jumped back.

"I knew you'd come running after me. Girls always do!" he announced proudly.

His crowd of puppets laughed.

"But you're running after me, too, aren't you, Trevor?" He stared at me, puzzled.

"It's true," I continued. "Tell your friends! They're all here. But I'm sure they knew it all along. Tell them why you're doing this!"

"What are you talking about, freak?" I could see by his expression he was ready for a battle, but he wasn't expecting to play this kind of game.

"I'm talking about love," I said coyly.

The whole crowd laughed. I had a weapon that was better than any two-hundred-dollar racket: humiliation. To accuse a soccer snob of being attracted to a Gothic girl was one thing, but to use this mushy gushy word in front of a sixteen-year-old macho guy was sure to bring the house down.

"You're really freaking out!" he shouted.

"Don't be so embarrassed. It's rather cute, really," I said smugly and smiled at the goalie. "Trevor Mitchell loves me. Trevor Mitchell loves me!" I sang.

Trevor didn't know what to say.

"You're on drugs, girl," Trevor declared.

"Lame comeback, Trevor." I looked at all his smiling soccer snob friends, and then glared at him. "It was so obvious the way you felt, I should have known all along." Then I said in my loudest voice, "Trevor Mitchell, you're in love with me."

"Right, you clown! Like I have a poster of you on my bedroom wall. You're nothing but a skank."

The skank bit hurt, but I let the pain fuel me for the next round.

"You didn't go to Oakley Woods with a poster. You didn't dress up like a vampire to impress a poster. And you didn't hide my dad's racket so you could gain the attention of a raging poster!"

The soccer guys must have been impressed by my argument, because they didn't attack me or defend Trevor, but instead waited to see what would happen next. "None of your friends here give me the time of day," I went on. "It's 'cause they don't care about me, but you care. You care like crazy. You're telling me the time every day."

"You're crazy! You're nothing but a drugged-up, freaked-out loser girl, and that's all you'll ever be."

Trevor looked at Matt, who only smiled awkwardly and shrugged his shoulders. There were snickers from his other mates and whispered words I couldn't hear.

"You want me so bad," I shouted in his face. "And you can't have me!"

He came at me, everything swinging, and it was a good thing I had my dad's tennis racket to defend myself against his punches. There must have been something pitiful about a furious jock trying to attack a girl, or maybe Trevor's gang of soccer dudes secretly enjoyed seeing him humiliated, because they pulled him back and Matt, along with the goalie, stepped in front of me like a handsome barricade.

Just then Mr. Harris blew his whistle for practice.

There was no time for thank-yous to Matt and the others or "Gee, this has been fun—we'll have to do it again some time." I ran back up the hill triumphantly. I couldn't wait to tell Becky.

Did I really believe Trevor was in love with me? No. It seemed as unlikely as the existence of vampires. Mr. Popular loves Ms. Unpopular. But I had made a good case, and the important thing was, everyone had bought it.

I was finally free.

Suddenly other Dullsvillians reported Gothic Guy sightings.

"He's really great looking, but a major weirdfest must be going on in that haunted house!" Monica Havers whispered to Josie Kendle in algebra class.

"He actually came out of his dungeon?"

"Yeah, and Trevor Mitchell spotted him coming out of the cemetery at night and said he had blood dripping from his mouth. And when Trevor drove closer, he suddenly disappeared!"

"Really? Hey, you're hanging out with Trevor again?"

"No way! Everyone knows he's in love with that Raven girl. But get this. I saw that ghost guy at the movies last Friday. Alone. Who goes to a movie by himself?"

"Only a loony loser crazy person," Josie said.

"Exactly!"

I rolled my eyes in total disgust.

Then after dinner I was at the 7-Eleven with Becky, picking up soda for my mom, when I noticed a tabloid headline that read, "I Gave Birth to a Two-Headed Vampire Baby."

"Well, it must be true then!" I joked. "Vampires do exist. I read it in the *National Liar*."

Becky and I giggled like little girls.

I turned around and there was Gothic Guy standing right in back of me, staring at the candy bars below the counter.

He was wearing Ray Bans, like a ghostly rock star, and was holding a pack of candles.

"Aren't you the guy—" I whispered breathlessly, as if I had spotted a celebrity.

"Next," the clerk said, summoning him to the counter.

He didn't even notice me. I followed him closely but was edged out by a red-haired fitness queen and her tanning-bed–addicted friend buying celebrity mags and bottles of imported water.

Gothic Guy took his bag and left the store, lifting his sunglasses as soon as he stepped into the dusk.

The two women leered at him like they had just seen a walking zombie.

"That reminds me, Phyllis," the fitness queen whispered. "I saw that kid at Carlson's Book Store. He's so pale! Hasn't he ever heard of the sun? At least he could use some fake tanning cream. He needs a makeover bad!"

"Did you notice what he was reading?"

"Oh, yes," she recalled. "It was a book on Benson Hill Cemetery!"

"I'll have to tell Natalie Mitchell. She's convinced they're vampires!"

"Maybe we'll see the Sterlings in the tabloids next week: 'Vampire Teen Plays Baseball with Real Bats.'" And they giggled like me and Becky had before.

"Hurry!" I said, impatiently.

By the time Becky and I raced into the parking lot he was gone.

The gossip continued at our dinner table.

"John Garver at the courthouse told me that the Sterlings didn't buy the Mansion, but they inherited it," my dad said.

"Jimmy Fields said he heard they don't eat real food, but bugs and twigs," Nerd Boy added, like only a nerd would.

"What's the matter with you guys?" I shouted. "They're just different—they aren't breaking any laws!"

"I'm sure they aren't, Raven," my mom agreed. "But at the very least, they are strange. Their clothes are bizarre."

They all looked at me—at my black lipstick, black nail polish, blackened hair, black spandex dress, and clunky black plastic bracelets.

"Well, I dress bizarre, too. Do you think I'm strange?"

"Yes," they said in unison.

We all had a good laugh at that one, even me. But deep down, I felt sad because I knew they really weren't kidding, and I could tell they felt sad, too, for the very same reason.

The sun had fallen from the sky and the moon was smiling over Becky and me. I was ready for the infiltration in camouflage night gear. I was wearing matte black lipstick instead of gloss, black turtleneck, black jeans, and a tiny black backpack with a flashlight and disposable camera. Mr. and Mrs. Sterling were in Europe. Their Mercedes was not in sight. Creepy Man must have gone to the store, and if he pushed his shopping cart as slowly as he drove, I'd have plenty of time.

The rusty iron gate stood in front of me. All the answers to the rumors lay on the other side. A quick climb over and the investigation would begin.

Unfortunately the adventure was going to be delayed, because Becky was terrified about climbing.

"You didn't tell me we'd have to climb the gate! I'm afraid of heights!"

"Please! Just get over. The clock is ticking."

Becky looked at the harmless old gate like it was Mt. Everest. "I can't. It's way too tall!"

"You can," I argued. "Here." I put my hands together for a boost. "You'll have to put your whole body weight into this!"

"I don't want to hurt you."

"You won't. Let's go."

"Are you sure?"

"Becky! I've waited months for this, and if you spoil it because you were afraid to step into my hand, I'll have to kill you."

She stepped and I grunted, and suddenly she was suctioned to the gate like a terrified spider.

"You can't just hang. You have to climb!"

She tried. She really did. I could see every muscle in her body strain. She wasn't heavy, but she wasn't strong either.

"Pretend you'll go to jail if you don't climb up."

"I'm trying!"

"Go, Becky, go!" I chanted like a cheerleader. She climbed slowly and finally reached the spiked top. Then she really freaked out.

"I can't go over. I'm scared."

"Don't look down."

"I can't move!"

I was starting to panic myself. She could have spoiled everything right then. A cop could have come by or some nosey neighbor. Or Gothic Guy himself might have come down from his attic to see what was making more noise than his blaring Cure CD.

"Here, I'll go." I pulled myself up the gate, maneuvered around Becky and flipped over the top. "Now you!" I whispered as I hung on the other side.

She didn't move. Her eyes weren't even open.

"I think I'm having a panic attack."

"Great!" I said, rolling my eyes. "You can't do this!" Maybe I should have brought Nerd Boy. "Becky?"

"I can't!"

"All right, all right! Slide down."

We both slithered down the iron gate on opposite sides. The iron bars separated us, but not our friendship.

"I hope I didn't spoil everything," Becky said.

"Hey, at least you gave me a ride."

She smiled appreciatively. "I'll keep an eye out here."

"No, go on home. Someone may see you."

"Are you sure?"

"It was fun hanging around with you," I joked. "But I gotta go now!"

"I hope you find everything you're looking for."

Becky drove off to the safety of her plaid couch and I continued on, minus one detective. I was the RBI—Raven Bureau of Investigation. I had to put an end to these rumors. And if they were more than just rumors, the world had to know.

The only light came from the curtained attic window. I could hear the faint wailing of an electric guitar, as I tip-toed around the side of the house. Fortunately, I didn't hear the sound of barking dogs. I found my favorite window. There were no boards or bricks, and the broken window had been replaced. If they fixed one thing in this Mansion, why did it have to be this particular window? I scrambled around and checked the other windows. They were all locked. Suddenly I noticed something catching the moonlight. I crouched over and lying by a bush was a hammer, and next to the hammer was the most beautiful thing I'd ever seen. It was a window, propped open with a brick. A caulking gun and putty were still sitting on the ledge. Someone had been working here and left their mess to dry. I kissed my new friend—the helpful brick—with my hand. Thank you, brick, thank you!

It was a much tighter squeeze through the window this time. I'd eaten a lot of candy since I was twelve.

I sucked in and pushed and pulled and grunted and heaved. I was through. I was in! I high-fived the air, the dark musty dusty basement air that filled the Mansion dungeon.

My flashlight guided me around crates and old furniture. I saw three rectangular objects leaning against the wall, covered with blankets. Paintings? My flesh tingled with anticipation as I grabbed the corner of the blanket and slowly pulled it back. I gasped. A face with two frozen eyes stared back at me. It was a mirror!

I clutched my racing heart. A covered mirror? I pulled the blankets off one after the other. They were all mirrors! Gold framed, wood framed, rectangular and oval. It couldn't be! Who covers their mirrors? Only vampires!

I continued to search the basement. I uncovered china dishes and crystal goblets, not the kind of glasses I was used to drinking from. Then I found a box that was labeled ALEXANDER'S WATERCOLORS, filled with drawings of an estate just like the one I was standing in.

There were other paintings, too: Spider-Man, Batman, and Superman. And a version of the big three together: Frankenstein, the Werewolf, and Count Dracula.

I started to put them into my backpack, but I had promised Becky I wouldn't take anything. So I took out my camera and took a photo instead.

I found a dusty rolled parchment with a faded family tree. There were long unpronounceable names of duchesses and barons going back centuries. And then at the bottom—Alexander. But no dates of births—or deaths!

Finally I uncovered three crates marked, SOIL. They had Romanian customs stamps on them.

As I made my way toward the stairs, I tripped over something covered with a white sheet. This was what I had come for—it had to be a coffin. The object was the right size for a coffin and sounded like wood when I tapped my knuckles on it. I was as afraid as I was excited. I closed my eyes and yanked the sheet off. I took a deep breath and opened my eyes wide. It was only a coffee table.

I replaced the dusty sheet and carefully walked up the creaky stairs. I twisted the glass door handle and pushed, but to no avail. I pushed again with all my might, and the door suddenly burst open. I went flying into the hallway.

Portraits of a silver-haired man and woman lined the hallway, along with some wild paintings that could have been van Goghs or Picassos. I'd have known for sure if I had ever paid attention in art. I felt like I was in a museum, except there were candles and not fluorescent lights.

I tiptoed into the living room. The furniture was art deco. Very stylish. Huge red velvet curtains hung over the windows—the windows I had once waved a red baseball cap through. I could hear the Smiths pulsing through the ceiling.

I looked at my glow-in-the-dark Swatch. It was already eight-thirty. Time to leave. But I paused at the bottom of the grand staircase. I couldn't go upstairs. It would be ultra-risky. But I had to see everything. When would I ever get a chance like this again?

The first room I entered was a grand study, books upon books, the Sterlings' very own library. But no librarian, thank goodness. "Just came to check out *Crime and Punishment*" would not go over very well with Creepy Man. I peeked quickly into the other rooms. I had never seen so many bathrooms on one floor. Not even a football stadium had so many. A small guest bedroom was surprisingly spartan with a single bed. The master bedroom had a canopy bed with black lace curtains dripping around the columns. There was a vanity, but no mirror! Little combs and brushes and nail polishes. Shades of black, gray, and brown. I was about to look into the closet when the music suddenly stopped. I heard footsteps overhead.

I slipped down the stairs fast. I didn't look back and made sure not to lose my footing and stumble or fall like those girls do in *Friday the 13th* movies. Fiddling with the door locks, my fingers shook uncontrollably, like those foolish horror-flick girls. I was making way too much noise. As I tried to unlock the top bolt, I saw the bottom bolt turning from the other side.

I ran down the hallway, but hearing footsteps coming from that direction, I doubled back and headed into the living room. There wasn't time to open the windows, so I threw myself behind the red velvet curtains.

"I'm back," I heard Creepy Man call in his thick Romanian accent. "Wexley's will be delivering tomorrow as usual. I'm going to retire now."

No one responded.

"You can't get them to shut up when they're three, but when they're seventeen they won't even open their mouths," I heard him mumbling to himself as he walked slowly past the grand staircase.

"Always leaving doors opened," I heard Creepy say and shut what must have been the door to the basement.

I peeled myself out of the curtain, ran, and unbolted all the front door locks in record time. I was ready to make my escape when I felt something familiar——a presence, again. I turned around and there he was standing in front of me. Gothic Guy. He stood motionless, like he was breathing in his uninvited guest.

When he extended his hand to me, to show I didn't have to be afraid, I noticed the accessory—he was wearing the black spider ring that I'd given Creepy Man on Halloween!

I had waited for a moment like this all my life. To see, to meet, to befriend someone who was different from everyone else, and just like me. Suddenly the reality of the situation hit me.

I had been caught.

I ran across the Mansion lawn and pumped and pulled and flung myself to the top of the rusty gate. And as I threw my booted foot over the top, I looked back and could see a distant figure standing in the doorway, watching me. I hesitated, feeling drawn back to the Mansion. I stared at him for a moment before sliding down to the other side.

I had found what I was looking for.

14

After calling Becky and describing my adventure in thrilling detail, I suffered from major insomnia. It wasn't nightfall keeping me awake, though; it was a guy with the deepest, darkest, dreamiest eyes that I had ever seen. My heart was spinning as much as my head. He was beautiful. His hair, his face, his lips. Absolutely amazing was the image of his extended hand—wearing my ring!

Why didn't he try to call the police? Why was he wearing my ring? Was he really a vampire? When would I see him again? I already missed Gothic Guy.

I was swinging high on the swing set the next morning at Evans Park, waiting for Becky, my head still dizzy from the previous night's encounter. I skidded to a stop when she finally arrived and I told her the whole incredible story again.

"You're lucky he didn't kill you!"

"Are you kidding? He was magnificent! I'd wait forever to meet someone half as cool!"

"So do you believe the rumors now?"

"I know it sounds crazy, but I think it could be true. There are so many signs. The drawing of Dracula, the candles, the sunglassses, the covered mirrors, the family tree."

"The mother's allergy to garlic and that the Sterlings have only been seen at night," Becky added.

"And what about the imported earth? Vampires always bring dirt from their native country."

"Are you going to call CNN?" she teased.

"Not yet. I need more proof."

"Would that involve trying to get me over that gate again?"

I began swinging, remembering Anne Rice, Bram Stoker, Bela Lugosi, *The Hunger*, *Lost Boys*, and all the Nosferatus that had ever graced the world with their wonderful smiles and slicked-back hair.

"No! It doesn't involve you at all," I finally answered her.

She let out a sigh of relief.

"There's really only one way to prove it, right? And then we can finally tell these gossip mongers to end their rumors for good. Then these Gothic angels can sleep peacefully, whether they go to bed during the night or day!" I joked.

"So what are you going to do, watch to see if he changes into a bat?"

"No. I'm going to watch to see if I do!"

"You can't change into a bat from watching him."

"I'll have to do more than look at him! There's only one way to tell if he's really a vampire."

"Yeah?"

"It'll be in his bite!" I screamed with excitement.

"You're going to have him bite you? Are you crazy?"

"Curiously crazy."

"But what happens if he is one? You'll turn into a vampire! Then what'll you do?"

"Then," I said, smiling, "I'll call CNN."

I sauntered home from Evans Park daydreaming about seeing my prince of darkness, when I spotted a black Mercedes turning the corner at the far end of my street.

I ran after it, as fast as I could, but combat boots can't compete with spinning wheels and motorized acceleration, even with Creepy driving.

At home I was greeted by a mischievously smiling Nerd Boy.

"I've got something for you!" he teased.

"Don't play games. I'm not in the mood."

"Seems as though the mail is now being delivered on Sundays. And the Sunday mailman is that weird butler from the Halloween Mansion!"

"What?"

"He delivered a letter for you!"

"Give it!"

"It'll cost you!"

"It'll cost you your head," I yelled, trying to jump on him.

He took off running and I followed in red-hot pursuit. "I'll get it. It's just a question of whether you're dead or alive when I do!"

If only I'd stayed home, Creepy Man would have given me the letter instead of Nerd Boy. Good thing my parents were out at lunch. They would have freaked if they'd seen a million-year-old man coming to the door and asking for me.

Nerd Boy waved the red envelope in front of my face, taunting me at every turn. Suddenly he ran upstairs. I grabbed his leg from behind and he fell. I pulled him toward me, but the envelope was in his outstretched arm, too far for me to grab.

I made a sharklike face to let him know I would bite his leg off if I had to, something you can do to a sibling and not go to jail. Panic set in, and he used his free foot to push my hands loose from his bony leg. He slammed his bedroom door in my face and turned the lock.

I banged and banged. My hands hurt but I wouldn't feel the throbbing till later, I was so mad.

"'Dear Raven,'" he pretended to read through the door. "I love you and want you to be my witchy wife so we can have scary butler babies. Love, Weirdo Butler."

"Give that to me! Now! Don't you know what I'm capable of? Just ask the soccer team. I can make life a living hell for you!"

"I'll give it back on one condition."

"How much?"

"I don't want money."

"Then what?"

"That you promise . . ."

"What, already?"

"That you promise to stop calling me 'Nerd Boy'!"

There was silence on both sides of the door.

I felt a pang in my heart. Guilt? Pathos? I guess I never realized that my little nickname could have been hurting him so much all these years. That I had already made his life a living hell.

"Then what should I call you?"

"How about my name?"

"What would that be?" I teased.

"Billy."

"Uh, well . . . okay. You give me the letter, and I won't call you Nerd Boy—for a year."

"Forever."

"Forever?"

"Forever!"

"Okay. For . . . ever."

He cracked the door open and slipped the envelope out. He peered at me with his deep-brown baby-brother eyes.

"Here. I didn't open it."

"Thanks. You shouldn't have made me chase you. I've had a long day!"

"It's only twelve o'clock!"

"Exactly!" Now I had the red envelope safely in my hands. "Thanks, Nerd Boy." I couldn't help it. It was habit.

"You promised!" he yelled, slamming the door.

I knocked again. This time I felt the pain from the previous banging.

"What, Witch Girl?" he yelled. "Anyone would be a nerd compared to you! Leave me alone and go back to your cave!"

I found the door unlocked and stepped inside. It had been years since I'd been in his room. There were pictures of Michael Jordan and Wayne Gretzky on the wall and fifty billion computer games stacked on his floor and desk beside his computer. Nerd Boy was actually pretty interesting.

"Thanks for the letter," I said.

He just sat mousing at his computer, ignoring me.

"Billy!" I shouted. He quickly looked up, with shocked eyes. "I said, 'Thanks.' But I can't hug you. We'll save that for TV."

I threw myself on my bed, my black down comforter soft against my arms, and stared at the blank red envelope. It could say anything inside like: "Stay off our property or we'll sue you and your parents."

But at least I had the threat safely in my hands.

I gently opened the envelope, fearing the worst.

It was an invitation! "Mr. Alexander Sterling requests the company of Ms. Raven Madison at his home December 1 at 8:00 P.M. for dinner."

How did he know my name? How did he know where I lived? And was this real? No seventeen-year-old guy in this town, state, or country invited girls over like this. It was straight out of some Merchant-Ivory–Emma Thompson movie where people have stuffy British accents and are sandwiched into corsets and never say the word "love." It was so medieval, old-fashioned, out of this world. It was so romantic my flesh tingled all over.

I looked at the envelope for any other message, but that's all there was. It didn't even say "R.S.V.P." What nerve! He expected I would come, and he was right. I had waited for this all my life.

I couldn't tell my mother about my mysterious invitation to the Mansion. She'd say no, I couldn't go. I'd say yes, I could. She'd ground me; I'd run away. It would all be very dramatic. I was certain nothing could stop me from going, until my dad dropped a bomb on the morning of December 1.

"I'm taking Mom to Vegas tonight!" he said, pulling me aside. "It's all very spur-of-the-moment. We're flying out this afternoon."

"Isn't that romantic?" My mom beamed, grabbing a suitcase from the hall closet. "Your father's never done anything like this for our anniversary!"

"So you'll be in charge of the house and watching Billy," my dad ordered.

"Watch Billy? He's eleven!" I yelled, following them into their bedroom.

"Here's where we can be reached if you have any problems," he said, handing me a slip of paper with a phone number. "Your employment at Janice's proved to me you can be responsible. We'll be back tomorrow after dinner."

"But I have plans!"

"So invite Becky over here tonight." He tossed a hairbrush into his travel bag. "You're always going to her house. But pick out a movie you all can enjoy."

"Becky? That's the only friend you think I have? Like all I do with my life is watch TV?"

"Paul, should I take this?" my mom interrupted, holding a red strapless dress.

"I'm sixteen, Dad. I want to go out on a Saturday night!"

"I know," my mom said, placing a pair of red stilettos in her bag. "But not tonight. Your father's just surprised me! He hasn't done that since college. Just this once, Raven, then you can have all the Saturdays you want." She kissed me on the head, not waiting for a response.

"I'll be calling in at midnight sharp," my father warned, "just to make sure you and Billy are getting along and that my tennis racket is still in the closet."

"Don't worry. I'm not going to throw a wild party," I said angrily.

"Good, I might have to use the house as collateral at the blackjack table."

He went into his closet and pulled a jacket out. I went into my room and pulled my hair out. In all the seventeen years my parents had been married, my dad had to pick tonight to surprise my mom?

It was seven-thirty that night when I broke the news to Nerd Boy—rather, Billy Boy. I was wearing my Saturday-night best: a black spandex sleeveless mini-dress with a black lacy undertop that peeked through, black tights, unscuffed combat boots, black lipstick, and silver-and-onyx earrings.

"I'm going out tonight."

"But you're supposed to stay here." He ogled my outfit like a protective father. "You have a date!"

"I do not. I just have to go."

"You can't! I won't let you. I'll tell." Billy Boy would have loved to stay by himself, but he loved his sudden power over me more.

"Becky's coming over to hang with you. You like Becky."

"Yeah, but does she like me?"

"She loves you!"

"Really?" he asked, with crush-boy eyes.

"I'll ask her when she gets here. Becky, do you love my little eleven-year-old brother?"

"Don't! You better not!"

"Then promise to behave."

"I'm going to tell. You're leaving me! Anything can happen. I could be on the internet and meet some crazy psycho woman that wants to marry me."

"You could only be so lucky," I said, looking out the window for Becky.

"You'll get in so much trouble!"

"Quit being a baby! Show Becky your computer games. She'll go mad over that alien spaceship stuff."

"If you leave, I'll call them in Vegas."

"Not if you value your life. I'll tie you to that chair if I have to!"

"Then do it, 'cause I'm going to call!" He ran for the cordless phone.

"Billy, please," I begged. "I really need to go. Someday you'll understand. Please, Billy."

He paused with the phone in his hand. He had never heard me beg him for anything, only threaten.

"Well, okay, just make sure you'll be here by midnight. I'm not going to pretend you're in the bathroom."

For the first time I can remember, I gave my brother a hug. And I gave him a real hug, a Ruby squeeze hug, the kind that lets you really feel the other person's warmth.

"Where's Becky already!" he yelled, now playing for my team. "You need to leave!"

Suddenly the doorbell rang and we both flew down the steps. "Where were you?" I asked.

Becky sauntered in with a box of microwave popcorn. "I thought you said eight."

"I have to be there at eight!"

"Shoot, and I thought I was early. Take the truck," she said, handing me her keys.

"Thanks. How do I look?" I asked, modeling my outfit.

"Wicked!"

"Really? Thanks!"

"You look like an angel of the night," my baby brother added.

I glanced in the hallway mirror and smiled. It might be the last time I would actually be able to see my reflection.

"Have fun, you two, and take good care of Billy, okay?"

"Who?" she asked, puzzled.

"Billy. My brother."

They both laughed. I grabbed my jacket and flew out of there like a bat.

Some hideous Dullsvillians had spray-painted GO HOME FREAKS! on the crumbling brick wall by the Mansion gate. It could have been Trevor. It could have been anyone. I felt an emptiness in my stomach.

I guess the Sterlings didn't get many visitors—there was no buzzer on the gate. Was I supposed to wait there, or climb over? But then I realized the gate was open. For me. I walked up the long driveway, looking at the curtained attic window, hoping I would be able to finally see it from the inside.

Anything could happen tonight. I really didn't know what to expect. What would we be eating for dinner? What do vampires eat anyway?

I gently rapped the serpent knocker.

The huge door slowly opened and Creepy Man greeted me with his crackly smile.

"So glad you could come," he said in his thick European accent, straight out of a black-and-white horror flick. "May I take your coat?"

He took my leather jacket somewhere.

I stood in the hallway, peering for signs of anything that seemed threatening. Where was my dinner partner anyway?

"Alexander will be joining you in a few minutes," Creepy said, returning. "Would you like to sit in the drawing room until he comes down?"

"Sure," I agreed, and was led to a huge room next to the living room. It was decorated simply with two scarlet Victorian chairs and a chaise longue. The only thing that didn't look dusty and old was the baby grand piano in the corner. Creepy Man left again and I took the opportunity to snoop around. There were leather-bound books in some foreign language, dusty music scores, and old crinkly maps, and this wasn't even their library.

I caressed the smooth oak desk. What secrets lay inside its drawers? Then I felt that same unseen presence I had felt the last time I visited the Mansion. Alexander had come into the room.

He stood, mysteriously handsome. His hair was sleek and he wore a silk black shirt hanging over black jeans. I was anxious to see if he was wearing the spider ring, but he held his hands behind his back.

"I'm sorry I'm late. I was waiting for the baby-sitter," I confessed.

"You have a baby?"

"No, a brother!"

"Right," he said with an awkward laugh, his pale face coming to life. He was even more handsome than Trevor but didn't come off as self-assured, more like a wounded bird that needed to be held. As if he'd been living in a dungeon all his life and this was the first time he'd seen another human. He seemed uncomfortable with conversation and chose his words carefully, as if once spoken he might never get them back.

"I'm sorry I kept you waiting," he began. "I was getting you these." And he timidly held out five wildflowers.

Flowers? No way!

"Those are for me?" I was completely overwhelmed. It was like everything moved in slow motion. I took the flowers from him, softly touching his hands in the process. The spider ring caught my eye.

"I've never gotten flowers before. They're the most beautiful flowers I've ever seen."

"You must have a hundred boyfriends," he said, glancing down at his boots. "I can't believe they've never given you flowers."

"When I turned thirteen my grandmother sent me a bouquet of tulips in a plastic yellow pot." As dumb as it sounded, it was better than saying, "I've never gotten flowers from my hundred boyfriends, because I've never had one boyfriend!"

"Flowers from grandmothers are very special," he replied strangely.

"But why five?"

"One for every time I saw you."

"I had nothing to do with the spray paint—"

Creepy Man appeared. "Dinner is ready. Shall I put those in some water, miss?"

"Please," I said, though I didn't want to part with them.

"Thank you, Jameson," Alexander said.

Alexander waited for me to exit the room first, straight out of a Cary Grant movie, but I was unsure which way to go.

"I thought you'd know the way," he teased. "Would you like something to drink?"

"Sure, anything." Wait a minute—anything? So I said, "Actually, water will be great!"

He returned a moment later with two crystal goblets. "I hope you're hungry."

"I'm always hungry," I flirted. "And you?"

"Rarely hungry," he said. "But always thirsty!"

He led me into the candlelit dining room, dominated by a long uncovered oak table set with ceramic plates and silver utensils. He pulled out my chair, then sat a million miles away at the other end of the table. The five wild-flowers stood in a crystal vase blocking my view.

Creepy Man—I mean, Jameson—wheeled in a creaky cart and presented me with a basket of steamy rolls. He returned with crystal bowls filled with a greenish soup. Considering the number of courses, the slowness of Jameson's service and the length of the table, we were guaranteed to be here for months. But I didn't care, I didn't want to be anywhere else in the world.

"It's Hungarian goulash," Alexander stated as I nervously stirred the pasty soup. I had no idea what—or who—was in it, and as Alexander and Jameson waited for my reaction, I realized I'd have to taste it.

"Yum!" I exclaimed, slurping down half a spoonful. It was way more delicious than any soup I'd ever eaten from a can, but one hundred times as spicy!

My tongue was on fire and I immediately chugged down my water.

"I hope it's not too spicy," Alexander said.

"Spicy?" I gasped, my eyes bursting. "You've got to be joking!"

Alexander motioned for Jameson to bring more water. It seemed like an eternity, but he returned with a pitcher. Eventually I got my breath back. I didn't know what to ask Alexander, but I wanted to know everything about him.

I could tell Alexander had fewer friends than I. He seemed uncomfortable in his own skin.

"What do you do all day?" I inquired like a TV reporter breaking the ice.

"I wanted to know the same thing about you," he offered.

"I go to school. What do you do?"

"Sleep."

"You sleep?" This was major news! "Really?" I asked skeptically.

"Is there something wrong with that?" he said, awkwardly brushing his hair from his eyes.

"Well, most people sleep at night."

"I'm not most people."

"True . . ."

"And you're not either," he said, staring at me with his soulful eyes. "I could tell when I saw you on Halloween dressed as a tennis player. You seemed a little too old to trick-or-treat. And you had to be different to think that was a costume."

"How did you get my info?"

"Jameson was supposed to return the tennis racket to you but gave it to a blond soccer player who said he was your boyfriend. I might have bought the story if I hadn't seen you smack his hand and drive off without him."

"Well, you're right, he's not my boyfriend. He's a totally lamoid jerk at school."

"But fortunately he also told Jameson your name and address to back up his story. That's how I knew how to find you. I didn't think I'd find you exploring the house again."

His dreamy eyes stared right through me.

"Well . . . I . . ."

Our laughter echoed in the Mansion.

"Where are your parents?" I asked.

"Romania."

"Romania? Isn't Romania where Dracula lived?" I inquired, hinting.

"Yes."

My eyes lit up. "Are you related to Dracula?" I asked.

"He never came to a family reunion," he teased in an

anxious voice. "You're a wacky girl. You certainly give life to Dullsville."

"Dullsville? No way! That's what I call this town!"

"Well, what else could we call it? There isn't any nightlife here, is there? Not for people like me and you."

Nightlife. People like me and you. You mean vampires, I wanted to say.

"I preferred living in New York and London," he went on.

"I bet there's a lot to do there at night. And a lot of night people." Just then Jameson came to take the goulash away and served us steak.

"I hope you're not a vegetarian," he said.

I peered down at my dinner. The steak was medium rare, more on the rare side, as the juice spilled onto the plate and into the mashed potatoes.

He was so mysterious, and funnier than I could have imagined. I was under his spell as I peered at him through the flowers.

"I'm sure it'll be delicious," I said. He watched as I took a bite. "Yum, once again."

Suddenly he looked at me with sad eyes. "Listen, do you mind—"

He picked up his plate and walked over to me. "All I can see are the wildflowers, and after all, you're much prettier."

He set his plate next to mine and dragged his oak chair over. I thought I would faint. He sat smiling as we ate, his leg softly touching mine. My body was electrified. Alexander was funny, gorgeous, and awkward in a sexy way. I wanted to know his whole life story. No matter how many years he had lived, seventeen or seventeen hundred.

"What do you do at night? Where else have you lived? Why don't you go to school?" I rattled on suddenly.

"Slow down."

"Um . . . where were you born?"

"Romania."

"Then where's your Romanian accent?"

"In Romania. We traveled constantly."

"Have you ever gone to school?"

"No, I've always had a private tutor."

"What's your favorite color?"

"Black."

I remembered Mrs. Peevish. I paused and asked, "What do you want to be when you grow up?"

"You mean I'm not grown up?"

"That's a question, not an answer," I said coyly.

"What do you want to be?" he asked.

I stared into his deep, dark mysterious eyes and whispered, "A vampire."

He stared at me curiously and seemed disturbed. And then he laughed. "You are a riot!" Then he looked at me sharply. "Raven, why did you sneak into the house?"

I looked away, embarrassed.

Jameson wheeled over some pastry on a cart. He lit a match and flames rose around the dessert. "Flambé!" he announced. And just in time.

Alexander extinguished our desserts and told Jameson we would finish our dinner outside. "I hope you aren't afraid of the dark," he said, leading me into the dilapidated gazebo.

"Afraid? I live for it!"

"Me, too," he said, smiling. "It's really the only way to see the stars properly." He lit a half-melted candle on the ledge.

"Do you bring all your girlfriends here?" I asked, fingering the used candle.

"Yes." He laughed. "And I read to them by candlelight. What would you like?" he asked, pointing to a stack of textbooks on the floor. "*Functions and Logarithms* or *Minority Group Cultures*?"

I laughed.

"The moon is so beautiful tonight," he said, staring out the gazebo.

"Makes me think of werewolves. Do you think a man can change into an animal?"

"If he's with the right girl," he said with a laugh.

I moved closer to him. The moonlight softly lit his face. He was beautiful. *Kiss me, Alexander. Kiss me now!* I thought, closing my eyes.

"But we have all of eternity," he suddenly said. "For now let's enjoy the stars."

He placed his dessert bowl on the ledge and blew out the candle, and I quickly grabbed his hand. It wasn't a Trevor hand or a skinny Billy Boy hand. He had the best hand in the whole world!

We lay down on the cold grass and gazed up at the stars, holding hands.

We relaxed in silence, our hands warming together. I could feel the prickly legs of the spider ring.

I wanted to kiss. But he just stared up at the stars.

"Who are your friends?" I asked, turning to him.

"I keep to myself."

"I bet you met tons of cool girls before you moved here."

"Cool is one thing. The kind of girls who accept you for who you really are is another. I'd like something . . . lasting."

Lasting? For eternity? But I couldn't ask that.

"I want a relationship I can finally sink my teeth into."

Really? Well, I'm your girl! I thought. But he didn't turn toward me; instead, Alexander gazed at the sky.

"So you don't have *any* friends here?" I asked, trying to pump him for more info.

"Just one."

"Jameson?"

"Someone who wears black lipstick."

We both stared up at the moon in silence. I beamed from his compliment.

"Who do you hang out with?" he finally asked.

"Becky is the only one who accepts me, and it's because I'm the only one who doesn't beat her up." We both laughed. "Everyone else thinks I'm weird."

"I don't."

"Really?" No one had ever said that to me in my whole life. No one.

"You seem a lot like me," he said. "You don't gawk at me like I'm a freak."

"I'll kick anyone who does."

"I think you already did. Or at least smacked him with a racket."

We laughed in the moonlight, and I placed my free arm on his chest and hugged him, as my Gothic Mate softly stroked my arm.

"Could those be ravens?" I asked, pointing to a flurry of dark wings circling high above the Mansion.

"Those aren't birds—they're bats."

"Bats! I've never seen bats around here, until you moved in."

"Yeah, we found some hanging in the attic. Jameson set them free. I hope they don't frighten you. They're wonderful creatures."

"It takes one to know one, right?" I hinted.

"But don't worry. They never swoop down and get tangled in jet-black hair like yours. Only in mall hair."

"They like hairspray?"

"They hate it. They know mall hair looks terrible!"

I laughed, and he began softly stroking my hair. His touch calmed me. I thought I was going to melt into the earth.

He was certainly taking much more time than Trevor had. I began stroking his hair, which was silky from his gel.

"Do bats like gel?" I asked.

"They love the way it looks with a silk Armani," he teased back.

I wriggled over him and pinned his arms down. He looked up at me with surprise and smiled. I waited for him to kiss me. But he didn't move. Of course, he didn't move—I was pinning him down! What was I thinking?

"Tell me your favorite thing about bats, Bat Girl," he asked, as I anxiously stared down at him.

"They can fly."

"You want to fly?"

I nodded.

He wrestled me over and pinned my arms down. Again I waited for him to kiss me, but he didn't. He just stared into my eyes.

"So what's your favorite thing about bats, Bat Boy?" I asked.

"I'd have to say," he began, thinking, "their vampire teeth."

I gasped, but it wasn't because of Alexander's comment. A mosquito had bitten my neck.

"Don't be afraid," he said, squeezing my hand. "I won't bite . . . yet." He laughed at his joke.

"I'm not afraid. A mosquito bit me!" I explained, scratching like mad.

He examined the mark like a doctor. "It's starting to swell. We'd better get you ice."

"It'll be okay. I get these all the time."

"I don't want you to tell your parents you came over to my house and got bitten!"

I wanted to tell the whole world I was bitten, but that mosquito had ruined everything.

He took me into the kitchen and put ice on my tiny wound. I listened to the grandfather clock chime away. Nine . . . *Chime* . . . Ten . . . *Chime*. No! Eleven . . . *Chime*. Frig! Twelve. It couldn't be!

"I've got to go!" I exclaimed.

"So soon?" he asked, disappointed.

"Any second my dad will be calling from Vegas, and if I'm not there to answer, I'll be grounded for eternity!"

If only I could stay and live with Alexander in his attic room and have Creepy Man serve me Count Chocula cereal every morning . . .

"Thanks for the flowers, and the dinner and the stars," I said hurriedly by Becky's truck, scrambling in my purse for the keys.

"Thank you for coming."

He looked dreamy and gorgeous, and somehow lonely. I wanted my Gothic Vampire Mate to kiss me now. I wanted his mouth on my neck and his soul within mine.

"Raven?" he said cautiously.

"Yes?"

"Would you like me to . . . "

"Yes? Yes?"

"Would you like me to . . . invite you again, or would you rather sneak back in?"

"I'd love to be invited," I answered, waiting. If he kissed me now, we'd be bonded for all eternity.

"Wonderful then. I'll call you." He kissed me softly on the cheek. The cheek? Still, it was softer and more romantic than the time Jack Patterson had kissed me outside the

Mansion, and much more romantic than Trevor pushing me against a tree. And as much as I wanted a real kiss—a vampire kiss—he was changing me. I was transforming into a swooning noodle-legged, goopy, googly-eyed, drippy marshmallow girl.

I could still feel his lovely, full lips against my face as I drove home. My body tingled all over with excitement, longing, passion—feelings I had never felt about a guy before. And as I scratched the bite that wasn't his, I could only hope I wouldn't turn into a blood-sucking mosquito.

"Dad's explaining to Becky the rules of blackjack," Billy whispered anxiously, as I ran through the door. "He's already told her about every casino and the history of Siegfried and Roy. He's running out of hotels on the strip!"

I whispered, "Thanks," to Becky and quickly grabbed the phone.

"Becky loves to talk," my dad began. "I had no idea she was so fascinated with Las Vegas. Next time I'll bring her. She tells me you guys have been watching vampire movies all evening."

"Yeah . . ."

"*Revenge of Dracula* for the fiftieth time?"

"No. It's a new one. It's called *Vampire Kisses*."

"Is it good?"

"I give it two thumbs up!"

Becky and I were eating ice-cream cones—Vanilla Royale and Chocolate Attack—outside Shirley's Bakery the next day.

"Alexander's the dreamiest! I can still feel his lips tingling against my cheek," I said. "Becky, for the first time I don't want to run away from this town, 'cause at the top of Benson Hill lives my Gothic dream guy. I can't stop thinking about him. I only wish you'd met him, too, then you'd know how spectacular he is!"

Suddenly a red Camaro pulled up.

"Matt saw Becky's truck parked outside Freaky Mansion last night," Trevor proclaimed in his ornery way as he sauntered over. He stared into Becky's face and asked, "Trying to spray paint the Mansion, Igor?"

"No," I defended, smiling, still thinking about last night. I wasn't going to let Trevor spoil my wonderful mood.

"So you weren't up to trouble, Werewolf Girl?" Trevor asked, continuing to stare at Becky.

Becky looked scared.

"Let's go, Trev," Matt said.

"We'd love to chat with you lovely gentlemen, but we're in the middle of a corporate meeting," I told him. "So you'll have to leave a message with my secretary."

"Is Shirley putting Prozac in her ice cream now?" Trevor said, laughing. "I don't think you'd know what a gentleman was if he bit you on the neck!"

I continued to lick the edge of my cone.

"Or was it you up there?" Trevor guessed. "You're always up to trouble."

"Maybe it was Becky's parents; it's their truck. It doesn't take a rocket scientist to figure that one out."

"I just thought that maybe you and Becky were dating the Osbournes! Oh, I forgot, he just bites the heads off bats—he doesn't turn into them."

"I think I hear your mother calling," I said.

"They're just like you, you know, miserably pale, and social outcasts. They haven't even tried to join the country club yet. But then again we don't accept vampires."

"Vampires?" I laughed uneasily. "Who says that?"

"Everyone, pinhead! The Sterling vampires. The dude hangs out in the cemetery. But I think they're just escaped lunatics like you. They're total freaks."

"C'mon, Trev, let's get out of here already. We've got practice," Matt said.

"Now I see who wears the pants in your relationship,"

I said. "But I forgot, your pants wound up on my locker."

Trevor grabbed the cone from my hand.

"Hey, give it back!" I shouted. Trevor had managed to spoil my blissful mood after all.

He took a huge lick.

"Great, now it has disgusting snob germs. You can keep it," I said.

"Baby, it had germs the moment you looked at it."

"Let's go, Becky," I said, tugging her arm.

"Leaving so soon?"

"I thought I was done with you!" I shouted.

"Done? You're always trying to break my heart, aren't you? Does this mean our engagement is off?"

"Let's go, Trev," Matt said. "We've got things to do."

"You know you love this, Monster Girl. If it wasn't for me, no one would pay attention to you."

"And I'd be the luckiest girl in the world."

"I'll see you in the car," Matt impatiently told Trevor.

"I'll be right there," Trevor replied, then leaned into me. "If you want to be the luckiest girl in the world, you'll go with me to the Snow Ball."

Trevor was asking me to a dance? And of all dances, the Snow Ball? The big school dance where plastic icicles and snowflakes hung from the gym rafters, and fake snow covered the gym floor? He'd show up with me on his arm in front of all his friends? The soccer snobs and the hundred-dollar-haircut girls? It had to be a big joke. I'd be gussied up, waiting at my house, and he'd stand me up, or he'd dump a bucket of red goo on me like in *Carrie*. But even if he was serious, even if by some miracle Trevor really did like me, I couldn't go to the ball with him. Not now that I had met Alexander Sterling.

"It'll be a night you'll never forget," he said seductively.

"I'm sure it will, but I don't want to have nightmares for the rest of my life."

"Just can't tear yourself away from Nick at Nite."

"No. I'm already going."

Trevor sneered. "Stag? Or with an inflatable doll?"

"I have a date."

Becky gasped, but she and Trevor weren't the only ones surprised by my rash words.

"In your dreams! I was only asking you out of pity. No one else would show up with you, unless he was dead."

"Well, we'll just see about that, won't we?"

"I'm leaving," Matt shouted from the car. "Are you coming?"

"Thanks for the ice cream, psycho," Trevor said, getting into the Camaro. "But next time remember, I prefer Rocky Road."

I watched my double-dip chocolate attack screech away.

"I'd offer you mine, but I know you don't like pure vanilla," Becky said consolingly.

"Thanks, but I have bigger things than ice cream to worry about. Like getting a date!"

Every time the phone rang, my heart jumped. Was it Alexander? And when it wasn't him my heart would break into a million pieces. It had been two long days since I had seen my Gothic mate. I was so preoccupied with Alexander, dreaming of the next time we'd be together, nothing else mattered. I didn't wash the spot where his tender love lips had pressed against my flesh. I was acting like I was straight out of a Gidget movie! What had happened to me? I was losing my edge! For the first time in my life I was really afraid. Afraid of never seeing him again, and afraid of being rejected.

If I asked Alexander to the dance, he might freak out. He might say, "With you?" or "No way, not a lame, school dance. I'm so beyond that! And I thought you were, too."

I was beyond that, even though I'd never gone to any dances to actually get beyond them. I wouldn't be going to homecoming or the prom or any of the other dances scheduled throughout the school year. I would stay home with Becky and watch the *Munsters* on TV. But Trevor's challenge had forced me to fight back, with a weapon that I didn't even have: Alexander.

This feeling of not being able to eat or sleep was new to me. To hang my heart on every ring of the phone, to scream at the top of my lungs for Billy Boy not to tie up the line with his addictive web surfing, not to be able to watch *Nosferatu* without crying, or to listen to a silly, sappy, drippy, lovesick Celine Dion song without thinking she had written it just for me—I wanted it all to go away.

I think some people call this love. I called it hell.

And then it happened. After two long, torture-filled days. When the phone rang, I thought it was for Billy Boy, and when Billy Boy called my name, I thought it was Becky. I was ready to pour my heart out to her. But before I could speak, I heard his dreamy voice.

"I couldn't wait any longer," he said.

"Excuse me?" I asked, surprised.

"It's Alexander. I know guys aren't supposed to call right away. But I couldn't wait any longer."

"That's a stupid rule. I could have moved."

"In two days?"

"It was only two days?"

He laughed. "It seemed a year for me."

His comment was like a love letter sent straight to my heart.

I waited for him to go on, but there was silence. He said nothing more. This was the perfect chance to invite him to the Snow Ball. The worst he could do was hang up. My hands were shaking and my confidence was oozing out with my perspiration. "Alexander . . . um . . . I have something to ask you."

"I do, too."

"Well, you first."

"No, ladies first."

"No, guys are supposed to do the asking."

"You're right." There was silence. "Well . . . would you like to go out? Tomorrow night?"

I smiled with delight! "Go out? Yeah, that would be great!"

"So what were you going to ask me?"

I paused. I can do this! I took a deep breath. "Would you . . ."

"Yes?"

"Do you . . ."

"Do I what?"

"Like to dance?"

"Yeah, but I didn't think this town had any hip clubs. You know of one?"

"No . . . but when I find one, I'll let you know." I was such a wimpola!

"Great! Then I'll see you tomorrow at my house, after sundown."

"After sundown?"

"You said you lived for the darkness. So do I."

"You remembered."

"I remember everything," he said, and hung up the phone.

17

Dream Date

My first date! Becky said my first date was dinner at the Mansion, but I didn't agree. Tonight we would be going out: to watch a movie, to play miniature golf, to share a soda at Shirley's. I spent all afternoon talking with Becky, speculating about where he'd take me, what he'd be wearing, and when he would kiss me.

I was so excited, I ran the whole way there. I had to meet Alexander at his iron gate. My mom would have freaked if she had known I had a date with the guy who lived in a haunted house. I couldn't bear the thought of his showing up at my door and my dad's asking him questions about tennis players and his plans for college. So I had to meet my Romeo on his balcony.

And there he was, leaning against the iron gate, sexy in his black jeans and black leather jacket, holding a back-pack.

"Are we going on a hike?" I asked.

"No, a picnic."

"At this hour?"

"Is there a better time?"

I shook my head, with a smile.

I had no idea where Alexander would take me, but I could imagine the response from our fellow Dullsvillians.

"Doesn't this bother you?" I asked, pointing to the graffiti.

Alexander shrugged. "Jameson wanted to paint over it, but I wouldn't let him. One man's graffiti is another man's masterpiece." He took my hand and led me down the street without any hints of our plans for the night. And I didn't care where we were going, just as long as it was a million miles away and he never let go.

We stopped at Dullsville's cemetery.

"Here we are," he said.

I had never been taken out on a date, much less a date to a cemetery. Dullsville's cemetery dated from the early 1800s. I'm sure Dullsville was much more exciting as a pioneer town—tiny dress shops, saloons, traders, gamblers, and those Victorian lace-up boots that were totally in.

"Do you bring all your dates here?" I asked.

"Are you afraid?" he asked.

"I used to play here as a child. But during the day."

"This cemetery is probably the most lively place in town."

The rumors were true. Alexander did come to the cemetery in the dark.

The creepy gate was locked to ensure uneasy access for Dullsville's vandals.

"We'll have to climb," he said. "But I know how you like climbing gates."

"We can get in trouble for this," I pointed out.

"But it's okay to sneak into houses, right?" he asked. "Don't worry. I know one of the people."

Dead? Alive? A corpse? Maybe a cousin of Jameson's worked the graveyard shift—literally.

Alexander turned away as I struggled to get over in my tight spandex dress.

After we both dusted off, he took my hand and led me down the middle path, where gravestones were lined up for miles. Some of the grave markers signfied a plague that devastated in the 1800s. Alexander walked briskly like he knew exactly where he was going.

Where was he leading me? Who did he know here? Did he sleep here? Had he brought me here to kiss me? And would I become a vampire?

I slowed down. Did I really want to be a vampire? And call this my home? For all eternity?

I tripped over the handle of a shovel, which sent me tumbling forward. I started to fall into an empty grave. Alexander grabbed my arm in the nick of time.

I hung over the empty grave, staring down into the darkness.

"Don't be afraid. It doesn't have your name on it," Alexander joked.

"I think I'm supposed to be home," I said nervously,

brushing graveyard dirt off my dress.

But he led me further into the cemetery with his strong hand.

Suddenly we were standing atop a small hill beneath a giant marble monument.

He picked up some fresh daffodils that had blown away and replaced them tenderly at the foot of Baroness Sterling's monument.

"I'd like you to meet someone," he said, looking at me gently and then at the grave. "Grandma, this is Raven."

I didn't know what to say as I stared at the marker. I had never *met* a dead person before. What was I supposed to say—"She looks just like you"?

But of course, he didn't expect me to say anything as he sat down on the grass and drew me next to him.

"Grandma used to live here—I mean in town. She left us the house and we finally got it after years of probate. I always loved the Mansion."

"Wow. The baroness was your grandmother?"

"I visit her when I feel lonely. She understood what it felt like to be alone. She didn't fit in with the Sterling side of the family. Grandpa died in the war. She said I always reminded her of him." He took a deep breath and looked up at the stars. "It's beautiful here, don't you think?" he went on. "There aren't many lights to block out the stars. It's like the universe is a huge canvas, with sprinkles of light that twinkle and glisten, like a painting that is always there, just waiting to be looked at. But people don't notice it because they're too busy. And it's the most beautiful work of all. Well, almost—"

We were silent for a few minutes, gazing at the heavens. I heard only his soft breath and the sound of crickets. All first dates should be as wonderful as this. It totally beat a first-run movie.

"So your grandma's the lady that stared out the wind—uh, I mean she, well . . ."

"She was a wonderful artist. She taught me how to paint superheroes and monsters. Lots of monsters!"

"I know."

"You know?"

"I mean, I know it must be hard for you. But I like vampires, too!" I hinted.

He seemed to be thinking of something else. "I traveled so much, and since I was home-schooled, I never had the chance to fit in anywhere."

He looked so lost, so soulful, so lonely. I wanted him to kiss me now. I wanted to let him know I was his for all eternity.

"Let's eat," he suddenly said, climbing to his feet.

He placed five black candles in ornate votive holders and lit them with an antique lighter. He unpacked a bottle of sparkling juice and crackers and cheese and spread a black lace tablecloth over the cold grass.

"Have you ever been in love?" I asked as he filled my crystal goblet.

Suddenly we heard a howl and the candles blew out.

"What was that?" I asked.

"I think it's a dog."

"It sounds more like a wolf!"

"Either way, we'd better go!" he said urgently.

I started to shove everything into his backpack.

"We don't have time for that!" he said, grabbing my hand.

The wind continued to howl. The noise was getting closer.

We hid behind the monument.

"If it's a ghost you've come to see," a familiar voice called to us, "I can assure you that the only ghost you'll be seeing tonight is your own."

A man followed with a flashlight. It was Old Jim, the caretaker, with Luke, his Great Dane.

If he recognized me here at this hour I'd have to bribe him with a year's supply of dog biscuits to keep him from telling my parents.

We peeked out and could see the dog licking juice off the grass.

"Give me that, Luke," Old Jim said and picked up the bottle. He took a long swig.

"Now!" Alexander whispered. He tightened his grip on my hand and we ran, scampering over the fence.

I don't think a real ghost and a phantom wolf could have scared me more than Old Jim and his rusty Luke.

"I guess I should have taken you to a movie after all," Alexander said with a smile after we caught our breath. "I'll walk you home."

"Can we go to your house?" I pleaded. "I want to see your room!"

"You can't see my room."

"We have time."

"No way."

There was an edginess in his voice I hadn't heard before. "What's in your room, Alexander?"

"What's in your room, Raven?" he asked, glaring at me. "Let's go back to your place."

"Uh . . . well . . ." He was right. I couldn't bring him into my house and subject him to Billy Boy and my white-bread parents. Not on our first date. "My room's a mess."

"Well, mine is, too," he said.

"I don't have to go home, really."

"I don't want to get you in trouble."

"I always get in trouble. My mom wouldn't recognize me if I wasn't in trouble."

But the streets we walked, hand-in-hand, led back to my house, and no matter how slowly I walked, before I knew it we were standing on my doorstep, saying good-bye.

"Well . . . until . . . next time . . ." he said, his face shining beneath the porch light.

"Next time the mortuary?"

"I thought we could watch a movie at my house."

"You have a TV?" I said. "It's powered by electricity, you know."

"Sassy girl, I have Bela Lugosi's *Dracula* on DVD, since you like vampires so much."

"*Dracula*? Awesome!"

"Then it's a date. Seven o'clock tomorrow, okay?"

"Sensational!"

We had made another date and there was nothing to do now but say good-bye. Primo moment for a luscious kiss. He put his hand on my shoulder and leaned in, his eyes closed and his lips full.

Suddenly the door locks rattled. Alexander stepped out of the light and into the bushes.

"I thought I heard voices," my mom said, opening the door. "Where's Becky?"

"She's at home." It was actually the truth.

"I don't like you running off without telling me," she scolded, holding the door open for me.

Longing to have that moment back and one moment more, I looked over at Alexander.

"Did you guys go to the movies?" she asked as I reluctantly stepped inside.

"No, Mom, we went to the cemetery."

"For once, I wish you would give me a straight answer!"

For once, I was giving her a straight answer.

And as I looked over my shoulder for a final glimpse of my Gothic Dream Mate, she closed the door on my heavenly first date.

18

Movie Madness

I was always late for everything—dinner, school, even movies—but tonight I was early, as I arrived at the Mansion at 6:45. Alexander opened the door himself and kissed me politely on the cheek. I was as shocked as he at his sudden display of affection.

"That never happened when Jameson opened the door!" I said.

"Well, you better tell me if it does. We have a rule, you know. I don't kiss his girls and he doesn't kiss mine!" Alexander glowed even more than he had that night I'd snuck in and he had extended the hand with the spider ring. He was growing confident.

He led me up the grand staircase to the family room. It was filled with modern art pieces—flowered paintings, an Andy Warhol print of Campbell's soup cans, Barbie doll sculptures, and flashy, furry, wild rugs. There was a black leather couch, a big-screen TV, and a glass table with a giant tub of movie popcorn, SnoCaps, Dots, Sprees, Good & Plenty, and two neon-green glasses filled with pop.

"I wanted to make you feel like you're at the movies," he explained.

He put in the DVD and turned out the lights, and we snuggled together in the darkness. I picked SnoCaps and he chose a pack of Sprees. The popcorn rested between us on the couch.

Dracula was getting ready to take a bite out of Lucy when Alexander gently pulled my face away from the screen.

He stared me at with his deep midnight eyes. He leaned toward me. And he kissed me. With passion. He kissed me! He finally kissed me! Right there in front of Bela Lugosi!

He kissed me as if he were drinking me in and filling my heart and veins with love. As I took a breath, he began kissing my ears and gently nibbling them. I giggled like crazy. His lips and teeth made their way down my neck, his mouth filling me with total passion. His soft biting on my neck tickled. I was so into his spell, I stretched my legs out clumsily on the coffee table, spilling Alexander's glass and then the popcorn over him. Alexander, startled, sunk his teeth into my neck so hard I screamed.

"Oh, no! I'm sorry!" he apologized.

Popcorn was scattered everywhere and I held my neck, which was pulsing like my heart.

"Raven, are you okay?"

The blood rushed from my brain, and the room began to turn one way then another, and my stomach felt nauseated. I did what any overexcited, sappy girl would do. I fainted dead away.

It seemed like hours later, but it was only seconds. I awoke to Alexander calling my name. Dracula was still in Lucy's room. The only difference was the lights were on.

"Raven? Raven?"

"What happened?"

"You fainted! I thought that only happened in old movies!"

"Here, drink this." He put my glass to my lips, like I was a baby.

Alexander's pale face was even paler. He took some ice that had spilled on the table and placed it on my neck. "I'm so sorry! I never meant to—"

"That's cold!" I cried.

"I've ruined everything," he said, holding the dripping ice on my neck.

"Don't say that. This happens all the time."

He looked at me skeptically.

"Well, just with you."

"I never meant to hurt you."

I could feel his fingers tracing the wound. "It's just a flesh wound. I didn't break the skin."

"You didn't?" I asked, almost disappointed.

"This is bigger than the mosquito bite. You'll have one major hickey!"

"Bela would be proud," I said, hanging on Alexander's reaction.

"Yes," he said. "I guess he would."

"I want to ask you something," I said nervously, as he walked me to my door. I was running out of chances to invite him to the dance, and I realized if I didn't ask him now, I never would.

"You don't want to hang out anymore? Listen, Raven—"

"No, I mean . . . I just wanted to say . . ."

"Yes?"

"Umm . . . I found a place to dance," I began.

"To dance? In this town?"

"Yes."

"Is it cool?"

"No, but—"

"But if you go there, it must be the trendiest place in the world."

"It's my school."

"School?"

"I thought you would think it was totally lame. I shouldn't have mentioned it."

"I've never been to a school dance before."

"Really? Me neither."

"Then it'll be the first time for both of us," he said with a sexy and suddenly confident grin.

"I guess it will. It's called the Snow Ball. I can wear a

woolen scarf to cover my bite," I joked.

"I'm sorry—it was an accident."

"It was the best accident that ever happened to me!"

He leaned in to kiss me and stopped suddenly. "I better not."

"You better!"

He leaned in again, and this time our lips melted together, his strong hand gently holding my chin.

"Until we meet again," he said, kissing me one last time. He blew me a final kiss when he reached the car.

I touched the mark where he had bitten me. I knew I was already changing. But I wanted to look in the mirror to see for sure.

The following day Becky and I went to Evans Park immediately after school. We opened our backpacks in a darkened corner of the empty rec center. My camera, my journal, and a compact mirror lay before us. Finally Becky placed a Tupperware bowl that held a clove of garlic and a cross wrapped in a leather pouch on the floor.

"Ready to see the bite?" I asked.

"Is it gross?"

"It's my love wound," I said and carefully unwrapped the black scarf I'd been wearing all day.

"Wow! He has a big mouth!" she said, wide-eyed.

"Isn't it cool?"

"I can see teeth marks. A few scrapes, but I don't think

he punctured the skin. Does it hurt?"

"Not at all. It's like getting your ears pierced—it stings at first, but the pain quickly goes away."

"Did you faint when you got your ears pierced, too?"

"Don't get smart!"

"And the mark will go away, too, won't it?"

"That's what we're here to find out. Get the camera."

Becky took pictures of my wound, front and side. We laid the Polaroids on the cement floor as they developed.

"You're showing up," Becky stated.

"Okay. Now the mirror," I said.

"Are you sure?"

"Yes."

"But if you are—you know, if you're really a . . . this could hurt."

"Becky, we don't have all day."

I took off my sunglasses.

"Ready?" she asked, holding the compact.

"Ready."

She opened the compact and pushed it against my nose.

"Ouch!"

"Oh, no!"

"You're not supposed to hit me with it! Give that to me!" I grabbed the compact with trembling hands and stared hard. Nothing—or rather, everything. I was still reflecting.

"Try the garlic!" I ordered, tossing the mirror aside.

Becky opened the Tupperware bowl and cut the clove in half.

"Now?" she asked.

"Now."

I could smell the garlic already. She held the clove under my nose. I took a deep whiff. And coughed wildly.

"Are you okay?"

"Man, that's strong! Gross! Put it away!"

"It's fresh—that's why."

"Put it away!" I said.

"I like the smell. It clears my sinuses."

"Well, it's not supposed to relieve me of nasal congestion. It's supposed to send me into a revolting frenzy."

"We have one more shot left."

She opened the leather pouch. "Ready?"

I took a deep breath. "Go for it!"

She pulled out a jeweled cross on a gold chain.

"Wow, that's cool," I said. "It looks very special."

"Does it bother you?"

"Yes, it bothers me. It bothers me that I was so foolish!"

We stepped into the sunshine—blinding for both of us.

"It's very glary after sitting in the dark," Becky commented as she put on her sunglasses. She looked up at me, relieved. "I don't think you're a vampire."

"What was I thinking? Alexander is so special. Why am I acting like Trevor?"

We both stared into the sunshine.

"I had gotten totally caught up in the rumor mill. Just

like all the Dullsvillians. I'm no better than they are, am I? We wear different clothes, but I'm just as shallow as they are," I said, disappointed in myself.

"But you wanted him to be a vampire because you like vampires!"

"Thanks. Maybe I'm supposed to give it twenty-four hours," I said as we started to walk home.

I awoke to another sunny day. Not only didn't the sun burn my skin on contact, but its warmth actually felt good against my flesh. Not only didn't mirrors shatter like they did for Gary Oldman in *Bram Stoker's Dracula*, but my reflection looked like it did every day—a pale girl in all-black. And the only thing I was thirsty for was a chocolate soda from Shirley's Bakery.

Still, my heart raced when my mother served linguini with garlic for dinner that night. Everyone stared at me as I played with my food, smelling and taking deep breaths.

"What's with you?" Billy Boy asked. "You're acting strange, even for you."

I twirled some pasta on my fork and raised it slowly to my mouth. "Here goes," I said.

My parents looked at me like I was an alien. The noodles touched my tongue and I chewed and chewed and took a huge swallow.

"Here goes what?" my mother asked.

I took a breath. I expected my throat to burn and my skin to crawl. I expected to choke and gasp at the first taste of garlic. And then it happened. Nothing. Nothing is what happened.

"Here's to what?" my mother repeated.

"Here's to . . . here's to another Sarah Madison gourmet dinner!"

Though I wasn't melting in the sun, shattering mirrors, or cringing from the sent of garlic, I was feeling Alexander's power in different ways. I was walking on air, as if I could fly like a bat. I couldn't possibly sleep at night, my mind was racing, dreaming of him, replaying his kisses over and over. I doodled our names surrounded by hearts in all my notebooks during class. I wanted to be with him every moment, because whatever he was, he was my Alexander. My funny, intelligent, caring, lonely, gorgeous, dreamy Alexander. He was more incredible and exceptional than I had ever imagined.

And I was glad I was changing, and not in the way I had fantasized about for so long. I was happy to see my mirrors didn't shatter, because now I saw a reflection of a girl in love, glowing with happiness. Why should I want to live in a cemetery for eternity, when it might be possible to live in Alexander's attic room? I didn't want to cringe from the sunlight but watch Hawaiian sunsets with him. I didn't want to drink blood but sip pop from Alexander's neon-green glasses. I wanted to enjoy the things I had always enjoyed—ice cream, horror movies, swings after dark—but now I wanted to share them with him.

"I heard you're hanging with the vampire," Trevor said the day before the Snow Ball as Becky and I walked through the hall after lunch. Signs for the dance hung from the ceiling and were plastered on the walls. "Isn't it enough that you're a freak, and Becky is a troll? Now you have to date a lunatic? Don't you know that the Mansion is haunted?"

"You don't know anything! You've never even met Alexander."

"Oh, Alexander. The monster has a name. I thought you just called him Frankenstein. If I do ever meet him, I'll kick his ass and run him out of town. We need to know that we can walk the streets safely at night!"

"I'll kick your ass if you ever even come near him. If you ever even look at him."

"If he looks anything like you, I'll need sunglasses to guard against the blinding ugliness."

Principal Smith walked by. "I hope everything is okay with you two. We haven't received a budget for new lockers." Then he put his arm around the jerk and said, "I heard you kicked the winning goal in yesterday's game, Trevor."

They turned away, Principal Smith engaging the reluctant Trevor in jock conversation.

"How did he know I'm seeing Alexander?" I asked Becky, puzzled.

"Uh, I guess people . . . you know how people talk in this town."

"Well, people in this town are stupid."

"Listen, Raven, I have something to tell you," she began in a nervous voice that was even more nervous than her normal nervous voice.

But I was distracted by the signs for the dance. Tickets On Sale Now. Save Five Dollars If You Pre-purchase.

"Tickets? Frig! I didn't know I needed tickets! Do I get them at TicketMaster? Charge by phone?" I laughed. "That's what happens when you're on the outside, you know?"

"I totally know. The outside gets worse and worse each day."

"Maybe they'll be sold out and we'll have to dance on the school lawn," I joked.

But Becky wasn't laughing.

"Maybe it's best you and Alexander have a private dance at the Mansion."

"And miss seeing Trevor's face when I walk in with Alexander?"

"Trevor knows a lot, Raven," she said oddly.

"Fine, so he'll get into a good college. What do I care?"

"I'm afraid of Trevor. His father owns half our farm."

"The corn or the sugar?"

"I have a confession—"

"Save it for Sunday. Forget about Trevor. He's just a bully."

"I'm not strong like you. I never was. You're my best friend, but Trevor has a way of making people say things they don't want to. But please—don't go to the dance," she said, grabbing my arm.

Suddenly the bell rang. "I've gotta go. I can't get another detention or I'll be banned from the dance."

"But Raven—"

"Don't be afraid, girlie, I'll protect you from the monsters."

19

The Snow Ball

I couldn't sit still through the rest of my classes. Not through algebra, history, geography, or English, which I spent underneath the football bleachers composing love poems to Alexander. I raced home and danced around my bedroom. I tried on every piece of clothing I owned in a million combinations until I had the perfect ensemble.

"Are you okay?" Billy Boy asked, peeking his head into my room.

"Just jumping around and dancing, my most precious little brother," I glowed, giving him a big squeeze and a kiss on the head.

"Are you insane?"

I sighed deeply. "You'll understand someday. You'll meet someone who is connected with you in your soul. And then everything will be exciting and peaceful at the same time."

"You mean like Pamela Anderson?"

"No, like a computer-math girl."

Billy Boy gazed off into the distance. "I guess that won't be so bad, as long as she looks like Pamela!"

"She'll look even better!" I said, messing up his hair. "Now get out. I have a ball to attend."

"You're going to a dance?"

"Yes."

"Well . . ." I could see he was revving up for a big sister major put-down. "Well . . . you'll be the prettiest one there."

"Are you sure you're not on drugs?"

"You'll be the prettiest one there . . . with black lipstick."

"Now that sounds more like your style."

I finally paraded into the kitchen, wearing high-heeled knee-high vinyl boots, black fishnet stockings, a black miniskirt, a lacy black tank top, and metallic black bracelets. A black cashmere scarf hid my love bite, and black leather fingerless gloves revealed my black nail polish—glittering like black ice, in keeping with the theme of the Snow Ball.

"Where do you think you're going dressed like that?" my mom asked.

"I'm going to a dance."

"With Becky?"

"No, with Alexander."

"Who's Alexander?"

"The love of my life!"

"What's this I hear about love?" my dad asked, entering the kitchen. "Raven, where are you going dressed like that?"

"She says she's going to a dance with the love of her life," my mom said.

"You're going nowhere in that! And who's the love of your life? A boy from school?"

"Alexander Sterling," I proclaimed.

"As in, the Sterlings that live in the Mansion?" my dad asked.

"The one and only!"

"Not the Sterling boy!" my mom said, shocked. "I've heard horror stories about him! He hangs out at cemeteries and is never seen in the light of day, like a vampire."

"Do you think I'd be going to a dance with a vampire?"

They both stared at me strangely and said nothing.

"Don't be like everyone else in this town!" I shouted.

"Honey, I've heard the stories all over town!" my mom gossiped. "Just yesterday, Natalie Mitchell was saying—"

"Mom, who are you going to believe, me or Natalie Mitchell? This night is very important. It's Alexander's first dance, too. He's so dreamy and intelligent! He knows about art and culture and—"

"Cemeteries?" my dad asked.

"He's not like what people say! He's the most fantabulous guy in our solar system—besides you, Dad."

"Well, in that case, have fun."

"Paul!"

"But not in that outfit," my dad quickly demanded. "Sarah, I'm glad she's going to a dance. Raven's actually going to school without being forced. This is the most normal thing she's done lately."

My mom glared at him.

"But not in that outfit," he repeated.

"Dad, this is all the rage in Europe!"

"But we're not in Europe. We're in a quiet little town where turtlenecks are the rage. Buttoned-up collars, long sleeves, and long skirts."

"No way!" I declared.

"This boy hasn't been out of his room in years, and you're going to let him escort your daughter looking like that?" my mom asked. "Paul, do something."

My father went to the closet. "Here, wear this," he said, handing me one of his sports coats. "It's black."

I stared at him in disbelief.

"It's this or my black bathrobe," he said.

I reluctantly grabbed the coat.

"And we'll be meeting the most fantabulous guy in the solar system when he comes to pick you up?" my mother chimed in.

"Are you kidding?" I was stunned. "Of course not!"

"It's only right; we didn't even know you were seeing him. We had no idea you were going to a dance."

"You want to interrogate and embarrass him. Not to mention me."

"That's what dating is all about. If your date can stand the questions and the parental embarrassment, then he's all yours," my dad teased.

"It's not fair! Do you want to come with us, too?"

"Yes," they both replied.

"This is hideous! It's the biggest night of my life, and you're going to ruin it!"

I heard a car pulling into the driveway. "He's here!" I screamed, peering out the window. "You guys have to be cool!" I said, running around frantically. "Channel those hippie days for me, please! Think about love beads and Joni Mitchell. Think bell-bottoms and incense, not golf pants and china," I begged. "And nothing about cemeteries!"

I wanted this night to be perfect, like it was my wedding day. But I felt like a bride who suddenly wished she had eloped.

Now that my parents were going to meet my date, my hands began to shake. I was hoping he wouldn't freak out sitting on their perky pastel furniture.

When the doorbell rang, I dashed to greet him. Alexander looked amazing. He was wearing a glossy, chic black three-piece suit and a red silk tie. He looked like one of the billion-dollar basketball players that I see on television interviews. He held a box wrapped in flowered paper.

"Wow!" he said, looking me over. My father nodded to me to put on the sports coat with a scolding eye. Instead I draped it over a chair.

"I should have worn a knit hat or snow boots," he said awkwardly. "I didn't really keep with the theme."

"Forget it! You'll be the best-looking guy there," I complimented, pulling him into the living room. "These are my parents, Sarah and Paul Madison."

"It's wonderful to meet both of you," Alexander said nervously, extending his hand.

"We've heard so much about you." My mother glowed, taking his hand.

I gave her a cold stare.

"Please sit down," she went on. "Would you like something to drink?"

"No, thank you."

"Make yourself comfortable," my dad said, motioning to the sofa, and settled into his beige recliner.

Uh-oh. I'd never had a guy over before. I could feel my dad taking full advantage. The "goals" inquisition. I prayed it went quickly.

"So, Alexander, how are you finding our town?"

"It's been great since I met Raven," he answered politely and smiled at me.

"So how did you two meet since you don't attend school? Raven neglected to tell us that part."

Oh, no! I started to squirm in my chair.

"Well, I guess we just ran into each other. I mean, it was just one of those things, the right place at the right time. Like they say, everything is about timing, and luck. And I'd have to say that I have been very lucky since I met your daughter."

My dad glared at him.

"Oh, no, that's not what I meant," Alexander added.

He turned to me, his ghostlike face bright red. I tried not to laugh.

"What do your parents do exactly? They aren't in town much, are they?"

"My father is an art dealer. He has galleries in Romania, London, and New York."

"That sounds very exciting."

"It's great, but he's never home," Alexander said. "He's always flying around somewhere."

My mom and dad looked at each other.

"Time to go or we'll be late!" I quickly interjected.

"I almost forgot," Alexander said, awkwardly standing up. "Raven, this is for you."

He handed me the flowered box.

"Thank you!" I smiled anxiously and tore it open, revealing a gorgeous red rose corsage. "It's beautiful!" I gave my mom and dad a look of "See? I told you so."

"How lovely!" my mom gushed.

I held the corsage over my heart as Alexander tried to pin it on. He fumbled out of nervousness.

"Ouch!"

"Did I stick you?" he asked.

"My finger got pricked, but it's okay."

He stared intensely at the drop of blood on the tip of my finger.

My mom stepped between us with a tissue she grabbed from the coffee table.

"It's nothing, Mom, just a little blood. I'm okay." I quickly stuck the pricked finger in my mouth.

"We better go," I said.

"Paul!" my mom pleaded.

But my dad knew better. There was nothing he could do. "Don't forget the coat" was all he said.

I grabbed the coat and Alexander's hand and dragged him out the door, afraid my mom would try to ward him off by making the sign of the cross.

We could hear dance music from the parking lot. No red Camaro anywhere. We were safe—for now.

"Don't forget your jacket," Alexander reminded me as I stepped out of the car.

"You'll have to keep me warm." I winked, leaving it on the backseat.

Two cheerleaders dressed for arctic temperatures stared at us with looks of horror.

I led Alexander away and we paused outside the main entrance. Alexander was like a child, inquisitive and nervous. He looked at the building with interest, like he'd never seen a school before.

"We don't have to go inside," I offered.

"No, that's okay," he said, squeezing my fingers.

Two jocks in the hallway stopped talking the instant they saw us and stared.

"You can pick up your eyeballs off the floor now," I said as I led Alexander past the gawkers.

Alexander examined everything: the Snow Ball signs, the bulletin board announcements, the trophy case. He ran his hand against the lockers, touching the cold metal.

"It's just like on TV!"

"Haven't you ever been in a school?" I wondered.

"No."

"Gosh! You're the luckiest guy in the world. You never had to eat a school lunch. Your intestines must be in great shape!"

"But if I went here we would have met sooner."

I hugged him close underneath the same Snow Ball banner that Trevor and I had argued beneath the day before.

Monica Havers and Jodie Carter passed us and did a double take. I thought their eyes were going to bulge right out of their pom-pom heads.

I was ready to fight if they said anything. But I could tell by the pressure on my wrist that Alexander wanted me to remain calm. The girls whispered and giggled to themselves and went on their gossipy way toward the gym.

"Here's where I don't learn chemistry," I said, opening the unlocked door to my chemistry lab. "I usually have to sneak into places. This is a breeze."

"By the way, I've always wanted to know why you snuck in—"

"Look at these!" I interrupted, pointing out the beakers on the lab table. "Lots of mysterious potions and explosions, but that wouldn't bother you, right?"

"I love it!" He was holding a beaker like it was a fine wine.

I pushed him into a desk, then wrote his name on the blackboard.

"Does anybody know the symbol for potassium? Raise your hand."

He raised his hand to the ceiling. "I do!"

"Yes, Alexander?"

"K."

"Correct, you pass the whole year!"

"Miss Madison?" he said, raising his hand again.

"Yes?"

"Can you come here for a moment? I think I need some tutoring. Do you think you can help me?"

"But I just gave you an *A*!"

"It's more along the lines of anatomy."

I stepped over. He pulled me onto his lap and kissed me softly on the mouth.

We heard some giggling girls run past the open door. "We better go," he suggested.

"No, it's okay."

"I don't want you to get expelled. Besides, we have a dance to attend," he said, making us both stand up.

I walked out hand-in-hand with the guy I had the most chemistry with, his name still etched on the blackboard.

As we approached the gym, I could already feel the cold stares. Everyone was looking at Alexander like he had come from another planet and at me like they always looked at me.

Miss Fay, my nosey algebra teacher, was collecting tickets by the door. "I see you arrived at the dance on time, Raven. Too bad you can't do the same for algebra. I've never seen this gentleman at school," she added, scrutinizing Alexander.

"That's because he doesn't go here." Just take the tickets, lady! I skipped the introductions and pulled Alexander inside.

We walked into the Snow Ball. I didn't know if it was because I was with Alexander, or because it was my first dance, but white had never looked so wonderful. Plastic icicles and snowflakes hung from the ceiling, and the floor was covered with powdery snow. Artificial snow softly sprinkled down from the ceiling. Everyone was dressed in shimmering winter dresses or corduroys with sweaters, mittens, scarves and hats. The blasting air conditioning sent chills through me.

Even the rock band, The Push-ups, fit the theme with their stocking caps and winter boots. Refreshments were set up underneath the scoreboard—snow cones, cider, and hot chocolate.

I could hear whispers, laughs, and gasps as we walked past the bundled-up students. The band, too, was looking at us.

"You want to get some hot chocolate before some senior spikes it?" I asked, trying to distract Alexander from all the attention.

"I'm not thirsty," he replied, watching the dancers.

"I thought you said you were always thirsty?"

The band started to play an electric version of "Winter Wonderland."

"Can I have this dance?" I asked, offering my hand.

I smiled with delight as we walked through the powdered snow to the dance floor.

I was in heaven. I had the best date at the Snow Ball—
there was no one more gorgeous than Alexander, and he
danced like a dream. We forgot that we were outsiders and
thrashed our bodies around like regulars in a trendy club.
We danced one song after another without stopping—
"Cold As Ice," "Ice Cream," "Frosty the Snowman."

The band started to sing, "I Melt with You." The gym
was spinning as tiny powdered snowflakes gently fell on
us. Alexander and I screamed with laughter as we tripped
over an inebriated soccer snob who was making a snow
angel on the floor. When the music stopped, I squeezed
Alexander like mad, like this was our own private dance.
But of course, we weren't alone, as a familiar voice
reminded me.

"Does the asylum know you've escaped?" Trevor
asked, appearing beside Alexander.

I led Alexander to the refreshment table and grabbed
two cherry snow cones.

"Does the warden know you're here?" Trevor asked,
pursuing us.

"Trevor, go away!" I said, shielding Alexander with my
body.

"Oh, is the Bride of Frankenstein having PMS?"

"Trevor, enough!" I couldn't see Alexander's reaction,
but I could feel his hands on my shoulders, drawing me
back.

"But this is just the beginning, Raven, just the beginning!

Don't they have dungeon dancing? You have to actually go to school to come to the dances," he said to Alexander. "But I guess in Hell there are no rules."

"Shut up!" I said. "Don't you have your own date? Or would that be Matt?" I asked sarcastically.

"Very good. She's clever," he said to Alexander. "But not too clever. No, my date is over there," he added, pointing to the entrance.

I looked over and saw Becky nervously standing at the door, dressed in a long pleated skirt, pale pink sweater and long white socks with loafers.

My heart sank to the floor. I felt sick.

"I've given her a little makeover," Trevor bragged. "And that's not all, baby."

"If you touch her, I'll kill you!" I screamed, lunging for him.

"I haven't touched her, yet. But there's time. The dance has just begun."

"Raven, what's going on?" Alexander demanded, turning me toward him.

Trevor signaled for Becky to come over. She didn't even look at me as she approached us. Trevor grabbed her hand and kissed her softly on the cheek. I cringed all over and felt nauseated.

"Get off her!" I grabbed her hand and tried to pull her away.

"Raven, is this the guy who's been hassling you?" Alexander asked.

"You mean he doesn't know me? He doesn't know about us?" Trevor asked proudly.

"There is no 'us'!" I tried to explain. "I pissed him off because I'm the only girl in school who doesn't think he's hot! So now he won't leave me alone. But Trevor, how dare you involve Becky and Alexander!"

Becky stood with her eyes glued to the floor.

"I think it's time to leave Raven alone, dude," Alexander said.

"Dude? Now I'm the freakoid's pal? We can hang out and play soccer? Sorry but there's a dress code. No fangs and capes. Go back to the cemetery."

"Trevor, enough! I'll kick you right now!" I threatened.

"It's okay, Raven," Alexander said. "Let's go dance."

"Becky, get away from him!" I yelled, not moving. "Becky, say something! Say something already!"

"She's already said something," Trevor announced. "She's said a lot. It's funny how the people in this town talk and can't shut up when their daddy's crops might suddenly catch fire from a dropped cigarette," Trevor said, looking straight at me.

He turned to Alexander. "You'll learn who these rumorholics are sooner than you think!"

I looked at Becky, who was staring at her loafers. "I'm sorry, Raven. I tried to warn you not to come here tonight."

"What's he talking about?" Alexander wondered.

"Let's go," I said.

"I'm talking about vampires!" Trevor declared.

"Vampires!" Alexander exclaimed.

"Shut up, Trevor!"

"I'm talking about gossip!"

"What gossip?" Alexander said. "I came here to be with my girlfriend."

"Girlfriend?" Trevor asked, surprised. "Then it's official. Are you going to spend all of eternity together?"

"Be quiet!" I ordered.

"Tell him why you broke into his house! Tell him what you saw."

"We're outta here!" I said, starting to go. But Alexander didn't move.

"Tell him why you threw yourself at him," Trevor continued.

"Don't say another word, Trevor!"

"Tell him why you went to the cemetery!"

"I said, 'Shut up!'"

"And why you fainted."

"Shut up!"

"And why you look at yourself in the mirror every hour!"

"What's he talking about?" Alexander demanded.

"And tell him about this," he said, thrusting the Polaroids of my bite mark at Alexander.

Alexander grabbed the picture and examined it. "What's this?"

"She used you," Trevor said. "I started a rumor that snowballed. I had everyone in town believing you were a vampire. The funny thing is, your dear, sweet Raven believed the rumors more than anyone!"

"Shut up!" I screamed and threw my melting snow cone in Trevor's face.

Trevor laughed as the cherry ice dripped down his cheeks. Alexander stared at the picture.

"What's going on?" Mr. Harris asked, running over.

Alexander looked at me in disbelief and confusion. He glanced around helplessly as the gawking crowd waited for his reaction. Then he angrily grabbed my hand and pulled me outside. We left the falling snow and went out into drizzling rain.

"Wait!" Becky shouted, running after us.

"What's going on, Raven?" Alexander demanded, ignoring her. "How does he know you snuck into my house? How does he know about the cemetery? How does he know you fainted? And what's this?" he asked, shoving the Polaroid at me.

"Alexander, you don't understand."

"You never told me why you snuck into my house," he said.

I stared at his lonely, deep, soulful eyes. His innocence. His sense of not belonging. What could I say? I couldn't lie. So I said nothing and just hugged him with all my might.

The photo dropped from his hand. And he pushed me away.

"I want to hear it from you," he demanded.

Tears started to well up. "I went there to disprove the

rumors. I wanted to put an end to them! So your family could live in peace."

"So I was just a ghost story to you, that you had to check out?"

"No! No! Becky, tell him it wasn't like that!"

"It wasn't!" Becky exclaimed. "She talks about you all the time!"

"I thought you were different, Raven. But you used me. You're just like everyone else."

Alexander turned away and I grabbed his arm.

"Don't go! Alexander!" I begged. "It's true, I was caught up in the rumors, but when I first saw you, I knew. I've never felt this way about anyone. That's why I did everything else!"

"I thought you liked me for just being myself—not for who you think I might be. Or for something you think you wanted to become."

He ran away.

"Don't go!" I cried. "Alexander—"

But he ignored me. He was gone, back to the solitude of his attic room.

I stormed into the gym. The band was on break, and everyone looked at me in silence as I crossed the floor.

"The end," Trevor announced and started clapping. "The end! And what a wonderful production it all was, if I do say so myself."

"You!" I yelled. Mr. Harris could see I was going for blood and grabbed me from behind. "You are evil incarnate, Trevor!" I screamed, my arms flailing as I tried unsuccessfully to wriggle out of the soccer coach's grasp. "Trevor Mitchell, you are the monster!" I looked at the faces around me. "Can't you see that? You all pushed away the most giving, lovable, gentle, intelligent person in this town while accepting the wickedest, vilest, most evil monster, just because he dresses like you! Trevor's the one who's destroying lives! And you just watch him play soccer and party with him while you cast out an angel because he wears black and is home-schooled!"

Tears streamed down my face, and I ran outside.

Becky ran after me. "I'm sorry, Raven. I'm sorry!" she shouted.

I ignored her and ran all the way to the Mansion, struggling over the slippery gate. Huge moths fluttered around the porch light as I banged the serpent knocker. "Alexander, open up! Alexander, open up!"

Eventually the light went out and the disappointed moths flew away. I sat on the doorstep crying. For the first time in my life I found no comfort in darkness.

20

Game Over

I cried all night and stayed home from school the next day. At noon I ran to the Mansion. I shook the gate until I thought it would fall over. Finally I climbed over and banged the serpent knocker. The attic curtains ruffled, but no one answered.

Back home I called the Mansion and spoke to Jameson, who said Alexander was asleep. "I'll tell him you rang," he said.

"Please tell him I'm sorry!"

I was afraid Jameson hated me as much as Alexander.

I called every hour; each time Jameson and I had the same conversation.

"I'm going to be home-schooled from now on!" I yelled when my mother tried to get me out of bed the next morning. Alexander wasn't taking my calls, and I wasn't taking Becky's. "I'm never going back to school!"

"You'll get over this, dear."

"Would you have gotten over Dad? Alexander's the only person in the universe who understands me! And I messed it all up!"

"No, *Trevor Mitchell* messed it up. You were nice to that young man. He's lucky to have you."

"You think so?" I started to cry mansion-sized tears. "I think I ruined his life!"

My mom sat on the edge of my bed. "He adores you, honey," she comforted, hugging me like I was a crying Billy Boy. I could smell the apricots in her shampooed velvet-chestnut hair and the sweet soft scent of her perfume. I needed my mom now. I needed her to tell me everything would be all right. "I could see how much he adored you when he came to the house," she continued. "It's a shame people talk about him the way they do."

"You were one of those people," I sighed. "And I guess I was, too."

"No, you weren't. You liked him for who he really was."

"I did—I mean, do. I really do. But it's too late now."

"It's never too late. But speaking of late, I'm late! I have to take your father to the airport."

"Call school," I called to her at the door. "Tell them I'm lovesick."

I pulled the covers over my head. I couldn't move until night. I had to see my Alexander, to shake some sense into his pale body. To beg his forgiveness. I couldn't go to the Mansion, and I couldn't break in—he might call the cops this time. There was only one place to go—one other place where he might be.

I climbed into Dullsville's cemetery with a bouquet of daffodils in my backpack. I walked quickly among the tombstones, trying to retrace the steps we had once taken together. I was as excited as I was nervous. I imagined him waiting for me, running up to me, and giving me a huge hug and showering me with kisses.

But then I thought, *Will he forgive me? Was this our first fight—or our last?*

Eventually I found his grandma's monument, but Alexander wasn't there.

I laid the flowers on the grave. My belly hurt, like it was caving in.

Tears started welling up in my eyes.

"Grandma," I said out loud, looking around. But who could hear me? I could shout if I wanted to. "Grandma, I messed up, messed up big time. There is no one in this world more wild about your grandson than I am. Could you please help me? I miss him so much! Alexander believes I think he's so different, and I do think he's different—but from other people, not from me. I love him. Could you help me?"

I waited, looking for a sign, something magical, a miracle—bats flying overhead or a loud thunderclap. Anything. But there was only the sound of crickets. Maybe it takes a little bit longer for miracles and signs. I could only hope.

One day of being lovesick turned into two days, which turned into three and four.

"You can't make me go to school!" I shouted every morning and turned over and went back to sleep.

Jameson continued to tell me Alexander couldn't come to the phone. "He needs time," Jameson offered. "Please be patient."

Patient? How could I be patient when every second of our separation felt like an eternity?

Saturday morning I had an unwelcome visitor. "I challenge you to a duel!" my father said, throwing his tennis racket on my bed. He opened the curtains and allowed the sun to blind me.

"Go away!"

"You need exercise." He threw a white T-shirt and white tennis skirt onto my bed. "These are Mom's! I didn't think I'd find anything white in your drawers. Now let's scoot! Court time is in half an hour."

"But I haven't played in years!"

"I know. That's why I'm taking you. I want to win today," he said, and closed the door behind him.

"You think you'll win!" I yelled through the closed door.

Dullsville's country club was just as I remembered it from all those years ago—snobby and boring. The pro shop was filled with designer tennis skirts and socks, neon balls, and overpriced rackets. There was a four-star restaurant that charged five dollars for a glass of water. I almost fit in, with my mom's white threads, except for the black lipstick. But my father let it go. I think he was happy I was in an upright position.

I ran after my dad's shots with a vengeance, each ball having Trevor Mitchell's face on it. I hit the balls as hard as I could, and naturally they either crashed into the net or into the fence.

"You used to let me win," I said after we ordered lunch.

"How can I let you win when you're slamming every shot into the net? Swing easy and follow through."

"I guess I've been hitting the ball in the wrong direction a lot lately. I never should have let Trevor get the best of me. I should never have believed the rumors, or wanted to believe them. I miss Alexander so much."

At lunch the waiter brought me a garden salad and a tuna melt for my dad. I stared at my tomatoes, eggs, and romaine lettuce. "Dad, do you think I'll ever meet someone like Alexander again?"

"What do you think?" he asked, taking a bite of his sandwich.

"I don't think I will. I think he's it. He's the special one people only find in movies and gushy romance novels. Like Heathcliff or Romeo."

My eyes welled up with tears.

"It's okay, honey," he said, handing me his napkin.

"When I met your mother, I wore John Lennon glasses and hair down to the middle of my back. I didn't know what a pair of scissors or a razor looked like! Her father didn't like me because of the way I looked and my radical politics. But she and I saw the world the same way. And that's all that mattered. It was a Wednesday when I first saw your mom, on the university lawn, in maroon bell-bottoms and a white halter top, twirling her long brown hair, gazing up. I walked over and asked what she was staring at. 'That mother bird is feeding its baby birds. Isn't it beautiful?' she said. 'It's a raven!' And she quoted some lines from Edgar Allan Poe. I laughed. 'What are you laughing at?' she asked me. And I told her it was a crow, not a raven. 'Oh, that's what I get for partying too hard last night,' she said, laughing with me. 'But aren't they beautiful just the same?' And I told her right there and then that yes, they were. But she was more beautiful."

"You said that?"

"I shouldn't be telling you this. Especially the part about the partying!"

"Mom always told me that's how I got my name, but she never mentioned the partying."

I thanked the universe my parents had been looking at a raven that day and not a squirrel. The results would have been disastrous.

"Dad, what do I do?"

"You'll have to figure that one out yourself. But if the ball lands in your court again, don't smash it into the fence. Just open your eyes and swing right through."

We got my salad to go as I couldn't chew on it and the tennis metaphors at the same time.

I was greatly confused. I didn't know what to do. Hit the ball or wait for it to come to me? My father was lolly-gagging with a friend when I heard a voice say, "You play a mean game, Raven!" I turned around and saw Matt leaning against the front counter.

"I can't play at all!" I replied, surprised. I looked around for Trevor.

"I'm not talking about tennis."

"I don't understand."

"I'm talking about school, about Trevor. Don't worry, he's not here."

"So, are you trying to start something with me?" I asked, clutching my racket. "Here at the club?"

"No, I'm trying to end it. I mean, what he does to you and Becky and everyone. Even me. And I'm his best friend. But you stick up for everyone here. And you don't even like us." He laughed. "We're mean to you and you still get Trevor back for all of us."

"Are we on *Spy TV*?" I asked, looking around for hidden cameras.

"You bring spice to this town, with your funky clothes and your attitude. You don't care what people think, and this town revolves on what people think."

"Is Trevor hiding in the gift shop?" I asked, peering over.

"The Snow Ball really changed a lot of people's minds. Trevor used the whole school, and in the end he made fools of everyone. I think it was our wake-up call."

I realized there were no hidden cameras or hiding Trevors. Matt wasn't joking.

"I wish Alexander could hear you say this," I finally said. "I haven't seen him, and I'm afraid I never will again. Trevor ruined everything," I said, my eyes starting to well up again.

"Screw Trevor!"

Several people looked over, as it wasn't polite to swear at the club, even though they did on the court after they missed a shot.

"Gotta run, Raven—see you," Matt said as he took off.

"I'd like you to meet an old acquaintance, Raven," my father said, approaching with a strikingly suntanned man after Matt left.

"It's nice to see you, Raven," he said. "It's been a while. You look so grown up now. I wouldn't recognize you without the lipstick. Do you remember me?"

How could I forget him? The first time I entered the Mansion, the basement window, the red cap. The warm kiss on my cheek from the handsome new guy trying to fit in.

"Jack Patterson! Of course I remember you, but I can't believe you remember me."

"I'll always remember you!"

"How do you two know each other?" my father asked.

"From school," Jack answered, with a glint in his eye.

"So what are you up to now?" Jack asked me. "Rumor

has it that you're going into the Mansion through the front door these days."

"Well, I was, but . . ."

"Jack recently moved back to town and took over his father's department store," my dad said.

"Yeah, stop by sometime," Jack said. "I'll give you a discount."

"Do you sell combat boots and black cosmetics?"

Jack Patterson laughed. "I guess some things haven't changed!"

Matt suddenly returned. "Ready to go, Matt?" Jack asked.

"You know Matt?" I asked, surprised.

"We're cousins. I'm glad I moved back—I have some reservations about the crowd he hangs around with."

21

It was Saturday evening. I was dressed in my Cure T-shirt and black boxers, watching *Dracula* in slow motion. I paused the part where Bela leans into a sleeping Helen Chandler and recalled the time Alexander kissed me on his black leather couch. I stared longingly at the screen and grabbed some more tissues.

The doorbell shocked me out of my self-pitying trance. "You get it!" I shouted, and suddenly remembered my family had gone to the movies.

I peered through the peephole but saw nothing. Then I looked again and discovered tiny Becky standing on the doorstep.

"What do you want?" I asked, opening the door.

"Get dressed!"

"I thought maybe you came here to apologize."

"I'm sorry, but you must believe me! You have to

come to the Mansion—now!"

"Go home!"

"Raven, immediately!

"What's going on?"

"Please, Raven, hurry!"

I ran upstairs and threw on a black T-shirt and black jeans.

"Hurry!"

I ran back downstairs. She grabbed my arm and pulled me out the door.

I bombarded her with questions as we got into her father's pickup, but she refused to tell me anything.

I imagined the Mansion covered with graffiti, its windows shattered, Trevor and his soccer snobs having it out on the hill with a bloody Alexander. And then another horrible image, but a silent one. A for sale sign in the yard and not even the dark curtains hanging in Alexander's attic window.

Becky didn't park at the Mansion, but a block away.

"What gives?" I asked. "Why don't you park closer?"

But as we jumped out, I saw several cars parked along the curb leading up to the Mansion, unusual for the desolate street.

In the distance I spotted two women dressed in black like they were going to a funeral. But they were swiftly walking, holding lighted torches.

My heart sank. "We'll never make it!" I shouted.

Worse still was seeing a man, also dressed in black and carrying a lighted torch. I freaked. Everything stopped inside of me. It was just like the ending of *Frankenstein*—where the townspeople gather to burn the castle and cast out poor Franky from his home. Only this was a smaller mob. I couldn't believe it had come to this. I could already smell the smoke.

"No, no!" I shouted, but the man had already turned the corner toward the gate.

My darkest imagination could not have prepared me for what I laid my eyes upon: A small crowd of Dullsvillians had gathered on the Mansion grounds. Conservative townspeople dressed in vampire black? Everyone was so dark I thought I must be wearing sunglasses, but a glowing Becky convinced me I was seeing a perfect picture. There were lively people hanging outside the front of the usually lonely Mansion—and they were all having a blast!

I didn't understand any of it. The gathering was more like a party, but it made no sense. Was it just another sick joke? And then I saw the banner on the open gate that made everything wonderfully clear: WELCOME TO THE NEIGHBORHOOD.

"Better late than never," Becky said.

Red streamers also hung from the gate, and lawn torches lit the hill.

"Hey, girl, don't ignore us!" someone called as Becky and I entered the grounds.

I turned around. It was Ruby! She was dressed in a skin-tight black-vinyl dress, and thigh-high black-vinyl go-go boots.

"I've gotten a date out of this outfit already, Raven. You'll never believe it—it was from the butler!" She grimaced like a smitten giggly school girl and fluffed her dyed black hair as she checked herself out in her compact. "He's older, but he's kinda cute!"

By the looks of Ruby, she had been pulled straight off a Paris fashion runway. Even her white poodle was wearing a studded black leash and a black doggie sweater.

"Recognize me?" It was Janice in a black mini and combat boots. "Think it's my color?" she said, revealing her black nail polish.

"Any shade of black will do!" I said.

"I tried to tell you not to come to the Snow Ball," Becky began quickly as we walked up the driveway. "But Trevor blackmailed me. You're always there for me when I need you and I wasn't there for you. Will you ever forgive me?"

"I was so caught up, I didn't listen to your warnings. And you're here for me now." I took her hand. "I'm just glad you're not under Trevor's spell anymore."

As Becky and I continued to walk up the hill of party goers, we ran into Jack Patterson wearing a black turtleneck and jeans.

"I've been waiting all these years for the right moment to pay you back," he confessed. "I've outfitted the party. There's nothing black left in the store!"

Now, after all these years, it was my turn to give him a grateful kiss on the cheek. "This is so unbelievable!"

"It wasn't my idea for the partiers to wear black," Jack

said, pointing to a guy in Doc Martens, a black T-shirt, and slicked-back hair.

"Hey, girl!" It was Matt. "I was afraid you wouldn't show. We had to send Becky for you. We couldn't properly welcome Alexander to town after all this time without you!" My eyes lit up. "Alexander's been asking about you all night."

I glanced around frantically, speechless. I wanted to throw my arms around everyone. But where was Alexander?

"I think you'll find him inside," Matt hinted.

"I can't believe you did this!" The thought of seeing Alexander again thrilled me. I gave Matt a Ruby squeeze-hug. I think he was as startled by my affection as I was.

"You better get up there—before the sun rises," he said.

I paused, remembering one Dullsvillian I hadn't spotted. "He's not going to be lurking in the shadows, right?"

"Who?"

"You know who!"

"Trevor? He wasn't invited."

"Thanks, Matt. Thank you so much!" I said, giving him a thumbs-up.

"You did this, really. It's been good for us to take a walk on the wild side."

Becky grabbed my arm and led me toward the Mansion. A refreshment table was set up by the door. Juices and pop, chips and SnoCaps, Sprees, Good & Plenty, and Dots. Everything that Alexander had that night we watched TV at his house.

"No way!" I exclaimed. I glared at Becky. "I even told you about the SnoCaps?" I realized.

"If I kept that a secret, too, we wouldn't have refreshments," Becky added.

She prepared herself for my fury, but instead I smiled and said, "I'm glad you have such a good memory. Whose idea was this welcome party?" I wondered.

Becky glanced toward the front steps.

Out of the corner of my eye I noticed two trendy honeymooners holding hands.

"Oh, there she is," I heard the hipster man say.

It was my parents! My mom was in black bell-bottoms, black platform sandals, and a silky black shirt, with a string of red love beads around her neck. My dad was wearing black-rimmed John Lennon glasses and had squeezed his body into black Levi's and a black silk shirt unbuttoned halfway.

"Are you on drugs?" I wondered aloud, astonished.

"Hi, honey," my mom said. "We had to do something to get you out of bed."

My dad laughed and two young kids in Dracula outfits came whizzing by. One extended his cape with his hands and pretended to fly toward me.

"I've come to suck your blood!" It was Billy Boy.

"You look divine! You're the cutest vampire I've ever seen," I said.

"Really? Then I'm going to wear this to school on Monday."

"Oh, no, you're not," my dad scolded. "One radical in the family is more than I can handle."

My father looked at my mother for help. Billy winked at me and flew off.

Jameson stepped out of the Mansion holding a black jacket.

"Here is your sports coat, Mr. Madison," he said, handing the jacket to my dad. "The boy wouldn't let it go. Something about your daughter's perfume."

I was totally embarrassed, but I melted inside.

"It's good to see you, Miss Raven."

I wanted to see Alexander. I wanted to see him right then. I wanted to see his face, his hair, his eyes. I wanted to see if he still looked the same, if he still felt our deep love connection. Or if he thought it was all a lie.

As if he could read my thoughts, Jameson said, "Won't you come in?"

I walked inside, thankful that the reunion—or the blowout—would be a private one. It was quiet inside, no music pulsing from the attic, and dark, with only a few candles lighting the way. I checked the living room, the dining room, the kitchen and the hallway. I climbed the grand staircase.

"Alexander?" I whispered. "Alexander?"

My heart was pounding and my mind frenetic. I peeked in the bathrooms, the library, the master bedroom.

I heard voices from the TV room.

Renfield was ratting to the doctor about Count Dracula. It was during this scene that Alexander had kissed me and I had fainted. I sat on the couch and watched impatiently for a minute, expecting him to return. But I grew anxious and wandered back out to the hallway.

"Alexander?"

I looked at the faded red-carpeted staircase leading to the attic. His staircase!

The door at the top of his squeaky stairs was closed. His door. His room. The room he wouldn't let me see. I gently knocked on the door.

No answer. "Alexander?" I knocked again. "It's me, Raven. Alexander?"

Behind that door was his world. The world I had never seen. The world that had all the answers to all his mysteries—how he spent his days, how he spent his nights. I twisted the knob, and the door creaked slightly open. It wasn't locked. I wanted more than anything to push it open. To snoop. But then I thought. This is how the trouble began: with my snooping. Haven't I learned anything? So I took a deep breath and acted against my impulse. I shut the door and hurried down the creaky attic stairs and the grand staircase with a new confidence. I paused at the open front door, and feeling a familiar presence once again, I turned around.

There he stood, like a Knight of the Night, looking straight at me with those dark, deep, lovely, calming, lonely, adoring, intelligent, dreamy, soulful eyes.

"I never meant to hurt you," I blurted out. "I'm not what Trevor said. I've always liked you, for who you are!"

Alexander didn't speak.

"I was so stupid. You're the most interesting thing that's ever happened in Dullsville. You must think I'm so childish."

He still didn't speak a word.

"Say something. Say I was totally third grade. Say you hate me."

"I know we are more similar than different."

"You do?" I asked, surprised.

"My grandma told me."

"She speaks to you?" I said, feeling a sudden chill.

"No, she's dead, silly! I saw the flowers."

He reached his hand for mine. "There's something I want to show you," he said mysteriously.

"Your room?" I asked, grabbing his hand.

"Yes, and something in my room. It's finally ready."

"It?" My imagination ran wild. What did Alexander do up in his room? Was "it" alive or dead?

He led me up the grand staircase and the creaky attic stairs. His stairs.

"It's time you knew my secrets," he said, opening the door. "Or at least most of them."

It was dark except for the moonlight that shone through the tiny attic window. A beat-up, comfy chair and a twin-sized mattress rested on the floor. A strewn black comforter exposed maroon sheets. A bed like any other teenager's. Not a coffin. And then I noticed the paintings. Big Ben with bats flying over the clock face, a castle on a hill, the Eiffel Tower upside down. There was a dark painting of an older couple in gothic outfits with a huge red heart around them. There was Dullsville's cemetery, his grandma smiling above her grave stone. A picture drawn from his attic window with trick-or-treaters everywhere. "Those are from my dark period," he joked.

"They're spectacular," I said, stepping closer.

Paint was everywhere, even splattered on the floor.

"You're totally awesome!"

"I wasn't sure you'd like them."

"They're unbelievable!"

I noticed a canvas covered with a sheet on an easel in the corner.

"Don't worry, it won't bite."

I paused before it, wondering what lay beneath the sheet. And for once my imagination failed me. I took a corner of the sheet and slowly peeled it back, just like when I had uncovered the mirror in Alexander's basement. I was stunned.

I was staring at myself, dressed for the Snow Ball, a red rose corsage pinned to my dress. But I carried a pumpkin basket over my arm and held a Snickers in one hand while on the other I wore a spider ring. Stars twinkled overhead and snow fell lightly around me. I grinned wonderfully through glistening fake vampire teeth.

"It looks just like me! I never imagined you were an artist! I mean I knew you did those drawings in the basement and then the paint on the side of the road. . . . I had no idea."

"That was you?" he asked, reflecting.

"Why were you standing in the middle of the road?"

"I was going to the cemetery to paint this picture of my grandmother's monument."

"Don't most painters use little tubes?"

"I mix my own."

"I had no idea. You're an artist. Now it all makes sense."

"I'm glad you like it," he said with relief. "We better get back to the party before we give them something to really gossip about."

"I guess you're right. You know how rumors spread in this town."

"Isn't it weird?" he asked, handing me a soda, back on the lawn after we'd mingled among the darkened Dullsvillians. "We're not the outcasts tonight."

"Let's enjoy it now. It'll all be back to normal tomorrow."

The party goers were smiling and having fun.

But then I noticed a figure in the distance slowly running up the driveway.

"Trevor!" I said, with a gasp. "What's he doing here?"

"He's a monster!" he yelled, approaching the party. "His whole family."

"Not this again!" I said.

All eyes were on Trevor.

"Alexander, go back inside," I urged. But he didn't move.

"He hangs out in the cemetery for freakin' sake!" Trevor said, pointing to my Gothic Mate. "There were no bats in this town before he came!" he shouted.

"And there weren't losers in this town before you came!" I said.

"Raven, calm down," my father admonished sternly.

"Enough of this!" Matt said, bursting forth, with Jack Patterson right behind him.

"Look here! I've been attacked!" Trevor exclaimed, pointing to a scratch on his neck. "By a bat! I'm going to have to get freakin' rabies shots!"

"Let it go, Trevor," Matt said, exhausted.

"It happened on the way here. I'd called your house and your mom said you were partying at freak Mansion. What's up with that? You were supposed to be hanging out with me!"

"You've done this to yourself," Matt answered. "I'm through driving you around town so you can spread your stupid rumors. You've played me long enough, Trev."

"But I was right! They are vampires!" Trevor shouted.

"And I was right when I didn't invite you," Matt said.

"You guys are crazy. Partying with freaks!" Trevor argued, glaring at us all.

"Okay, Trevor, that's enough," my father said, stepping toward him.

"I didn't have anything to do with this," Alexander said, confused.

"I think we know that," I confirmed.

"But—" Trevor began, his angry eyes thirsting for blood.

"I'd rather not have to call your father," my dad finally

said, putting his hand on Trevor's shoulder.

Trevor was fuming, but he was running out of steam. There was no one here who'd fall for his jokes, take his side, think he was wonderful for scoring a winning goal. No giggling girls who wanted to date a soccer snob or hang with him anymore because he was popular. There was nothing left for him to do but leave.

"You just wait—my dad owns this town!" he said, as he stormed off. It was the only thing he could say.

"Don't forget to use some ice on that," my mom advised as if she were Florence Nightingale.

"He needs a tranquilizer gun, not ice, Mom."

We all watched as Trevor reached the gate and was finally gone.

"Well, we had planned on a singing telegram, but they must have gotten the instructions wrong," my dad joked. The crowd laughed with relief.

Alexander and I hung onto each other for comfort. The children began running around, pretending to be vampires.

Later, after Alexander had said good-bye to his neighbors, Becky found me cleaning up the refreshment table.

"I'm sorry," she said.

"Are you going to apologize for the rest of your life?"

I gave her a Ruby squeeze-hug. "See you tomorrow," Becky said with tired eyes.

"I thought your parents already left."

"They keep farm hours, you know. Early to bed and early to rise."

"Then who are we riding with?" I asked, confused.

"Matt."

"Matt!"

She smiled an I-have-a-crush smile. "He's not as snobby as he seems."

"I know. Who would have thought?"

"He's never ridden on a tractor before," Becky said. "Do you think he says that to every girl?"

"No, Becky, I think he really means it!"

"C'mon, Becky," Matt called, just like he used to call Trevor.

"I'll catch up in a minute," I said.

I was helping Jameson with the last of the party trash when Alexander descended the stairs, wearing a cape, slicked-back hair, and fake vampire teeth.

"My dream vampire," I said.

He pulled me close in the hallway.

"You tried to save me tonight," he said. "I will be eternally grateful."

"Eternally," I said with a grin.

"Hopefully someday I'll return the favor."

I giggled as he nibbled on my neck. "I don't want to go," I whined. "But Becky is waiting. See you tomorrow?" I asked. "Same bat time? Same bat channel?"

He walked me to the door and playfully bit me on the

neck with his vampire teeth.

I laughed and tried to pull the fake teeth out of his mouth.

"Ouch," he exclaimed.

"You're not supposed to Superglue them on!"

"Raven, you don't still believe in vampires, do you?" he asked.

"I think you've cured me of that," I answered. "But I'm going to keep the black lipstick."

He gave me a long, heavenly good-night kiss.

As I turned to leave, I noticed Ruby's monogrammed compact on the doorstep and picked it up. I opened it to smooth out my lipstick. I saw the Mansion's open door reflected in its glass.

"Sweet dreams," I heard Alexander say.

But he didn't appear in the mirror.

I turned around. Alexander was clearly standing in the doorway.

But when I checked the mirror again, he was gone!

When I turned around once again, I found the serpent door knob staring me in the face. I rapped on it desperately.

"Alexander! Alexander!"

I backed away from the door in disbelief. I slowly retreated and stared up at the attic window. The light came on.

"Alexander!" I called.

He peered out from behind the ruffled curtains, my

Gothic Guy, my Gothic Mate, my Gothic Prince, my Knight of the Night. Looking down at me, longingly. He touched the window with the palm of his hand. I stood motionless. As I began to reach toward him, he withdrew from the curtain and the light vanished.

My childhood dream had come true, but it was more of a nightmare than I could have imagined. I lay awake all night, trying to make sense of it all.

The guy I was in love with was really a vampire? Would I spend eternity as a cool ghoul?

I didn't react to this development in the way I'd always dreamed. I didn't pick up the phone to call CNN. In fact, the whole ride home with Becky I didn't say a word, only stared out the window in disbelief as she flirted with Matt.

At home I locked myself in my bedroom. I scoured my vampire books for answers but found none. I rehearsed telling him that I loved him, no matter who or what he was. That his secret was safe with me. But was I prepared to leave everything I knew? Trade my world for his? Leave my parents? Becky? Even Billy Boy? I stared at my reflection in the full-length mirror, as if for the last time.

I spent the next day at the cemetery, pacing in front of the baroness's monument. As soon as the sun set behind the trees, I took off for the Mansion.

When I came around the hill, I noticed the gate was locked. I scaled the fence to find the Mansion even more eerie and lonely than usual. The Mercedes was gone and the lights were off. I rang the bell, over and over. I rapped on the serpent knocker. No one answered. I peered through the living room window. White sheets were draped over the furniture. I ran around back and pressed my nose against the basement window. I couldn't breathe. The crates of earth were no longer there!

My heart sank. I couldn't swallow.

I reached for the loose brick I had formerly used to sneak in. But when I pulled on it, an envelope with my name written across it in large letters fell out.

I raced to the front gate and held the letter under the light.

I saw my name clearly.

I pulled out a black card. In blood-red letters were four simple words: BECAUSE I LOVE YOU.

I caressed the words with my fingertips and held the letter to my heart. Tears fell from my face as I wearily slunk against the Mansion gate.

It was a stake shoved into my heart.

Birds chirped overhead and I looked up to see them

hovering over the trees. One swooped down and landed above me on the iron gate.

It was a bat.

Its wings remained solemnly still as it fixed its gaze upon me. Its shadow prominent on the pavement, its breath in time with mine. Bats are blind, but this one seemed to be staring right into my soul.

I slowly reached for it. "Alexander?"

And then it flew away.

Acknowledgments

A million thanks to my editor, Katherine Brown Tegen, for your experienced advice, talent, and friendship.

Many thanks to Julie Hittman, for your hard work and communication, and the wonderful staff at HarperCollins.

I'm deeply grateful to my brother, Mark Schreiber, for your generosity and expertise.

XOXO to Suzie, Ben, and Audrey Schreiber, for your support and the memorable trip to New Orleans.

Vampire Kisses 2

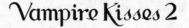

To my father, Gary Schreiber,
with all my love,
from your little ghoul

"Here's to new blood."

—Jagger Maxwell

1

I t was like a final nail in a coffin.

Becky and I were camped out in my darkened bedroom, engrossed in the eighties cult horror classic *Kissing Coffins*. The femme fatale, Jenny, a teenage, malnourished blond wearing a size negative-two white cotton dress, was desperately running up a serpentine rock footpath toward an isolated haunted mansion. Bright veins of lightning shot overhead in the pouring rain.

Only the night before had Jenny unearthed the true identity of her fiancé when she stumbled upon his hidden dungeon and found him climbing out of a coffin. The dashing Vladimir Livingston, a renowned English professor, was not a mere mortal after all, but an immortal blood-sucking vampire. Upon hearing Jenny's blood-curdling screams, Professor Livingston immediately covered his fangs with his black cape. His red eyes remained unconcealed, gazing back at her longingly.

"You cannot bear witness to me in this state," I said along with the vampire.

Jenny didn't flee. Instead, she reached out toward her fiancé. Her vampire love growled, reluctantly stepped back into the shadows, and disappeared.

The fang flick had gathered a goth cult following that continued today. Audience members flocked to retro cinemas in full costume, shouted the lines of the movie in unison, and acted out the various roles in front of the screen. Although I'd seen the movie a dozen times at home on DVD and knew all the words, I'd never been blessed with participating in a theatrical showing. This was Becky's first time watching it. We sat in my room, glued to the screen, as Jenny decided to return to the professor's mansion to confront her immortal lover. Becky dug her gnawed-on blood-red-painted fingernails into my arm as Jenny slowly opened the creaky wooden arch-shaped dungeon door. The ingénue softly crept down the massive winding staircase into Vladimir's darkened basement, torches and cobwebs hanging on the cement brick walls. A simple black coffin sat in the center of the room, earth sprinkled beneath it. She approached it cautiously. With all her might, Jenny lifted the heavy coffin lid.

Violins screeched to a climax. Jenny peered inside. The coffin was empty.

Becky gasped. "He's gone!"

Tears began to well in my eyes. It was like watching myself on-screen. My own love, Alexander Sterling, had vanished into the night two evenings ago, shortly after I had discovered he, too, was a vampire.

Jenny leaned over the empty casket and melodramatically wept as only a B-movie actress could.

A tear threatened to fall from my eye. I wiped it off with the back of my hand before Becky could see. I pressed the "Stop" button on the remote and the screen went black.

"Why did you turn it off?" Becky asked. Her disgruntled face was barely illuminated by the few votives I had scattered around my room. A tear rolling down her cheek caught the reflection of one of the candles. "It was just getting to the good part."

"I've seen this a hundred times," I said, rising, and ejected the DVD.

"But *I* haven't," she whined. "What happens next?"

"We can finish it next time," I reassured her as I put the DVD away in my closet.

"If Matt were a vampire," Becky pondered, referring to her khaki-clad new boyfriend, "I'd let him take a bite out of me anytime."

I felt challenged by her innocent remark, but I bit my tongue. I couldn't share my most secretest of secrets even with my best friend.

"Really, you don't know what you'd do" was all I could say.

"I'd let him bite me," she replied matter-of-factly.

"It's getting late," I said, turning on the light.

I hadn't slept the last two nights since Alexander left.

My eyes were blacker than the eye shadow I put on them.

"Yeah, I have to call Matt before nine," she said, glancing at my *Nightmare Before Christmas* alarm clock. "Would you and Alexander meet us for a movie tomorrow?" she asked, grabbing her jean jacket from the back of my computer chair.

"Uh . . . we can't," I stalled, blowing out the votives. "Maybe next week."

"Next week? But I haven't even seen him since the party."

"I told you, Alexander's studying for exams."

"Well, I'm sure he'll ace them," she said. "He's been cracking the books all day and night."

Of course, I couldn't tell anyone, even Becky, why Alexander had disappeared. I wasn't even sure of the reason myself.

But mostly, I couldn't admit to myself that he had gone. I was in denial. *Gone*—the word turned my stomach and choked my throat. Just the thought of explaining to my parents that Alexander had left Dullsville brought tears to my eyes. I couldn't bear accepting the truth, much less telling it.

And I didn't want another rumor mill circulating throughout Dullsville. If word got out that Alexander had moved without warning, who knows what conclusions the gossipmongers would jump to.

At this point, I wanted to maintain the status quo: keep up appearances until the RBI—Raven Bureau of Investigation—had a few more days to figure out a plan.

"We'll double-date soon," I promised as I walked Becky outside to her truck.

"I'm dying to know. . . ," she said, climbing into her pickup truck. "What happens to Jenny?"

"Uh . . . She tries to find Vladimir."

Becky closed her door, rolled down the window. "If I discovered Matt was a vampire and then he disappeared, I'd search for him," she said confidently. "I know you'd do the same for Alexander."

She started the engine and backed out of the driveway.

My best friend's remark was like a package of Pop Rocks blasting off in my brain. Why hadn't I thought of it sooner? I'd spent the last several days worrying how long I'd have to keep making excuses for Alexander's absence. Now I wouldn't be forced to wait an eternity in Dullsville wondering if he'd ever return. I didn't have to jump every time the telephone rang to find out it was for my mother.

I waved to Becky as she drove down the street. "You're right," I said to myself. "I have to find him!"

"I'm going to Alexander's. I won't be long—" I called to my mother as she sat devouring a J. Jill catalogue in the living room. I had a jolt of electricity coursing through my veins, which had been stagnant since my goth guy departed.

I grabbed my coat and ran back to the Mansion to find any clues of Alexander's whereabouts. I couldn't let my true love disappear without a full report from the RBI— Nancy Drew dipped in black.

Although becoming a vampire had always been a dream of mine, when faced with it, I didn't know what I'd do. Alexander already did what all great vampires do—he transformed me. I craved his presence every minute I was awake. I thirsted for his smile and hungered for his touch. So did I need to literally transform into a diva of darkness to be with my vampire boyfriend? Did I want to spend my life in greater isolation than I already did as an outcast goth? However, I had to let him know that I loved him no matter who or what he was.

I had spent a lifetime as a nocturnal-loving, rebellious, black-on-black-wearing outcast in the pearly white cliquey conservative town of Dullsville. I was relentlessly teased and bullied by soccer snob Trevor Mitchell. I was stared at like a circus freak by Dullsvillians, classmates, and teachers. The only friend I'd ever had was Becky, but we never shared the same taste in music or fashion, and our personalities were polar opposites. When Alexander Sterling moved to the Mansion on Benson Hill, for the first time in my life I felt like I wasn't alone. I was drawn to him before I even met him—seeing him standing in the darkened roadway, Becky's headlights illuminating his fair skin and sexy features. He took my breath away. Then, when he caught me sneaking into the Mansion and I got a glimpse of him again, I had a feeling I'd never known before. I knew I had to be with him.

Not only was he a pale-skinned, combat-boot-wearing goth like me, but as we began dating, I found out we listened to the same music—Bauhaus, Korn, and Marilyn

Manson. More important than tastes, we shared the same desires and dreams. Alexander understood loneliness, isolation, and being different. He knew firsthand what it was like to be judged for what he wore, how he looked, for being homeschooled and expressing himself through a paintbrush instead of a soccer ball.

When I was with him, I felt like I finally belonged. I wasn't judged, bullied, or teased for what I wore but was accepted, and even celebrated, for who I was inside.

With Alexander gone and his whereabouts unknown, I felt lonelier than I had before I met him.

I removed the brick that held the broken window open and crept inside the Mansion's basement. The full moon illuminated mirrors covered with white rumpled sheets, carelessly stacked cardboard boxes, and a coffin-shaped coffee table. My heart sank when I saw again that the earth-filled crates were gone.

The last time I had searched the Mansion uninvited, I had hoped to make chilling discoveries. I unearthed crates stamped by Romanian customs and marked SOIL. I found an ancient family tree, including Alexander's name, with no dates of births—or deaths. Now I was apprehensive about what I *wouldn't* find.

Upstairs, the portraits that once lined the walls were gone. I followed the hallway to the kitchen, where I opened the refrigerator. Only leftovers remained. Antique china dishes and pewter goblets still lined the cabinets. I spotted an unlit candle and a box of matches on the black granite countertop.

I wandered the empty halls by candlelight. The wooden floorboards creaked beneath my feet as if the lonely Mansion were crying.

In the living room the moonlight shone through the cracks in the red velvet drapes. The furniture was once again covered with white sheets. Disheartened, I headed for the grand staircase.

Instead of the music of the Smiths pulsing from upstairs, all I heard was the wind blowing against the shutters.

The ghoulish Mansion no longer sent waves of excitement through my veins, only lonely chills. I ascended the stairs and crept into the study, where I'd once been greeted by my knight of the night, holding fresh-picked daisies. Now it was just another abandoned library—books collecting dust, empty of readers.

The butler's bedroom was even more spartan, with a single perfectly made bed, Jameson's closet cleared of clothes, cloaks, and shoes.

The master bedroom was furnished with a canopy bed with black lace that dripped around its gothic columns. I stared at the mirrorless vanity directly across. The little combs, brushes, and nail polishes in shades of black, gray, and brown that had belonged to his mother were gone.

I'd never even had the opportunity to meet Alexander's parents. I wasn't sure if they even existed.

Tormented, I paused at the bottom of the attic steps. I wondered how Alexander felt leaving so suddenly, after finally being accepted by so many Dullsvillians.

I climbed the narrow attic stairway and blew out the

dripping candle. I entered his abandoned bedroom, which only two nights ago he had invited me into. His twin-sized mattress rested on the floor, unmade. Typical for any teenager, vampire or not.

The easel in the corner was bare. I gazed at the paint splattered on the floor. All his artwork was gone, even the painting he had made for me—a portrait of me dressed for the Snow Ball, holding a pumpkin basket and a Snickers, sporting a spider ring and fake vampire teeth.

A black letter-sized envelope lay on top of a blood-red paint can, sitting underneath the easel. I held the piece of mail up to the moonlight. It was addressed to Alexander and had a Romanian stamp. There was no return address and the postmark was illegible. The envelope had been ripped open.

Curiosity getting the best of me, I reached my fingers inside and pulled out a red letter. In black ink it read:

Alexander,
HE IS ON HIS WAY!

Unfortunately the rest of the letter had been torn off. I didn't know who it was from or what it meant. I wondered what vital information it held—maybe a top secret location. It was like watching a movie and not seeing the ending. And who was *he*?

I walked to the window and stared up at the moon—the very window where his grandmother's ghost was rumored to have been seen. I felt a kinship with the baroness. She had lost the love of her life and was left to keep his secret in isolation. I wondered if that would be my fate as well.

Where was Alexander headed? Back to Romania? I'd buy a ticket to Europe if I had to. I'd walk mansion door to mansion door to find him.

I wondered, if Alexander had stayed, what would have happened to him. If the town found out his identity, he could have been persecuted, taken away for scientific research, or paraded around as the top act in a sideshow. I imagined what would become of me. I might be interrogated by the FBI, hounded by tabloids, or forced to live in isolation, forever known as the Vampire Vulture.

I turned to leave his room when I saw a small booklet poking out from underneath his mattress. I took it to the attic window for closer inspection.

Had Alexander forgotten his passport? There was an empty spot where his photo had been torn out. I touched the space, wondering what picture a vampire could have taken.

I flipped through the pages. Stamps from England, Ireland, Italy, France, and the United States.

If I had Alexander's passport in my hand, he couldn't have gone back to Romania. No one can travel out of the country without a passport.

Now I had one thing I didn't have before.

Hope.

"Slow down!" my mom said when I burst through the kitchen door. "You're tracking mud all over the floor."

"I'll clean it later—" I said hurriedly.

"I'd like to invite Alexander over for dinner this week," she offered, catching up to me. "We haven't seen him since the party. You've been keeping him all to yourself."

"Sure—" I mumbled. "We'll talk later. I'm going to study."

"Study? You've been studying since the party. Alexander has had a positive effect on you," she said.

If my mother only knew I had been holed up in my room, waiting for e-mails, calls, and letters that never arrived.

Billy Boy and my dad were watching a basketball game in the den.

"When's Alexander coming over?" Billy asked when I passed by.

What could I tell him? Maybe never?

I quickly settled for, "Not for a while. I don't want to overexpose him to suburbia. He might want to start playing golf."

"I think you've found yourself a keeper," my dad complimented.

"Thanks, Dad," I said, stopping for a moment, thinking of the family picnics, holidays, and vacations Alexander and I wouldn't be able to share. "Please don't disturb me," I ordered, heading toward my bat cave.

"Could she actually be doing homework?" Billy Boy asked my dad, surprised.

"I'm doing a report," I called back. "On vampires."

"I'm sure you'll get an A," my dad replied.

I locked myself in my bedroom and feverishly searched the Internet for any info on vampire hangouts where Alexander might be. New Orleans? New York? The six months sans sunlight of the North Pole? Would a vampire want to hide among the mortal population or isolate himself with his own kind?

Frustrated, I lay on my bed, boots still on, and stared at my bookshelves of Bram Stoker novels, movie posters of *The Lost Boys* and *Dracula 2000*, and my dresser top adorned with Hello Batty figures. But nothing gave me insight into where he might have gone.

I reached over to switch off my *Edward Scissorhands* lamp when I noticed on my nightstand the object that had gotten me into this mess: Ruby's compact!

Why hadn't I thought of her sooner? At the party, Jameson had asked her out for a date.

No one stands up Ruby—not even the undead!

The following morning I ran full throttle to Armstrong Travel, arriving before the agency opened.

I heard keys rattling and heels clicking behind me. It was Janice Armstrong, the owner.

"Where is Ruby?" I asked breathlessly.

"She doesn't come in on Tuesdays until the afternoon," she answered, opening the door.

"The afternoon?" I groaned.

"By the way," she said, moving close, "do you know anything about Alexander's butler?"

"Creepy Man?" I asked. "I mean, Jameson?"

"They were supposed to have a date," she confessed, switching on the office lights and adjusting the thermostat.

"How was it?" I asked naively.

Janice put her purse in her top drawer, turned on her computer, and looked at me.

"Don't you already know? He didn't show," she said. "And with a stunner like Ruby he was lucky she even looked in his direction!"

"Did he say why he canceled?" I pressed.

"No. I thought Alexander would have told you," she said.

"Not directly."

She shook her head. "A good man is hard to find, you know. But you have Alexander."

I bit my black lip.

"Hey, aren't you late for school?" she inquired, looking up at the Armstrong Travel clock.

"I'm always late! Janice, can you give me Ruby's address?"

"Why don't you stop back at the end of the day?"

"It's just that she left her compact—"

"You can leave it here," Janice suggested.

The front door opened and in walked Ruby.

I imagined a jaded woman in jeans holding a cigarette and a beer, but even being jilted, Ruby was in style. She was wearing full makeup and a white sweater and matching tight white slacks.

"You're in early today," Janice said.

"I have a lot to catch up on," Ruby replied with a sigh. "What are you doing here?" she asked, surprised to see me.

"I have something of yours."

"If you are here on behalf of Jameson," she said, "you can tell him I'm sorry *I* had to cancel."

"You? But he was—" I began.

Ruby settled in at her desk and turned on her computer, accidentally knocking over her cup of pens.

"Darn it!" she exclaimed, agitated, trying to grab the pens as they fell to the floor.

Janice and I raced over to help her pick them up.

"This has never happened before!" Ruby said angrily. "Now everyone will know."

"I knock things over all the time," I comforted.

"No, she means about Jameson," Janice whispered to me. "I got stood up several times before I met my Joe. But I must admit I'm surprised about the butler. It was doubly rude, since we came to the party to support the Sterling family." Janice glared at me as if Jameson's no-show was my fault. "I feel as though he stood me up, too."

"It's not the biggest deal," Ruby said. "Anyway, he's more . . . shall I say, eccentric than I am."

"He's a fool," Janice said.

"This really surprises me. He was such a gentleman," Ruby lamented. "And that accent. I guess that's why I was taken by him."

"He likes you, too," I said. "Only—"

Both women looked at me as if I were going to reveal national secrets.

"Only what?" Janice asked.

"Only . . . that he should have called."

"You're darn right! I hope you haven't told anyone about this," Ruby said worriedly. "In a small town like this, being stood up could ruin my reputation."

"You must know something, Raven," Janice pried.

"Yes, did Alexander allude to anything?" Ruby asked.

I had to console my former boss. After all, I was the one who caused Jameson to abandon their date. I couldn't let Ruby take it personally.

"Just that the reason he canceled had nothing to do with you," I said evasively.

"I bet he has a girlfriend," Ruby speculated. "I read in *Cosmo*—"

"Of course he doesn't!" I exclaimed with a laugh. "But I need to know something as well. Did Jameson have a trip planned?"

"Do you know something I don't?"

"Did he buy any airline tickets? Or come in asking for any road maps?" I hinted.

"What aren't you telling us?"

Ruby and Janice stared at me hard. I wasn't about to tell them the truth—that Alexander didn't reflect in her compact.

Ruby's compact! I almost forgot.

I began to pull it out from my purse when a man dressed in chinos and a red polo shirt entered the office with a grand bouquet. Distracted, I replaced the compact and zipped up my purse.

"Ruby White?" he asked.

"I'm Ruby," she said, her hand waving in the air like she'd just won the coverall at bingo.

He handed Ruby a bouquet of white roses. She blushed as she took the flowers.

Flowers for Ruby? They could have been sent from any number of Dullsvillian suitors.

"What does the card say?" Janice asked eagerly. "I wonder if they're from Kyle the golf pro."

"'I'm sorry these had to greet you instead of me,'" Ruby read. She looked up in astonishment. "'Fondly, Jameson.'"

"Jameson?" I asked, suddenly wide-eyed.

"How sweet!" Janice said, filling a glass vase from the watercooler. "I told you all along he was wonderful."

"Can you believe this?" Ruby wondered aloud, holding the bouquet close.

"What else does it say?" I asked.

"Isn't that enough?" Janice said, inhaling the scent and placing the flowers in the vase. "They're beautiful!"

"No info on where the order was placed from?" I inquired.

Ruby shook her head, distracted.

"But there has to be—" I mumbled. I looked out the window and saw the deliveryman stepping into a white van with the words FLOWER POWER spelled out in daisies.

I raced out the door as the van began to drive off.

"Wait!" I called, running hard in my combat boots. "You forgot something!"

But it was too late. The van sped around the corner.

Breathless and frustrated, I retreated back to the travel agency. I began to open the door when I noticed a piece of paper lying on the sidewalk. It was a Flower Power delivery order. It must have fallen out of the van. I quickly grabbed it, scanning the document for any vital info. The travel agency address was fully disclosed. But the sender's address was blank. No name. No e-mail. Nothing.

Then, hidden in the right-hand corner, I noticed a ten-digit number.

"Can I use your phone, Ruby?" I asked, running inside. "I'll only be a minute."

"Of course," she said, arranging the roses. At that moment, I could have called Africa and she wouldn't have cared.

The area code seemed oddly familiar. I racked my brain. It belonged to a town a couple hundred miles away, where my aunt Libby lived.

I dialed. Would Alexander's voice greet me? *Ring.* Or Creepy Man's? *Ring.* Or would it be a dead end? *Ring.*

"Thank you for calling the Coffin Club," a zombie-like voice finally answered. "Our business hours are nightly from sunset to sunrise. Leave a message—if you dare!"

I let the phone slip from my hand. Ruby was still arranging her flowers.

"Good goth!" I whispered. "The Coffin Club!"

At school I now experienced a newfound popularity. It wasn't as if I were a celebrity, but schoolmates who had never even looked my way before called, "What's up, Raven?"

But besides a hello wave, nothing had changed. No one except Matt and Becky invited me to eat lunch, offered me a ride home, or asked me to join their study group. Not one classmate secretly passed me a note or bothered to share his pack of gum. Thankfully, I was too distracted to appreciate any rise in status and spent a morbidly long afternoon in front of the library computer searching the Internet for the Coffin Club.

"I want to visit Aunt Libby," I told my parents that night at dinner.

"Aunt Libby?" my dad asked. "We haven't seen her in ages."

"I know. And it's about time. Spring break starts Wednesday. I'd like to leave tomorrow afternoon."

"I can't imagine you'd want to be away from Alexander for a minute, much less a few days," my mom said.

"Of course I'll die being away from Alexander," I exclaimed, rolling my eyes. I could feel my family staring at me, waiting for my next response. "But he's going to be tied up with his homeschooling exams. So I thought I'd take the opportunity to see Aunt Libby."

My parents looked at each other.

"Are you sure you're not going there to see a Wicked Wiccas concert?"

"Dad! They broke up five years ago."

"Well, Libby's not a very good role model," my dad remarked. "And who knows what neurotic guy she's involved with this time."

"Dad, she's more like you than you think. You just don't drive a hippie mobile anymore."

"I remember visiting *my* aunt when I was a teenager," my mom said. "She took me to see *Hair*."

"See—I need these memorable teen experiences to shape my life."

"Libby gets such a kick out of Raven," she admitted. "It would be good for her as well."

"All right," Dad said reluctantly. "I'll call her tonight. But if she's still practicing voodoo, you're not going."

After dinner I met Becky by the swings at Evans Park.

"I had to talk to you, pronto," I began.

"Me, too! Life is so good. Can you believe we both have boyfriends?"

Even if Alexander weren't a vampire, the idea of us having boyfriends was still unreal. We'd both been social outcasts for so many years, it was incomprehensible to be accepted by anyone but each other.

"I need you to come on a little trip with me," I told her.

"Trip?"

"I'm going to visit my aunt Libby and I need you to come!" I exclaimed excitedly.

"This weekend? I'll have to ask."

"No, I'm leaving tomorrow afternoon."

"Matt asked me to watch his soccer game after school."

"You just started seeing him!" I argued.

"I thought you'd be happy for me. Besides, I was going to ask you to come."

The thought of watching a soccer game made me want to hurl, but Becky's glow made me realize I was being selfish. "I *am* happy for you, but—"

"Can't you go another time?" she begged. "We have all spring break to hang out with Matt and Alexander."

There was no point arguing. Becky was going to watch Matt's game tomorrow, just as I was going to search for Alexander. No amount of pleading would make us change our minds. Now that Matt had abandoned his best friend, my nemesis, Trevor, the thorn in my side since kinder-garten, he would hang out with Becky all the time. And I was jealous of Becky for having a boyfriend who hadn't disappeared into the night.

"Why is this trip so important?" she asked.

"It's top secret."

"What's top secret?" Matt inquired, appearing behind us.

"What are you doing here?" I asked, startled. "This is a private meeting."

"Becky and I are going to Ace's Arcade. She told me to meet her here."

It was bad enough I was losing Alexander to the Underworld, but when I needed my best friend the most, I was losing her to 3-D pinball.

"I gotta go," I said, turning away.

"So what was your top secret news?" Matt asked. "It'll be great to hear something other than Trevor's bogus stories for once."

I stared at the happy couple—Cupid's newest bull's-eyes.

"Trevor was right. The Sterlings really *are* vampires," I said impulsively.

They stared at me like I was crazy. Then they burst into laughter.

I, too, laughed and then walked away.

I packed my suitcase full of black garments, unsure of what I was preparing for. To be safe I also packed a clove of garlic in Tupperware, Ruby's compact, and a can of Mace.

To calm my nerves, I opened my Olivia Outcast journal and made a list of Positives of Dating a Vampire:

1. He'll be around for eternity.
2. He can always fly for free.
3. I'll save hundreds of dollars on wedding photos.
4. No mirrors to Windex.
5. He'll never have garlic breath.

I closed my journal. I had one more thing to pack.

I opened the door to my brother's room. Billy was tapping his skinny fingers on his computer keyboard.

"What do you want?" he snapped when I peeked in.

"Want? It's not what I want, but rather what I have to give. I picked this up after school today from Software City. They said it was the latest."

I showed him *Wrestling Maniacs 3*.

"Did you steal it?"

"Of course not—I may be weird, but I'm not a thief!"

He reached for the game, but I held it firm. "I just need one thing in return."

He rolled his eyes. "I knew it!"

"It's just teensy-weensy."

"Answers to a test?" he guessed.

"Not this time."

"Need a paper written?"

"Not yet."

"Then what?"

"I need a fake ID," I whispered.

"Aunt Libby is not going to take you to a bar!"

"Of course she's not. But it's really for identification, since I won't have my driver's license for a few months."

"Use your school ID, then."

"I need to be eighteen!" I started to shout. Then I took a deep breath. "There's a library convention, and I need to be eighteen to check out books."

"Whatever! Mom and Dad will kill you! You're too young to drink."

"I'm not going to drink. I just want to hang out."

"What would Alexander say if he found that you were going cruising without him?"

"I'm hoping to meet him there," I whispered.

"I knew it! You couldn't care less about 'my favorite aunt Libby,'" he said in a girlie voice.

"Pretty please?" I asked, dangling the game before his computer-strained eyes.

"Well . . ."

"You'll make it?"

"No, but I know someone who will."

For the first time ever I walked my brother to school— Dullsville Middle. The redbrick building, front lawn, and playground looked surprisingly smaller than when I had attended several years ago.

"I used to skip class and hide out over there," I said, pointing to a small athletics equipment shed.

"I know," he said. "'Raven was here' is scratched all over the side."

"I guess I skipped more than I thought," I said with a grin.

I felt like a towering gothic giant as I walked up the

front lawn among girls sporting Bratz T-shirts and Strawberry Shortcake notebooks and boys with overstuffed Pokemon backpacks.

I figured we were meeting a corrupt shop teacher, but instead we were greeted at the entrance by an eleven-year-old red-haired wunderkind named Henry.

"What do you need to make fake IDs for?" I asked him. "Getting into Chuck E. Cheese's after hours?"

Billy Boy's friend gazed up at me, like he'd never seen a real girl up close.

"You can stare at my picture *after* you take it," I joked.

"Follow me," he said.

In the hallway we were stopped by Mrs. Hanley, my sixth grade math teacher.

"Raven Madison! You look so grown up!"

I could tell she had expected me to wind up in juvie hall or shipped off to a boarding school. She stared at my brother and me, obviously wondering how two such different human beings could come from the same shared DNA.

"I never realized Billy was your brother," she confessed.

"I know," I whispered. "I'm amazed, too."

"Well, some things haven't changed," she said, walking off. She kept looking back as if she had seen an apparition. I knew who'd be the subject of today's talk around the microwave in the teachers' lounge.

We stopped at Henry's locker, the only one with a combination lock that was hooked up to a garage door opener. Henry flipped the control switch and the combo lock sprung open. Computer games, electronics, and programming manuals were organized in racks like a miniature computer store.

He pulled out a digital camera hidden underneath a shelf.

"Let's go."

I followed them around the corner to the computer room. But it was locked. My heart sank.

"This can't happen! Break a window if you have to," I said, half jokingly.

Both geeky preteens looked at me as if I were the odd one.

Henry dug into the back pocket of his chinos and pulled out a worn brown leather wallet. He opened it and got out a credit card. He slid the card into the door, jiggled it a little, and within a moment the door slipped open.

"I like your style," I said with a smile.

Twenty minutes later I was staring at an eighteen-year-old Raven. "I look good for my age," I said with a wink, and headed for home.

Mom, I'm not going to Siberia. I'll be back in two
days." We were sitting at Dullsville's Greyhound bus
stop, outside Shirley's Ice Cream Parlor. She was trying to
strangle me with kisses when the bus squealed to the curb
in front of a few other young Dullsvillians heading out
early for spring break.

As the bus pulled away and I waved good-bye from my
window seat in the back, I actually felt a pang in my stomach. This would be my first trip away from Dullsville on
my own. I even wondered if I would return.

I sat back, closed my eyes, and thought what it would be
like if I became Alexander's vampiress.

I imagined Alexander waiting for me at Hipsterville's
bus stop, standing in the rain, wearing tight black jeans and
a glow-in-the-dark Jack Skellington shirt, a small bouquet
of black roses in one hand. Upon seeing me, his pale face

would flush with just enough pink to make him look alive. He'd take my hand in his, lean into me, and kiss me long. He would whisk me off in his restored vintage hearse, adorned with painted spiders and cobwebs, the music of Slipknot blasting from the speakers.

We'd park in front of an abandoned castle and climb the creaky spiral stairs that led to the desolate tower. The ancient castle walls would be lined with black lace and the rustic wooden floors sprinkled with rose petals. A million candles would flicker around the room, the skinny medieval windows barely letting in moonlight.

"I couldn't be without you anymore," Alexander would say. He would lean into me and take my neck into his mouth. I'd feel a slight pressure on my flesh. I'd become dizzy, but feel more alive than I'd ever felt before—my head would slump back, my body become limp in his arms. My heart would pulse in overtime as if beating for both of us. Out of the corner of my eye, I would be able to see Alexander lift his head proudly.

He'd gently let me down. I'd feel lightheaded and stumble to my feet, holding my red-stained neck as the blood trickled down my forearm.

I'd be able to feel two pointy fangs with the tip of my tongue.

He would open a tower window to reveal the sleeping town. I'd be able to see things I'd never seen before, like smiling ghosts floating above the houses.

Alexander would take my hand, and we would fly off into the night, above the sparkling lights of the town and beneath the twinkling stars, like two gothic fairies.

The sound of clanging bells interrupted. Not the tinkling of bells signaling my arrival into the Underworld, but rather a railroad crossing warning of an incoming train, signaling the end of my overactive imagination. The bus was stopped in front of a railroad track. A toddler in the seat across the aisle from me waved excitedly as the black engine approached.

"Chug-a-chug-a-choo-choo!" he exclaimed. "I want to be a conductor," he proclaimed to his mother.

I, too, stared as the conductor waved his blue hat while the train began to pass us. Instead of new boxcars whizzing by us, a string of dilapidated, graffiti-laden freight cars lagged in front of us. Like the toddler across from me, who was likely dreaming of the glamorous life of a conductor—too naive to realize the demands of the job, isolation, long hours, and little pay—I, too, wondered if my dream of becoming a vampire was more romantic than its reality.

I was stepping into a world of the unknown, knowing only one thing: I had to find Alexander.

The official welcome sign to Aunt Libby's town should read, "Welcome to Hipsterville—Inhabitants must check all golf pants at the city limits." The small town was an eclectic mix of hip coffee shops, upscale secondhand stores, and indie cinemas where all forms of cool people presided—granola heads, artists, goths, and chic freaks. Every kind was acceptable here. I could see why Alexander and Jameson might have escaped to this particular town. It was in close proximity to Dullsville and they could easily blend in with the smorgasbord of other motley inhabitants.

I could only imagine what my life would have been like if I had grown up in a town where I was more accepted than ostracized. I could have been on the A-list to Friday night "haunted" house parties, been crowned Halloween Queen, and received straight A's in Historical Tombstones class.

Dad and Aunt Libby had both been hippies in the sixties, but while Dad morphed into a yuppie, Libby stayed true to her inner Deadhead. She had moved to Hipsterville, majored in theater at the university, and now worked as a waitress in a vegan restaurant to support her acting. She was always performing in an avant-garde play or a performance-art piece in some director's garage. When I was eleven my family watched her stand onstage for what seem liked days, dressed as a giant snow pea and speaking in broken sentences about how she sprouted.

When I arrived in Hipsterville, I wasn't shocked to find that Alexander wasn't waiting for me, but I was surprised my aunt wasn't. *I hope she isn't this late for her curtain calls,* I thought, as I waited at the bus stop in the hot sun beside my suitcase. Finally I spotted her beat-up vintage yellow Beetle sputtering into the lot.

"You're so grown up!" she exclaimed, getting out of her car and giving me a huge hug. "But you dress the same. I was counting on that."

Aunt Libby had a youthful face, decorated with sparkling purple eye shadow and pink lipstick. She wore red dangly crystal earrings beneath her auburn hair, a sky blue halter dress spotted with white beads, and beige Nairobi sandals.

Her warmth spilled over me. Even though we differed

in our tastes, we immediately bonded like sisters, talking about fashion, music, and movies.

"*Kissing Coffins?*" she asked when I told her what I recently watched. "That's like *The Rocky Horror Picture Show.* I remember going to the midnight show and dancing in the aisles. 'Let's do the time warp again,'" Aunt Libby sang, as passersby gave us strange looks.

"Uh, *Kissing Coffins* isn't a musical," I interrupted before my aunt got a citation for disturbing the peace.

"Isn't that a shame. Well, I've got a great place to take you," she raved, and led me around the block to Hot Gothics.

"Wow!" I shouted, pointing to a pair of black patent-leather boots and a torn black mesh sweater. "I've only seen this store on the Internet."

I was in goth heaven, and it was beautiful! Wicked Wiccas T-shirts, Hello Batty comics, and fake body tattoos.

The multipierced fuchsia-haired clerk in black shorts over black leggings, three-inch-heeled Mary Janes, and a gray mechanics shirt that said "Bob" walked over to me. She had the kind of style that in Dullsville could be seen only on satellite TV. And instead of my usual retail experience of either being ignored or seen as a potential thief, she greeted me as if I were a movie star at a Beverly Hills boutique.

"Can I help you? We have tons of stuff on sale."

I eagerly followed her around the store until I was exhausted from rack after rack of gothic clothing.

"Feel free to ask, if you need anything else," she said.

I had my arms stuffed with fishnet stockings, knee-high black boots, and an Olivia Outcast purse.

Libby modeled a black T-shirt that read "Vampires Suck."

I felt a pang in my heart and a lump in my throat.

"I'll buy it for you," she insisted, taking it to the cash register.

Normally I would have screamed with delight at a shirt like that. But now it only reminded me that Alexander was gone.

"You don't have to."

"Of course I do. I'm your aunt. We'll take this," she said, handing the clerk the shirt and her credit card.

I held my gothic goodies. Everything reminded me of Alexander.

"I'll just put these back," I said. But then I thought about how sexy I'd look in boots and black fishnets, if I found him again.

"We'll get these, too," my aunt said, seeing through me, and handed the clerk my merchandise.

Aunt Libby lived on a tiny tree-lined urban street with skinny row-house apartments from the 1940s—a sharp contrast to my contemporary suburban house and neighborhood in Dullsville. Her one-bedroom apartment was small but cozy, with a bohemian feel—flowered rugs, pillows, wicker chairs, and lavender potpourri filled the living room. Italian masks decorated the walls and Chinese lanterns hung from the ceiling.

"You can crash here," Aunt Libby said, pointing to a paisley futon couch in the living room.

"Thanks!" I said, excited about my new digs. "I appreciate you letting me visit you."

"I'm so happy you came!" she replied.

I placed my suitcase by the futon and glanced at a Pink Floyd clock hanging above the antique "just for show" fireplace, which she had filled with unlit candles. I had only a few hours until sunset.

Libby poured me carrot juice as I unpacked. "You must be hungry," she called from her tiny art deco kitchen. "You want an avocado wrap?"

"Sure," I said, plopping down at her vintage weathered-yellow dinner table with a beaded napkin holder and a wobbly leg. "I bet you have a hot date tonight," I hinted, as she topped my sandwich with sprouts. "But that's okay. I can take care of myself."

"Didn't your father tell you? I guess he wanted it to be a surprise."

"Tell me what?" I asked, envisioning Libby handing me VIP passes to the Coffin Club.

"I have a show tonight."

A show? I didn't travel all the way to Hipsterville to spend three hours sitting in a garage.

"It's downtown," she said proudly. "We're having a private performance tonight for the town's senior citizens, so I'm sorry to say you'll be the only one there without gray hair. But I know you'll love it." She grabbed an envelope hanging on her fridge by a rainbow magnet.

She opened the envelope, pulled out a ticket, and presented it to me.

THE VILLAGE PLAYERS PRESENT
Dracula

The Village Players performed in a former elementary school. The actresses' dressing room was a classroom that still smelled of erasers, and the large windows were covered with heavy shades. Mirrors replaced the chalkboard, and a long vanity lined with makeup cases, flowers, and congratulations cards sat in place of a teacher's desk.

As Aunt Libby applied her makeup and squirmed into her white Victorian dress, I spun a forgotten globe in the corner, letting a black-painted fingernail come to a rest on Romania.

Of course, under any other circumstances I would have loved to see a performance of *Dracula*. I would have gone every night, especially to see my aunt as an admittedly old, but I'm sure convincing, Lucy. I would have ordered front-row seats. But why would I want to see a fake Dracula when I could see the real thing sipping a Bloody Mary down the street at the Coffin Club?

The stage manager called from the hallway, "Five minutes."

I hugged Libby and told her to break a leg. I hoped she wouldn't notice my empty seat during the performance, but I couldn't worry about that as I hurried up the aisle to the back of the theater.

I pulled aside an elderly usher who looked like he might be one of the undead. "Which way to the Coffin Club?"

Some people spend all their lives searching for their soul mates. I had only an hour and a half to find mine.

I turned the corner to a sight I'd never seen before: More than a dozen young goths waiting in a line. Spiked, dyed black-and-white hair, purple floor-length extensions, billowy capes, knee-high black boots, and Morticia dresses. Lips, cheeks, tongues, foreheads pierced with metal studs and chains. Tattoos of bats, barbed wire, and esoteric designs covered their limbs, chests, and backs and, in many cases, their entire flesh.

Above the line of ghoulish goths, two coffins were outlined in red neon on the black brick building.

Impatience being my virtue, I snuck in front of a girl who was tying up loose corset laces in her medieval gown.

A Marilyn Manson look-alike standing in front of me turned to face me. "You from around here?"

"I don't think any of us are from around here, if you know what I mean," I said, all knowing.

"I'm Primus," he responded, extending his hand. His

fingernails were longer than mine.

"I'm Raven," I replied.

"And I'm Poison," a girl in a tight black-and-red-striped rayon dress snapped, grabbing Primus's hand away.

The crowd continued moving forward. Primus and Poison showed their IDs and disappeared inside.

A bouncer in a *Nosferatu* T-shirt scrutinized me, blocking the black, wooden coffin-shaped door.

I held my card proudly. But when the devilish-looking bouncer started studying it, my confidence waned and my heart began to pound.

"This looks like it was taken yesterday."

"Well, it wasn't," I said with a sneer. "It was taken today."

The bouncer cracked a smile, then laughed. "I haven't seen you here before."

"Don't you remember me from last time? I was the girl in black."

The bouncer laughed again. He stamped my hand with an image of a bat and wrapped a barbed-wire-shaped plastic bracelet around my left wrist. "Here alone?" he asked.

"I'm hoping to meet a friend. An older dude, bald with a gray cloak. He was here recently. Have you seen him?"

The bouncer shrugged. "I only remember the girls," he said with a smile. "But, if he doesn't show, I'm off just before sunrise," he added, letting me pass and opening the coffin door.

I stepped through and entered a dark, crowded, smoke-filled, head-banging Underworld. I had to pause to let my eyes adjust.

Dry-ice fog floated over the clubsters like tiny ghosts. The cement walls were spray-painted black, with flashing neon headstones. Pale mannequins with huge bat wings hung from the ceiling, some bound in leather, others in Victorian suits or antique dresses. The bathroom doors were shaped like giant tombstones; one read MONSTERS and the other GHOULS. Spiderwebs clung to the bottles behind the bar. A sign underneath a broken clock read NO GARLIC. Next to the dance floor a mini gothic flea market was set up on folding tables. A vampire clubster could buy anything from fake teeth to body tattoos and tarot card readings. A balcony loomed above the dance floor, accessible by a spiral staircase. Clubsters, with blood-filled amulets dangling from their necks and grimacing vampire teeth, seemed to be a mix of harmless outcast goths and maybe a few truly deranged. But if I had to bank that there were real vampires in this part of the world, some had to be mixing it up here, where they could walk hidden among the masses.

The thrashing music of Nightshade blasted from the speakers. I could feel the stares as I walked by. Instead of the usual glares I was used to enduring whether walking down the halls of Dullsville High or sauntering past Prada-bes milling about town, I felt self-conscious for a different reason—I was being checked out. Hot Goths, Gorgeous Goths, even Geeky Goths were eyeing me as if I were a gothic Paris Hilton catwalking down a medieval runway. Even girls, sporting shrunken T-shirts that read SIN or pretentiously exposed their concave, multipierced bellies, scrutinized me territorially, as if threatened by any other single female with black eye shadow in a tight black dress. I fingered my raven-colored hair nervously, trying to be careful whom I made eye contact with. Were they real vampires smelling the scent of a mortal? Or just goths looking for a ghoul?

I pushed my way to the bar, where a long-haired bartender wearing lipstick and eye shadow was pouring red liquor into a martini glass.

"What can I get for you?" he asked. "Blood beer or an Execution?"

"I'd like an Execution, but make it a virgin," I replied with confidence. "I'm driving. Or should I say *flying*."

The grim bartender broke into a smile. He took two pewter bottles off the shelf and poured them into an iron-maiden-shaped glass.

"That'll be nine dollars."

"Can I keep the glass?" I asked. I sounded like an excited kid at an amusement park instead of an underage teen trying to be cool at a bar.

I handed him a ten. "Keep the change," I said proudly, like I'd seen my dad do a thousand times. I wasn't even sure I was leaving a proper tip.

I took a sip of the red slush, which tasted like tomato juice.

"Was a bald man wearing a dark cloak here the other night?" I asked, shouting over the blaring music. "He made a phone call from the club."

"That guy's here every night."

I smiled eagerly. "Really?"

"And at least fifty guys just like him," he answered loudly.

I turned around. He was right. There were as many shaved heads as there were spiked ones.

"He has creepy-looking eyes and a Romanian accent," I added.

"Oh, that dude?" he asked, pointing to a skinny, bald man with a gray cloak, talking to a girl in a Wednesday Addams dress in the corner.

"Thanks!"

I quickly pushed my way through the crowd.

"Jameson!" I shouted, tapping him on the shoulder. "It's me!"

He turned around. But instead of actually being a senior citizen, he just looked like one. I fled before he could ask me to bond with him for eternity.

I scooted by the gothic marketplace, not having time to stop and purchase pewter, crystal, or silver amulets or have my tarot cards read.

But when I passed the last booth, a palm reader grabbed my hand. "You are looking for love," she said.

A single girl in a club looking for love? What were the odds of that?

"Well, where is he?" I challenged, shouting over the blaring music.

"He's closer than you think," she answered mysteriously.

I glanced around the packed club. "Where?" I hollered.

The reader said nothing.

I slipped a couple of dollars into her palm. "Which direction?" I asked loudly.

She looked into my eyes. "East."

"The bar?"

"You must look in here," she said, and pointed with her other hand to her heart.

"I don't need pithy sayings. I need a map!" I chided, and continued to make my way through the crowd.

I stopped at the DJ booth.

"Did you see a bald man here recently?" I asked the DJ, who was dressed in a white lab coat with fake blood splattered on it.

"Who?"

"Did you see a bald man here last weekend?" I repeated.

He shrugged his shoulders.

"He may have been wearing a gray cloak."

"Who?"

"The man I'm asking about!" The music was so loud, even I couldn't hear myself.

"Ask Romeo at the bar," he hollered back.

"I already did!" I grumbled.

As I returned to the bar, I spotted a dark-haired guy in jeans and a charcoal gray T-shirt leaning against a Corinthian column on the dance floor.

I pushed past the clubsters, my heart beating full force. "Alexander?"

But on closer inspection, I was confronted with a twenty-something wearing a BITE ME T-shirt and reeking of alcohol.

Frustrated, I headed back to the bar once again.

"That wasn't him," I said to Romeo. "The guy I'm talking about made a phone call from the Coffin Club."

Romeo turned to his Elviraish counterpart, who was placing a tip into her bra.

"Hey, this girl's looking for a bald guy who came to the club the other night," Romeo said. "He made a phone call from here."

"Oh, yeah, that sounds familiar," she said.

"Really?" I perked up.

"I remember because he asked to use the phone. No one asks anymore. Everyone has a cell."

"Did he tell you where he was staying?"

"No. He just said thank you and gave me a twenty for handing him our phone."

"Was he with anyone?" I asked, eager to receive news of Alexander.

"I think I saw him hanging out with a guy in a Dracula cape."

"Alexander?" I asked excitedly. "Was his name Alexander Sterling?"

Romeo looked at me as if he had recognized the name, but then turned away to wipe down the bar.

"I didn't have time for introductions," Elvira said. She turned away from me and waited on a guy dressed in leather waving a twenty.

Jameson *had* been here! And possibly Alexander, in the cape he had worn on the last night I saw him.

I looked around the club for any signs that might help me find him. Maybe Alexander found this place completely bogus. Was this club just full of outcast goths like me, or were any of them real vampires? Then I remembered the way to spot a true vampire was by *not* looking at them.

I reached into my purse and pulled out Ruby's compact. Every fanged clubster around me reflected back. I had to think of another plan. I replaced the compact and headed for the door.

Suddenly I felt a cold hand on my shoulder.

I turned around.

"I think I know who you want to see," Romeo said.

"You do?"

"Follow me."

I hung close to my gothic usher, half exhilarated, half terrified.

He led me up the spiral staircase to the balcony. A shadowy figure sat on a coffin-shaped couch, a large goblet and a candelabra before him on a round coffee table.

The mysterious figure glared up at me. I felt a sudden chill. I could barely whisper, "Alexander—"

The lone figure pulled the candelabra close, illuminating his features.

It wasn't Alexander.

Instead, sitting in front of me was a cryptic-looking teen, his cadaverous yet attractive face almost hidden beneath dripping white hair with red ends, as if they had been dipped in blood. Three silver rings pierced his eyebrow, and a pewter skeleton hung from his left ear. His seductive eyes pierced through me, one metallic green, the other ice blue. The whites were filled with spiderwebbed veins, as if he'd been awake for days. His skin was the color of death. His fingernails were painted black, like mine, and he wore a tattoo on his arm, which read POSSESS.

It took all my strength to turn away from his intoxicating gaze, as if I were trying to break an unearthly spell.

"You look disappointed," he said in a seductive voice, forcing me to gaze back at him. "You were expecting to meet someone else?"

"Yes. I mean . . . no."

"Hoping for someone to bond with for eternity? Someone who won't run away from you?"

"Aren't we all?" I snapped back.

"Well, I just may be your man."

"I think Romeo was confused," I said. "I was looking for someone who made a phone call from here. An older, bald man."

"Really? He doesn't seem your type."

"I was obviously mistaken—"

"One person's mistake is another man's destiny. I'm Jagger," he said with a piercing glare that made my blood boil. He stood and offered a pale hand.

"I'm Raven, but—"

"You are looking for someone who can help you fulfill your darkest desires."

"No, I was looking for . . . ," I began naively.

"Yes?" Jagger asked, with a cunning smile.

Something didn't feel right. Hadn't Romeo already told him who I was looking for? Intuition overcame me.

Jagger seemed too eager to hear me name someone.

"I've really got to go," I said, clutching my purse close like a shield.

"Please, join me." He grabbed my arm and pulled me onto the couch. "I believe we have a lot in common."

"Maybe next time . . . I really have to go—"

"Romeo, get the lady a drink," Jagger commanded. "How about a Death Sentence? It's the club special."

Jagger inched toward me and gently stroked my hair away from my shoulder.

"You're quite beautiful," he said.

I avoided his gaze and clutched my purse in my lap while he continued to eye me. I sensed that this seductive good-looking goth was no more my friend than Trevor.

"Listen, you have been—" I began, trying to stand up, when Romeo returned with two goblets.

"Here's to new blood," said Jagger with a laugh.

I hesitantly clinked my goblet with his. He took a long gulp, then waited for me to do the same. With a guy this nefarious, I could only imagine what the drink might have been laced with.

"I've gotta go," I said, standing up.

"He's not like you think he is," he said.

I paused, almost frozen. "I don't know who you are talking about," I replied, and turned to leave.

"We'll find him together," Jagger said, and rose from the couch to block my path.

He winked at me, and then grinned, revealing sharp vampire fangs that glistened in the candlelight. I stepped back, and then realized that in the Coffin Club everyone had fangs.

There was only one way to confirm who or what Jagger was.

"Okay. I'll give you my number," I said, turning away from him. I reached into my purse and sheltered the compact from his view. "Just let me find my pen."

My fingers shook as I opened Ruby's compact and angled it in his direction. I closed my eyes and hesitated. I took a deep breath and opened them.

But Jagger had already disappeared.

6

Dracula Delivers

I returned to the Village Players Theater just in time for curtain call. I hurried backstage, where I was greeted by a worried Lucy in the dressing room.

"I didn't see you in the audience!" Aunt Libby said in a tone that resembled my mother's.

"Aren't you supposed to be concentrating on the show?"

"How could I concentrate when all I saw was your empty seat?" she snapped.

"A woman next to me kept falling asleep on me," I fibbed, "so I moved to the back row. But you were wonderful!"

"So you did see it," she responded, relieved.

"Of course!" I gave her a big squeeze. "Wild vampires couldn't pull me away."

I fiddled through her makeup kit while she greeted a few fans in the hallway. I couldn't shake my encounter with Jagger from my head. Had I met a second Dracula? Or was Jagger just some tattooed teen thirsting for a date?

"You have to meet Marshall," Aunt Libby called when she returned to the dressing room.

I was peeking beneath the window shade at a lone figure lurking in the darkened alley by the Dumpster.

"Raven!" Aunt Libby called.

I turned around to face the Village Players version of Dracula—a malnourished, overpowdered, middle-aged man with slicked-back, gelatinized gray hair, ultra-red lips that resembled Bozo the Clown's, and oversized press-on fingernails. He wore a traditional satin cape.

How could an overaged, uncharismatic man play the sexy, seductive Dracula? He must have been a good actor.

"I'd like to introduce you to your biggest fan," Aunt Libby told him.

My mind was still on the figure lurking outside. "Aunt Libby, we really should—" I began.

"I've come to suck your blood!" Dracula said in a ghoulish voice, lunging at me.

I had to keep from rolling my eyes.

There was a time not too long ago when meeting an actor who played Dracula in a professional production would have been the highlight of my existence. I would have become a gushy groupie in his presence and kept his framed autograph on my bookshelf. Now it was more like meeting a shopping mall Easter Bunny.

"Libby has told me so much about you," Dracula continued.

"Nice to meet you," I said. "We were just—"

"Come, sit down," Aunt Libby suggested, offering a

folding chair to the ghoulish lead.

"Your aunt tells me you are obsessed with vampires," he said, draping his cape over the chair and sitting down.

Actually, I'm dating one, I wanted to say.

"Have you been to the Coffin Club?" he asked me.

"She's too young," Aunt Libby reminded him as she sat in her dressing-room chair and began taking off her makeup.

"Have *you*?" I asked eagerly.

"Yes. For research purposes only."

"Did you see anything unusual?" I inquired, like a gothic Nancy Drew.

"Everything there is unusual." He laughed. "Kids walk around wearing medieval cloaks and vampire teeth, with metal spears piercing through their eyebrows and lips, and amulets of blood hanging from their necks. I think I was the only one there above thirty. Except for one other man."

"Older than you?"

"Well, stranger, if you can imagine."

"I didn't mean—"

"I know. He stuck out, too. But not in the way I did. He could have played Renfield."

"Creepy Man?" I blurted out. "I mean, was he creepy?"

"Well, I guess he was."

Unfortunately it must have been this dime-store Dracula, and not Alexander, whom Elvira had spotted talking with Jameson.

"He was quite eccentric," Marshall continued. "He

asked if I was aware of any abandoned mansions in the area. Dark, secluded, near a cemetery, with an attic."

"Are there any? I love old mansions."

"I confessed I was starring in *Dracula*," Marshall said proudly, "and I'd been to the Historical Society to research mansions and local cemeteries. I explained to him that he was better off going to the Historical Society than a real estate agent."

Dracula got up to leave. "It was a pleasure meeting you."

I could still see the figure creeping outside through the partially covered window. When I turned to look at Aunt Libby as she thanked Marshall for his visit, I could see their reflections in the long mirror, as well as the reflection of the window through which I'd been peering. The alley appeared empty. But when I turned back to the window, the figure was still there.

Alexander?

I quickly headed for the door, pushing past the exiting Dracula.

"Raven," Aunt Libby scolded.

"I'm sorry," I began. "I think I saw one of your fans outside. I'm going to see if they want to meet you!"

I rushed outside, past a smelly Dumpster, some discarded antique chairs, and stage scenery. Fire escapes hung from overhead.

When I came to the other side of the dressing-room window, the figure had already gone.

Disappointed, I looked around for any signs. The alley was empty of people. A glistening object on the cracked blacktop underneath the window caught my eye.

On closer inspection, I saw a pewter skeleton earring lying next to a puddle. I'd vaguely remembered seeing someone wearing an earring just like this. But Alexander wore studs. Then it hit me—it had been Jagger.

I checked all around me, making sure the coast was clear. I picked it up, stuck the earring in my purse, and ran back inside the theater.

Aunt Libby and I walked to her car with some of the other cast members. With each step, I couldn't help but feel as if someone was watching me.

I looked up and spotted a small dark object dangling from the telephone wire above the alley.

"Is that a bat?" I asked as she unlocked my door.

"I can't see anything," she said.

"Over there." I pointed.

Aunt Libby squinted. "I'm sure it's a bird," she commented.

"Birds don't hang upside down," I said.

"You're creeping me out!" she hollered, and swiftly raced around to her side and got into the Beetle.

Could it be Alexander? Or were my suspicions right about Jagger?

As my aunt started the car, I looked back at the wire, which was now bare.

"What are you doing?" Aunt Libby asked, back at her bachelorette pad, as I turned on all the lights. "Are you paying for the electric bill this month?"

She followed behind, turning them off.

"We have to keep them on," I declared.

"All of them?"

"Didn't my dad tell you? I'm afraid of the dark."

She glared at me in disbelief. "This from a girl who has sleepovers at cemeteries?"

She had a point. But I couldn't tell her my most secretest of all secrets. "The show really spooked me," I said instead. "You gave such a realistic performance, I'm afraid I could be bitten at any moment."

"You thought I was that believable?" she asked, surprised.

I nodded eagerly.

"Well, I prefer candlelight," she said. She lit some votives and placed them throughout the living room. Her apartment began to smell of roses and flickered with shadows of Italian masks.

Had I really met a second teen vampire? Maybe Jagger had been afraid I'd spotted his unreflected image in my compact. He might have been spying on me in the alleyway, or watching me as he hung from a telephone wire. I took a deep breath, realizing I was no better than an overreacting gossipmonger like Trevor Mitchell. I should be spending my time planning my continuing search for Alexander instead of pointing fingers to a white-haired goth's mortal existence. Jagger could have dropped his earring on his way home from the Coffin Club. The lurking figure could have been a clubster, weaving back and forth by the Dumpster after having a few too many Executions.

I picked up Aunt Libby's Lava lamp phone and called my parents.

"Hello?" Billy Boy answered.

"It's me. Are Mom and Dad home?"

"They're next door, visiting the Jenkins's new baby," he replied.

"They left you alone?" I asked, ribbing him.

"Give it a rest."

"Well, don't touch my room! Or anything in it," I warned, wrapping the telephone cord around my fingers.

"I've already read one of your journals."

"You better be kidding!"

"'Alexander kissed me!'" he said in a girlish voice. Then I heard him leaf through pages.

"You better—"

"'Trevor was right,'" he continued. "'Alexander really is a vampire.'"

I froze. How had Billy Boy gotten hold of one of my journals?

"Close it right now!" I cried. "It's not a journal. It's a story I'm writing for English class!"

"Well, you have a lot of spelling mistakes."

"Right now, Nerd Boy! Shut it or I'm coming home and melting all your computer games!"

"Calm down, spaz. I'm in my room, leafing through my NASA book," he confessed. "You think I want to go in your messy room? I could be missing for days!"

"I knew that," I said, with a sigh of relief. "Well, tell Mom I called." I was amazed how accurately Billy Boy had guessed the contents of my journal. Maybe he should perform crystal-ball readings at the Coffin Club.

"Oh, someone called for you," he remembered.

"Becky?"

"No. It was a guy."

I held my breath. "Alexander?"

"He didn't leave his name. When I said you weren't home, he hung up."

"Did you check the caller ID?"

I waited an eternity for his response.

"Out of area," he finally answered.

"If he calls again, ask who it is," I demanded. "And then call me immediately!"

Aunt Libby was munching on carrots dipped in hummus while sitting on the floor on a purple corduroy pillow. I was too distraught to eat.

"So tell me about your boyfriend," she asked, as if reading my thoughts.

"Well, he's a goth like me," I answered, beginning to tell her the part of Alexander's identity that wasn't secret. "And he's delicious!"

"What does he look like?"

"Luscious, long midnight hair. Deep, dreamy eyes. He's taller than me, about your height. Thin, not malnourished, but not beefy like he has to be in a gym twenty-four-seven. I just can't believe he left," I added, remembering the farewell note.

"He left you?"

"No, I mean he left for spring break." I scrambled, trying to cover my mistake. "To visit his family."

"I'm glad you found someone special you can identify

with. It must be hard for you growing up in that town."

I appreciated that Libby understood what it was like to be different. Because she felt more comfortable in Hipsterville, maybe Alexander had found a place where he felt more comfortable, too.

"Aunt Libby, can I ask you a personal question?"

"Of course."

"Do you believe in vampires?"

She laughed. "I thought you were going to ask about sex."

But I was serious. "Do you?"

"I once dated a guy who kept a vial around his neck. He claimed it was blood, but it smelled like strawberry Kool-Aid."

"Did he creep you out?"

"Actually the ones who claimed they weren't vampires scared me more," she teased. "We should get some sleep. We've both had a long day," she said, blowing the votives out and putting the carrots away. "I'm so glad you're here," she said, giving me a squeeze.

"Me, too."

As soon as Aunt Libby went into her bedroom, I tip-toed through the apartment and turned the other lights back on, just to be safe. I climbed onto the futon, pulled the covers over me, and closed my eyes.

Suddenly I felt a shadow on me. I squeezed my eyes shut. I imagined Alexander standing over me with flowers, begging my forgiveness for leaving so abruptly. But then I realized it could be Jagger, about to plunge his fangs into my neck.

I opened my eyes slowly.

"Aunt Libby!" I shouted with relief.

"Still spooked?" she asked, standing over me. "You can leave the living room light on."

Libby turned all the other lights off and returned to her bedroom, unaware I was trying to protect her from a tattooed teen of darkness. I pulled the covers back over my head, but still felt as if someone were watching me. I tried to calm myself by thinking of Alexander. I recalled lying in the grass with him, in the backyard of the Mansion, staring at the stars, our fingers intertwined.

I heard a scratching sound coming from the kitchen. I was probably the only girl in the world who hears a scratching sound and hopes it's a mouse. I imagined myself back at the Mansion, the dark sky brightened by luminous clouds above us, the smell of Drakar cologne in the air, and Alexander kissing me. But when Alexander spoke into my ear, all I heard was that scratching sound.

I decided to confront it and walked toward the kitchen in my black socks. A white mouse running across my feet was the least of my issues.

I switched on the kitchen light. The sound seemed to be coming from outside.

I peeled back the curtain above the sink, expecting to see Jagger's ghost-white face staring back. But it was only a tree branch swaying against the window in the wind.

Just to be safe, I opened my Tupperware container and placed a clove of garlic on the windowsill above the futon.

The next morning, I was jarred awake by the music of the Doors. The bright sun beaming in through the open windows made my head pound. I was exhausted from the bus ride to Hipsterville, searching for Alexander, and my nocturnal meeting with the inhabitants of the Coffin Club. As I looked outside, the mortal world seemed the same. Jeeps parallel parked. Hipstervillians pushed chic strollers. Birds hung on telephone wires.

But the morning sun shed new light on last night's events. Maybe my Coffin Club experience was just a dream and Jagger just a concoction of my nighttime imagination.

I rose from the futon with a gentle laugh, thinking about my overimaginative nocturnal dreams, when I spotted a charm on Aunt Libby's wooden footlocker, next to my bracelets.

Jagger's skeleton earring. It hadn't been a dream.

I held it in my hand. The bony charm stared up at me.

If Jagger was a vampire, I wondered what frights it had observed, dangling from his ear. Was it witness to late-night bites on unsuspecting girls? Had the tiny pewter bones seen Alexander?

I reminded myself that I was doing to Jagger what Trevor had done to Alexander. Trevor had started rumors that the Sterlings were vampires, not because he knew their true identity, but because he wanted to make them a town scandal. Now I was making judgments and jumping to my own conclusions about Jagger without having any facts. I had to spend my energies searching for what I had come to Hipsterville for—a real vampire instead of a wannabe.

I remembered my conversation with the Village Dracula. I had to get to the Historical Society as soon as it opened.

I found Aunt Libby in the kitchen cooking eggs.

"Good morning, honey," she said. "Did you sleep well?"

"Like a baby."

"I'm surprised you did," she said, cutting me off. "Something in the living room smells funny," she said, turning off the stove and placing the skillet on another burner.

"My mom packed me some goodies for the bus ride," I said, following her into the living room. "Maybe something spoiled."

"It seems like it's coming from over here," she said, pointing toward the window above the futon.

She quickly pulled back a broken window shade before I could stop her.

"I found it on the floor last night when I went to the bathroom," I improvised. "I thought it was a seashell."

I paused, waiting for her response.

She looked at me skeptically.

"Well, after watching your show last night, I just couldn't sleep," I added.

"But I thought you liked vampires."

"I do, but not at my window."

"You remind me of your father when he was growing up. Loved scary movies, but must have slept with the light on until college," she said.

"Then I guess it's in my genes," I said, retrieving the garlic from the windowsill and sticking it back in the Tupperware container.

"I can throw that away for you," she offered, extending her hand.

"I want to keep it," I said, as I put the container in my purse. "Until college."

Aunt Libby laughed, and I followed her into the kitchen. "I have a list of things we can do," she said, as we sat down to breakfast. "We can start by going to the art museum. There's an exhibition on Edward Gorey I think you might enjoy. We can go to the Nifty Fifties diner for lunch; they make a great bacon cheeseburger. Of course, I've never had it, but that's what I hear. After that, we can go antiquing in the neighborhood. Then I have my show. But you can hang backstage. I'm afraid it might be too scary for you to see again," she teased. "Sound cool?"

"I'd like to check out the Historical Society," I requested.

"All that talk about mansions last night with Marshall?" she guessed.

"I think I'll do a report on one for history class."

"During spring break? I figured you'd rather have a picnic in the cemetery," she said, putting down her coffee.

"Great idea! Let's do that afterward."

"I was joking," she responded.

By the time Aunt Libby got ready and I showered and dressed, the morning hours were dwindling. Libby was everything my dad wasn't—while he was an uptight type-A personality, she was a laid-back type-ZZZ. He was fifteen minutes early to a movie, and she was lucky to make it before the credits rolled.

I couldn't convince Aunt Libby to pack a basket of tortilla-wrapped tofu sandwiches and sit by empty graves, but I was able to trade in the art museum for the Historical Society. I grabbed my Olivia Outcast journal from my suitcase and put it in my backpack, and we finally headed out the door.

Dullsville's Historical Society was in an unhaunted late-nineteenth-century church. I had visited it only once on a school field trip and spent most of the time exploring the three tombstones in the cemetery until a teacher discovered my whereabouts and threatened to call my parents.

Hipsterville's Historical Society proved to be more interesting, located in two Pullman railway cars at the old train station.

Inside, I rummaged through pictures of Victorian houses, original menus from Joe's Eats, and letters from early residents. From the second car emerged a woman wearing a lime green pantsuit with matching sandals and a red-hair *That Girl* do.

"Can I help you?" she asked.

"My niece is visiting and would like to do a report on our historical mansions," Aunt Libby said, peering at black-and-white photos of streetcars that hung next to the emergency brake.

"Well, you came to the right place," she said, and pulled a book from a shelf.

"I'm interested in an abandoned estate near a cemetery."

The woman looked at me as if I were a ghost. "Strange. A man was in here the other day asking about the very same thing!"

"Really?" I asked, surprised.

"Was it Marshall Kenner?" Aunt Libby inquired. "He's starring in *Dracula*."

"No, Marshall was in earlier in the month. This was a gentleman who was new to town."

My ears perked up.

She pulled out several more books and leafed through them as Aunt Libby explored the museum.

"Here's the Landford Mansion," the woman pointed out. "It's in the far north part of town. And the Kensley Estate, toward the east."

I studied all the pictures, imagining which one Jameson would have selected. Nothing remotely resembled the Mansion on Benson Hill.

"Which one was the man interested in?" I whispered.

She looked at me strangely. "You should do your report on what *you* like."

I looked again at all the mansions, each one statelier than the last. I wrote down their names and addresses on the back of the Historical Society's brochure and realized it would take me several spring breaks to visit them all.

As I was ready to close the book, I noticed the edge of a bookmark peeking out toward the back. When I turned to the noted page, I lost my breath. A black-and-white photo of a gloomy nineteenth-century grand estate stared back at me. A wrought-iron gate surrounded the towering house, and at the top of the mansion was a tiny attic window. I envisioned ghosts hiding behind the curtains, too shy to be photographed.

Underneath, the picture read "Coswell Manor House."

"What's this?" I asked the woman, who was organizing the bookshelf.

She glanced at the picture. "I didn't think to mention that one because it's on the outskirts of town. It's been abandoned for years."

"It's perfect," I said.

"Weird. That's what that gentleman said, too."

The woman jotted down an address and handed it to me. "It's on Lennox Hill at the far end of the road."

I dropped a donation in the "Friendly Funds" jar as we left the museum.

"That was nice of you," my aunt said, as we walked through the parking lot to the Nifty Fifties diner.

"I'd have given her my college fund if I could've."

While Aunt Libby gathered her belongings for the theater and the sun made its final descent, I sat cross-legged on her futon and made notes in my journal.

My investigation was almost complete. In only a few hours, I would be reunited with Alexander. Once he understood I loved him no matter who or what he was, we could go back to Dullsville and we'd be able to be together.

Then I wondered what exactly that would mean. Would he want me to be like him in every way I could? And if faced with the choice, would I really want to choose the lifestyle I'd always dreamed of?

To quiet my mind, I made more notes:

Positives of Being a Vampire
1. Save on electric bills.
2. Could always sleep in late—very late.

3. Wouldn't have to worry about keeping a low-carb diet.

"Are you sure you want to stay alone?" Aunt Libby asked, holding her makeup bag.

"I am sixteen."

"Your parents let you stay by yourself?"

"I could have been babysitting at twelve, if anyone in Dullsville would have hired me."

"Well, there's plenty of food in the fridge," she offered, heading for the door. "I'll call at intermission to check in."

Aunt Libby may have been laid back when it came to her own lifestyle, but when I was under her roof she was just like my dad. I guess she would have been like my father and left her hippie days behind if she had had kids, too.

I quickly changed into my Hot Gothics fashion merch—black-and-white-striped tights and a torn black minidress revealing a blood-red chemise. I applied my standard black lipstick and dark eye shadow. I barely had enough time to put a red rose body tattoo on my neck.

I checked to make sure the container of garlic was tightly sealed, as I didn't want to expose Alexander to the two-inch weapon I'd use to ward off any lurking vampires. I must have brushed my hair and rearranged my red extensions a million times before I rushed out the door and waited at the bus stop for the number seven.

With every passing number eleven or sixteen, I paced the bus stop. I was considering returning to my aunt's apartment and calling a cab when I saw the number seven turn onto the street and slowly lumber toward me. Anxiously, I boarded the crowded bus, a mixture of granola heads and urbanites, slipped my cash into the change receptacle, and grabbed the slippery aluminum pole. I held on to the pole for dear life, trying to keep my balance and avoid bumping into the other passengers as the bus jolted with every acceleration. As soon as the number seven lurched forward and reached the speed limit, it began to slow down again, stopping at every bus stop in town. I checked my watch. It would have been quicker if I'd walked.

After letting off a few dozen passengers and picking up a few more, the bus driver turned the corner and passed my destination—Lennox Hill Road.

I ran toward the front of the bus.

"You passed Lennox Hill Road!" I called in a panic as the bus driver continued accelerating.

"There is no bus stop there," he said to me, looking in his rearview mirror.

"But that's my destination," I argued.

"I only stop at bus stops," he recited, continuing to drive.

"If it's a dollar fifty to get on the bus, how much is it to get off?"

I heard a few of the passengers laugh behind me.

"Pull the cord," the woman said, pointing to a white wire that ran above the bus windows.

I reached across her and pulled the wire hard.

A few seconds later, the bus driver slowed down and pulled over.

"See that?" he asked, pointing to a square sign on a pole with the number seven next to the curb. "That's a bus stop."

I gave him a dirty look and jumped off the bus, dodging an elderly couple trying to board. I ran down the road the bus had just driven up until I reached Lennox Hill Road. I turned the corner and walked past gigantic pristine estates with lush green lawns and purple and yellow flowers until I found an unkempt, overgrown weed-filled lawn. A decaying house sat on it at the end of a cold and ominous cul-de-sac. It looked as if a storm cloud were hovering over it. I had finally arrived at the stately gothic manor house.

Gargoyles sat on top of the jagged wrought-iron gates. Untamed bushes lined the front of the manor. The dead grass crunched beneath my boots. A broken birdbath sat in the center of the lawn. Moss and ivy grew on the roof like a gothic Chia Pet. I skipped along a fractured rock path, which led to an arched wooden front door.

I grabbed on the dragon-shaped knocker, and it came off the door and fell into my hand. Embarrassed, I quickly hid the knocker underneath a bush.

I rapped the door again. I wondered if Alexander was standing on the other side, ready to greet me with a colossal kiss. But there was no answer. I banged my fist against the door until my hand began to throb.

I turned the rusty handle and tried to push against the wooden entrance, but it was locked.

I snuck behind the dead bushes alongside the front of the manor. The windows were boarded up, but I spotted a slender crack. The ceilings in the manor house were so high, I was surprised that there were no clouds wafting through the rafters—plenty of room for a ghost to fly around in without even being noticed. From what I could see, the walls in the living room were as bare as the room itself.

Frustrated, I walked around to the side of the manor house and discovered a butler's entrance. I twisted the iron knob on the skinny oak door, but that, too, was bolted shut.

My heart pulsing hard, I ran to the back of the house. A few broken steps led down to a lone dingy window. It wasn't boarded up, so I eagerly pressed my face to the glass.

Nothing unusual. I saw a few cardboard boxes, a dusty tool rack, and an old sewing machine.

I tried to open the window, but it was stuck. I ran back up the broken steps and stood on the lawn.

"Hello?" I called. "Jameson? Alexander?"

But my words were answered only by the barking of a neighbor's dog.

I stared up at a single attic window. A tree starved of leaves leaned toward the manor house, one of its branches reaching out just below the window. The huge oak must have been centuries old—its trunk was as wide as a house, and its roots clutched the ground like a spider's legs. I was used to climbing, whether it was over the Mansion's wrought-iron gate or up apple trees in Becky's backyard. But scaling this tree seemed like ascending Mt. Everest in the dark. Clad in combat boots and a minidress, I stuck my heel onto the lowest branch and pulled myself up. I continued to climb at a steady rate, slowing down only to catch my breath or when I needed to feel above me for a limb hiding away from the moonlight. Weary but determined, I scooted along a heavy branch stretching underneath the attic window.

A dark curtain hid most of the room from view, but I managed to peek inside. I could make out an empty box and a wooden chair. Then, I saw the most amazing sight staring back at me—resting in the corner was the portrait Alexander had painted of me dressed for the Snow Ball. A pumpkin basket hung over one arm. A two-dimensional Raven grinned, flashing fake vampire teeth.

"Alexander!" I called. I tried to tap against the window, but my fingers were just out of reach.

"Alexander!" I called again.

I could hear the dog's bark getting louder.

"Alexander! Jameson!" I yelled with all my might.

Just then, the next-door neighbor opened his back door and stepped onto his deck. He was built like a professional wrestler.

"Hey! You kids back again?" he called over.

"What's going on, Hal?" a petite woman asked, following him out of the house.

"I told you, kids are playing in that house next door," he said to her. "I'm calling the police!" he yelled, and pulled out a cell phone from his back pocket.

I scurried down the tree, wanting to avoid being placed in a full nelson or, worse, handcuffs. Plus, I didn't want law enforcement to arrest Alexander and Jameson or force them to find another home—and this time it might be Romania.

When I reached the bottom branch, I saw, out of the corner of my eye, a rustling of the dark curtain in the attic window.

I quickly stepped back to get a better view.

But the curtain was still.

Suddenly, a chocolate-colored Doberman pinscher sprinted out of the neighbor's house, down the deck stairs, and scratched against the brown picket fence that ran parallel to the manor house.

Afraid the dog would wriggle his way through the skinny spaces between the boards and devour me like Kibbles 'n Bits, I took off around the other side of the manor and tore down the road to the bus stop.

I boarded the westbound number seven, taking a seat in the back behind a college-aged couple. I was excited to find that Alexander was indeed in Hipsterville. I imagined that he was painting portraits in a spooky cemetery. Searching a haunted mansion for furniture to decorate his attic room. Or maybe he was out for a night flight.

I was still confused why Alexander had come to Hipsterville. It was a small town with eerie abandoned manors, and with enough goths and artists to be hidden among. What else did it offer a lone vampire?

The couple seated in front of me began making out, oblivious to the other staring passengers.

I saw their reflections in the bus window. I wondered if they knew how lucky they were. Two humans who could share their nights and days together. Take pictures. Sit in the sun. Then I realized those were just small sacrifices I'd make to be with Alexander again.

The bus approached the Village Players Theater, and I disembarked with several other passengers. I walked alone down the alley toward the back entrance of the theater, conjuring excuses I could tell Aunt Libby and my parents so I could stake out the manor house for the next few nights until I made contact with Alexander. I saw a figure lurking behind the Dumpster.

"I hoped to find you here," a deep voice said, stepping out to block my way.

I froze. It was Jagger. I held my purse close; inside was my Mace and, possibly more important, my container of garlic.

"I have information that may be of interest to you."

"Information?" I asked skeptically.

"About Sterling," he said, with a knowing glance. "Isn't that who you are looking for?"

Shocked, I inched back. I knew where Alexander was staying, but I didn't know where he was. The promise of any new leads on Alexander's whereabouts made my heart pulse in overtime. Plus, my curiosity about Jagger's identity still lingered. I had to know how he knew Alexander.

"I can help you. I've known him for an eternity," he said with a grin.

I glanced back at the Village Players Theater. If I went back inside, I was guaranteed to have a safe night with real unreal vampires. Or I could just wait for Alexander outside the manor house—unless he and Jameson spotted me and left for another town. Then I was guaranteed to never see my Gothic Mate again.

"You better tell me everything you know," I said, clutching my purse to my side. "Otherwise—"

"You are free to go whenever you like," he reassured me.

I stood still as Jagger began walking down the alley.

Curiosity eating away at me, I decided to catch up to him. I followed Jagger down the street and toward a back entrance to the Coffin Club.

He led me into the warehouse and down a darkened hallway to an empty freight elevator. The rickety door shrieked out in pain when he shut it. Instead of pushing the button for the Coffin Club, he pressed the "B" button.

The elevator slowly lowered to the basement, screeching as if it were a coffin descending into hell.

"I thought we were going to the Coffin Club."

The elevator stopped. Jagger opened the door and held it for me as I stepped into a corridor.

He followed behind me so closely I could feel his warm breath on the back of my neck. We walked down the narrow hallway, the walls adorned with graffiti and the cement floor cluttered with discarded chairs and boxes. The dance floor music pulsed above. When we reached what looked like a wide storage-room door, I could hear the elevator slowly grind its way back up to mortal level. Jagger lifted the metal-gray door above our heads to reveal a windowless apartment.

I stepped inside.

"Welcome to my dungeon," he said.

Dozens of medieval candelabras filled the spacious apartment.

And then I saw it. In the far corner lay an open coffin, adorned with gothic band stickers like a mortal teen's skateboard. Dirt encircled the coffin like a walled city.

My eyes grew wide. "So you are. . . ," I began, but could barely speak.

"Oh, the coffin," he said. "Cool, huh? I got it at a vin-tage store."

"And the dirt?"

"Saw it in a vampire mag. Creepy, huh?"

I didn't know what to think. Even Alexander slept on a mattress.

"It's really comfortable. Want to give it a try?" he asked with sexy eyes.

"I'm not tired."

"You don't have to be."

Jagger confused me. I couldn't figure out if he was a vulpine vampire or just a goth-obsessed teen like me.

I looked around for any other unusual clues—but everything was unusual. Maps were spread out on the floor. The cement walls were decorated with gravestone etchings.

Next to the radiator an aquarium, without water, was filled with rocks.

His kitchen counter and sink looked as if they had remained untouched. Metal cabinets were missing their doors. I was afraid to think what was in the refrigerator—or, rather, who.

"You are the first girl I've ever brought down here," Jagger confessed.

"I'm surprised. You must meet a lot of girls at the Coffin Club."

"Actually, I'm new to town. Just like you. Visiting."

The hairs on the back of my neck rose. "How do you know I'm visiting?"

"It doesn't take a psychic to figure it out. Someone as

goth as you would be a regular at the club. Romeo had never seen you before."

"Uh . . . I guess you're right."

"Can I get you anything to drink?"

"No, thank you," I replied. "I want to know—"

Jagger walked over to the aquarium. He placed his hand inside and pulled out a huge tarantula.

"I just bought him. Would you like to pet him?" he asked, stroking the potentially poisonous spider as if it were a sleeping cat.

Normally I would have loved to pet a tarantula, but I wasn't sure of Jagger's motive.

"Where's your big-screen TV?" I asked, noticing the lack of televisions or computers.

"I find them offensive."

"So you don't watch movies? You've never even seen the original *Dracula*?" I hinted. "*Nosferatu*? *Kissing Coffins*? Someone as goth as you would seem to have the lines memorized."

"I would rather experience life than be a voyeur."

He returned the spider to the aquarium. I dug my hand into my purse.

"You left this behind," I said, and revealed the skeleton earring in my hand. He smiled brightly as if I were reuniting him with a long-lost friend.

As he took the charm from my hand, his fingers lingered, gently touching my palm, sending chills through my veins. It took some strength, but I withdrew.

"Now that this has been in your possession, it is even more special to me," he said, placing it back in his ear.

"Can I give you a reward?" he asked.

"You can tell me about Alexander."

"Shall I tell you? Or should I just show you," he asked, stepping toward me.

"Tell me," I said, defiant. "Is he a friend of yours?"

"Maybe yes," he said with an inviting smile. "Maybe no," he said with a wicked grin.

"Forget it, I'm outta here."

"I know him from Romania," he said quickly.

"Have you seen him in America?"

He shook his head, his white hair flopping over his blue and green eyes.

"Do you know where he is?" I asked.

"What if I do? How much is it worth?" he asked, licking his lips.

"You don't know, do you?" I challenged. I backed away from him, stepping on a map.

"But you know quite a lot," he argued.

I pulled my purse close.

"You knew enough about my Romanian friend to come to the Coffin Club and ask for him," he said, approaching me again.

"I don't know anything—"

"Then why do you want to find him?" he whispered softly in my ear as he gently stroked my hair off my shoulder.

"I must have been mistaken—" I said, looking away from his gaze, wanting to run, but not being able to move.

"Really?" he whispered. "He made you feel like his breath was yours," he said, circling me, his words landing softly on the back of my neck.

"I don't know what you are talking about," I lied, my heart pounding in my chest.

"That your flesh and his are one," he said, as his lips gently caressed the nape of my neck.

I could barely speak, my heart racing, the map crinkling underneath my boot.

He stepped close in front of me, his eyes piercing through my own, and gently touched my onyx necklace.

He leaned into me and kissed the top of my chest. He whispered, "That you are just a kiss away from being bonded with him for eternity."

I could barely breathe. My heart raced as he held me.

"Get off!" I cried, wedging my arms between us and pushing him away.

A map tore underneath my boot. Jagger tried to pierce me with his gaze, but I stared down at my feet. It was a map of Hipsterville. The cemeteries were highlighted in yellow, with several crossed out in black marker.

Then I noticed, lying a few feet away on the floor, the other maps—neighboring towns of Hipsterville and Dullsville. Cemeteries were highlighted and crossed out in black.

I glanced up at Jagger as he tried to lock his blue and green eyes with mine. He gently grabbed my hand like he'd done in the Coffin Club. "We can find him together," I recalled him saying. Then I remembered the note I'd found in Alexander's room—"HE IS ON HIS WAY!"

I backed away from Jagger and reached into my purse. It was worth a shot. My fingers shook as I tried to pry open the container of garlic.

The container's suction was like Super Glue. I struggled with the lid when Jagger stepped toward me.

I raced out the door and ran down the hallway. I pressed the elevator button and glanced back. Jagger stepped through his doorway and began running down the hall after me. I could hear the screeching elevator above me, but it was nowhere to be found. I looked up. The number "3" lit up; "2" lit up. "G" lit.

"Hurry! Hurry!" I mumbled, pressing the button repeatedly.

I could hear Jagger coming closer. Suddenly the "B" lit up, and the elevator stopped in front of me. I pulled the rickety door to one side and jumped in. I used all my strength to pull the accordion door shut just as an angry Jagger stepped in front of the elevator.

I darted back, away from the door, as his gaze caught me. He reached out for the door, realizing I hadn't yet pushed a button. I quickly pressed my finger against the "G" button.

As the elevator began to lift, I leaned against the wall, away from him. "I hope you find him," I heard Jagger call. "Before I do."

"What are you doing here?" Aunt Libby asked when she found me peeking underneath the shades in her dressing room after curtain call. "I called you at intermission, but you didn't pick up."

"I must have been in the shower," I rambled. "But I wanted to see you."

"You did? That's so cute!" she said, wiping off her makeup.

"I'm having such a fabulous time. But I have something to tell you."

"Yes?"

"I have to go back home tomorrow."

"So soon?" she asked, putting down her makeup sponge.

"I know," I whined. "I don't want to leave, but I still have tons of homework to do."

"When I was in school, spring break was just that—a break."

"And I'll need to leave early. Before sunset."

"Still afraid of the vampires?" she teased.

The truth was, I wasn't sure—I didn't know who or what Jagger was. The one thing I was sure of was that he was following Alexander.

It was just moments ago that I had barely escaped Jagger's lair. If I attempted to find out Jagger's reason for his search, I might be putting myself—and, more important, Alexander—in danger.

Now that Jagger was following me—outside the theater yesterday and waiting for me in the alley tonight—I knew if I returned to the manor house, or anywhere I thought I might find Alexander, I would lead Jagger right to him. Although it broke my heart, I had no choice. I would have to leave Hipsterville.

A unt Libby and I sat together on a wooden bench outside the Greyhound bus station waiting for the eight
o'clock to pull in. There was only one bus each day out of
Hipsterville, and it departed just as the sun was setting.

I looked forward to returning to Dullsville and hopefully Alexander, but I was sad to leave Aunt Libby. I
enjoyed our visit together, and I really admired her. She had
followed her dream of being an actress and in the process
lived independently, with her own style, tastes, and view of
life. She saw me as unique and special, instead of as a freak.
And most important, she treated me like I was normal.

I'd also miss the excitement of Hipsterville, knowing
there was a place like the Coffin Club for goths to hang
out and dance, and Hipsterville's Hot Gothics—a store
where I could purchase gothic clothes, spiked jewelry, and
body tattoos.

Libby put her arm around me, and I leaned my head on her shoulder as the bus pulled in.

"I'm going to miss you so much, Aunt Libby," I said, squeezing her with all my might before I climbed aboard the bus.

As I walked down the aisle, I opened my compact to check the other travelers. After everyone reflected back, even a gothic couple snuggling in back, I chose a seat next to the window. Aunt Libby waved to me as we waited for the bus to leave. I could see in her eyes that she would miss me as much as I'd miss her. She kept waving as the bus drove off. But as soon as the station was out of sight, I breathed a sigh of relief. The nefarious, mysterious, feud-seeking shock-goth Jagger was now behind me. Hopefully, a new plan to contact my handsome Gothic Prince Alexander was before me.

The bus ride back to Dullsville was painfully long. I called Becky from my cell phone, but she was at the movies with Matt. I jotted notes about my encounter with Jagger in my Olivia Outcast journal, but writing gave me motion sickness. I imagined why Jagger was searching for Alexander—maybe it was a feud between the two families over the baroness's Mansion—but it only made me worry about my boyfriend. I dreamed about reuniting with Alexander, but I also couldn't stop thinking about the maps Jagger had lying on his floor.

It seemed like an eternity until the bus finally pulled into Dullsville's bus stop. I even hoped against hope that

Alexander would magically be waiting for me, but instead I was greeted by Mom, Dad, Billy Boy, and his nerd-mate Henry.

"You're leaving already?" my dad asked after we arrived back home and I dropped my suitcase off in my room. "We want to hear more about your trip."

I didn't have time for my parents' well-meaning questions. "How did you like Aunt Libby? What did you think of her performance in *Dracula*? Did you like eating tofu sandwiches?"

I wanted to go to the place where I did my best thinking.

"I have to see Alexander!" I said, shutting the front door behind me.

I raced to the Mansion and found the iron gate ajar. Out of breath, I hurried up the long, winding driveway and noticed something peculiar—the front door was also ajar.

Maybe he'd seen me from the manor house attic window and followed me back to Dullsville.

"Alexander?" I called as I walked inside.

The entranceway, living room, and dining room were as I'd last seen them, covered and empty of paintings.

"Alexander?" I called, walking up the grand staircase. My heart beat wildly with each step.

I whisked through the second floor and up Alexander's attic steps. I reached his bedroom. I could barely breathe. I gently knocked on his door. "Alexander, it's me, Raven."

No one responded.

I turned the knob and opened the door. This room also looked like I'd last seen it, bare except for a few remaining items. But on his unmade bed lay a backpack. *He had come back.*

I picked up the rustic black bag and hugged it. I knew it would be rude to look through the backpack, especially if Alexander suddenly walked into the room. But I couldn't help it.

I sat it back on the bed and began to unzip it when I heard a noise coming from the backyard.

I looked outside his attic window and saw a candle flickering in the gazebo. A bat was hovering above the roof.

I took off, bolting out of his room, down the attic stairs, around the second floor, and down the never-ending staircase.

I flew out the front door and raced around to the backyard.

"Alexander!" I called, and ran into the darkened gazebo, barely able to make out his features in the shadows.

Then the candlelight flickered. I saw his eyes first. One green and one blue, before he stepped fully into the moonlight.

I tried to run, but it was too late. Jagger's gaze had already begun to make me dizzy.

10

The Covenant

I awoke on my back, on cold wet grass, with raindrops kissing my face, as if in a Sleeping Beauty slumber. The silvery sky held a bright, shining moon. A spidery tree loomed over me, its skinny, naked branches reaching toward me with witch-like fingers.

I sat up, my head aching. Then I saw it. A tombstone. Then another. Not one, but hundreds. I saw the baroness's monument. I was in Dullsville's cemetery.

As I rose, I felt light-headed. I caught my balance on a graveyard marker. I used to seek comfort among the tombstones, but because I was unsure of how I got here, I was anxious to leave before I ended up in an unmarked grave.

Jagger, wearing black cargo pants with red seams and a white T-shirt emblazoned with the words THE PUNISHER, was standing before me.

"How did you get here? Did you follow my bus?" I asked, confused.

"It will all be over in just a few minutes."

"What—my life? Forget it. I'm getting outta here!"

"Not so fast." Jagger grabbed my hand and began leading me toward the middle of the cemetery. I tried to pull away from him, but his grip was too strong and my strength had been depleted from whatever means he used to get me there.

I'd snuck into Dullsville's cemetery many times, and invariably Old Jim, the caretaker, and Luke, his Great Dane, would chase me out. They seemed to be nowhere, now when my life depended on them.

"I thought you were looking for Alexander," I said, but Jagger ignored me and continued pulling me toward the monuments and tombs. We stopped at a closed coffin laid upon a cement bench. I could hear strange music, a mixture of wailing violins and an underlying harpsichord, coming from one of the tombs. On the coffin, a candelabra flickered among the raindrops, wax dripping down its pewter spine. A medieval goblet sat next to it.

It looked like a scene from a gothic wedding.

"What's this?" I asked, my mental fog beginning to wear off.

"A covenant ceremony."

"But where are the guests? I didn't bring a gift," I said, giddy from my daze.

"The bride doesn't have to."

"Bride? But I didn't even register yet!"

Jagger didn't smile. Instead he relit a candle.

A few feet away, I spotted a shovel lying next to an

empty grave, glistening in the moonlight. I backed up slowly, inching my way to the shovel until the caretaker's tool lay at my feet.

My heart was beating so loudly, I was afraid Jagger would hear it. I took a deep breath. As he centered the candelabra on the coffin, I bent over and reached for the handle. But as soon as I grabbed it, Jagger's boot pinned it to the earth. He stood over me as I tried in vain to pry it from the ground. In the struggle, the shiny new shovel shook, and a few bits of clinging dirt fell off the metal head. I saw myself in the shovel's curve, upside down like a spoon's reflection. However, I didn't see a reflection for Jagger right behind me. I looked back up at him. He smiled a wicked smile. I hastily wiped the shovel with my sleeve and shifted to one side, peering into the shiny metal surface. All I could see were the stars above him, but his boot remained on the handle behind me.

I gasped.

"Something missing?" he teased.

I rose quickly and stepped back. "You—" I began, breathless.

I tried to run, but Jagger lunged forward and grabbed my arm. He flashed his fangs at me and licked his lips.

My reality spun out of control. I was standing face-to-face with a real vampire. One who wasn't Alexander. Jagger was the kind I'd read about and seen in movies—the kind who meant to snatch me away from my family and friends and take my blood as his own. I faced pledging my life to a stranger for all eternity. The radical dreams I'd wished for as just a curious goth were about to come true.

But this wasn't my dream. I'd dreamed of eternal love, belonging, and fitting in. Not danger, deceit, and evil. Dullsville hadn't been so dull after Alexander had moved into town. After meeting him, I'd realized all I'd ever wanted was to become one of the living—experiencing movies, metal concerts, and love—and not one of the undead. I wanted to sleep in Alexander's arms, not alone in a coffin. I wanted to turn into a gothic beauty, not a creepy bat. And most important, if I had to make the choice to transform, I would only do it for Alexander.

"My parents are expecting me home. They'll be sending out the SWAT team any minute now."

He held my hand with a strength I'd never felt before. I looked around for anything else to help my escape.

Jagger led me to the front of the coffin. He picked up the goblet and raised it to the moon, spoke a few words in a language I didn't understand, and then took a long drink.

"Now you," he said with a wicked grin, offering me the goblet.

"Forget it!" I said, pushing the goblet away with my free hand.

"But isn't this what you wanted all along? Why else would you follow Alexander?" he asked.

"Because I love him!" I said, trying to wriggle free. "And I will never love you!"

"But you don't have to," he said, and forced the goblet to my mouth.

Drops of thick, sweet liquid spilled against my lips.

I spit the liquid from my mouth. "I will never become like you, whoever or whatever you are!"

Jagger's face grew strange, as if my words had been a silver stake driven through his heart.

"And I say you will!" His blue and green eyes gazed into mine as if trying to cast a spell. "With this kiss, I take thee for all eternity."

Jagger flashed his smile, and his white fangs glistened in the moonlight. He leaned into me.

"I bite back!" I yelled defensively, gritting my teeth.

Suddenly a burst of lightning struck, illuminating the sky and all of the graveyard.

I plunged my teeth into Jagger's arm as hard as I could and dug my nails into his bony hand. He quickly released his death grip. I turned to run but slammed hard into something—or, rather, someone.

"Old Jim?" I cried, confused.

But when I looked up and stared into two midnight eyes, I realized it wasn't the caretaker I'd run into.

Instead, standing before me was my Gothic Guy, like a knight of the night. His dark, shoulder-length hair was hanging in his face. His white, moonlit skin was covered by a black T-shirt and jeans. The plastic spider ring I'd given him was resting on his finger. His eyes were deep, lonely, adoringly intelligent, just as they were the first time I'd seen them.

"Alexander!" I exclaimed, and fell into his arms.

"Just as I thought!" Jagger proclaimed, as if he'd won a contest. "I knew she'd bring me to you!"

Alexander embraced me hard as if he would never release me. Then he pushed me away. "You must go," he commanded.

"Are you crazy? I can't leave you!" I held his hand tightly. "I thought I'd never see you again!"

He stared into my eyes and warned me. "You have to go."

"But I—"

"You shouldn't have brought her into this!" Alexander told Jagger, with an anger I'd never seen before.

"She found *me*. Besides, I'm surprised to see that you're letting her go so soon, after she came all the way to the Coffin Club to find you. . . ."

"Leave Raven out of this!" Alexander exclaimed.

"I couldn't have planned my revenge any better than this. I could destroy you and gain an eternal partner with just one bite."

"You wouldn't dare—" Alexander warned.

"I knew she'd bring you to me, Sterling. You think you're not like one of us, but the truth is you are," Jagger argued.

"What is he talking about?" I asked.

"Not now," Alexander answered.

"Why do you think Sterling left Romania?" Jagger asked me. "Do you think it was an accident he came to a small town in America where there weren't any vampires?"

I didn't really know, after all.

"But I found you, Sterling," Jagger bragged. "And I found Raven."

"She has nothing to do with this," Alexander said,

stepping in between Jagger and me.

"I have nothing to do with what?" I asked curiously.

"Don't worry, Raven, he breaks promises all the time. Right, Sterling?" Jagger said.

Alexander clenched his fist.

"What promise? Why revenge? What does he mean?" I asked, confused, wondering what kind of agreement Alexander had made but couldn't keep.

"Well, I'm not going to leave her! I'm going to hold on to her for all of eternity!" Jagger proclaimed.

He flashed his teeth with a wickedly gnarled grin and leaned in to sink his fangs into my neck.

Frightening Farewell

I found myself flat on my back again, wet grass underneath me. Raindrops hit my face. I anxiously felt my neck for any wound.

Alexander leaned over me, his eyes filled with worry.

"Are you okay?" he asked sorrowfully. "You got in the way."

"Am I a . . . ?" I didn't even want to finish my thought.

He shook his head and helped me to my feet. "You have to go!" he commanded again. "You shouldn't be here—you're in danger."

I turned to look around for Jagger. But all I saw were grave markers. "But I may never see you," I pleaded.

"You must leave now," he persisted.

Alexander was breaking my heart again. If I left, it could be for the last time. How could I be sure Jagger wouldn't harm him? Alexander could disappear into the night forever. But if I didn't listen to his instructions, I might actually be doing Alexander more harm by getting in his way.

I saw Jagger stumbling by the baroness's monument and wiping his mouth. His green and blue eyes had turned fiery red. His lean muscles tensed. He grinned at me and licked his lips like a rabid animal ready to rip into its prey.

I didn't even have time to kiss my Gothic Mate good-bye. I ran without looking back, tears and raindrops dripping down my face, the graveyard mud splashing against my boots, my heart pulsing. Thunder clapped against the trees and seemed to echo against the tombstones.

I raced to the entrance of the cemetery and climbed over the fence.

When I turned around, Jagger and Alexander were gone.

Risky Reunion

I sobbed as I ran as fast as I could from the cemetery. I could barely see the pavement through my watery eyes. I headed through downtown Dullsville in the pouring rain where drivers in their Saabs, Mercedeses, and Jeeps looked strangely at the sight of a miserable, soaking wet goth girl.

I ran down the main street and tore through shoppers with umbrellas, knocked into couples coming out of the movie theater, and barreled past patrons escaping from the rain into restaurants.

With every flap of a bird's wing or sound of a honking horn, I was startled, thinking it was Jagger following me. I raced on.

I didn't want to go home. I needed to be alone, away from my family. I didn't want to talk—no one, not even Becky, would understand this unearthly experience. I had to hide out and seek comfort in the only place I had ever really felt at home.

I hurried through the open Mansion gates, my legs numb and my feet tingly inside my boots. I rushed up the long, windy driveway and around to the back of the Mansion. I glanced toward the gazebo to see if any two-colored eyeballs were staring back at me. When I found the gazebo empty, I climbed through the open basement window and made my way through the deserted Mansion. My tears dropped onto the creaky wooden floors beneath my squeaky boots. I wiped my eyes as I ascended the grand staircase and made my way into Alexander's attic room.

I touched the empty easel. I gazed at his bed, still creased from when he'd slept there days ago. I held his black knit sweater left behind on his beaten-up comfy chair.

I walked to the attic window and gazed out into the lonely moonlight. The heavy rain had ceased. I felt exhausted, abandoned, like a complete failure. Had I just stayed in Dullsville, Alexander would have returned for me. But my impatience had put me, and Alexander, in danger. He had been safely hiding in Dullsville from Jagger's thirsty revenge, and I'd pointed his nemesis right in his direction. As clever as I thought I was, I'd just been a pawn in Jagger's wicked game.

I heard a floorboard creak behind me. I slowly turned around but could barely make out the dark figure standing in the doorway.

"Jagger—" I said with a gasp.

The floorboard creaked again as the figure took a step toward me.

"Get out!" I yelled, backing up. I had nowhere to go. The figure was blocking the doorway, and my only escape was the narrow attic window ledge.

I stepped away, anxious about making a dangerous escape.

"I'll call the police!" I warned.

The figure drew closer. I decided I'd have to make a run for it by going around him. I took a breath and counted to myself. One. Two. Three.

I speedily darted around the figure, and was close to making my escape through the doorway when the figure grabbed my wrist.

"Get off!" I cried, trying to wriggle away. But when the moonlight gleamed down on his hand, a black plastic spider ring shined back at me.

I gasped, ceasing my struggle. "Alexander?"

He stepped completely into the light.

There he was, like a dream, standing before me. He'd returned. Handsome and now weary looking.

"I thought I'd never see you again!" I exclaimed. My body, tense with fear, melted into him as I wrapped my arms around him. He squeezed me back, so hard I could almost feel his heart beat through my own chest.

"I'm not letting go," I said, squeezing him harder and smiling. "Not ever!"

"I shouldn't have . . ." he began, softly.

I looked up, as if I were seeing an apparition. "I just

can't believe you're here!"

He took my hands and raised them to his mouth, kissing the back of them with his full lips, sending shivers through my veins. He gazed back into my eyes and smiled.

And then he did what I had so longed for him to do. He kissed me. His full lips pressed tenderly against mine, slowly, softly, seductively. It was as if we'd been separated for an eternity.

We continued to kiss, passionately, moving from our mouths to our cheeks to our ears as if drinking in each other's flesh. He gently stroked my hair, then nibbled my ear. I giggled as he sat on his comfy chair and pulled me onto his lap. I looked into his eyes, wondering how I could have breathed the last few days without him near me.

I ran my fingers through his messy, licorice-colored locks.

He brushed my hair away from my neck and made his way up my shoulder with sexy kisses. I could feel his teeth, seductively sliding against the skin of my neck. Touching, toying, tingling, giving me playful nibbles. The nape of my neck hung tenderly in his mouth.

Suddenly Alexander pulled away, a look of terror in his eyes.

"I can't," he said shamefully, looking away.

"What's wrong?" I asked, surprised by his change in mood.

Alexander stood up, helping me to my feet. He anxiously drew his hand through his hair and paced the room.

"It's okay," I said, catching up to him by his easel.

"I thought I wasn't like Jagger," he said, and sat on the

edge of his bed. "But . . . maybe I am."

"You are nothing like him," I said. "In fact, you are the opposite."

"I just want you to be safe. Always," he said, looking at me soulfully.

"I am, now that you are here," I said, stroking his hand.

"But don't you see?" he said seriously. "My world is not a safe one."

"Well, mine isn't either. Don't you watch the news?"

His sullen face turned bright, and he laughed. "I guess you're right."

"See? I'm more at risk going to school with Trevor than I am kissing a vampire."

"I've never met anyone like you," he said, turning toward me. "And I've never felt before the way I feel about you."

"I'm so glad you came back for me." I hugged him around his waist.

"This won't happen again," he assured me.

"How can you be so sure? Jagger seems bent on getting even with you," I asked, sitting beside him.

"Because he couldn't get even."

"Wow, so you showed him who's boss? Like in a school yard brawl?"

"I guess. . . . Only in our case it was a graveyard brawl."

"Is he gone?"

"His family is in Romania. There is nothing for him here now. He can go back and tell them he found me."

I fingered my necklace.

"What promise did you break?"

"I didn't break it. I never made it. . . . But we don't

have to worry about that anymore," he said wearily.

"What were all the candles in the cemetery for?" I asked.

"A vampire can take anyone at any time. But if he takes another at a cemetery or some other sacred ground, then she is his for eternity."

"Then I'm glad you showed up when you did!" I squeezed Alexander with all my might. "I'm sorry I led Jagger to you," I confessed.

"I should be the one apologizing to you. I couldn't imagine you'd come for me," he said, staring off into the moonlight. Then he turned back to me. "But I should have known. That's what I love about you."

"Now tell me everything!" I exclaimed suddenly. "What's it like being a—?"

"What's it like being human?" he interrupted.

"Boring."

"How can you say that?" he asked, holding me close. "You can wake up in the daylight, go to school, and see your reflection."

"But I want to be like you."

"You already are," he said with a smile.

"Were you born a vampire?"

"Yes. Were you born a human?" he teased.

"Yes. Are there millions of vampires around?"

He nodded. "But we are a minority, so we like to stick together. Obviously there is safety in numbers. We can't reveal our identities or we'd be persecuted."

"It must be so hard to cover up who you really are inside."

"It's very lonely, feeling like an outcast. Like you are invited to a costume party, but you are the only one in a mask."

"Do you have a lot of vampire friends in Romania? I bet you miss them."

"My dad procures art for his galleries in several countries. So we traveled quite a bit. By the time I made a friend, it was time to leave."

"What about humans, like me?" I asked, curling up next to him.

"There is no one like you, vampire or not," he said with a warm smile. "It's hard making human friends when you don't attend school, and it's even harder keeping them when they're eating their evening dinner and you are just rolling out of bed."

"Are your parents upset that you have a human girlfriend?"

"No. If they met you, they would immediately fall in love with you, just like I did," he said, and stroked my hair.

"I'd love to travel and live in the nighttime and sleep during the day. Your world seems so romantic. Being bonded to one another for an eternity. Flying off into the night together. Thirsting for no one but each other."

"I feel that way about your world."

"The grass is always greener, I guess. Or, in our case, blacker."

"When I'm with you," he began, "I don't care which world we are in, just as long as we're in the same one together."

Wake up," Alexander gently whispered in my ear.

I opened my eyes to find that I had crashed out on the couch in his TV room as he stroked my hair. *Kissing Coffins* was playing on his oversized flat screen.

Jenny had desperately entered Professor Livingston's office at the university.

"I knew I'd find you here!" she exclaimed, finding Vladimir seated at his desk, his head buried in a textbook.

"You weren't supposed to come," he warned, without looking up, "to my house or to my study. You have put yourself in danger."

In the distance, there was an eerie howling.

"Why did you let me fall asleep?" I asked Alexander, lifting my head from his shoulder. "Did you put a spell on me?"

"You suggested we watch this," he replied. "But you conked out as soon as I pressed 'Play.' Besides, it's late and you've been through a lot."

"Late?" I asked, stretching my arms. "For you it's the middle of the day."

Jenny looked toward the window. "They are coming for me," she confessed to Vladimir nervously. "They want me to be one of . . . you."

Vladimir methodically turned the page of his book. He didn't look up. Another eerie howling was heard in the distance.

"I'll walk you home," Alexander offered as we rose to our feet. He kindly handed me his black leather jacket.

"But I want to stay here," I whined.

"You can't. Your parents will be worried."

"I'll tell them I'm babysitting."

"For a seventeen-year-old?"

He put the coat around my shoulders.

"I had better go—" Jenny started, looking out the window of the study into the fog-layered darkness. "It was foolish of me to come."

"You'll be all alone here in this huge mansion," I said to Alexander, as I adjusted my wrinkled dress.

"I'm safe. Besides, I've sent for Jameson."

"As slow as he drives? It'll take him years to get here. I'll stay until he arrives," I said, sitting back down.

"Wait!" Vladimir called, his head still focused on his book.

Jenny stopped at the door. The professor rose and slowly walked to her. "Since I've met you, I haven't been myself," Vladimir confessed.

The howling continued.

"Come on, girl," Alexander said, nudging me.

"I was afraid I'd never see you again," Jenny said. "If I leave here without you, I may not be able to find you next time."

I stared at Jenny as if she had just proclaimed my own fear.

"But what if I never see you again?" I asked Alexander, pulling him close.

"Is tomorrow after sunset soon enough?"

"I can't leave," I told Alexander. "I thought I'd see you after the Welcome to the Neighborhood party. And the next night you were gone."

"I left to protect you, not to hurt you," he answered in a serious tone, sitting down next to me.

"Protect me from what?"

"From Jagger. From me. From my world."

"But you don't have to protect me."

"My world is not just filled with romance, like you think it is. There is danger."

"There can be risk anywhere. It's not exclusive to vampires. You just have to be careful."

"But I don't want you to be near danger in any world."

"I won't if we are together," I argued.

"I don't want you to think you have to change who you are to be with me," he said earnestly.

"I know that," I assured him.

"Or ask that you change."

"That's why you left Dullsville," I realized out loud. "You were afraid I'd want to become a vampire."

"Yes. But there was a more imminent danger presiding. A vampire with white hair."

"Jagger."

He nodded.

"Then why did you go to Hipsterville?"

"Hipsterville?" he asked, confused.

"That's what I call it," I confessed with a grin.

"Of course," he said with a laugh. "I got word from my parents that Jagger had found an apartment in 'Hipsterville' and was searching cemeteries in neighboring communities for my grandmother's monument. Once he'd found it, he would know which town I was living in."

"That was what the note meant," I remembered. "A warning that Jagger was on his way to find you. To seek revenge."

"What note?" he asked, confused.

"In your room," I confessed.

"You snuck into the Mansion after I left?"

I flashed him a cheesy grin.

"I should have known," he said, and smiled back. Then his playful tone turned serious. "But more important than finding me, he may have found you."

"Well, he did, but that was my own fault."

"I was going to head him off at the pass before he came to Dullsville—confront him before he confronted me. Jameson and I found an abandoned manor house so we could hide while I made my plan. But I didn't plan on one thing."

"I'd follow you?"

"I saw the most beautiful girl climbing down the back-yard tree."

"That was you in the attic window?"

"Yes."

"So why didn't you—"

"I kept a close eye on you. I had to, didn't I?"

"So why is Jagger out to get you?"

A sharp howl came from the screen, distracting Alexander from my question.

"We need to get you to the cemetery—to sacred ground," Vladimir warned. The handsome professor led her through the dark, marshy woods, riddled with fog. Vladimir held Jenny close as the howling sounds grew louder.

Alexander and I were fixed on the movie.

"How can we be together," Jenny asked, "if I'm not a vampire?"

Suddenly the TV screen went black. Alexander placed the remote he was holding on the coffee table.

He stood up and held his hand out for me.

"How *can* we be together?" I asked, rising.

"How can we *not* be?" he reassured me. Alexander grabbed my hand, and I reluctantly followed him out of the Mansion and toward my house. I felt like a kid at Disney World at closing time.

The night air in Dullsville felt fresher than ever, the dark sky clearer, the wet grass crisper. "So why was Jagger seeking revenge?" I asked.

"It's a long story," he said, with a yawn.

Alexander seemed so content forgetting the past, our hands entwined as we walked side by side. But I wouldn't rest until I knew.

"I have all night. And you have 'til sunrise."

"You're right," he said, as we walked down the street.

"It was about a promise I never made."

"A promise?" I asked.

"To take a girl for all of eternity."

"What girl?"

"Jagger's twin sister, Luna."

"He has a twin?"

Alexander nodded.

"Well, who made the promise?" I questioned aloud.

"My family did the year the three of us were born."

"Like an arranged marriage?"

"It's more than marriage."

"So why Luna?"

"When she was born, it was said she didn't respond to the darkness but seemed to flourish in the light. She refused to drink anything besides milk. Desperate, her family took her to a local underground doctor who pronounced her 'human.'"

I laughed. Alexander didn't seem to find it funny.

"It just sounds strange to me, that's all," I said, as we turned a corner.

"Well, it wasn't funny to the Maxwells. They were devastated. Luna had to live her life in daylight, while her family lived at night. She never even bonded with Jagger. At that time of the agreement, my family and his were very close. It was understood that when Luna was eighteen, we'd meet for a covenant ceremony and unite together for eternity, ensuring her a place in the vampire world."

"So what happened?" I asked, as we cut across the lawn through Oakley Woods.

"As I grew up, my family traveled and our families

became distant. Because Luna and I lived in different worlds, I never even knew her. When it came time for the ceremony, I had seen her only a few times. She didn't know me, and she was going to be with me forever?"

"Well, you are quite handsome," I said coyly. "So what did you do?"

"When it came time to kiss her for eternity, I leaned over and kissed her good-bye."

"That must have been hard for you, being a vampire and all," I whispered.

"I was doing it for both of us. Of course, the Maxwells didn't see it that way. They felt that I had spurned Luna, therefore offending her entire family. They were outraged. My parents quickly arranged for me to come here with Jameson and live in my grandmother's Mansion."

"Wow. It really had to have been tough following your heart when it went against your vampire community," I said. "And even more difficult to have been forced to leave Romania because of that decision."

"When I saw this raven-haired beauty trick-or-treating from my attic window, I knew I'd rather spend an eternity alone waiting to see her again than spend one with some-one I didn't love."

Just then we reached my front door. Alexander gave me a long good-night kiss.

"Tomorrow after sunset," I reminded him.

"And not a second later," he said.

Alexander waved to me as I opened the front door. I walked inside and turned around to wave good-bye.

He had already disappeared, just as I knew he would.

14

I t's after midnight," my dad warned as I tiptoed past him watching ESPN in the family room.

"Dad, I'm sixteen. It's a weekend."

"But this is—". he began in a stern voice.

"I know, your house. And I'm your daughter, and until I'm on my own I'll live by your rules."

"Well, at least you were paying attention."

"You've been saying it to me since I was two."

"You've been sneaking out since you could walk."

"I'm sorry, it won't happen again," I said.

I handed him his soda that was sitting on the coffee table and gave him a good-night hug.

"I'm glad you had a good time at Aunt Libby's," he said. "But I'm also glad you're back home."

"Me, too, Dad. Me, too."

Exhausted, I crawled into bed without even removing my rain-dampened clothes. I switched off the *Edward*

Scissorhands light on my nightstand and licked my lips. Alexander's kisses still lingered on my mouth. I curled up with my Mickey Malice plush, wishing I were holding Alexander instead. As I lay in bed, I tossed and turned. I couldn't wait for tomorrow's sunset.

Moments later, I felt a presence stirring in the quiet. I glanced around, but all the shadows were from the furniture. I checked under my bed; even a bat couldn't squeeze between all the junk I had stashed underneath it. I opened my closet door, but the only clothes I found were on hangers or strewn on the floor. I tiptoed to my window and pulled back the curtain, looking out into our backyard.

"Alexander?"

I saw a darkened figure walking away from the house, into the night.

"Good night, my love," I said, pressing my hand to the window.

I returned to bed and fell asleep.

The next morning, I awoke with a jolt. Yesterday's events seemed like a dream.

When I rose in my stiffened clothes, I realized that those events were real.

"Why are you still in your outfit from yesterday?" my mom nagged when I entered the kitchen. "Don't they talk about proper hygiene in health class?"

I wiped my haggard eyes and stumbled to the bathroom. I peeled off my day-old clothes and stepped into the shower.

Warm water flowed over my pale skin. My black nail

and toe polish looked stark against the clear white tub and tile that surrounded me.

I was back in Dullsville and Alexander was in his Mansion. We could finally live our lives together. But my boyfriend was a vampire and his nemesis had come to hunt him down. I'd never thought Dullsville could be so, well, not dull!

My whole life had changed in just a few days. For sixteen years I'd been living the same monotonous existence. My greatest concern had been finding black nail polish in a pastel town. Now it was getting through a sun-filled day alone while Alexander slept peacefully in his Mansion. We wouldn't be able to go for afternoon bike rides, meet after school, or spend our weekend days hanging out.

It was hard to imagine that I wouldn't ever be able to share sunlight with him. I was beginning to have doubts that I could handle this new world.

"It was a blast! I bought you this," I said, and handed Becky a package as we sat on the Evans Park swings.

She opened a Hello Kitty journal. "Cool. Thanks!"

"They have the best stores ever! And I went to a place called the Coffin Club. I met this weird guy."

"Really? Matt and I just went to the movies."

"If I tell you a secret, a super-duper colossal secret, do you promise not to tell anyone?"

"Can I tell Matt?" she asked eagerly.

Matt, Matt, Matt—who cared about Matt when I was bursting to tell her about my encounter with Jagger and the truth about Alexander.

"Why are we talking about Matt when I have the biggest news of a lifetime?"

"Well, you always talk about Alexander," she barked back. Her porcelain cheeks flushed ruby red. "And I listen to you all the time. Just 'cause you went away and had exciting things happen doesn't mean I didn't, too."

I was surprised by Becky's outburst. It had been only a few days since she had hooked up with Matt, but if she felt for him half of what I felt for Alexander, I'd have to understand her intensity. Becky had always been so mousy. Now that she had her own beau, she had become more confident. Our relationship had changed. We had never had anyone before but each other.

"Fine," I said, reluctantly. "You're right. I'm glad you are going out with Matt. Someone as awesome as you should have an awesome boyfriend."

"Thanks, Raven. Now, what were you going to tell me?"

I paused, debating if she could handle the vampirey info.

"Is Matt going to show up here again?"

She nodded. "He's right behind you."

I guess I had my answer.

"So, Monster Girl, how's Monster Boy?" a male voice called as I left the park. I glanced around to find Trevor in his red-and-white soccer uniform.

"I thought I was done with you. Are you always going

to be in my face?" I asked.

"As long as you wear black I will be. Have you two made any Monster Babies yet?" he asked.

"No, but when we do, I'll be sure to name one after you."

I walked away, and Trevor continued to follow.

"How do you do it? Play soccer, spend your daddy's money, and annoy people, all at the same time?" I asked.

"I could do more than annoy you, if you'd let me," he said, coyly fixing his green eyes on me.

"So that line isn't working on the cheerleaders anymore?"

If Trevor had ever truly bothered me before, he was now just a pest given what I'd recently been through.

"I still think there's something fishy going on in that mansion," he said, unrelenting.

"Give it a rest."

"Don't you think it's strange that Alexander's never seen during the day?"

"I wish *you* weren't seen during the day. Besides, he's homeschooled."

"My mom told me she spotted that freaky butler man hanging out at the butcher."

"Yeah. That is strange. The butler eats food. Who knew?"

"He requested 'the freshest, bloodiest meat you have.'"

"Would you prefer they drink your blood?" I teased.

He looked at me in shock.

"Get a life," I said. "Maybe your mom should be

paying attention to you more and gossiping less."

"You leave my mother—"

"I really don't have time for you or your mother anymore. Maybe it's time you get a new best friend," I said, and walked away.

15

Nightmare

Impatient, I arrived at the Mansion before sunset. Jameson's Mercedes was once again parked in the driveway.

I sat on the uneven front steps, picking at the dandelions and weeds growing between the cracking cement. The door slowly creaked open.

Jameson greeted me.

"I'm so glad you're back," I said, squeezing his bony frame.

"I am, too, Miss Raven. I missed the Mansion and our favorite guest."

"I missed you, too. And I know one fabulous lady who was bummed that you were gone. . . ."

"Miss Ruby?" he asked, his eyes coming alive.

"Are you going to call her?" I asked.

"After what I've done? I couldn't."

"You have to! Besides, it wasn't your fault. Just tell her

you were unexpectedly called out of town."

"She'd never forgive me. And she shouldn't."

"Ruby loved the flowers. Besides, there's a carnival this weekend. She'll need a date. And you'll need one, too."

I could see Jameson pondering the decision, excited about seeing Ruby again, but unsure if he could muster the courage to call her.

Alexander bounced down the grand staircase, wearing black jeans and a black HIM T-shirt. He gave me a long hello kiss.

"That was sweet of you to come by last night," I said, in his arms.

"I didn't come by," he said, confused.

"You didn't? I saw a guy in my backyard."

Alexander looked worried.

"I bet it was Trevor," I guessed. "I saw him after school. I think he still blames me for his plummeting popularity."

"If you need me to talk to him, I will."

I'd always defended myself from Trevor. It was refreshing to finally have someone who would stand up for me. "You are my superhero!" I exclaimed, and gave him a hug.

"I found this really cool place."

"Cool place? In Dullsville?"

He grabbed my hand and led me out of the Mansion and down the street.

"It's so ironic that the rumors Trevor started turned out to be true," I said to my vampire boyfriend.

"About me, or you?" he teased.

"I mean, I thought you were . . . then I didn't. But then I did. And then when I totally didn't again, I found out you were."

"Now I'm confused. Am I? Or am I not?"

"That is the question." I squeezed his hand.

"I just don't want to lose you or put you in danger."

"I love danger."

When we passed Dullsville's cemetery, I wondered where we were going.

"Just a little bit farther," he assured me.

I would walk to China if Alexander were by my side. I had so many questions burning inside me, I didn't know which to ask first.

"Did you grow up with Jagger?"

"Our families were close when we were born. I think he was jealous of Luna. With her living as a human, he knew what he was missing—school, sports, friends. He is scrawny, but I think he really dreamed of being a jock like Trevor. I kind of feel sorry for him. He wasn't able to find something he enjoyed, besides revenge. But then my family traveled. My parents were bohemians, and we really never fit in with our kind. We were what was known as vampire vegetarians."

"Cool. So how do you survive? Connections with the butcher?" I joked, referring to my conversation with Trevor.

"How did you know?" he asked, surprised. "We also have family who have ties to blood banks."

"Uh . . . I just guessed," I replied. "My parents were hippies, too. They wouldn't eat anything with eyeballs. But they traded their hippie threads and beaded satchels for Armani suits and briefcases, and they drive their BMWs past PETA protesters on their way to work."

"Sounds like our parents would make great friends."

"Just like us."

Alexander squeezed my hand.

"I sometimes wonder what it would be like if you changed me. We could stay up all night long, fly into the night, and be bonded for eternity."

"I've imagined what it would be like if I were born like you. We could go to the same school, lie out in the sun, have picnics in the park. I'd be able to see us reflected together in a mirror. I'd fill my walls with pictures of us at the beach."

"We share similar dreams."

"You're a human who wants to be a vampire, and I'm a vampire who wants to be human."

I gazed up at Alexander with empathy. I hadn't realized he felt as alone in his own world as I did in mine.

"It's just over there," he said, pointing to an abandoned barn across the train tracks.

The red barn had seen better days. Boards from the gray roof and side were missing, like teeth on a smiling kindergartner.

We stepped through the door frame. The door was missing, but the wooden beams that held the barn together still remained intact. Vacant stalls stood on one side, an empty hayloft on the other. Alexander grabbed a gas lantern that hung from a hook on the wall and turned it on. He took my hand and led me toward a darkened corner.

"Are we going up into the hayloft?" I asked coyly.

"Follow me," he said. "Don't be afraid. They won't bite," he said with a laugh.

"Who's they?" I wondered. I imagined a family of vampires, hiding out in the stable. Maybe long-lost relatives of his.

I held his hand hard as he pulled me into the corner of the abandoned barn. I could see two slanted eyes staring back at me from the corner. I stepped into the moonlight to discover a powder white mama cat with a litter of snowball white baby kittens—and there in the mix by herself was one teeny black cat.

"She's just like me!" I exclaimed.

"I thought you'd like her."

"She's the cutest thing I've ever seen! I want her to come home with me," I said wishfully, kneeling down and staring at the kitten.

"I found them last night."

"You want me to keep her?"

"She's finished nursing. And the mother can't care for them all."

Alexander and I sat off to the side and watched as the kittens purred and the mama fell asleep.

"I'm surprised she isn't hissing at us," I said.

"She understands we're not here to hurt her, but to help her."

"So, you're like Dr. Dolittle with a bite."

He grimaced at my joke. "Do you want the cat or not?"

I nodded my head eagerly.

Alexander picked up the tiny black kitten, who looked like a small ball of yarn in his handsome hands.

"It's okay," he said, handing her to me.

I held the tiniest black baby kitten I'd ever seen. She licked her mouth and looked up at me as if she were smiling.

"I can keep her?"

"I wanted you to have something to remember me by."

"Remember you?"

"To keep you company during the day."

"That is the sweetest thing!"

I stared down at my Gothic Gift gazing up at me with teeny lime green eyes.

"I'll call her Nightmare."

16

"W here did you get that?" Billy Boy asked when I brought Nightmare into the house.

"Alexander gave her to me."

"She's so cute. But you'll have to hide her from Dad. You know how he feels about pets."

"I know, but I'm not bringing a lizard home this time. It's just a kitty."

"Where'd you get that?" my dad asked, coming down the stairs.

"Alexander gave her to me."

"I don't care if the president gave it to you. It has to go."

"Paul, she is really cute," my mom commented, petting Nightmare's head. "And Raven is certainly old enough to be responsible for a cat."

"Her age is not what I'm concerned about," he warned.

"Dad, didn't I prove enough to you by working at Armstrong Travel? I'm not a little girl anymore."

He paused as I held my Nightmare up to his face.

"Fine. But she stays in your room. I don't want her running all around the kitchen countertops or scratching on my couch."

"Thanks, Dad." I gave him a huge hug and kiss on his cheek.

"Now I'll show you your new home," I said to Nightmare as I took her to my bedroom.

I looked around my room. I didn't know where to put her.

"I have an old box in the garage filled with clothes from college that would be a perfect bed for her," Mom said, peeking in. "It's above the tools. Bring me the box and I'll repack the clothes."

"Thanks."

I started to close my bedroom door when Nightmare began to follow me.

"I'll be right back, sweetie," I said, putting her in the middle of the floor. "I'm going to make you a bed."

Nightmare's ears perked up, and she looked at the window. She darted up onto my computer chair and then onto my desk. She stared out the window, hissing. I picked her up and placed her on my bed.

"I'll be right back. Sleep here for now."

When I reached my bedroom door, Nightmare was back at my feet, her lime green eyes squinting at me. She hissed at me and pawed at my boots.

I picked her up. "Mommy will be right back." I kissed my new kitty on the nose, placed her back on the floor, and quickly closed the door. I could hear her scratching against the wood as I ran down the hall.

I walked to our garage at the end of our driveway. I stood on my dad's toolbox as I searched for the box. I could hear the crickets.

There was a lot of rustling in the tree by my bedroom window. I froze.

More rustling. It could be a squirrel. Or having just seen Trevor last night, I thought he could be toilet papering my window.

I turned off the garage light and tiptoed over to the tree. But now the leaves were still. Not a bird. Not a squirrel. Not a soccer snob.

I headed back to the garage, and then I saw Jagger.

I gasped.

"What are you doing here?"

"I just wanted to see you."

"I thought you went back to Romania," I said, stepping back.

"I was hoping you would come with me."

"Alexander assured me that the feud was over and you were gone for good."

"That is why you can't tell him," he said. "Otherwise, not only will your safety and Sterling's be in jeopardy, but the whole town's."

"The whole town?" I asked.

"Don't tempt me," he said, licking his lips. "You

wouldn't like to know what happens when a small town finds out a vampire is living among them and dating one of their daughters."

I froze. I remembered how easily Dullsville was sucked into Trevor's rumor, resulting in gossip and graffiti. If the town had proof of Alexander's true identity, there was no predicting what people would do.

"Fine, I won't tell him. But you must leave now!"

Jagger only stepped closer.

"I'm not going back to the cemetery with you," I argued, backing up. "I'll scream if I have to. My father is inside and he's a lawyer."

"That won't be necessary. Why spend your life sitting in a mansion with a sensitive artist watching paint dry when we could see the world together?"

"I'm not going anywhere with you!"

"Well, I'm sure you could persuade me to stay in town. In fact, I'm beginning to like it here."

"I don't want you! Your feud is over with Alexander. Go home already—"

"Feud? I have other things on my mind now. Alexander might be able to deny who he is, but I can't deny who I am."

His blue and green eyes shot through me. I looked away, afraid he'd make me dizzy again. He began to lean into me.

"Raven!" Billy Boy called from the back door.

My brother ran down the steps holding Nightmare. Jagger stepped back into the shadows.

"Billy Boy! Go inside. Now!" I exclaimed, running toward him.

"What's taking you so long?" Billy Boy asked. "Nightmare is throwing a freak attack. I found her pawing against your bedroom door."

I blocked Billy Boy's step. Frantically, I turned around, shielding him.

The backyard was empty. Jagger was gone.

I pulled Billy Boy inside and locked the door.

"I've never been so happy to see you!" I said, squeezing my little brother, Nightmare in his hands.

"What's wrong with you?" he asked, cringing like I had cooties.

"I just thought I saw the bogeyman."

"You watch too many scary movies," he said.

"I sometimes feel like I'm starring in them," I replied.

17

As much as I hated going back to school after spring break, I knew at least my daylight hours brought a safe reprieve from Jagger.

I returned to Dullsville High a different person than when I had left—as if being the only goth in a conservative town hadn't made me different enough. I couldn't concentrate in class, knowing I was privy to a secret world of vampires.

Classmates continued to bury their heads in textbooks and anticipate the next soccer game, while I doodled in my journal and couldn't wait for the next sunset.

I was still an outcast, but I think my classmates got a rise that Trevor had been dethroned from his kingdom. And although they didn't high-five me in the hallway or invite me to their parties, I was actually given a cutter's privilege at the drinking fountain.

"It's a shame Alexander is homeschooled. It would be nice to eat lunch as a foursome," Becky said at lunch on the baseball bleachers.

"Yeah, that would rock."

"But still, we should do something together."

"How about going to the drive-in?" Matt asked, as he walked up the bleachers behind me. "*Kissing Coffins* is playing tonight. Admission is half price if you wear a costume."

"Cool! I've always wanted to see it on the big screen. I'm sure Alexander would love to go."

"And I'll be able to see what happens to Jenny," Becky said excitedly. "I can dress as one of the town's vampires and wear a cape."

"And fangs!" I added.

Just then Trevor walked onto the field with his soccer-snob groupies. He looked up at Matt, who sat down next to Becky.

As much as Trevor tormented me and as pathetic as I thought he was, I felt a tinge of pity for him. He was an even sadder case now that he was Matt-less. I watched Matt offer Becky his sandwich.

"I'm glad you got traded to our team," I said to Matt, who closed his brown bag and gave me a warm smile.

After school, Becky and I searched through my closet to find her a costume to wear to the drive-in.

"Man, you do have a lot of black," she said, as I tossed out dozens of skirts and shirts for her to choose from.

Becky modeled black tights, a black miniskirt, and a lacy black chemise.

"That's perfect. You'll be one of the members of the vampire gang who tries to convert Jenny. I just need my outfit."

I heard my mom's SUV pull into the driveway, and Becky and I raced to meet her at the back door.

"Can I have an advance on my allowance?" I asked hurriedly.

"Calm down," she advised. "Don't I even get a hello?"

"Hello," I replied. "Now, can I have an advance on my allowance?"

"I hope you didn't bid on a Hello Batty toaster on eBay again. I thought we told you—"

"I want to dye my hair blond."

"Blond?" she asked, shocked. "You are not going to ruin your gorgeous black hair."

"But it needs to be blond to complete my costume."

"Are you in a play?"

"Well, sort of."

"For school?"

"No, I just need your help."

"Well, I have some wigs from college in the box I emptied for Nightmare. I know there's an auburn one. There may be a blond one, too."

"Can we go see?" I begged.

Mom reluctantly put her purse down on the kitchen table, and Becky and I followed her into my parents' bedroom.

She rummaged through an old Harrod's shopping bag. "Here it is!" she exclaimed, as if she'd found a sunken treasure. She handed me a weathered blond wig. "I wore this in college. Your father loved it!"

I rolled my eyes. "I also need a white dress," I confessed.

She looked at me, pleased, as if her rebellious daughter were finally asking to borrow pearls. "I'll see what I have!" she replied gleefully.

She picked up a pair of flared denims with rhinestones from the box. "Do you believe I once wore these?" she asked, holding them against her pleated Ann Taylor skirt.

"I have a white blouse," she said.

"Ahh. Here's a white eyelet skirt."

"Perfect."

My mom stuck the wig on my head, and I held the clothes in front of me.

"It's like looking at a teenage version of myself," she said fondly.

I threw the skirt and blouse in the wash, and Becky and I returned to my room.

"We are so going to rock!" I said. "But we just need one thing to complete our outfits."

I hunted through my dresser drawers, closet shelves, and boxes underneath my bed.

Halloween was months ago, and in a town like Dullsville it was easier to find a fake Prada purse than fake teeth.

Frustrated, I banged on Billy Boy's door. He opened it

slightly, sticking his Charlie Brown–shaped head out. I could barely see Henry typing at my brother's computer.

"Did you take my vampire teeth?" I accused him.

"Why would I want your nasty saliva near me?" Billy Boy said, starting to close the door on me.

"Well, I can't find them, and I have to have them for tonight," I argued, pressing the door back open.

Henry rushed over to the door. "I have some," he offered. "Never been used."

Henry and Billy Boy rode their bikes, and I followed with Becky on mine. We must have been quite a sight as we headed to Henry's house at the edge of Oakley Woods— two goths and two nerds riding alongside one another.

We parked our bikes in Henry's driveway and entered the colonial-style five-bedroom house.

We were greeted by his housekeeper, who was folding laundry.

We walked up the pristine wooden stairs to his bedroom. A NO YUPPIES ALLOWED sign hung on his door.

"I like that," I said.

A spongy black doormat rested on the floor, and a million dead bolts sealed his door.

"What are you hiding inside? Secret recipes of cafeteria food?" I asked.

After he unlocked the outside dead bolts, he stepped onto the mat. His bedroom door sprung open automatically.

Henry had a loft bed, with a metallic blue computer

underneath. Stars were pasted on his ceiling, I'm sure in astronomically correct order. A solar system mobile hung from his ceiling fan. A telescope stood by his window.

He slid open his walk-in closet doors to reveal neatly stacked, clear plastic shoe boxes.

"Five dollars gets you samples," he said, pointing to them.

Each box was labeled: ACNE. BLOOD. PIMPLES. PUKE. SCARS.

"Who wants to have more pimples?" I asked.

"And I have smells. Here," he said, opening a beaker and pushing it under my nose.

"Gross!" I said, repulsed. "It smells like the bathroom after Billy Boy uses it."

"Shut up!" my brother said.

"I like to pour this on Mrs. Louis's chair sometimes," he said proudly. "Look around. I have them alphabetized."

"I should have known."

Becky and I each handed over our money and loaded our pockets with ghoulish goodies.

When we were finished, Henry held a box before me as if he were holding the Holy Grail. He opened it, revealing two exact replicas of human teeth in the shape of fangs.

"With the glue, seven dollars."

I knew I had only six in my purse.

"Five dollars and a stick of gum," I offered.

"Six. And your school picture," he countered.

I looked hard at him, then at Becky.

"But you inscribed it to me!" she said.

"Please," I begged, flashing her my puppy-dog eyes.

She opened her wallet and handed Henry the picture.

I handed him the money and left before he changed his mind.

As I headed out to meet Alexander for our date, I found my parents in the kitchen, paying bills.

"I'm going to be out a teensy bit late tonight," I advised.

"It's a school night," my mother said.

"I know, but we're going to the drive-in," I said with a smile.

"Why don't you wait until the weekend?" my mom asked.

"Because tonight's half price if you wear a costume. Becky and Matt are going, too."

"Becky?" my mother asked, surprised.

"Yes, my little Becky. It'll be our first double date. Besides, I already did my homework, and we have a sub for first bell anyway."

"Seems like you had all your excuses lined up," my father said.

"I'll take care of the dishes all week," I said to my mother. "And Dad, I'll wash your car."

"Last time you washed my car, you put Wicked Wiccas stickers on it."

"But you have to admit, it looked cool."

"And last time you took care of the dishes, you broke

Grandma's teapot," my mother remembered.

"Fine. Then we have a deal," I began. "I'll just go to the movie, and I'll save you trouble by not doing your chores."

"How did that just happen?" my dad wondered, as I headed for the front door. "And when you're finished with that blond wig, your mother needs it back."

I slung my backpack filled with my *Kissing Coffins* accessories on my shoulder and grabbed a container of garlic powder from the kitchen. I held it tightly in my hand, as if I were holding a can of Mace, as I walked to the Mansion. If Jagger jumped out at me, I wanted to be protected.

I felt a familiar lurking presence as I turned the corner to Benson Hill. I saw a rustling in a bush and blond strands poking through the branches. I took a deep breath, and I quietly opened the container of garlic powder and threw it hard, directly into the brush.

"Ouch!" a male's voice cried.

Trevor jumped out of the bush and held his forehead.

"What are you doing?" I shouted at him.

"I saw you coming up the road and wanted to scare you," he said, rubbing his wound.

"You don't have to hide. Your face alone could scare Frankenstein."

I grabbed the container from the sidewalk and replaced it in my purse.

I walked away, and Trevor continued to follow me as we drew closer to the gate.

"I really don't have time for you anymore," I said. "I'm going to the drive-in." And I slipped past the slightly open iron gate.

"You have a pretty good arm. You should try out for the baseball team. And tell your gothic boyfriend," he called, "if he wants to apply, they could use a batboy."

I left Trevor and was walking up the Mansion's driveway when I overheard him talking to someone outside the gate. I glanced back and saw my nemesis from behind, standing next to a guy with white hair.

I stopped. Jagger and Trevor? A dangerous duo.

I sneaked back down the driveway and hid behind a bush next to the wrought-iron gate.

"Hey, watch out, dude!" Trevor hollered. He must have bumped into Jagger in the darkness.

I could only imagine Trevor's reaction to the shock of seeing the pale, tattooed, multipierced Jagger walking alone on a darkened street. I wasn't sure if Trevor would hit him or take off running.

"Sorry," Jagger said in a cool voice. "I didn't see you coming.

"It's so dark around here," Jagger continued, shifting his feet.

"Yeah, I think the Sterlings knock out the streetlamps on purpose."

Jagger laughed. "That babe you were walking with. She's your girlfriend?" he asked.

"Raven? She's my nightmare. No, she hangs out with

the dude who lives in the Mansion. I've never seen you around here before," he said, scrutinizing him.

"I'm just visiting. I'm Sterling's friend."

"Friend? I didn't think he had any," he said with a laugh. "Well, you better catch him before they go to the drive-in."

"The drive-in?" Jagger asked.

"Yeah. It's built on an ancient burial ground," he whispered, as if revealing a secret. "I've heard that late at night, you can see ghosts eating popcorn."

"Burial ground?" Jagger wondered aloud. "Perfect."

"For what?" Trevor asked, confused.

"Uh . . . a club initiation," Jagger rambled. "But it's a very exclusive club. . . . Maybe in the future you could join."

"Thanks anyway. Soccer takes all my free time. Besides, Sterling doesn't seem like the type to belong to a club."

"He's already a member. I just have to persuade Raven to join. Maybe I'll surprise them there," Jagger said. "Can you point me in the right direction?"

"Follow me," Jagger's new ally said. "It's on the way to the game."

As the two left together, my mouth hung open in disbelief.

Jagger was planning to have a covenant ceremony tonight at the drive-in, with me as his covenant girl!

I needed a plan fast.

I took a deep breath and tried to think. If I canceled our double date, Jagger could return to my house, putting not only me but my family in danger.

I didn't have much time to find a way to keep Jagger away for good without ending up as his dinner. Why couldn't Alexander and I just enjoy a movie together? Like *Kissing Coffins*, which reflected my own imminent situation—a movie about the vampire Vladimir Livingston, who tried to save the innocent mortal ingénue Jenny from the depths of the darkened Underworld.

And then it hit me.

Jagger was planning to take me tonight at the drive-in? But he couldn't. Not if I was already taken by someone else first.

I t's hard, you know, without a mirror," I commented anxiously in Alexander's room as I awkwardly tried to glue my fake fangs onto my teeth. The soundtrack to *Kissing Coffins* was blaring in the background. "Are they straight?" I flashed him a sexy vampire smile.

"Wow!" he said, impressed. "Are you sure they are plastic?" He touched them with his fingers. "They look so real."

"Be careful. They aren't dry," I snapped.

"Why are you so nervous? It's just a movie."

"But it's not. I have something to tell you. Promise you won't be mad at me."

"Okay. Does it involve another guy?"

"Yes, but not in the way you think. Jagger's still in Dullsville."

"How do you know?" he asked, shocked.

"I just saw him," I confessed.

"Where?"

"Outside the Mansion with Trevor."

"Trevor? That's the last person he should be talking to."

"Well, I saw Jagger the other night, too, at my house. But he warned me that if I told you, he would tell everyone about you."

"He was at your house?" he asked angrily. "Did he hurt you?"

"No," I assured him. "But he plans to, tonight, at the drive-in. Trevor told Jagger it was built on sacred ground and Jagger persuaded Trevor to show him where it was. Before, Jagger wanted me just to get even with you. Now I just think he wants me for himself—unless he is convinced that I have already been taken."

"But—"

"I'll need you to convince him."

"But that means—"

"Just like Vladimir saves Jenny in the movie. It will be so romantic."

"I don't know if I can."

"You have to. We have no other choice."

I gave him a reassuring kiss. "It will be okay. Trust me."

I fluffed my hair. I spun around and modeled my outfit. "How do I look?"

"I like you as a blond," he said, half distracted.

"And you look like Vladimir," I complimented him, as I smoothed his dark suit and straightened his black cape.

"You look just like Jenny," he said.

"But I want to see for myself."

I grabbed my purse off his bed, opened it, and reached inside, searching for Ruby's compact.

Alexander pulled at his stomach. "I don't feel so well."

"You're just nervous. I promise you, it will be okay."

"I really don't—"

"Wait a minute," I said, scrounging for a peppermint.

"What's that?" he asked, repulsed when I offered it to him.

"It's just a mint," I answered. "Don't they have them in Romania? It settles your stomach."

"Get it away from me," he said, refusing the mint and stepping away.

Then I smelled something odd coming from inside my purse.

I stuck my hand inside, and buried underneath my wallet and a huge wad of tissues was the cause.

"Oh no! It's my garlic powder," I said, holding the plastic container toward him. The lid had opened.

"Put that away!" he said, holding his stomach.

"I'm sorry!" I said, fumbling and stepping away from him.

"Farther. Like in Utah!"

"I didn't mean to—" I apologized.

His ghost-white face grew even more gaunt with every breath he took.

I opened the attic window and threw the plastic container as hard as I could, far into the night sky.

Alexander was still stepping back from me, his breathing getting heavier.

"I'll throw my purse out, if I have to."

But he said nothing as he gasped for air.

"Jameson!" I called, but the *Kissing Coffins* soundtrack was playing too loudly for anyone to hear.

I ran out of the bedroom and down the attic steps. "Jameson!" I cried. "Jameson!" I didn't hear a sound as I barreled through the second floor. I flew down the grand staircase. Why did he have to live in such a big house?

I burst through the kitchen door and found Jameson putting dishes into the dishwasher.

"Alexander!" I gasped. "He was exposed to garlic! Call nine-one-one!"

Jameson's eyes grew even buggier than usual, making me even more terrified of the tragic state of the situation. But then he collected himself and opened a cabinet door.

Lying on the shelf was an antidote. Jameson handed me the shot.

"You must give it to him in his leg," he ordered.

"I must?" I said, shocked.

"By the time I climb those stairs, Miss Raven, it may be too late."

I grabbed the shot from his slender hand and ran.

My heart raced as I took off up the grand staircase, doubtful I would get to Alexander in time.

I rushed into the room to find Alexander lying on his back on his bed, his skin turning blue and his eyes growing vacant. His breath was shallow.

I remembered watching *Pulp Fiction*. A nervous John Travolta wound up his arm and slammed a shot into Uma Thurman's arrested heart. I wondered if I could be so brave.

I placed a shaking hand on Alexander's thigh and raised the shot. "One. Two. Three." I bit my lip and jammed the injection into his leg.

I waited. But Alexander didn't move. How long did it take? Was I too late?

"Alexander! Talk to me! Please!"

Suddenly, Alexander sat up, rigid, his eyes wide open. He breathed a full breath of air as if sucking in all the oxygen in the room.

Then he breathed out, and his body relaxed.

He looked up at me with weary eyes.

"Are you okay?" I asked. "I didn't mean to—"

"I need some—" he tried to say.

"Blood?" I asked, worried.

"No. Water."

Just then Jameson came into the room with a tall glass.

I held the glass to his lips. Alexander quickly drank it down. With every gulp his eyes grew more alive.

"Your face looks almost pale again," I said eagerly.

Jameson and I breathed a sigh of relief as Alexander recovered.

"Why were you carrying garlic?" Alexander finally asked.

"In case Jagger visited me again."

"Jagger?" Jameson asked, alarmed. "He's here?"

Alexander and I nodded.

"Then shouldn't we go? Is Miss Raven safe?"

I grabbed Alexander's hand. "Batman saved me from his evil nemesis before. And tonight he will for good."

The closest I'd been to Dullsville's drive-in was when Becky and I were in elementary school. We would sit outside the surrounding fence and watch a blockbuster movie in the crisp grass, eating popcorn and candy we brought from home. If we were lucky enough, the patrons would have their movie speakers turned on full blast. If not, Becky and I would provide our own dialogue and crack up until a security guard shooed us away.

Never in my wildest dreams did I imagine that Becky and I would be driving through the gates of Dullsville's drive-in with two boyfriends.

When the rumors about Dullsville's drive-in being built on an ancient burial ground began, it was forced to shut down. But the only thing excavators discovered buried in the dirt were worms, and the theater had recently reopened. The smell of fresh paint mixed with the night air. Metallic gray speakers hung on stands next to the arriving cars. A yellow-and-white snack bar and picnic tables sat fifty yards behind the last parked car.

As Alexander drove Matt, Becky, and me through the parking lot, couples were wearing homemade capes and slicked-back hair, while little kids sporting pajamas and bat wings hung out on hoods and roofs of cars. Schoolmates from Dullsville High wore black T-shirts and jeans. It was obvious that no one but Alexander and me had actually seen the film. Alexander and I were the only patrons who came dressed as Vladimir and Jenny; everyone only knew it was a vampire movie, so they just wore black. The moviegoers stared at us as we drove through the crowd.

We found a spot in the back of the drive-in, and the four of us got out of the car to decide on snacks.

I had other things on my mind besides popcorn. As the three of them discussed "to butter or not to butter," I tiptoed around the parking lot. Jagger could be anywhere, waiting to sink his fangs into my neck.

Alexander found me hunting around the bushes.

"Come here," he said, leading me back to the car. "He's spoiled enough of our fun. We should at least try to enjoy ourselves. Look around. Tonight, we're not outcasts," Alexander said, and gave me a squeeze. He was right. I glanced at the crowd, larger than Alexander's Welcome to the Neighborhood party.

"This is way cool," I said, for a moment forgetting about the impending danger.

Matt and Becky returned with popcorn and drinks. The previews started, and we got back into the car—Matt and Becky in the backseat and Alexander and me in the front.

I immediately locked the doors.

"What are you doing?" Matt asked. "It's a drive-in."

"Keeping out the riffraff," I said.

Just then a preteen boy with straws stuck on his teeth for fangs pressed his face against my window.

"See!" I said, as we all laughed. I leaned against the window, bugged my eyes, and flashed my vampire teeth.

The boy's mouth dropped open, and his straws fell to the ground. "Mom!" he cried, and ran off.

"That was awful," Becky admonished.

"But funny," Matt confirmed.

We munched on our snacks and cuddled as the previews ended and the movie began. All the while, Alexander and I anxiously glanced outside for any vampire activity.

"I don't think I can do this," Alexander whispered when he caught me focusing on the picnic tables instead of the movie screen.

"Of course you can." I could see the concern in his eyes. I leaned over and gave him a kiss on the mouth.

"Hey, we can't see," Matt and Becky said.

Alexander and I laughed, a great relief from the nervous tension that had been building up in us. I cuddled next to him and, for a while, forgot about Jagger. We got lost in the moment, and Alexander and I recited the lines of the movie together.

Three-quarters of the way through the film, at the moment that the vampire Vladimir was bringing Jenny to a graveyard wedding, the screen turned yellow, and the film burned and crumbled. We could hear a flapping sound.

The crowd began yelling "Boo!"

"Aw, man," I heard Matt say.

"It's all a conspiracy to make us buy more popcorn," I said.

We climbed out of the car and stretched.

"I could use a drink. You guys want anything?" Matt asked.

"Thanks anyway," I said.

"I'll go with you," Becky offered. Matt grabbed her hand, and they left for the snack bar.

"Should we be concerned about them?" I asked, feeling uneasy.

"Jagger wants you, not a soccer match."

I looked around. My heart started to race.

"Now I'm getting nervous," I said.

"Why don't you relax in the car. I'll stand guard."

I opened the driver's-side door, jumped in, and quickly locked the door.

I turned to lock the passenger door and gasped.

Jagger was sitting next to me!

"You thought I wouldn't recognize you with blond hair," he sneered.

I tried to open the door, but he grabbed my arm.

"I've come to collect what I didn't collect before," he said, looking into my eyes, his fangs primed. I pushed him away just as I heard a banging on my window. I looked up to see an enraged Alexander.

He tried to open my door as I struggled to keep Jagger's fangs at bay.

Frustrated, Alexander ran to the other side as Jagger automatically locked all the doors.

"Help!" I cried, pushing him at arm's length.

Alexander returned to my window, balling his fist to

punch through the glass, when I managed to wedge my feet in front of Jagger. I stretched one hand toward the window, my fingers reaching as far as they could, and barely touched the lock. With all my might, I managed to lift the knob with my index finger.

My door flung open, but Jagger pulled me out the passenger door before Alexander could reach me.

He dragged me away from the car and toward the back of the drive-in.

But before Jagger reached the exit, Alexander caught up and grabbed his arm. "Let her go!" he demanded, "before I—"

Jagger's grip remained tight around my wrist.

"I came to do what you could never do," Jagger said.

"What does he mean?" I asked.

Alexander flashed his fangs at Jagger and stepped in between us. "Don't make me do this in front of those people," Alexander said, referring to a few patrons in the distance who were looking at us curiously.

I backed away, out of reach of Jagger.

"This would never have happened," Jagger continued. "My sister just wanted to be like everyone else. She could have had anyone. But we chose you! And you left her standing all alone!"

"You know why. I never meant to hurt her or your family," Alexander defended.

"You'll do the same thing to Raven. You really were never like one of us. You may deny who you are," Jagger yelled, "but I won't deny who I am!"

He ran toward me and grabbed my arm just as Alexander grabbed the other.

Then Jagger flashed his fangs and lunged at my neck.

"It's too late!" I hollered, ducking away. "Alexander already has me." I leaned in and bit Jagger's arm.

Suddenly the parking lot lights dimmed and the movie started again. The vampire Vladimir was leading Jenny by the hand through the cemetery. A gang of vampires was following them, trying in vain to stop the ceremony and take the ingénue for their own.

Jagger howled out in pain as I pulled Alexander toward the movie screen.

Alexander resisted. "Where are you going? We can't turn our backs on him."

I gazed up at the screen. Vladimir was leading Jenny to the tombs. "We don't have much time."

But Alexander stared back at Jagger, whose pale face was turning red.

"Just like we planned. Please, trust me," I begged him, tugging his hand.

Alexander glanced over his shoulder. Jagger was heading straight for us.

I could see Becky and Matt coming through the parking lot with drinks in their hands.

"Hey, what's going on?" Becky asked as she got closer.

"I can't talk now, but get in the car and lock the doors!" I commanded.

Alexander and I hurried toward the front of the lot, where the movie screen was.

An angry Jagger lurked behind us.

"What is Raven doing?" I heard Becky ask, as she and Matt got into the Mercedes.

Alexander and I stood in front of the movie screen and our *Kissing Coffins* mirror images.

Patrons began hollering, "What's going on?"

I looked out into the crowd, but I couldn't see Jagger.

Then I noticed him hovering behind a family, only fifty feet away from us. When he caught my eye, he took off toward us.

"Hurry!" I exclaimed. "We don't have much time!"

As Vladimir lifted his beloved Jenny into his arms, I placed my arms around Alexander's neck. He lifted me up.

The crowd roared, clapping and tapping their horns as we acted out the movie behind us.

I could see out of the corner of my eye that Jagger was now only a few feet away, coming after me.

"Just like the film," I whispered.

Alexander anxiously looked into my eyes. My fist clenched by my side, primed for what was about to happen.

"Bite me, Alexander!" I cried. "Bite me!"

Jagger reached out. Alexander put his mouth on my neck just as the on-screen vampire did to his bride. I felt a slight pressure on my flesh. I grabbed my neck and cried out. My head slumped back, my body lay limp in his arms. My heart pulsed in overtime as if beating for both of us. I could feel the warm red liquid slowly dripping down my neck, the smell of blood permeating the air around us. Alexander lifted his head proudly, mirroring the on-screen vampire, holding his bride in his arms, a red river flowing from both vampires' lips.

The crowd cheered.

I glanced over to Jagger, whose blue and green eyes were now red with rage. Alexander gently let me down.

I was light-headed. I stumbled to my feet, holding my red-stained neck, as the liquid trickled down my forearm. As the camera moved to a close-up of Jenny's face, I looked at Jagger with a wicked grin and flashed my vampire fangs.

He began to howl with such a rage his body shook, but his cry was masked by the audience hollering and honking their car horns.

There was nothing left he could do to Alexander, nothing he could take.

Jagger's eyes grew redder, his muscles rippled, and he licked his fangs. He withdrew into the darkness and disappeared.

I loved the way you acted out the movie last night!"
Becky complimented me the next day at our lockers. "I
had no idea you planned to do that. You totally rocked!"

"Thanks. I just had to wait for the right moment."

"Who would have known Vladimir would only pretend to bite Jenny so the vampires wouldn't covet her as
one of their own."

"He does it so the vampires will believe Jenny has
bonded eternally to him. They are forced to flee London
and return to Romania, never to harm her again."

"Yeah, but you would think Vladimir would want to
make her a vampire for himself."

"Well, the lesson is, not all vampires are bad," I said
with a smile.

"They aren't?" Matt asked, standing behind us.

"Yes, just like soccer snobs," I teased.

"Well, I thought Alexander really bit you. Can I see your flesh wounds?" he added.

"Isn't that a personal question?" I kidded. "Besides, Alexander only pretended to bite me—just like Vladimir does to Jenny. He gave an award-winning performance," I said proudly. "I think he actually liked acting in front of all those people."

"Well, the blood looked real, too," he said.

"My brother's nerd-mate, Henry, has all these special effects. That's where I got these vampire teeth," I said, and flashed them.

"Why are you still wearing them?" he asked.

"I can't get them off. I think Henry charges extra for glue remover."

Just then two of Dullsville High's junior varsity cheerleaders stopped at our lockers.

"Like, can you tell me where I can get those costumes you wore last night?" one asked.

"You looked like Marilyn Monroe," the other cheerleader said to me. "And you looked like Elvira," she said to Becky. "I want a costume like Elvira."

Costume? I wondered. Hadn't they ever noticed I'd always dressed like that? I considered telling her about Hot Gothics in Hipsterville, or inviting her to come over to my house to borrow from my closet. But the thought of preppy cheerleaders dressing goth just because they thought it was "in" turned my stomach. I'd been an outcast for so long, I might have a hard time being an incast.

"You were awesome last night," her friend complimented. "Where did you get that blood?"

I was thinking of telling her about Henry, but decided to keep him my secret.

"It was real," I said.

"Ooh, gross!" they both exclaimed, and scurried away.

I had to admit, I liked the attention the drive-in performance brought me. Even if I knew it was going to last only as long as a ditzy cheerleader's attention span.

The bell rang.

"The drive-in's going to have another costume night," Matt added. "And people are already talking about acting out the movie."

"Maybe Alexander and I should get a cut of the admissions. Where's my agent when I need her?"

"Who was that creepy white-haired kid who came over to you by the movie screen?" Becky asked.

"I guess someone wanting to play one of the vampire gang," I replied, and slammed my locker shut. "But I thought he sucked," I added. "He wasn't convincing as an evil vampire at all."

20

Dancing in the Dark

There was a new girl in Dullsville—me. After all, I'd spent sixteen years living a monotonous existence. Now Dullsville wasn't so dull anymore. A few blocks away from me on Benson Hill lived the love of my life— Alexander Sterling. My boyfriend. My Gothic Mate. My vampire.

I was reunited with Alexander, and his nemesis was out of our lives. I had to wonder what would be normal for us. I was dating a vampire. I would have to keep a secret I'd never be able to share with Becky, my parents, or anyone. To keep him in my life, I needed a padlock on my black lips.

Alexander and I would always have to meet after sundown. I would never be able to eat breakfast or lunch with him. We'd have to avoid sitting near mirrors at fancy restaurants and make sure garlic wasn't being minced anywhere in the vicinity.

And most important, I wondered whether I would have to become a vampire for us to have a future.

That evening, I met Alexander at the Mansion door, a backpack slung on his shoulder and an umbrella in his hand.

"Let's go," he said proudly, taking my hand.

"Where are you taking me tonight? A tomb?"

"You'll see . . ."

"You were awesome that night. Everyone at school thought you totally rocked! For a moment, I thought you were really going to bite me."

"For a moment, I really wanted to," he said with a wink.

"It must be hard for you, resisting your impulses."

"You have impulses, too, that you resist, don't you?" he asked playfully, tickling me. "Why should I be any different?"

I giggled.

After a few blocks we stopped in front of Dullsville's country club.

"You're kidding. My dad belongs here."

"Well, he has good taste."

"I never thought so."

Bushes standing eight feet high lined the property of the golf course, surrounded by a low chain-link fence.

We quickly climbed over the metal blockade and walked onto Dullsville's golf course. Of all the places I've snuck into before, this was not on my list.

"If I get caught sneaking in here," I joked, "this could really ruin my reputation."

At night, the course seemed mysteriously spooky and gorgeous.

We walked across the tee, down the fairway, and onto the green, avoiding the sand traps and bunkers just like golf balls.

Alexander and I sat on the green of the third hole, which overlooked a small lake with a lit fountain. A few weeping willows, which offset the lake, in the darkness looked like they were crying black lace instead of leaves. The course was eerily quiet. The only sounds we could hear were crickets and the gentle splashing of the waterfall.

"I like to be surrounded by beautiful scenery—but you overshadow even that."

I gave him a quick kiss.

"I also like to dance in unusual places." He opened his backpack and pulled out a portable CD player. He switched it on, and Marilyn Manson began to wail.

"Can I have this dance?" he asked, offering his hand.

At first we slow danced on the green to one of the morbidly sluggish tunes. We must have looked like quite a sight—two goths dancing in the dark on a golf course.

As the songs picked up pace, we danced around each other and the flagpole until we were exhausted.

We ran to the lake and cupped our hands in the water. The light from the fountain caught my reflection in the water. What should have been Alexander's reflection was only ripples of water from where he dipped his hands. I looked up at him. He smiled back joyfully, not even aware of his missing image. I felt a pang of loneliness for him, wondering what it must be like to live a life of empty reflections.

Breathless, we plopped down on the green and looked up at the stars. The sky was clear except for some clouds in the distance. Lying on the open golf course without hovering trees and glaring streetlights, we could see what seemed like a million stars twinkling just for us.

Alexander sat up and pulled out two drinks from his backpack.

"Gummi worms, spiders, or lizards?" he asked, reaching back inside.

"Worms, please."

We both drank and chewed on the brightly colored candy insects.

"What's it like never seeing your reflection?" I asked, his missing image still on my mind.

"It's all I've ever known."

"How do you know what you look like?"

"From paintings. When I was five, my parents commissioned one of their artists to make a portrait of us. We have it hanging over the fireplace in our home in Romania. It was the most beautiful thing I'd ever seen. How the artist captured the light, the details of my mother's dimples, the joy in my father's eyes, all through gentle strokes from his palette. The artist made me look alive when I felt lonely and grim inside. That's the way this man saw me. I decided then that that's what I wanted to do."

"Did you like the way you looked?"

"I'm sure I looked much better than if I'd seen myself in a reflection." Alexander's voice became impassioned, as if he were expressing his thoughts for the very first time. "I always felt sorry for humans, spending so much time in front of the mirror. Fixing their hair, makeup, and clothes, mostly to impress others. Did they really see themselves in the mirror? Was it what they wanted to see? Did it make them feel good or bad? And mostly I wondered if they based their self-image on their reflected one."

"You're right. We do spend a lot of time worrying about our looks, instead of focusing on what's inside."

"The artist has the power to capture that. To express what he thinks about the subject. I thought that was much more romantic than seeing myself in a cold, stark glass reflection."

"So that is why you paint portraits? Like the one of me at the Snow Ball?"

"Yes."

"It must be hard to be an artist among vampires."

"That's why I never fit in. I'd rather create than destroy."

Alexander suddenly looked up at the moon. He got up and grabbed a sturdy branch that had fallen from one of the trees and was lying by the lake. He took off his belt and bound the branch to the umbrella handle. He removed the flagpole and stuck the umbrella stick in the third hole.

"What are you doing? Want to keep out the moon?"

Suddenly I could hear the sound of a sprinkler turning on. Water began to drizzle down over us like a gentle storm.

I giggled as the cold water hit my legs.

"This is so awesome! I never knew a golf course could be so beautiful."

We kissed underneath the sprinkling water until we noticed lightning flashing in the distance.

I quickly packed up our drinks and CD player while Alexander dismantled the umbrella.

"I'm sorry we have to call this short," he said as we headed for home.

"Are you kidding? It was perfect," I said, giving him a quick hug. "I'll never look at golf the same way again."

21

Creepy Carnival

For the next few days, I went to school, hung out with Becky and Matt, dodged Trevor, came home, and took care of Nightmare. After sunset, I spent as much time as I could with Alexander, watching movies, cuddling, and listening to music in the darkness.

By Saturday, I was exhausted. I slept the day away and met Alexander by dusk at his Mansion. It was the night of Dullsville's Spring Carnival.

In the past, Becky and I had always attended the carnival together. This time, we would be arriving separately on the arms of our respective dates.

Alexander and I entered, hand in hand, shortly after sunset. We stepped through the two arches made of multi-colored balloons, a white wooden admission booth in between. Alexander approached Old Jim, who was selling tickets; Luke, his Great Dane, was sitting at his feet.

"Two, please," Alexander requested, paying for us both.

"I see you've been sleeping in one of the vacant coffins," Old Jim warned.

"I haven't slept at the cemetery for months," I replied. "Maybe it's—"

He looked at me skeptically. "Well, if I catch you, I have to tell your parents, you know."

Alexander grabbed my hand and led me away from Old Jim and through the balloon-filled entrance. The carnival was spread over Dullsville High's soccer field. There were booths of homemade pies, corn dogs, snow cones, rides like the Ferris wheel and the Scrambler, a fun house, and games of tic-tac-toe, a ring toss, and a dunking booth. The air smelled of cotton candy and grilled corn on the cob. Alexander and I walked through the crowd like the prince and princess of darkness. But he was oblivious to the stares and looked like a wide-eyed kid not knowing what to play with first.

"Haven't you been to a carnival before?" I asked.

"No. Have you?"

"Of course."

"You made it," I heard a familiar voice say. It was my dad.

I turned around to find my parents eating hot dogs at a picnic table.

Alexander shook my dad's hand and politely said hello to my mother.

"Would you like to sit with us?" my mom offered.

"They don't want to spend all day with us old fogies," my dad interjected. "You guys have fun," he said, reaching into his wallet and offering me a twenty.

"I've got it covered, Mr. Madison," Alexander said.

"I like your style," my dad replied, returning the money to his wallet.

"Thanks anyway, Dad," I said. "We'll see you later."

As Alexander and I walked past the booths, patrons and workers stared at us like we were part of the sideshow.

"Hey, Raven," Becky said, when I found her selling homemade pies at her father's booth. "Dad had to run home. We sold out of the caramel apples and only have two pies left."

"Congratulations," I complimented her. "But I was looking forward to some."

"I'll reserve two for you when he gets back," Matt said, as he handed a piece of apple cobbler to a customer.

"I think you've found your calling," I said to him.

We said good-bye to Becky and Matt as they tried to keep one step ahead of their customers.

On our way to the carnival rides, I spotted Ruby, who was standing in between two booths. "Hi, Ruby, are you here with Janice?" I asked.

"Oh, hi, Raven," she said, giving me a friendly hug. "No, I'm here with a friend," she added with a wink.

Just then Jameson, minus his usual butler uniform and wearing a dark suit and black tie, walked over with a fresh swirl of blue cotton candy.

"Hello, Miss Raven," he said, gently handing the candy to Ruby. "I'm glad to see Alexander is in such good hands, as I have the night off."

Alexander gave the Creepy Man a smile.

"I'm glad that you and Jameson are back in town," Ruby said to Alexander.

"I am, too," he replied, and squeezed my hand. "Is Jameson treating you right? I know he can get kind of wild," he teased.

"He's been nothing but a perfect gentleman," she said, but then whispered, "Hopefully that will wear off as the evening continues."

Alexander and I laughed. "We'll leave you two kids with your candy. I promised Raven I'd take her on the Ferris wheel."

We cut away from the food booths and past the carnival games.

"Raven," Billy Boy called from behind.

We turned around, and my brother ran up to us, holding a plastic bag with a frantic fish inside. Henry followed close behind with his own swimming prize.

"Look what we just won!" Billy Boy exclaimed.

"Cool," Alexander commented.

"He's a cutie," I said, tapping the side of the bag. "Just make sure you keep him out of reach of Nightmare. She's small now, but she'll be growing."

"Not to fear, I'm going to make a safety roof for their fishbowls," Henry proudly proclaimed.

"I'm sure you will," I said to my brother's nerd-mate.

"We're all out of tickets," Billy Boy whined. "Did you see Dad around?"

"Here," Alexander said, reaching in his back pocket

before I could answer. He handed Billy Boy some cash.

My brother's eyes bugged out as if he'd just won the lottery.

"Thanks, Alexander!" he exclaimed.

"Yeah, thanks, man," Henry said, and they took off back to the goldfish booth.

"That was so nice of you. You didn't have to do that," I said.

"Don't worry about it. Now let's go ride the Ferris wheel," he suggested.

Normally I hated waiting for rides and would cut in line, dragging along a reluctant Becky. Now I enjoyed the wait, because it meant I had more time with Alexander.

Soon we were ascending into the night sky. We slowly came to the top when the ride stopped, letting off the riders at the bottom.

"Do you think it will be difficult because we are different?" I asked, staring down at the couples.

"We are more alike than most."

"Does it bother you that we are not the same on the inside?" I asked, looking at him.

"But we are in here," he said, pointing to his heart.

"If I were Luna, would you have left the ceremony?"

Alexander looked confused. "What do you mean?"

"Do you want me to become a . . . ?" I asked.

Suddenly the ride started up, cutting our conversation short. We cuddled as our car finally descended to the ground.

Alexander helped me off the Ferris wheel. We paused,

overwhelmed by the choices of food, games, and rides that still awaited us.

"Let's do the ring toss," he said when we got off.

Alexander and I went over to the ring toss booth as a couple finished, walking away empty-handed.

I gazed at the stuffed animals as the blue-and-white-uniformed clerk, wearing a black top hat, picked up the rings off the floor.

"They're rigged. I never win. I usually spend all my allowance and I don't even get Mardi Gras beads," I lamented.

Alexander placed some money on the counter, and the clerk stood up and handed him three rings.

"Harder than it looks," I said.

Alexander stared at the single wooden pole as if he were a wolf staring at an unsuspecting deer.

He threw the rings in quick succession like a dealer at a casino. The clerk and I were stunned. The three rings were resting around the pole.

I jumped up and down. "You did it!"

Alexander beamed as the clerk handed me a giant purple bear. I squeezed it hard and gave Alexander a huge kiss.

I glowed as I held the bear, almost bigger than me.

"Snow cones are on me," I announced, as we turned to make our way back through the crowd. My stride was broken when I bumped into someone.

"Excuse me," I said, and placed the bear on my hip so I could see.

"Hey, monster, watch out!" Trevor hollered, holding two tickets. "On your way to get your face painted?" he asked. "Perhaps you should."

"Nice seeing you, too," I said sarcastically.

I grabbed Alexander's hand, and we headed toward the snow cones.

"Hey, Luna!" I heard Trevor call from behind.

Alexander and I stopped dead in our tracks. He couldn't have just said what we thought he said.

"Luna!" Trevor called again.

Alexander and I looked at each other in disbelief.

Luna? It couldn't be! Jagger's twin sister? What would she be doing in Dullsville?

We turned around to find Trevor looking toward the fun house—a huge multicolored rectangular building. On the upper left-hand side of the structure was a gigantic clown's head, his mouth the entrance to the exhibit. On the bottom right-hand side, patrons exited through the red fabric laces of the clown's enormous brown shoe.

"That *is* her," Alexander said, shakily pointing to a petite girl standing near the front of the ramp that led to the entrance. She had long, flowing powder white hair and pale porcelain white skin, and she was wearing a pastel pink dress and black boots.

"It's like seeing an apparition. The last time I saw her was in Romania."

"What is she doing here?" I asked. "It's not like this town is vacation central."

"That's what I want to know!"

I handed the bear to Alexander, and we hurried after her, catching up to Trevor.

"You know that girl?" I asked Trevor, my pulse racing.

"A friend of Alexander's introduced us and asked me to bring her here. She's really pretty," he said in my face. "Why, are you jealous?"

"Jagger? He's still here?" I asked, confused.

"If you really were a good friend of his, you'd know that."

"He's not a friend. He's evil. You can't trust him," I warned.

"Well, he is kind of freaky like you guys, but he said he'd had a falling out with Alexander, so I figured that made him cool."

"He talked to you more than that night outside the Mansion?"

"What, are you spying on me? He came to a night game and told me his sister was coming to town. He asked me if I'd want to meet her. The coach wouldn't let him on the field, though. That dude has more metal on his face than a pair of cleats."

"Jagger's not a replacement for Matt, you know," I tried to tell Trevor. "He's nothing like Matt. Jagger's just trying to play you."

"Sounds like someone is jealous."

"He's not what you think he is," Alexander urgently cautioned.

"Listen, it was wonderful talking to you, but I have a date. Besides, you better get back to your cage. I think the zoo has reported you missing."

He took off into the crowd. We began to follow but were stopped when a burly man holding a toddler stepped in our way. I could see Trevor and Luna racing up the red, tongued ramp of the fun house.

"The end of the line is back there!" the burly man ordered, pointing behind us.

"It's urgent," I said.

I peered past the disgruntled fun house customer and saw Trevor handing his tickets to the clerk. They stepped into the clown's mouth and disappeared.

I grabbed Alexander's hand, and we raced around the man as he wiped ice cream off his child's mouth.

We hurried up the plank and around the patrons in line. "Hey, no cutting!" a few kids started shouting.

When we reached the entrance, the clerk blocked our way. "Tickets, please."

"I don't . . ." I reached into my pocket and pulled out a handful of change and put it into his palm.

"That's only enough for one."

Alexander pulled out a wad of dollars, stuck it into the clerk's hand, and placed the bear at his feet. "I'll be back for him," Alexander said. He grabbed my hand, and we raced through the clown's mouth.

We stepped into a room filled with multicolored plastic balls up to our knees. We waded through the balls, trying to move as quickly as possible.

"At this rate, we'll never find her," I said.

When we finally reached the end of the room, we saw

that to the right of us was a red door, to the left a black-and-white tunnel.

"Oh no! It's a maze!" I groaned. "Should we flip a coin?"

"We don't have time," Alexander said.

I followed him through a huge black-and-white tunnel that twisted around us as we walked. I got dizzy, stumbling, holding on to the railing and Alexander for support. We had to walk over a glass bridge. I could see Trevor below. I banged on the glass, but he didn't look up.

At the end of the bridge, there was a red slide. I went down first, with Alexander following behind. When we rose to our feet, I saw Trevor's blond hair ten feet ahead of me.

"Trevor—" I called.

But he turned the corner, heading into the next room. I pushed past a family of three and opened a polka dotted door.

Alexander and I were alone.

"Trevor?" I called.

The lights went out. I stood frozen. We could hear the maniacal laughter of a clown as soft lights slowly dimmed. And then Luna appeared before us.

She was beautiful. Ocean blue eyes, puffy pink lips, brilliant baby-doll black eyelashes. Her pale bubblegum-colored cotton dress outlined in fuchsia lace hung on her. Her skinny alabaster white legs poked out of her chunky black knee-high boots, a plastic pink Scare Bear dangling from the zipper. On her upper arm was a tattoo of a black rose.

Before we could speak, it went totally dark.

Alexander grabbed my hand just as the room slowly began to brighten, the black walls now glass. Luna was still standing before us.

I caught my reflection. The wall wasn't glass after all, but a hall of mirrors.

Dozens of Ravens reflected on and on. Alexander, still standing beside me, didn't reflect back. There was one other reflection that was missing.

I was breathless.

"What have you come for?" Alexander challenged her.

"Luna!" I could hear Trevor call from another room. "Where are you?"

Luna smiled a wicked pale smile, two sparkling fangs glistening. I gasped.

"Well, if you've gotten your wish—to become a vampire," Alexander said, "then why are you here?"

"Jagger sent for me. Now I want to live the life I was never able to before. Jagger gave me an opportunity to get out of Romania."

"What about the vampire who bit you? Shouldn't you be with him?" Alexander argued.

"He was just a fling, on unsacred ground. After you left me, I realized I could find someone else—anyone else—to transform me and find true love later."

"You can find that in Romania," Alexander disputed.

"*You* didn't," she said with an evil glare. "Besides, Jagger told me he met a guy who he thought might be perfect for me."

"Trevor?" I asked. "You've got to be kidding."

"But you can't trust Jagger," Alexander argued. "He's not looking out for your best interest, only his own. He's motivated by revenge."

"Now that I'm in your world, I see things differently. I saw it in your eyes at the cemetery, Alexander. We both want the same thing," she said. "Vampire or human. I just want a relationship I can sink my teeth into."

The lights went out. I squeezed Alexander's hand tightly. I reached out blindly. I had to find Trevor before Luna did.

"Trevor!" I called. "Don't—"

The light flashed on again.

Luna was gone.

Acknowledgments

I am forever grateful to my editor, Katherine Tegen, for your extreme talent, friendship, direction, and enthusiasm. A sequel would not have been possible without you.

To my agent, Ellen Levine, I am extremely thankful for your advice, expertise, and friendship.

Many thanks to Julie Hittman, for all your hard work, helpful e-mails, and upbeat nature.

And hugs to my brother, Mark Schreiber, for your continuing generosity and support.

Vampire Kisses 3

Vampireville

To my parents,
Gary and Suzanne Schreiber,
with love and vampire kisses

"I'm looking for someone
to quench my thirst—for all eternity."
—Luna Maxwell

I was ready to become a vampire.

I stood alone in the middle of Dullsville's cemetery, dressed in a black corset minidress, fishnet stockings, and my signature combat boots. I held a small bouquet of dead black roses in my black fingerless gloves. A vintage midnight-colored lace veil dripped down over my pale face, gracefully shrouding my black lipstick and eye shadow.

My vampire to be, Alexander Sterling, wearing a gray pallbearer's suit and hat, waited a few yards ahead of me by our gothic altar—a closed coffin adorned with a candelabra and a pewter goblet.

The scene was breathtaking. Fog floated through the graveyard like wayward ghosts. Candles flickered atop tombstones and were scattered alongside graves. A group of bats hovered over a cluster of lonely trees. Raindrops began to fall as the faint sound of screeching violins and a discordant harpsichord sent icy chills through my veins.

I had waited an eternity for this moment. My childhood fantasy was now coming true—I would be a dark angel of the night. I was as excited as a groupie who was about to marry a rock star.

Tiny torches lit my path, like a gothic runway. But as I took my first step toward Alexander, I began to wonder if I was making the right choice. My heart started to race as I proceeded forward. Images of the life I would be leaving behind flashed before me. My mom helping me sew a black velvet tote for my home ec. project. I took a step. Watching *Dracula* on DVD with my dad. Another step. Even my nerdy brother, Billy Boy, kindly helping me with my math homework. Step. My best friend, Becky, and I trying to climb the Mansion's gate. Step. My new kitty, Nightmare, gently purring in my arms. Step. They all began to haunt me.

In one bite my life would change forever.

I was leaving a boring, safe, yet love-filled world of the living and committing an eternity to a dangerous, unknown, darkened world of the undead.

As I continued to walk down the cemetery aisle, I could see the back of Alexander who, now only a few feet away, lifted a goblet from the coffin.

I reminded myself I was making the right decision. I wouldn't have to spend morbidly long daylight hours in Dullsville High. I'd have the ability to fly. And most important, I would be bonding with my true love, for all eternity.

I finally reached the coffin and stood alongside Alexander. He slid his white-gloved hand in mine, his plastic spider ring shining in the candlelight. He raised the pewter goblet to the moon and took a long drink. My heart raced as he passed it to me and I hesitantly lifted my veil from over my mouth. My hand was shaking, so the dark liquid wavered in the goblet.

"Maybe you aren't——," Alexander started, and put his hand over the glass.

"I am!" I argued defiantly. I pulled the goblet back and gulped the sweet, thick liquid.

I began to feel light-headed. The fog thickened around us. I could barely see Alexander's silhouette as he replaced the goblet on the coffin and then turned to me. With his white gloves, he gently lifted the black veil away from my face.

Now I could see clearly. Only I wasn't sure of what I was seeing. Instead of Alexander's usual long black hair, I noticed light-colored hair poking out from underneath his pallbearer's hat.

I gasped. It couldn't be!

"Jagger——," I exclaimed, frozen.

But when I looked into his eyes, I didn't see Alexander's rival's blue and green eyes that had once hypnotized me by the Mansion's gazebo. And they weren't the dark soulful eyes I had fallen in love with. These hypnotic eyes were green, and I'd seen them all my life.

"Trevor!" I declared, the words barely escaping my lips.

My childhood nemesis flashed a wicked grin, two

razor-sharp fangs hanging from his mouth.

I stepped back.

It was only last night at Dullsville's Spring Carnival that Alexander and I had tried to warn Trevor about Jagger's twin sister, Luna, who was looking to sink her newly formed fangs into the soccer snob's neck. Jagger had been seeking revenge on Alexander for not turning Luna into a vampire, and now that she'd been turned by another vampire, the nefarious teens were in Dullsville to find her a lifelong partner. But Trevor had failed to heed our warning. When Alexander and I arrived outside the Fun House and searched through the carnival, Trevor was gone.

Only now my nemesis had found me.

I tried to run, but Trevor grabbed my hand as I pulled away. "I've got you now, Monster Girl. Forever." He licked his lips and leaned into my neck.

I looked around for anything to help my escape. But when I reached out for the candelabra, I felt dizzy. Suddenly Trevor's mouth was on my neck.

"Get off!" I cried. "Let go of me!"

He pulled me into him with the force of a whole soccer team. I wedged my boot between us, and, with all my strength, I managed to push him away.

Trevor stumbled back and grabbed my arm. He tried to pull me close, but I bit his hand. I broke free as he stood up confidently and grinned a wicked smile. Blood began to drip from the corner of his mouth.

I reached for my neck. My palm felt warm and wet. I

gasped. When I held my hand before me, it was covered in blood.

"No!" I cried.

Just then I saw a confused Alexander, also sporting a gray pallbearer's uniform, running up the cemetery aisle. I turned to Trevor, who just stood and smiled.

"Not you! Not for an eternity!" I yelled.

I sat up, screaming so hard my throat hurt.

I opened my eyes to darkness. I could hardly breathe. Where was I? In a coffin? A tomb? An empty grave?

Soft material covered my legs, but my eyes couldn't adjust to my surroundings. I figured I must be wrapped in a burial shroud.

My heart was throbbing. My skin perspiring. My mouth dry.

Flashing, bloodred numbers caught my eye: Two fifteen A.M.

I breathed a sigh of relief. I wasn't lying in an unknown coffin in Dullsville's cemetery but rather in my own bed.

Was I as safe as I thought? Maybe this was all part of my nightmare. My fingers shaking, I switched on my *Edward Scissorhands* lamp and ran to my dresser mirror. I closed my eyes, anticipating what I might *not* see. When I opened them, my ghostlike reflection stared back. I pulled my bed-head hair away from my shoulders and examined my neck.

My bedroom door flung open and my dad appeared in the doorway, sporting flannel boxers, a Lakers T-shirt, and messy hair. "What's wrong?" he asked, more annoyed than worried.

"Uh, nothing," I replied, startled. I dropped my hair and stepped away from the mirror.

"What happened?" my mom asked, barging in.

"I heard a scream," Billy Boy said, nosing his way behind them, his tired eyes heavy.

"I'm sorry I woke you guys. I just had a bad dream," I confessed.

"You?" my father asked, raising his eyebrow. "I thought you loved bad dreams."

"I know. Can you believe it?" I asked, my heart still racing. "Who knew?"

"What was it about? You ran out of black lipstick?" Billy Boy teased.

"Yes. And I found a new one in *your* dresser drawer."

"Dad!" Billy Boy hollered, ready to pummel me.

"Now I know I'm not dreaming," I said, and playfully tousled my brother's hair.

"All right. Enough excitement for tonight. Let's all go back to sleep," my dad ordered, putting his arm around my brother as they left the room.

I settled back into bed.

"So what were you *really* dreaming about?" my mom asked curiously.

"It was nothing."

"Nothing woke up the whole house?" she asked.

She shook her head and started for the door.

"Mom . . . ," I said, my words stopping her. "Does my

neck look okay to you?" I whispered, pulling my hair back.

She returned to my bedside. "Looks like a regular neck to me," she said, examining it. "What were you expecting—a vampire bite?"

I gave her a quick smile. She pulled the covers over me as if I were still a child.

"I remember when you were a little girl and you stayed up all night with your father watching *Dracula* movies on our black-and-white TV," she reminisced fondly.

She handed me my Mickey Malice plush that had fallen beside my bed. "You never had nightmares then. It was as if you were comforted by vampires the way other kids are comforted by lullabies."

She kissed me on top of the head and reached for my lamp.

"Maybe you should leave it on," I said. "Just for tonight."

"Now you are scaring *me*," she said, and left my room.

The Almost Great Escape

The official welcome sign to my town should now read, "Welcome to Vampireville—come for a bite, but stay for an eternity!"

The town that I'd grown up in and had always called Dullsville was no longer dull. Not only was I dating a vampire, but now two other teen Nosferatus were living among Dullsvillians, whose biggest concern was getting the best price on the newest Prada purses or the latest Big Bertha golf clubs.

I was the only mortal who knew about the secret identity of the new bloodsucking inhabitants and I was dying to spill my guts to the *Dullsville Dispatch*. The front-page headline would read: GOTH GIRL GETS THE GOODS! Raven Madison Wins Nobel Peace Prize for Unearthing the Undead. Below, a color photograph would feature me standing next to Luna, Jagger, and Alexander—and I'd be the only one reflected in the picture.

If I came forward with my discoveries, my outcast life would be broadcast nationwide. I might be picked up in a chauffeur-driven hearse and my awaiting publicist would whisk me away on my Gulfstream jet for a media blitz tour; I'd be booked on CNN, *Oprah*, and MTV to plug my memoir, *Vampire Vixen*. My personal assistant would be in charge of making sure I had a bowl of black gummy bats and total darkness in the greenrooms at every talk show. My personal stylist would follow closely behind me, reapplying body tattoos, attaching blue hair extensions, and outfitting me in the latest Drac Blac dresses.

But in lieu of blabbing my discoveries to the world, I would have to keep Jagger's and Luna's ghastly secret to myself—that the twins were really vampires.

It had not always been so. Alexander shared with me that when the Maxwell twins were born, it was quickly discovered that Luna was not a vampire like everyone else in her family but rather a human—a genetic link that went back generations to a great-great mortal grandmother. A promise was made between the Sterlings and the Maxwells that on Luna's eighteenth birthday, Alexander was to meet Luna on sacred ground for a covenant ceremony—turning Luna into a vampire and bonding each to the other for eternity. When the day came, however, Alexander decided that Luna and he should both spend eternity with someone they love. After Alexander broke the two families' promise, Jagger sought revenge on Alexander. Once Luna was turned into a vampire by another vampire on unsacred ground, she joined her brother in Dullsville to meet a mortal teen with whom Luna could spend eternity. I knew that if I revealed the twins' true identity, then I'd be giving away Alexander's as well. I'd be putting my boyfriend in danger and could lose him forever.

So instead of being on the cover of *Gothic Girl,* I was going undercover.

The irony was that I'd have to convince Trevor, who had started the rumor in the first place that the Sterlings were vampires, that he had been right all along and now was in line to be the newest victim of Jagger and Luna's deadly duo. Though no one on earth repulsed me as much as Trevor, there was a gnawing inside me to warn him about the impending danger. And more important, if someone as wicked as Trevor became a vampire, all of Dullsville would be unsafe after sunset.

At Dullsville's drive-in, during the showing of *Kissing Coffins,* Alexander and I had tricked Jagger into believing I'd been bitten and turned into a vampiress. But several days later, at Dullsville's carnival, when Alexander and I confronted Luna in the Fun House's Hall of Mirrors, I was the only one whose image reflected. Would Jagger believe his sister or what his own eyes had witnessed at the drive-in?

"I'm not concerned," Alexander said, gently reassuring me that night when he pulled his butler Jameson's Mercedes into my driveway. "Jagger is seeking revenge on us through Trevor now. We can easily explain the Hall of Mirrors. Besides, Jagger's ego is too big to admit he was double-crossed."

"So we should continue to keep up appearances that I am a vampire," I said. "It would be easier if we just go to the cemetery and you take my blood as your own."

Alexander turned off the engine.

I know he dreamed of being in my world as much as I dreamed of being in his. But when he turned to me, his shadowy eyes reflected the loneliness of living in a mysterious world that was filled with darkness and isolation.

As I gazed back at him, I wondered if I really wanted to be a part of a world that Alexander didn't want to be in. Was I just going through a phase that would seemingly last forever? At this point, it was irrelevant, as we sat parked in the driveway, on unsacred ground. Alexander was making the decision for us both, by saying nothing.

"Then I'll start just by ditching school," I thought aloud. "I'll replace my bed with a coffin, sleep in all day with the shades pulled, wake up just in time for dinner. We can feast on bloody steaks and party among the tombstones. I'm going to love being a vampire!"

He turned to me and placed his hand on my knee. "I've already caused you enough disruption by entering your life," he said softly. "First with Jagger, now with Luna. I'm not going to let this interfere with your family or school."

Frustrated, he pushed back his black hair, his earrings catching the moonlight.

"Don't say that—you've brought me a life I never knew existed. Adventure, belonging. True love."

His sullen eyes sparkled.

"Well, if you don't act normal, we'll have your parents, friends, and the whole town questioning your behavior," he argued.

I gnawed on my black fingernail. "But they already do."

A sweet smile came over his pale face. Then he furrowed his brow.

"Besides, you can do what I can't—attend school. That's where Trevor will be, if he's not already turned. Then you'll have a shot at convincing him to stay away from Luna."

I felt a sudden surge of pride. "You're entrusting me with a secret mission?"

"You'll be like a gothic Charlie's Angel."

"What if Jagger finds out I'm at school?" I asked. "He may wonder why I'm out in the daylight. I've never seen any vampires attending Dullsville High."

"That's the exact reason Jagger and Luna will never find out. Since they'll be hidden from the sun, they won't ever be able to see you," he reassured me.

"But what if Trevor or his soccer snob friends tell Jagger they saw me at school?" I pressed.

"They won't have proof," Alexander said with certainty. "Jagger isn't likely to believe what he hasn't seen. And he did see me bite you, or pretend to bite you," he admitted, "at the drive-in."

Alexander walked me to the door. He leaned in to me and gave me a long good-night kiss. "While you're at school, I'll be fast asleep dreaming of you."

Alexander blew me a kiss, got in his car, and drove down the driveway. When I turned to wave, he had already vanished from view.

That night, as I lay in bed, I tried to calm my anxious nerves. I closed my eyes and imagined Alexander alone in his attic bedroom, skillfully painting a portrait of us at Dullsville's carnival, blasting Korn from his stereo.

I wasn't sure Alexander could remain so calm, knowing Luna and Jagger were in Dullsville. After the sun rose, I wouldn't be able to see my vampire-mate until nightfall. As Alexander slept the day away, I would return to school and find Trevor on my own.

The next morning, I awoke to the sun scorching through the cracks between my curtains like a burning torch. I pulled the drapes tightly closed, covered myself with a blanket, and tried to go back to sleep. But I kept thinking about my mission—to save my nemesis from a thirsty vampiress.

I was in my bedroom scrounging for clothes for school when I heard the sound of a honking horn.

"Becky's here!" my mom called up to me from the kitchen.

"She's always ten minutes early!" I barked, pulling black-and-white tights over my legs. My best friend had always kept farm hours, but now that she was dating Matt, Trevor's former silent shadow, she insisted on arriving at school even earlier.

The sound of a horn blasted again. "You'll see him for the next six hours!" I murmured to myself.

"Raven," my mom called again. "I can't take you in today. I have a meeting—"

"I know! I'll be down in a minute!"

The truth was if Alexander was waiting by the bleachers for me at Dullsville High each day, I'd set my *Nightmare Before Christmas* alarm clock for five thirty, too. But as I put on a black miniskirt and a torn *Donnie Darko* T-shirt, all I could think of was handsome Alexander sleeping in his darkened bedroom. I would face the sunny day without him.

As Becky impatiently honked again, I covered my already blackened, tired eyes with charcoal eye shadow and eyeliner. Finally I grabbed my backpack and waved to my mom, and climbed into Becky's truck.

"I'm disconnecting that horn immediately," I said in a grumpy tone as I climbed into Becky's pickup.

"I'm sorry, Raven, it's just that—"

"I know, I know. 'I'm meeting Matt by the bleachers before school.'"

"Am I getting annoying?" she asked.

"I'd be the same way if Alexander was waiting for me at school, instead of Trevor Mitchell."

"Thanks for understanding."

Becky passed a yellow bus loaded with preteen students heading for Dullsville Middle. Several students gathered at their windows. Some gawked at me, while the others pointed and laughed. I would have been surprised and perturbed, except that they did that every day.

"Well, speaking of Trevor . . . I have some major dirt on him."

"What's the buzz factor?"

"On a scale of one to ten, it's a nine and a half."

"Bring it on," I said, checking my ghoulish makeup in her broken visor mirror.

"Trevor has a girlfriend."

"You mean Luna?" I said, slamming the visor back.

"Luna?" she asked, confused.

"I mean, luna . . . tic. She's got to be a lunatic to date him. Anyway, who told you?"

"Matt said Trevor was seen with a goth at the carnival. I thought he meant you until he said she had ghost white hair."

"Goth? That's what people are saying about her?"

She nodded her head. "Yes. And that she's a major hottie. Matt didn't say that, of course, but he said that's what the soccer snobs are saying. You know how guys are, checking out the new girl."

"But Trevor despises anyone not sporting school colors."

"Yeah, but she dotes on him like he's a prince. She and her brother worship him. So it's like he's captain of the soccer snobs *and* the goths. His head is going to explode.

"He probably likes her," she went on, "but it's you he really loves. It's obvious he's had a crush on you since you were kids. He can't have you, so he's trying to get second best."

I rolled my eyes and pretended to gag. "Thanks for the compliment," I said sarcastically.

"The good news is maybe Trevor will stop torturing you."

If Trevor became a vampire, his bite would be worse than his bark.

"Apparently she showed up at their soccer practice last night, cheering for Trevor," Becky continued.

"She did? I was afraid this would happen."

"Afraid of what?"

"Uh . . . ," I began, stalling. "That Trevor would be popular again. After we've worked so hard to expose his inner monster."

"Without Matt by his side, no one cares what he says or does anymore."

"But who knows what . . ."

"We have our own lives now," Becky said proudly. "So who cares if he has one too."

I looked out the window and reflected on the rivalry Trevor and I had had since childhood. Deep down, I knew Becky was right, but I felt torn. Even though I detested Trevor and I was in love with Alexander, there was still a teeny competitive part of me that didn't want Trevor to be popular and have a girlfriend—vampire or not.

Becky and I arrived late at the soccer field and spotted Matt walking down the bleachers, listening to his iPod. Becky raced over to him as if he had just disembarked off a military vessel.

I reached the slobbering pair. "Eh hem!" I said, coughing, and tapped Becky on the shoulder.

They broke apart their superglued embrace.

"Becky tells me Trevor has a girlfriend," I blurted out.

"I didn't say that," Matt said, looking strangely at Becky.

"But Becky said a girl was at practice rooting for Trevor."

"I guess. I thought you were done with him."

"I am, but gossip is gossip. Did Trevor leave with her?" I asked.

"She was with a creepy guy in a black knit hat. I think you'd like him. Pale with a lot of tattoos. When the team came out of the locker room, they had already gone."

Matt adjusted his backpack, grabbed Becky's hand, and started heading for school.

"Wait—did Trevor look different?" I interrogated.

"He wasn't wearing any tattoos," Matt said with a laugh.

"No, I mean unusually pale. Really thirsty. Redder eyes."

He thought for a moment. "He said he wasn't feeling well," he remembered. "Why all this interest in Trevor?"

The smitten couple looked at me curiously, waiting for an answer.

Suddenly the bell rang.

"I'd love to stay and chat, but you know how I like to be punctual," I lied, and took off.

During my first three classes I was preoccupied with confronting Trevor, so to distract myself I daydreamed about Alexander. I wrote our names in my journal—Raven

Madison x Alexander Sterling, TRUE LOVE ALWAYS—surrounded by black roses.

When the lunch bell finally rang, I skipped meeting Becky and Matt at the bleachers. Instead I combed the campus searching for Trevor.

I couldn't find my nemesis on the soccer field, the gym, or the steps where all the soccer snobs ate their filet mignon baguettes.

"Where's Trevor?" I asked a cheerleader who was tying her sneaker.

She eyeballed my outfit with contempt. She glared at me as if she were a queen and I were a serf who had dared to stumble upon her castle. She picked up her red and white pom-poms and turned away as if she had already wasted too much time.

"Have you seen Trevor?" I repeated.

"He's home," she snarled.

"You mean I could have stayed home too?" I mumbled. The only reason I came to school today was to find him.

She rolled her eyes at me.

I glared back, imagining what it would be like if I was a real vampire. I'd transform into a spooky bat, swoop around her as she let out a bloodcurdling scream, and tangle myself in her perfectly combed blond hair.

"Duh. He's sick," she finally said, scrutinizing me as if I, too, were spreading contagions.

Sick? Matt said that last night Trevor was pale and wasn't feeling well. My mind raced. Sick from what? The sunlight? Garlic? Maybe Luna and Jagger had already managed to lure him to Dullsville's cemetery. Right now Trevor could be sleeping in a red and white coffin.

I had to act fast.

I'd spent most of my life sneaking in and out of places—my house, the Mansion, Dullsville's elementary and middle schools. But since I was still a mere mortal and did not yet possess the powers of a shapeshifting bat, Dullsville High was getting harder to just walk, climb, or tunnel out of.

Principal Reed hired security guards to patrol both entrances of the campus, cutting down on kids leaving for lunch and not returning to school. Dullsville High was becoming like Alcatraz. All that remained was for the school board to encircle the campus with frigid water and killer sharks.

Instead of sneaking out, I'd have to make my exit known.

I opened Nurse William's office door to find three other kids wheezing, coughing, and sneezing in the waiting room, glaring at me as if I were the one who was ill.

I realized this might take longer than waiting until school let out.

I jotted down notes in my Olivia Outcast journal when Nurse William, the poster woman for health, bounced out. Exposed to seasonal colds, allergies, and excuses, Nurse William was impervious to dripping noses. Looking more like she stepped out of a gym than an examination room, she could probably snap off her own blood pressure band with a single bicep curl.

"Teddy Lerner," she called, reading from a chart. "It's your turn," she said, flashing a Colgate smile.

"I need to see you immediately," I interjected, standing up and holding my stomach. "I don't think I can wait much longer."

Teddy stared at me, his nose as red as Rudolph's, and sneezed. I almost felt bad, but I knew all Teddy needed was a big Kleenex and a bowl of chicken soup. If I didn't get to Trevor Mitchell soon, there might not be any blood left to draw in town.

"All right, Raven."

Nurse William, like Principal Reed, knew me on a first-name basis, since I'd been to each of their offices on numerous occasions.

I followed her into her office—a small, sterile room with the usual jars of tongue depressors, Band-Aids, extra long Q-tips, and a blue cot.

I sat on a metal chair next to Nurse William's desk.

"I've had the chills since I woke up," I fibbed.

She examined my eyes with a small pen light.

"Uh-huh," she said.

She held up her stethoscope.

"Take a deep breath," she said, putting her instrument on my chest.

I slowly breathed in and then fake sneezed and coughed so wildly, I thought I'd pulled a lung.

She quickly drew back the stethoscope.

"Interesting."

Nurse William opened her glass cabinet and pulled out an ear thermometer and sterile cover and took my temperature.

After a minute, she read the results.

"Just what I thought."

"I'm sick?"

"I think you have a case of either 'testitis' or 'I Didn't Do My Homework Syndrome.' It's common in the spring."

"But I feel awful!"

"You probably just need a good night's rest."

"I think I need to go home," I choked out. "You are keeping me against my will. I have a stomachache and headache, and my throat hurts," I said, talking through my nose.

"We can't release you unless you have a fever," she said, returning the thermometer to the glass cabinet.

"Haven't you heard of preventive medicine?"

"You do look like you haven't slept. Well, you'll have to get approval from Principal Reed," she said with a sigh, exhausted.

Great. New rules to be broken.

I stepped into Principal Reed's office with a note from Nurse William.

I fake sneezed and coughed.

"You've used up all your school sick days," he said, perusing my file. "You've requested to leave school one hundred and thirty days out of the one hundred and forty days of school so far."

"So thirty-one might be the magic number?"

"Well, you do look awful," he finally said, and signed my school release form.

"Thanks!" I said sarcastically.

I wasn't planning on appearing so convincing.

"I'm sorry, Raven," my mom said as she pulled our SUV into the driveway. "I feel terrible leaving you alone, but I have an off-site meeting that's been scheduled for months."

She walked me to the front door and gave me a quick hug as I stepped inside.

"Funny," I began. "I'm feeling better already."

I closed the door, and as soon as I saw my mom drive down the street, I grabbed my usual vampire detectors—garlic powder and a compact mirror belonging to Ruby White of Armstrong Travel—and headed straight for Trevor's.

No wonder vampires didn't venture out in daylight. I hungered for the safe haven of shade from trees and hovering clouds and thirsted for the warm blanket of nightfall. The hot sun began to bake my pale skin as I rode my bike up the Mitchells' driveway and passed a Ferguson and Son's Painting pickup parked in front of their four-car garage. I laid the bike against the side of the screened-in porch and rang the Mitchells' bell. Their dog began to bark from the backyard.

When no one answered, I rang the bell again.

Suddenly a small, elderly white-haired man carrying a

ladder came out of the garage.

"Hi, Mr. Ferguson," I said, running over to the familiar painter. "Is Trevor home?"

The elderly worker looked at me oddly.

"It's me, Raven," I said, pulling down my shades.

"Hi, Raven. Shouldn't you be at school?" he wondered.

"I'm on lunch break," I replied.

"I didn't think they let kids go home for lunch anymore. In my day, there was no such thing as school lunch," he began. "We had to—"

"Really, I'd love to hear all about it, but I don't have much time—"

"I just dispatched my sons for takeout. If I'd known you were coming . . . ," he began politely.

"That's very sweet of you, but I just need to see Trevor."

"It's probably not a good day for a visit. He's been in his room since sunrise."

Sunrise? I wondered.

"Well, I'll just be a minute," I said, walking past him toward the garage.

Mr. Ferguson put down the ladder.

"Raven, I can't let you in."

"But why? It's only me—," I whined.

Didn't he know I was on a mission to save Dullsville?

"Not when I'm on a job. It could cost me my contract."

More rules to be broken.

I plastered on my best puppy-dog face, the one I used with my dad when I wanted to stay out late. But the old man was steadfast. "The Mitchells should be home after five."

"I'll come back later then," I responded. "It was nice seeing you."

I walked over to my bike as Mr. Ferguson awkwardly carried the ladder to his truck. With his back to me, I knew I had only seconds. I dashed into the garage, snuck past a vintage Bentley, and opened the door to the laundry room. The smell of fresh paint wafted through the house as I raced over the plastic drop cloth, past the newly painted sunflower yellow kitchen. I would have complimented Mr. Ferguson on his paint job if it wouldn't have given away my dubious location.

I ran toward the front hall.

I'd been to Trevor's house only once, for his fifth birthday party, and that was only because he had invited everyone in our kindergarten class. My parents always told me that when they grew up and returned to their childhood homes, the houses looked smaller. Well, if Trevor's house seemed like a castle when I was in kindergarten, then as a sophomore, it had only downsized to a mansion. Mr. Mitchell owned half of Dullsville, and Mrs. Mitchell made her living by serial shopping. And it showed.

The entranceway alone seemed three stories high. A marble balcony was accentuated with two descending bleach white wooden staircases forming a semicircle around an indoor fountain. A grand dining room sat off to the left with a white diamond teardrop chandelier and a glass table with twelve beige linen-covered chairs. It was almost the same style as the living room at the Mansion— but without the cobwebs. On the right, a sitting room the size of my house was decorated in African art and adorned with enough fertility statues to impregnate an entire country.

I remembered standing in this exact spot when I was five, just after my mom dropped me off. For what seemed like hours, my classmates were running past me, giggling as if I weren't even there.

Finally we were called outside to the Mitchells' football-size backyard where a clown, a merry-go-round, and a pony were awaiting us. Watching my classmates dance, sing, and ride, I sat alone on the patio until Trevor opened one perfectly wrapped present after another containing Hot Wheels, LEGOs, or Nerf footballs. Then Mrs. Mitchell handed him a black box complete with a black bow, wrapped by yours truly.

Trevor ripped the package open and pulled out a brand-new mint-condition Dracula action figure. His eyes lit up and he exclaimed, "Wow!"

Mrs. Mitchell cued him to "show and share."

Wide-eyed, he proudly passed it to the pigtailed party-goer sitting next to him.

"That looks like Raven!" the girl shouted.

"Gross. It probably has cooties," another warned, returning it to him.

Trevor's gorgeous smile turned into a hideous frown.

He glared at me and threw my gift back in the box.

I remained alone on the patio steps for the rest of the party while the other kids ate cake and ice cream.

My stomach turned as I remembered that day. I paused for a moment and wondered if instead of running up to Trevor's room and warning him about Luna's intentions, I should sneak back out the way I came in.

I heard the laundry room doorknob turn.

I quietly raced up the pristine staircase and past more doors than were in the MGM Grand Hotel. After peeking in a million guest bedrooms and bathrooms down a hallway the length of an international runway, one final door awaited.

I'm not sure what I expected to find—Trevor had been sleeping since sunrise. It had been confirmed by several sources that he was sick and pale. If Trevor had already been bitten, I was putting myself in danger.

I had no other choice. I double-checked the garlic stashed in my purse.

I knocked gently.

When I didn't get a response, I slowly twisted the handle and opened the door. I took off my glasses and my hood. I crept inside.

Light from the hallway shined softly through the bedroom. The dark curtains were drawn closed—one sign Trevor could already be turned.

The soccer snob must have had his own personal interior decorator. His bedroom could have graced the cover of *Architectural Digest Teen*.

Next to the curtains, a giant flat-screen computer sat on a white modular desk. On one side of the room was a wall-mounted gazillion-inch plasma TV. Underneath it was a teen's dream lounge—a red futon couch, a soccer-themed pinball machine, and a foosball table.

Lastly and most ghastly was his midnight blue king-size bed with a soccer-goal headboard.

I almost gagged.

I could see Trevor's golden blond hair sticking out from underneath his comforter.

As much as I would have liked to short-sheet his bed or stick his hand in warm water, I decided to open his computer desk to search for any hidden clues. All I found were unsharpened pencils, a school lock, and loose batteries.

I opened two shutter doors, which led to something more like a sporting goods store than a teen's closet. A few feet away a glass bookshelf was adorned with a million soccer trophies and medals, and on the wall hung ribbons, a half dozen framed soccer pictures, and *Dullsville High Chatterbox* articles. I glided my finger across a dust-free gold trophy when I noticed something dust-filled hidden behind it—a decade-old Dracula action figure.

For a moment I almost felt a warming sensation filter through my icy veins. Then he stirred.

I quietly tiptoed over to him. I stood frozen. The normally sun-kissed soccer snob looked like one of the undead. But even when he was sick, Trevor was gorgeous. It almost made me ill that he had gotten so much by having a pretty face and a fast kick to midfield.

I wondered why this conservative snob was so attracted to the gothic Luna. Was it because she was pursuing him? Was it to get back at me? Or had my nemesis found the true love of his life? The major issue that perplexed me was why I cared.

I opened my purse and pulled out Ruby's compact. My fingers quavering, I angled it toward Trevor. All at once, he turned over and knocked it out of my hand. I scrambled on the floor to find it.

"What's going on?" he asked, his voice hoarse.

I curled up alongside his bed, breathing the shallowest of breaths.

"Jasper? Is that you?" he asked.

I lifted up his blue duvet so I could squeeze underneath his bed. Instead of an open space to hide, I found a handle to a king-size trundle drawer—as if he didn't have enough closet space.

I had nowhere to escape. I'd have to switch to plan B.

"Hi, Trevor," I said, popping up.

Startled, the soccer snob let out a scraggly yell. "What the hell are you doing here?" he shouted, sitting up.

"I just—," I stammered, fumbling with the compact and trying to shove it back into my purse.

"How did you get in?"

"Your nanny let me in," I teased. "I'm not surprised you still have one."

"What are you doing in my room?" Trevor wondered, fingering his tousled blond hair.

"I heard you were sick."

"So?"

"I wanted to know if you needed anything."

"Are you insane?"

"I'm fulfilling my health class assignment: Help some-one in need."

"But I'm not in need, especially from you."

"I'll be the judge of that. I think you should start with some sunshine," I said, like a gothic Mary Poppins. "I'm the only one who likes it this gloomy." I went to his win-dow and pulled back the heavy drapes.

"Stop!" he said, shielding his eyes.

But I continued to draw the curtains as far as they could go.

"Get out of here, freak!" he hollered, squinting.

I waited to see if there was any reaction. He could recoil. Maybe he'd melt.

I got a reaction from Trevor all right, but it wasn't what I expected. He got up, his pale face now flushed with anger.

"Get out already," he ordered. "Go back to the troll hole you live in. You've contaminated my house enough already."

I grabbed the garlic container from my purse and held it out to him.

"What's that?" he asked.

"Garlic. It helps clear out the system. Why don't you breathe it in," I said, stepping closer.

"Get that away from me, you freak."

Trevor didn't recoil like Alexander had when I acci-dentally exposed him to garlic powder. Instead, Trevor got madder.

I pulled out a pen and a Hello Batty paper pad. "Now," I said like a nurse filling out a patient's records, "have you kissed anyone in the past forty-eight hours?"

"What's it your business?"

"I have to fill out a communicable diseases questionnaire. You don't want your new girlfriend, Luna, to get your diseases, do you?"

"Why, are you jealous?"

"Of course not," I replied with a laugh.

"That's what this is really about," he said, his raspy tone suddenly brightening. "Why you are here, in my house. In my room—," he said, stepping closer.

"Don't flatter yourself—"

"You couldn't handle seeing me with Luna—," he said with a smile.

"Frankly, I can't handle seeing you at all."

"I knew it. I saw it in your eyes at the carnival," he said, taking another step toward me.

"That's not what you saw in my eyes."

I tried to get a quick glance at both sides of his neck. But he mistook the reason for my gaze. He stepped toward me and leaned in to kiss me.

I held him at bay with my pad of paper.

"Get off!"

"But I thought that's why you came—"

I rolled my eyes. "I need to know—have you been bitten by anything or anyone?"

"Of course not. But I won't tell if you don't tell," he said with a clever grin.

"Then my work is complete," I said, racing for the door. "Now take two dog biscuits and don't call me in the morning."

Trevor stood still, weary and confused.

"And most important," I offered as I opened the door, "stay away from the cemetery."

"I'm sick," he said. "Not dead."

I hopped on my bike. Coasting back home, I was relieved that Trevor wasn't a vampire—for the town's sake and for mine.

As the sun set, I lay in bed under the covers.

"I hate to leave you again," my mom said, "but they are honoring your father at the country club. It's been such a busy day, I feel like I'm neglecting you."

"I feel tons better. I took a nap and I'm totally recovered."

"Well, Billy is over at Henry's. We'll pick him up after the ceremony."

As soon as I heard my dad's BMW pull out of the driveway, I jumped out of bed, fully dressed, and headed over to the Mansion.

I found Alexander in his attic room. He was staring pensively out the window. When I tapped at his door, his mood quickly changed. He gave me a long hello kiss, and for a moment I forgot all about my childhood nemesis and a lurking vampiress named Luna.

"We have to do something," Alexander said suddenly. I was quickly pulled from a heavenly cloud nine and back into the threat of the Underworld.

"I can think of a few things. Shall we stay in here?" I teased coyly. "Or take our party to the gazebo?"

But Alexander didn't smile. "I'm serious," he said.

I missed Alexander so desperately during the day, I felt grateful to be with him now. Though I was excited by the adventures of the town I now called "Vampireville," I also resented that Jagger and Luna took romantic time away from Alexander and me.

"But now that we're together, it's hard for me think of anything but you. I've been waiting all day to see you," I said.

"I know, me too," he said with a sigh. "But until Jagger and Luna are gone, we can't sit around. Did you see Trevor?"

"Yes," I began, sitting in his beat-up comfy chair. "He was sick today and stayed home from school."

"Sick?" he asked, worried. "Is it already too late?"

"No," I said. "Fortunately Luna hasn't sunk her fangs into him yet. He just has the flu."

"Great!" he said, relieved, and leaned on the arm of the chair. Then he turned serious. "If he was home sick, how did you see him?"

"Uh . . . ," I stammered, turning away.

"You didn't," he said in a scornful voice.

"Well—"

"You went to his house? Alone?" he asked, glaring down at me.

"No, the painter was there," I said, fiddling with a

loose string from the fabric of the chair.

Alexander knelt down and took my hand. "Raven—I don't want you to be alone with him. If Trevor isn't a vampire, he is still a vulture."

"I know. You are right," I replied, his dark eyes melting me.

When my mom and dad were protective of me, it was annoying; when it came from Alexander, it was sexy.

"Promise me—"

"I promise," I said.

"Well, if they didn't get to Trevor already, then they must be waiting for the right moment."

"That would be ironic. Trevor, who hates anything goth, gets to be a vampire, and I, who would love nothing more, don't."

"It is important to be whoever you are, for the right reason," he said, stroking my hand reassuringly.

"I know."

"Besides," he began, rising and returning to the attic window, "Trevor has no idea what Luna has in store for him."

I followed him and nestled in the dusty window seat. "What do we do?" I asked.

"Somehow we have to force them to go back to Romania."

"With an iron stake?" I wondered. "Or a fiery torch?"

Alexander shook his head, still thinking.

"Maybe I could swing a discounted fare from Ruby at Armstrong Travel," I suggested, pulling at a tear on my black leather boot. "We could convince Jagger and Luna that their parents miss them and demand their immediate return."

"But at this point we don't even know where they are," he said, frustrated. "They're hiding somewhere in the shadows."

"If we can take away the shadows, then we take away their defense," I said.

"You're right," he agreed suddenly.

"I am?" I asked, excited by my unlikely genius. "How do we take away a shadow?"

"Not a shadow . . . ," he said, scooching next to me. "We have to take away the one thing that makes Jagger safe, no matter where he is."

I looked at Alexander curiously.

"The one thing that protects him from humans, other vampires, and the sun," he continued.

"Yes?" I asked eagerly.

"We have to find Jagger's coffin."

"Wow. That's perfect. Then he won't have anywhere to hide."

Alexander smiled, exhilarated that we finally had a plan.

"But wait," I said. "Can't Jagger just sleep in a bed like you, with the shades drawn? Or hide in the loft of a barn? You don't sleep in a coffin."

Alexander looked at me with deep, almost shameful eyes.

Then he rose and pushed aside his beat-up comfy

chair, revealing a small attic door. He reached into his back pocket and pulled out a skeleton key.

"I do," he whispered.

He unlocked the bolt and slowly opened the door, and we stepped inside a dark, dusty ancient hideaway.

There, sitting in the shadows, was a secret in the shape of a casket—a simple black coffin, with dirt haphazardly sprinkled around it. Next to it was a wooden table with an unlit half-melted candle and a small, softly painted portrait of me.

"I had no idea—," I said with barely any breath.

"You weren't supposed to."

"But your bed—it's always unmade."

"It's where I rest and try to dream that I am like you."

I grabbed his hand and held it close. "You never had to hide anything in your world from me," I said, looking up into his lonely eyes.

"I know," he said. "I was hiding it from myself."

Alexander closed and locked the small attic door, once again concealing his conflicted true identity.

To find a vampire, you have to think like a vampire," Alexander said, grabbing his backpack. "I won't be gone more than an hour." He gave me a quick kiss.

"Gone?" I asked, following him toward his bedroom door.

"You'll have to stay here. I'm going to sacred ground."

"I'm going with you. If Jagger thinks I'm a vampire, then I'll be safe," I argued.

"And if he doesn't?"

"Then I have this." I pulled out my container of garlic powder from my purse.

Alexander quickly retreated.

"It's tightly sealed," I said, referring to the time it spilled out in my purse, causing Alexander to have an allergic reaction and forcing me to inject him with an antidote. "I'll wait outside," I pleaded.

Alexander paused. He wiped his flopping rock-star

hair away from his gorgeous face and slung his backpack on his shoulder. He glanced at the door, then back at me. Finally he held his pale hand out. While it was hard enough to be separated during the daylight, it was unbearable during the moonlight. As Alexander and I walked down the windy streets and toward the cemetery, I realized it was a dream come true—to be walking with one vampire and searching for another.

I'd never seen anyone in the moonlight as handsome as Alexander, vampire or not. His pale face seemed to glow, and his smile seemed to illuminate what the moon and the stars couldn't.

"Where are we going?" I finally asked.

"Your favorite place."

"My favorite place is here—by your side."

"Mine too," he said, squeezing my hand.

"Will Jagger know I'm still mortal?"

"It's not written on your forehead, is it?" he teased.

As he led me to an unknown destination, he walked with an air of confidence and determination I hadn't seen before.

We arrived at the entrance to Dullsville's cemetery.

"Remember when Old Jim took our tickets at the carnival, he accused you of sleeping at the cemetery?" he asked.

"But I wasn't," I defended. "I haven't done that in months!"

"I know. So if it's not you, then who do you think it is?" he asked.

I answered like an eager student. "Jagger."

"Trevor is safe for the night—but we're not." Then he paused. "You better stay outside the cemetery," he warned, changing his mind about our plan. "It's sacred ground and you would be in danger."

"You mean you bring me to the scene of the crime and don't let me dust for fingerprints? Or at least leave any?"

"You'll be safe only if you remain on the outside." He tenderly brushed my hair away from my face.

As Alexander climbed over the gate, I reluctantly stayed behind. I anxiously dug my boot into the wet grass, feeling as if I were being left out of the adventure of a lifetime. What could I accomplish by staying behind? Alexander and I could cover more terrain if there were two of us searching the graveyard. Besides, if Jagger still thought I was a vampire, it would be more natural for me to be standing inside a cemetery than outside one.

I could barely see Alexander's shrinking silhouette in the distance. Then I quickly climbed the gate and jogged after him.

I ran among the tombstones, as quiet as a wandering ghost following Alexander's shadowy figure.

As I approached him, I realized the figure I was running to was a monument.

I didn't see Alexander anywhere.

"Alexander?" I called.

I wondered where he could have disappeared to so quickly. He must have turned behind the caretaker's shed.

I raced around to the back of the shed, but all I saw was an abandoned shovel.

"Alexander?" I called again.

I continued to walk in the direction of the baroness's monument. Maybe Alexander was paying his respects to his grandmother as he searched the graveyard. When I approached the monument, however, the only thing visiting the stone memorial was a curious squirrel.

I walked on. Underneath a weeping willow tree, I saw a newly dug grave. I carefully walked toward it when I noticed a familiar pattern of dirt. Gravediggers make piles, not circles. I tiptoed closer. Jagger's stickered coffin could be lying inside, Jagger himself sitting on top, waiting for a mortal to be lured into his trap. I took a deep breath and peered down.

The grave was empty. No stickered coffin. No fang-toothed teen of darkness.

Where was Jagger? And more important, where was Alexander? I was standing in the middle of three acres of sacred ground. I'd picnicked alone a million times at Dullsville's cemetery, feeling as comfortable as if it were my own home. Tonight, though, I realized I'd perhaps made the biggest mistake of my life. Alexander had been right when he told me to stay outside the cemetery's gates. If Jagger was lurking in the shadows, he could easily sink his fangs into me before my true love had a chance to realize I was no longer standing by the graveyard's entrance.

My heart began to throb. My blood pressure soared.

I did have some mace, but I wasn't sure it would work against teen vampires.

I stuck my hand in my purse and clutched the container of garlic powder in my sweaty fingers and tiptoed through the tombstones.

"Alexander?" I whispered.

The howling wind was the only audible sound.

I turned around and could barely see the entrance to the cemetery. If I ran at top speed, I could reach the safety of the gate, though I wasn't sure I could outrun a flying vampire bat.

There was no other choice.

I took a deep breath, but as I took my first step, a strong hand bore down on my shoulder.

"Let go!" I cried.

I turned around to pry it off with one hand and aim the garlic container with the other.

"Don't!" a voice shouted.

I froze.

"What are you doing here?" Alexander asked sternly. "I told you to wait by the entrance."

"But I found something—an empty grave encircled with dirt."

"I did too," he said. "And I discovered something else."

I followed Alexander toward the back of the cemetery to a lone, dead sycamore. A brown package was sitting at the foot of the tree. Alexander picked up the package and held it in front of me. In crooked handwriting was marked: Jagger Maxwell.

The upper-left-hand corner was stamped: COFFIN CLUB.

It was the nocturnal gothic club where I'd first encountered Jagger.

The box had been ripped open, as if severed with razor-sharp teeth. Alexander pulled back the flaps and showed me the contents. It was a vampire's treasure chest: a box full of crystal, pewter, and silver amulets, filled with the sweet red nectar vampires crave. Fresh off the necks of the Coffin Club clubsters, who I'd seen wearing their blood as innocent charms, these vials now in turn were serving as a teen vampire's nourishment.

"Without a Coffin Club to hide in," Alexander explained, "Jagger could be chased out of town quickly. He couldn't make his presence known. This was his only means of survival."

Alexander eyed the amulets like a child eyeing a gumball machine. Instead of returning the box underneath the tree, he stuck it in his backpack.

"Should we wait here until he comes back?"

Alexander grabbed my hand. "He's not coming back."

"How do you know?"

"There is only one empty grave. He needs two now."

As we quickly walked through the cemetery, I imagined Jagger sitting underneath the dead tree, secluded in the back of the cemetery, waiting for Luna to arrive from Romania. He would be tipping back several amulets, like the tiny bottles of liquor anxious travelers sip on airplanes, while he plotted her visit and their next location.

"Shouldn't we continue searching for Luna?" I asked Alexander as we approached my house on our way back from Dullsville's cemetery. I wasn't ready for my vampire hunting to end.

But instead of walking hand in hand with Alexander, his hands were buried in his pockets. He seemed unusually cold and distant.

"I think your cemetery searching days are over," he said sternly.

"You're mad at me for not listening?" I asked, sincerely concerned.

Alexander stopped and turned to me. "You put yourself in grave danger. I only want you to be safe."

"But if Jagger thinks I am a vampire, I was safer in the cemetery," I said, attempting to cozy up to him.

"You may be right. But . . ." He folded his arms, leaned against a parked SUV, and looked toward the moon.

It was one thing to push my parents over the edge with my princess of darkness wardrobe, or to stay out past curfew, or even to boss Becky into climbing over the Mansion's gate or to convince her to sneak into movies, but I'd never felt as rotten as I now did, disappointing the one person who meant the most to me.

"I should have listened," I admitted.

He put his hands back in his oversized pockets and avoided eye contact.

"I want so badly to be a part of your world," I said, knitting my arms through his. "I want to taste the adventure alongside you."

Alexander softened and gently stroked my hair. "You are already a part of my world," he said with a smile that lit up his pale face. "You know that. I'm just asking you to be careful."

"I understand. I just don't want us to be apart—even for a moment. But I'll try harder."

Alexander grabbed my hand and we continued down the street, past houses, trees, and mailboxes.

"Okay now, I have to come up with a plan," he said.

"Plan? I'm all about plans! Where do we start?"

Alexander looked buried in thought and led me toward my house.

"I still want to hang out," I whined. "Darkness is our only time together," I continued, staring up into his midnight eyes.

"I know, but—"

"And daylight seems like an eternity without you. I have to endure unbearably boring teachers, classmates who ostracize me, and two yuppie parents who don't get black lipstick."

"I feel the same," he revealed, stopping at the bottom of my driveway. "Except for me it's not daylight, but starlight and moonlight. During the long midnight hours, I hang out underneath your window and imagine what you're dreaming of. I used to thrive in the darkness; now I almost resent it."

Alexander and I walked up my driveway. Instead of taking the path that led to my front door, Alexander escorted me toward my backyard.

"Yay! We can't let Jagger spoil our night," I cheered.

"We do have to be careful," he warned. "But you're right. I'm not ready to say good-bye just yet," he confessed. "Not now, not ever."

Suddenly a motion detector light above the garage triggered, illuminating the driveway, Billy Boy's basketball hoop, Mom's SUV, and a mortal girl and her vampire boyfriend.

"No!" Alexander shouted. He quickly shielded his pale face and retreated into the shadows.

"Are you all right?" I called, squinting into the darkness.

Alexander didn't answer. I followed him into the grass, toward our east-side neighbor's fence.

It took a moment for my eyes to adjust, though I still couldn't see him. "Alexander, where are you? Are you hurt?"

I heard a fluttering above the power lines behind me. I followed the sound, which continued back over the driveway in the opposite direction from where I had been standing. When I walked through my backyard, there was a rustling in the bushes by our west-side neighbor's fence. Alexander was standing in front of them.

"How did you get over here so fast?" I asked curiously, all the while knowing the answer. "That was cool. It's like dating a superhero."

Alexander dusted off his black jeans, unfazed by his unearthly abilities.

"Are you okay?" I asked. Before he could answer, I was in his arms.

"Now that you are with me," he said, caressing my hair.

"I forgot—"

"I didn't melt," he said. "I can handle softer light, like candles or lamps. But a burst of high-powered light repels me."

"I didn't even think—," I began when he pulled back and placed his frosty white index finger on my black lips.

"I'll be able to think better out here," he said, and stared up to the sky. "With you, underneath the stars. We don't have much time."

He led me over to the rickety wooden swing set Billy Boy and I had outgrown but my parents hadn't bothered to get rid of.

"It's been an eternity since I've hung out here," I told him. I could feel my pale face flush, exhilarated that I was finally able to share a place I'd spent in childhood isolation. "I used to bury my Barbies over there," I said, pointing to a mound of soil underneath an oak tree.

We each sat on a faded yellow plastic swing.

I began swinging, but Alexander remained still. He picked up twigs and threw them into the bushes, as if he were tossing Jagger out of Dullsville.

I skidded my combat boots into the weathered patches of grass.

"What's wrong?" I asked, now standing before him.

Alexander pulled me close. "It's hard for me to relax, knowing Jagger and Luna are still plotting revenge."

"Well, let's think like them. If he isn't in a cemetery

and we don't have a Coffin Club in Dullsville, where could they be?"

"I know we are both vampires, but our instincts are different. He sees the world in black and red—*blood* red. I see the world in all different colors."

I grabbed his icy hand and fingered his spider ring.

"Just because you and Jagger are vampires doesn't mean you are the same. Look at Trevor and me. We're human, but total opposites," I reassured him.

Alexander broke into a smile. "I just want to be spending the darkness with you; instead I'm thinking of *him*."

"That's my fault," I insisted. "I wish I hadn't gone to the Coffin Club. Then we'd never be in this mess. I led Jagger right to you, and Luna straight to Trevor."

"You had nothing to do with this. If I'd said yes to Luna at the covenant ceremony in Romania, none of this would have happened."

"Then we wouldn't be together. And that is the most important thing."

"You're right," he said, and pulled me onto his lap. "But now we have a couple of vampires to catch."

We gently swung back and forth on the swing. The stars shone in the night sky. The sweet smell of Drakar filled the air. The crickets seemed to be singing for us.

Just then my bedroom light switched on.

"Who's in my room?" I snarled.

Billy Boy jumped in front of the window, with his back toward us, hugging himself. From our vantage point, he appeared as if he were making out with a girl.

Alexander laughed at my little brother's antics.

"Get out of my room!" I yelled.

Billy Boy held Nightmare in his hands and waved her paw at me.

"Let her go! You'll give her fleas!" I shouted.

"He just wants your attention," Alexander said, dragging his boots into the dirt and holding one arm around me like a safety belt. "It's cute. He adores you."

"Adores me?"

"He has the coolest sister ever."

I turned to Alexander and gave him a long kiss. I'd spent my whole life as an outsider. Even though Alexander and I had been dating for a few months, it was still hard to get used to the fact that anyone would think I was normal, much less cool.

"It's getting late," he said. He grabbed my hand and began walking me to the front door. "You get your rest while I figure out where Jagger is."

"The night has just begun," I argued.

"Not for someone who has classes at eight in the morning."

"They always go on without me," I said with a shrug.

Alexander smiled at my tireless efforts but then turned serious. "Jagger's somewhere out here," he began, "hidden in a dark, secluded area or building big enough for two coffins," he said. When we reached the front doorstep, he went on, "You understand, I'll have to search for them alone."

"Just because I jumped the fence tonight?"

"I can't risk putting you in danger again."

"But I can't spend the days *and* nights without you! And you need me—it's like Batman without Robin. I know all the creepy places to hide in this town."

"Well . . . you're right, but not quite—"

"Why not?"

"It's more like Gomez without Morticia," he said with a wink.

I leaned in to him and gave him a huge squeeze.

"We'll meet at sunset," he said, resigned. "And you can take me to one of those creepy places you are so fond of."

He gave me a lingering kiss, the kind that made my knees weak and my heart flutter like a hovering bat.

I unlocked the front door. "Till sunset," I said in a romantic daze and slowly turned to him.

Alexander had already vanished, just like any great vampire would.

I was sitting on my black beanbag chair recording the evening's events in my journal. I was too preoccupied with thoughts of Luna and Jagger to sleep. I imagined the two of them flying through Dullsville's night sky together, looking down on Dullsvillians who would look like tiny nobodies as they got stuck in traffic, played golf, and dined in outdoor restaurants. I imagined the twins hiding in a basement-turned-dungeon, Jagger with pet tarantulas, and Luna dolled up in dresses made out of spiderwebs.

A scratching sound began outside my window.

Nightmare jumped up on my computer desk and hissed at the darkness.

I raced to my window. "Alexander?" I called softly.

There were no signs of anything living or undead outside.

I closed the curtains and held an anxious Nightmare in my arms. There could have been a number of vampires lurking outside my window under the night sky. I just didn't know which one. I pondered placing a garlic clove on the windowsill, but I might repel the very vampire I wanted to attract.

4

Freaky Factory

The next evening I exclaimed, "I have great news!" as Alexander opened the Mansion door. He was sporting a black Alice Cooper T-shirt and oversized black pants riddled with safety pins. His dark eyes looked tired.

"What's wrong, sweetie?" I asked.

"Last night I searched all over town until I could feel the sun rise behind me," he began as we sat on the red-carpeted grand staircase. "I went to a vacant church and the abandoned farmhouse where we found Nightmare. I even found a dried-up well. The only thing in it was a broken bucket. I've been rattling my brain ever since and I didn't sleep all day.

"What's your good news?" he asked.

"Trevor is sick and will be absent from school all week. Plus that means he'll have to miss games and practices. It'll make it very hard for Jagger and Luna to take him to sacred ground if he's stuck inside."

Alexander's weary face came alive. "That's awesome! We'll have more time to find the Maxwells before they find him. But we have to do it quickly. The longer that Jagger and Luna wait for Trevor, the hungrier they will get. Literally."

"I spent all of algebra making a list of places they may be hiding out. It was hard. There aren't that many creepy places in this candy-colored town. I came up with ten—if you include my algebra class itself."

"Where's the list?" he asked eagerly.

"Well, Mr. Miller caught me writing in my notebook instead of figuring out what x plus y equaled and he confiscated my list."

"That's okay. I found a place I'd like to check out. But you have to promise me—"

"That I will love you forever? That's easy," I said, running my finger along one of the safety pins adorning his pants.

"Promise me you will stay out of trouble."

"That one is harder to commit to."

He leaned back. "Then you'll have to stay here."

"All right," I reconciled. "I'll behave."

"We won't be on sacred ground, so you'll be safe, but you need to stay close."

"Of course," I agreed. "Where are we going?"

"An abandoned factory at the edge of town."

"The Sinclair mill? That is totally dark, secluded, and big enough for a cemetery full of coffins."

Alexander borrowed his butler Jameson's Mercedes and we embarked on our own Magical Mystery Tour.

We left behind the twisty road of Benson Hill and headed past Dullsville High, through downtown, and finally over the railroad tracks into what the country clubsters called the "wrong" side of town.

"It's just up over there," I reminded him as I pointed to a covered bridge.

We drove over the shaky bridge, around a winding, dark, fog-covered road, until the Mercedes's headlights shone upon a NO TRESPASSING sign on the gravel road leading to the vacant factory.

Spanning thirty-five acres, the Sinclair mill was surrounded by trees, overgrown bushes, and weeds. On the west side, a stagnant, murky creek barely rose during sporadic rainfalls. Fragrant wild flowers never seemed to mask its pungent smell.

The mill thrived in the 1940s, manufacturing uniforms for the war, employing hundreds of Dullsvillians. The once proudly puffing red-tiled S smokestack now stood silent. After the war the mill was bought by a linen company but ultimately couldn't compete with outsourcing, and the factory went bankrupt.

Now the Sinclair mill loomed over Dullsville like a listless monster. Half the factory's windows were blown out, and the others needed a gazillion liters of Windex. Police cars routinely patrolled the area, trying to deny graffiti artists a thirty-acre canvas.

Alexander parked the Mercedes next to several rusty

garbage barrels. As soon as we stepped foot onto the grounds, we heard a barking off in the distance. We paused and glanced around. Maybe it was Jagger. Or maybe it was my own boyfriend's presence that was disturbing the dogs.

Supposedly, when the factory first opened, a fateful accident occurred when an elevator malfunctioned and plummeted to the basement, claiming several employees' lives. A rumor spread throughout Dullsville that on a full moon, a passerby could hear the mill workers' screams.

But the only ghosts I'd heard shrieking were actors covered in sheets when I was a child. We were visiting the factory for WXUV's Haunted House with my family.

"This was the haunted house's entrance," I recalled, heading for the broken metal door at the front of the mill. The words GET OUT WHILE YOU CAN! were still spray painted on the door from Halloweens past.

Alexander lit the way with his flashlight. I pulled the heavy door open and we crept inside.

A few spray paintings of humorous epitaphs remained on the concrete walls.

Alexander and I cautiously walked over discarded boxes and headed for the main part of the factory. The twenty-five-thousand-square-foot room was empty of everything but dust. Round, discolored markings remained on the wooden floors where the machines had been bolted in place. Half the panes of glass were gone after decades of vandals, baseballs, and misguided birds.

"This room draws in too much daylight," Alexander

said, looking at the missing windows. "Let's keep looking."

Alexander kindly held out his hand, like a Victorian gentleman, and with his flashlight led me down a dark two-flight staircase.

We passed through what must have been an employee locker room. The windowless room seemed ripe for a vampire to call home. Several metal lockers remained against the wall and even a few wooden benches. It now seemed like a dumping ground for garbage, littered with pop cans, bags, and a few discarded bicycle tires. No coffins were evident.

The basement was huge, cold, and damp. Several mammoth-size furnaces filled the center of the room. I could almost hear the deafening roar of the once-burning kindling. Now the metal doors were rusty and unhinged, and a few were lying against the cement wall.

"Wow, with a few more spiderwebs and a couple of ghosts, this place would be perfect," I said.

"This could be ours," Alexander said, holding me close.

"We could put your easel over here," I said, pointing to an empty corner. "There would be plenty of room for you to paint."

"We could make shelves for your Hello Batty collection."

"And bring in a huge TV to watch scary movies. I wouldn't have to go to school and it could be dark twenty-four hours a day."

"No one would bother us, not even soccer snobs or

vengeful vampires," Alexander said with a smile.

Just then we heard a barking sound.

"What was that?" I asked.

Alexander raised his eyebrow and listened. "We'd better go." He offered his hand and he led me out of the basement toward the front of the building.

In a small alcove Alexander found another staircase and lit our way back to the main floor.

While Alexander explored an office room, I investigated a hallway filled with boxes, a piece of cardboard covering a window, and a Stone Age freight elevator.

I removed the cardboard from the window to shed streetlight into the oversized lift.

The heavy metal elevator door hung partially open. I couldn't see clearly into it, so I snuck underneath the rusty door. When I stepped into the elevator, I heard a horrible screeching sound. I quickly turned around as the door slammed shut.

I stood in total darkness. I couldn't even see my own hands.

"Alexander! Let me out!" I called.

I banged my hands against the door.

"Alexander! I'm in the elevator!"

I felt along the side panel, vehemently trying to find a button to push. The surface was smooth. I fingered the adjacent wall and discovered what I thought might be a lever. I tried to pull it, but it didn't budge.

Normally I was comforted by darkness and found solace in tightly enclosed places. But now I was trapped.

My mind began to think of the poor souls who found their fate sealed in an elevator at the Sinclair mill.

I imagined bloody fingernails stuck to the inside door from decades of entombed young vandals.

I felt like I was going to be trapped forever.

I heard the cables rattling. Then heavy footsteps walked on the boards above me.

"Alexander! Get me out! Now!"

I wondered if the cables were still intact; if not, the elevator could plummet to the bowels of the basement at any moment.

I even thought I heard the screams of the ghosts—until I realized the screams were coming from me.

Suddenly the door pulled open, and I could barely see the oversized black pants and combat boots standing before me. My eyes squinted, trying to adjust to the moonlight that shined through the uncovered hallway window.

I was standing in the middle of an oval-shaped ring of dirt, the front part messy, as if something heavy had dragged over it.

Alexander pulled me out before the door closed again.

I squeezed him with the little breath I still had in me.

"You saved my life."

"Hardly. But I think you found something."

We stood at a distance and examined the elevator's contents. Gravestone etchings covered the walls. In the corner sat an antique candelabra and a pewter goblet.

"Jagger had the same etchings at his Coffin Club apartment!" I said excitedly. "It's just missing the coffin."

"He must have left in a hurry."

"Why would he leave? Jagger could remain undiscovered for several eternities in this place. And this elevator could easily fit two coffins."

"He must have felt threatened."

"By the ghost story?"

"This old elevator isn't moving anywhere," Alexander reassured.

"Then what could possibly threaten Jagger?" I wondered.

While Alexander examined the elevator, I tried to catch my breath and combed the hallway for any more clues. Next to the boxes I noticed something silver catching the moonlight.

"What would this be doing here?" I asked, holding a garage door opener in my hand.

Alexander came over to me and examined my discovery.

At that moment, standing in the window right behind him, was a ghostly, attractive teen with white hair, the ends dyed bloodred. His eyes, one blue and one green, stared through me.

"Jagger!" I whispered.

"I know," Alexander answered, repeatedly clicking the opener in frustration. "He was here."

"No. He's here now! He's right outside!" I said, pointing to the window again.

Jagger flashed a wicked grin, his fangs gleaming.

Alexander quickly turned around, but Jagger had vanished.

"He was standing right there!" I cried, pointing to the window.

Alexander took off and I followed him back through the factory, past the ghostly Halloween props and out the front door.

When we reached the gravel drive, Alexander suddenly stopped next to the Mercedes.

He pressed the keys to the car in my hand and handed me the flashlight.

"Drive to the Mansion. I'll meet you there in half an hour," he said.

"But—"

"Please," he said, opening the door for me.

"Okay," I agreed, and reluctantly got inside.

Alexander closed the door. When I glanced back to say good-bye, he had vanished.

I locked the door and put the key in the ignition. As the crickets chirped and Alexander continued his search alone, I grew anxious. What if something happened to him? I couldn't hear his calls if I was miles away atop Benson Hill. I checked my container of garlic sealed safely inside my purse. I got out of the car and stuck the keys into my back pocket. I raced toward the east side of the factory with the flashlight in my hand.

The mill grounds had an eerie quietness to them. I felt as if someone were watching me. I looked up at the sky. I saw what appeared to be a bat hanging from the power lines above me. When I shined my light on the wire, it was gone.

I turned the corner of the factory to find Alexander pacing outside the hallway window.

"He was standing right here," I said.

"I should have known—," Alexander murmured.

"That I wouldn't stay in the car?"

Alexander shook his head and pointed toward the smokestack. Not twenty feet from where we were standing I could see plain as daylight what had threatened Jagger—a giant wrecking ball.

5

The Key

T hat night I sat in my computer chair, holding the garage door opener in my hand. I felt I held the key to cracking the Case of the Missing Twin Teen Vampires.

In fact, an empty garage was an awesome hiding place for a vampire. If a family were on vacation, they would have to drive the hour and a half to the nearest airport, therefore giving vacancy to a waiting coffin. With no one in the residence, Jagger and Luna could go undetected long enough to seduce Trevor into their vampirey lair.

If Alexander and I walked from garage door to garage door, it could take decades to discover which one Jagger and Luna were calling their latest batcave. By then Trevor would be "fluless" and return to practice in enough time for Luna to have sunk her fangs into him and the entire Dullsville High soccer team.

I hardly spoke to anyone in this town, much less knew

the travel plans of the other Dullsvillians. I had to figure out a way to find out who was traveling, their destinations, and the durations of their stays. How could I get access to that information? Just then an idea struck me like a bolt of lightning. Of course I couldn't get the information—but I knew someone who could.

The next day, after school, Becky drove me to the Armstrong Travel Agency.

I missed the old girl. Since she'd begun dating Matt Wells and I'd met Alexander, we didn't have the endless free time to hang out, talk on the phone, or climb the Mansion's gates. So when we did have girl time, we made the most of it.

"I've heard rumors about that white-haired girl from Romania," she said when I got into her truck.

"What did you hear?" I asked, perking up after a long, mind-numbing school day.

"Well, that dude that was lurking at the drive-in when we saw *Kissing Coffins* was her brother."

"Yes . . . ," I began, hinting for more info.

"Matt says they've been asking around for Trevor. I think the dude wants to play on the soccer team, but he doesn't even go to our school."

"That's it?" I asked, disappointed. "I wouldn't worry about it. No one will take Matt's position away. Not even a vampire," I mumbled.

"What did you say?" she asked as she pulled the pickup in front of Armstrong Travel.

I stepped out of the truck.

"Are you sure you and Alexander aren't going to elope in Romania?" Becky teased.

"No, but if we do, I'll get *four* tickets."

I was happy to walk into Armstrong Travel in full goth garb—Herman Munster-size black boots, purple tights, and a black torn T-shirt dress—instead of their Corporate Cathy dress code of tailored skirts and blouses.

I smiled at Ruby, who was seated at her desk, handing pamphlets to two customers. Ruby's friendly expression strained as I stood like an ill-mannered eyesore in the very conservative business.

"I'll be right with you," Ruby said, hinting at an out-of-the-way chair behind a rack of luggage tags.

"I'm just browsing," I said, and began glancing at a map of Hawaii.

Finally the young couple with Mexico brochures in their hands rose. They looked at me oddly, then cowered past, as if at any moment my bat body tattoo was going to jump off my arm and bite their heads off.

"I'll call you to confirm," Ruby said with a wave as the couple scurried out the door.

"Raven, it's great to see you," she greeted sincerely. "What brings you by?"

"Is Janice in?" I asked, secretly hoping she wasn't.

"No, she's at the post office. Is there something I can help you with?"

"Well . . . has anyone in town booked a vacation in the last few days?"

"People book vacations every day. This *is* a travel agency, you know," she said with a smile.

"I mean—"

"Why would you want to know?"

Well, there are these two teen vampires who are hiding out in town, waiting for the right moment to bite Trevor Mitchell. I believe they are living in a vacant garage, probably belonging to a vacationer, I wanted to say. I imagined Ruby's pleasant face turning to shock, then horror, then her plugging away at her keyboard for a list of addresses. "You go, Raven Madison. Save Dullsville. Save the world."

"Uh . . . for a school report," I said instead. "I'm doing statistics on spring vacations."

"I'm sorry, hon, but I can't give out that information. You ought to know that; you worked here."

"But that's precisely the reason I thought you'd tell me."

"I'd love to help, but I just can't give out names, addresses, and itineraries," she said with a laugh. "In the wrong hands that information could be used for home invasions."

"Or at least garages," I said.

Ruby appeared confused just as the phone rang.

"Armstrong Travel, Ruby speaking. Can I help you make a reservation?" she said in an ultra-perky voice.

I fiddled with the white pens on her desk.

"Of course, let me see," she said, and began plugging away at her computer keyboard.

The phone rang again, this time lighting up line two of Ruby's white phone.

"Can I put you on hold?" Ruby asked. "Oh . . . you are calling from where?"

As the red light flashed and the phone continued to ring, I spun Ruby's lucite organizer and wondered how I could hack into their computer without the FBI finding out.

Ruby covered the receiver with her hand. "Do you mind answering that?" she asked, pointing to Janice's phone.

Who did she think I was? I didn't work here anymore, and I most certainly wasn't on the clock.

I went to Janice's desk, pressed line two, and picked up the phone. "Armstrong Travel, where Spain is hot and the men are hotter. Can I book you a trip there?"

"Do you have any specials on cruises?" a woman's voice asked.

"Janice?" I said. "Janice, is that you?"

Ruby glanced over at me.

"No, my name isn't Janice," the caller answered. "It's Liz. I'm interested in a vacation cruise to Alaska."

"Keys?" I asked loud enough for Ruby to hear. "You need car keys?"

"No," Liz corrected. "I said 'cruise.'"

Ruby looked over.

"You're at the post office? Your cell is breaking up. You need Ruby to pick you up?"

"I thought you said this was Armstrong Travel," Liz said.

"Let me talk," Ruby said to me. "Excuse me," she said politely to her caller, "I need to put you on hold."

"I'm sorry, I must have the wrong number," the inquiring Liz said, and hung up.

Ruby switched lines just as line two's red light went dead. "Janice? Janice?"

"Her cell kept dropping, then went dead. Maybe it wasn't her—"

"No, she's been frazzled all day."

Ruby hurried over to her business partner's desk and found a spare set of keys in her top drawer.

"Do you mind riding these over to the post office for me?"

This plan wasn't for *me* to leave. Ruby was making this difficult.

"I don't have my bike."

"Do you have your driver's license?"

"I have my temps."

Ruby glanced at me, then outside at her white Mercedes parked in front of the agency. I could see her mind race as she imagined me screeching down the street, blasting Marilyn Manson, and returning her car with newly painted black widow spiders running alongside the exterior.

"I'll have to close the agency," she said.

"Well . . . ," I began, twisting a lock of hair. "I could watch the office, if that would help you."

"You really aren't dressed appropriately," she said, eyeing my morose-looking outfit. "But I guess I don't have a choice. You wouldn't mind staying here for just a few minutes? I hate to close the agency."

"Well—"

"I won't be long, really," she said, gathering her purse and keys. "It would be a big help."

"Will I be paid the same rate as before?"

"Paid?" she asked with her hand on her hip. "I'll only be gone for a few minutes."

"How about throwing in a few plane tickets, too."

Flustered, Ruby paused. "I'll give you ten dollars and a coupon for a free movie."

"Deal."

"You drive a hard bargain. That's what I've always liked about you," she said as she raced out the door.

I sat at Ruby's desk. I flipped through a *Condé Nast* magazine until I saw her get in her white Mercedes and drive off.

Now that I was employed again, even if only for twenty minutes, it was part of my job to be informed. I logged on to her computer using the same password I had when I was in her employ. Within moments I was surfing through the itineraries of vacationing Dullsvillians.

After my brief re-employment at Armstrong Travel, I arrived home, and geared up for my continuing mission. Wearing my Olivia Outcast backpack, I hopped on my mountain bike and headed for Loveland.

On the good side of the tracks sat Loveland, a quiet, middle-class community filled with vintage and modern homes.

I stopped at the corner of Shenandoah Avenue. I put on my sunglasses and Emily the Strange hoodie, so I wouldn't be recognized, though no one else in town dressed like I did. I pulled out my list of three Dullsvillian vacationers. For seven days and six nights, three Matten families—all related—were traveling to Los Angeles.

I felt like a gothic Goldilocks as I crept up the first driveway. The senior Matten Victorian-style house was gigantic. Their three-car garage could easily fit a few cars and a few sleeping vampires. I pressed the silver button and waited for the white door to open. It remained still.

A few houses down, the Mattens' eldest son's home appeared to be way too small. The one-car detached garage could barely fit a car, much less a coffin. I pressed the door opener anyway, but the door didn't budge.

Determined to find my nocturnal bounty, I made my way across the street, to the third Matten house. The Tudor-style home had a backyard garage hidden by a few trees. Their two-car garage seemed just right. Only it wasn't. The door didn't move.

Frustrated, I checked my list again.

By the time I headed for Oakley Village, I felt like I needed a few blood-filled amulets to recharge my pounding heart.

Oakley Village was a prosperous community of ultra-upscale homes. A who's who of successful Dullsvillians. I discovered on Ruby's computer that the Witherspoons, a retired couple who had just sold Witherspoon Lumber, were booked on a trip to Europe. They had departed three days ago and were scheduled to return in thirty days.

I rode up Tyler Street and turned into number 1455. The Witherspoons lived in a beautiful yellow-shuttered Victorian-style home with an attached three-car garage.

I quickly snuck up their driveway.

I checked out my surroundings to make sure there weren't any nosy neighbors eyeballing me. When I saw I was in the clear, I aimed the opener at the door. I took a deep breath and pressed the silver button.

The door didn't move. I pressed it again.

Nothing happened. This couldn't be!

I tapped it over and over. Still, the door remained fixed.

I ran to the front of the house and pressed my face against the carport's yellow-shuttered window. The garage was empty of cars *and* coffins.

I stormed down the driveway to retrieve my bike and checked my Hello Batty watch. I had only a few more hours left of sunlight until this hunter would become the hunted.

I held the door opener in my hand. Which garage did it belong to?

Frustrated, I decided to return home, wait until sunset for Alexander to awake, then confess I hadn't made any Underworldly discoveries. I coasted down the winding road, heading for a shortcut through the Oakley Woods.

I began riding over the bumpy terrain, but then I saw something odd. Sticking out from behind a large pile of wood chips was a vintage hearse!

I pulled my bike up alongside the ghastly car. The circa 1970s Cadillac midnight mobile was beautiful; it had a sleek, long black hood with a silver bat ornament, white-walled tires, a black carriage adorned with a chrome S-shaped insignia, and black curtains. On the left rear quarter panel was a decal of a white skull and crossbones.

I hopped off my bike and peered into the driver's seat, where I could see restored shiny black vinyl upholstered seats and a tiny white skeleton hanging from the rearview mirror.

I tried to peer in the back window, but the curtains were drawn. The license plate's county sticker was from Hipsterville—the town a few hundred miles away from Dullsville where the Coffin Club was and where I first encountered the nefarious Jagger. The license plate read: I BITE.

"What are you doing here?" a familiar voice asked.

I nearly jumped out of my boots.

I turned around to find Billy Boy and Henry standing right in front of me.

"I told you it was for real," Henry proudly proclaimed.

"Wow. It is freaky," Billy Boy remarked. "But why is it parked in the woods?"

"I don't know. I discovered it yesterday on my way home from math club," Henry replied.

"Is there a body inside?" Billy Boy asked, nervously trying to peer into the back window.

"No. But I think we could arrange that," I said.

Billy Boy backed away from the macabre mobile.

"Have you seen anyone driving it?" I inquired.

Henry shook his head.

"You still haven't told me why you are out here," Billy Boy charged.

I fingered the garage door opener in my hand. And then it hit me.

There was only one person I knew in Dullsville who could help me whittle down my search—one person who could figure out how to use a garage door opener to unlock his locker or even unbolt his bedroom door. And his five-foot-two-inch nerd body was standing right in front of me.

"I found this," I said, showing Henry. "I'm sure the person who lost it would like to get their car out—or back in."

"You want to know which door it is so you can break in," Billy Boy alleged.

"I wouldn't be breaking in if I had the opener, now would I?" I snarled. "Besides, I'm not a thief. It's my civic duty to return it to its rightful owner."

"Let's see it," Henry said like a jeweler inspecting a precious stone. "This is an Aladdin. I'd say one out of ten homes use this manufacturer. It's the same kind we use."

"You do?" I asked curiously.

"Yes. And this one looks familiar."

"You've seen it? Can you tell me which homes might use them?"

"I was missing one the other day," he said, wrinkling his face in thought. "Hey—"

Henry lived in a five-bedroom Colonial-style house just up the road. I'd visited his house once before, when Becky and I were in need of accessories for our *Kissing Coffins* outfits. Henry supplied us with fangs, blood pellets, and scars.

I imagined bloodthirsty vampire twins anxiously waiting in coffins in his family's garage as he innocently played with fake blood and fangs above them in his bedroom.

"This couldn't be it," I said protectively, and immediately grabbed back the opener.

"But I swore—"

"Are your parents home?" I asked.

"No, they went to San Diego for a medical convention."

My heart stopped pulsing. "Did they plan their trips through Armstrong Travel?" I asked.

"They booked their tickets online," he answered, confused.

"Then who is home with you?"

"Our housekeeper, Nina," he continued.

"Do you want Raven to be your babysitter?" Billy Boy teased.

Then my thoughts turned serious. Behind that mechanical shield of wood might lie two sleeping teen vampires.

"I'll walk you to your house," I said. "You can never be too careful these days."

I followed the two nerds up the steep road to Henry's house. When we reached his driveway I saw the three-car garage attached to his home. And then, a few yards back, sat another two-car detached garage.

One garage wasn't good enough? I thought as we approached Henry's house.

"I'll tell Mom you are doing your homework *inside* Henry's," I said. "You should stay indoors today trading your Pokémon cards or whatever it is you do. It's supposed to rain."

"I told you she's weird," Billy Boy whispered as the two went inside.

I waited for a moment, walked my bike halfway down the driveway, then quietly doubled back.

I rested my bike against the side of his brick house.

Since Henry was staying with Nina, I assumed the attached garage, with the comings and goings of a preteen and a hardworking housekeeper, was too exposed for a hiding vampire. But I peered into it anyway. I saw a vintage Rolls and shelves of tools.

Now that Henry and Billy Boy were safely inside the house finding square roots, I ran to the detached garage. I took a deep breath and aimed the door opener.

I pressed the silver button.

Nothing happened. The door didn't budge. The opener didn't click.

I pressed it again.

The door remained still.

"It's not for that," Henry said as he and Billy Boy came out of the house.

I jumped back.

"I open it this way," Henry said, and stepped on a WEL-COME HOME mat.

The garage door began to open.

"No! Cover your eyes!" I cried, and put my hand out in front of them as if my lanky arm could block them from seeing two coffins.

It was too late.

The garage door slowly opened like a creaky coffin lid. My heart stopped beating. I could barely open my eyes.

Then I saw them. Not one but two silver BMWs, both

emblazoned with red Dullsville Middle School "I'm the proud parent of an honor student" bumper stickers.

I went inside the garage and looked around, underneath, and inside the back of the luxury vehicles.

"What is wrong with you?" Billy asked. "You're not used to cars without skulls and crossbones?"

"Well, if this doesn't open the garage," I argued, now fatigued and angry, "what does it do?"

We followed Henry into his gigantic backyard, which was the size of a football field, complete with a mosaic-tiled patio, an Olympic-size pool, and a million-dollar flower garden.

He aimed the opener toward the house and pressed the button. Suddenly floodlights, scattered around his property, illuminated the already sunlit backyard.

"Nina gets freaked out when she house-sits," Henry stated. "She claims she sees shadows and things moving in the backyard. I keep the lights on when my parents are out of town. But since I lost it, it's been pitch-black back here."

I didn't understand. What did this have to do with Jagger? Why was he returning for it? Or was he making sure it was still there?

I walked past Henry's pool and garden and into his backyard to see what he needed to illuminate. The huge field was wasted on a boy who was more interested in throwing around scientific theories than footballs.

Then I saw it. In the far corner of the yard—at least sixty yards from where we stood—was an A-framed treehouse.

"That is perfect!" I exclaimed.

"I used to spend a lot of time out here until my dad built me a lab in the basement—now I'm down there more," Henry said. "He just bought me a telescope to entice me outdoors and into the treehouse again, but it's still in the box in my room."

"Yeah, it's been forever since we've been up here," Billy Boy added.

"What's that?" I asked, pointing to a rope with a rusty pulley dangling from one of the massive branches.

"It's a principle similar to one used in canal houses in Europe," Henry said behind me. "I had it installed to lift up furniture."

Or coffins? I wondered.

"Want to take a look?" he asked proudly.

I still had the protection of the sun's rays and the unyielding curiosity of a cat, but if I rode to the Mansion and waited for Alexander to wake up, then Jagger and Luna would be rising, too. The moon was ticking. My heart was pounding. First I had to make sure Henry and Billy Boy were far away from the treehouse.

"How about putting together that telescope your dad bought you?" I suggested.

Henry's face lit up as if I'd just invited him to see a private screening of *Lord of the Rings*. "I didn't know you were into astronomy," he said.

Billy Boy looked at me skeptically. "She probably just wants to look in your neighbor's windows."

I glared at my brother.

"And we'll need maps of the constellations," I added. "And don't forget charts and any diagrams you might have."

"There are quite a few constellations you can see in the daylight."

"We'll be able to see more clearly when the sun sets. So take your time. Don't come out here until you have everything ready. I'll wait here."

As soon as the two nerd-mates reached the back patio, I started to climb the thick wooden ladder that led up the tree, the boards creaking underneath my combat boots.

I stepped onto the uneven treehouse deck.

The wooden door slowly creaked open.

If Jagger and Luna were hiding here, then I realized why Jagger left the door opener at the factory. If Henry continued to use it to illuminate the treehouse, Jagger and Luna risked being discovered and scorched by the light.

When I opened the wooden door, I expected to find the coffins I had been searching for.

Instead I saw a run-down 3-D version of *Dexter's Laboratory*. On a folding lab table sat dusty beakers, petri dishes, and a microscope. The periodic table and a photosynthesis chart were taped to the slanting walls.

The treehouse interior was divided by a black curtain. I slowly pulled it back.

What I found took my breath away. Hidden in the shadows of the sloping wooden wall was a black coffin adorned with gothic band stickers, encircled in dirt. And resting next to it was a pale pink coffin!

I'd dreamed about a moment like this all my vampire-obsessed life, never to believe it would actually come to fruition. This was my chance to witness up close and personal a modern-day Nosferatu in his natural habitat. And with Luna, the moment was even more meaningful, because she, once human, was now a vampiress. I was looking firsthand into a world that I'd always envisioned being part of.

I crept toward the pink casket, hoping for a peek at what it was like inside. It was as fashionable as it was spooky. The once mortal Luna was now living in the Underworld next to her twin brother. I wondered if she regretted her decision.

I tiptoed over to Jagger's coffin. I gently touched the wooden top with the tip of my fingers. I held my breath and pressed my ear to the lid. I could hear the faint breathing of someone who was in a heavy stage of sleep. And then I heard him stir.

"Raven!" yelled Billy Boy.

I jumped back.

"Where are you?" he shouted.

I raced out of the room and promptly closed the curtain.

Billy Boy, with rolled-up maps under one arm, was fiddling with the microscope. "If you think this place is cool, you should see his basement."

"I've seen enough petri dishes to last me a lifetime. Let's go." I pulled my brother by the sleeve of his striped Izod T-shirt and led him to the treehouse door.

Even though I had daylight protecting me, I glanced back, expecting Luna and Jagger to somehow be following me.

We reached the bottom of the creaky ladder to find Henry carrying the telescope.

"Let's take this over to our place," I said, grabbing the telescope. "This treehouse isn't up to code."

"But my dad just—"

"Speaking of your dad, I think you should stay at our house for the week," I said to Henry.

My brother and his nerd-mate's eyes perked up.

"Seriously. You shouldn't be in this huge house without your parents. And I'm sure Nina could use a vacation."

"That'll be awesome. Your parents won't mind?" Henry asked politely.

"Pack your briefcase, and not another word," I ordered as we headed for his house.

Shortly after dusk I put on my Emily the Strange sweat-shirt hoodie and secured Henry's garage door opener safely inside the pouch pocket. I raced to the Mansion and tore up the broken cement stairs to the front door and anxiously rapped the serpent knocker.

Alexander opened the door. I was greeted by my hand-some boyfriend, standing in a black-and-white bowling shirt and black jeans with hanging silver chains, wearing a smile that could melt any sixteen-year-old vampire-obsessed goth. Before he even had a chance to say hello, I blurted out, "I've got major news. I've found the coffins!"

"That's awesome! Where?"

"I'll show you," I said, grabbing his hand and leading him out of the Mansion and toward the Mercedes.

Alexander drove me to the edge of the Oakley Woods, and we hopped out of the car. "Jagger's hearse was right here," I said, pointing to a pile of wood chips.

We followed fresh tire marks leading out of the woods, which turned into muddy tracks heading up the street.

"They must have left in the hearse. If we move quickly, we can remove the coffins."

Alexander parked the Mercedes outside Henry's house and we crept through the backyard.

"There it is," I said proudly, pointing to the treehouse.

Alexander and I watched for any signs that Jagger and Luna might still be inside. There were no candles flickering, or movement from the white-curtained windows.

"This is the pulley Henry used to hoist his furniture into the treehouse," I whispered, holding the dangling rope. "Jagger must have used it, too. This is how we'll get the caskets down."

"Stay here," Alexander said. "If you see anything, don't hesitate to take off. I can handle myself."

I glanced around. "But—"

When I turned back, Alexander was gone.

Once again Alexander was protecting me. Didn't he know we could move the coffins quicker if we both helped? I searched around the tree and found no signs of Luna or Jagger.

I tiptoed up the ladder and entered the treehouse.

"What are you doing up here?" Alexander asked. "I thought we had an agreement."

"We did. But I missed you," I said, giving him a quick

hug. "Besides, I've been up here before and I can show you around."

Alexander shook his head, went to the window, and peered out.

"We don't have much time," he said. "Where are they hiding? In the petri dishes?"

"No, silly." I pulled the black curtain open.

The darkened room was different from what I'd seen a few hours earlier—the coffin lids were open!

I peeked into Luna's casket. It held a neatly made pink satin comforter with a black lace border, a pink faux fur pillow, and a black Scare Bear plush.

The gravestone etchings Alexander and I had seen at the linen factory lining the rustic elevator were now tacked up to the slanting treehouse walls. The antique candelabra and pewter goblet Jagger had used at Dullsville's cemetery during his attempted covenant ceremony were resting on the floor. A black duffel bag and a Little Nancy Nightmare backpack were shoved in the corner. Next to them was an open box from the Coffin Club, loaded with blood-filled amulets from the mortal clubsters—the only way for the pair to survive without drawing attention or blood from Dullsville's mortals. Then I noticed a blood-red party-size cooler. I knelt beside it and fingered the edge of the white Styrofoam lid. What was being chilled inside? Packets or bottles of blood? Transplanted organs? A human head? I took a breath and began to lift the lid.

"Raven!" Alexander said.

I almost jumped out of my own pale skin.

"I need you to hold the door open for me," Alexander whispered. "I'll have to drag the coffins through."

"Let me help you," I offered.

"I'll do it," he said, always the gentleman. "I don't want you to hurt yourself."

Alexander started to close Jagger's coffin lid when we heard voices coming from outside.

"That might be Henry and Billy Boy," I said. "We can't let them up here."

"Stay here. I'll divert them."

I hid in the shadows and, naturally curious, began to further search the teen vampires' hideout. A plastic end table was turned into a goth makeup counter. I examined Luna's neatly arranged pink and black eye shadows, gray lipsticks, and mud-colored glosses. I opened a small bottle of Cotton Candy nail polish.

"So how do you like being a vampire?"

I dropped the nail polish and quickly turned around.

Jagger, wearing a white "Bite Me, I'm Transylvanian" T-shirt and black army fatigues, was standing before me.

"What are you doing here?" I questioned.

"Shouldn't I be asking you that?" he asked. His white hair hung in his face.

"I was just leaving—"

"I thought you'd be happy to see me. After all, haven't you been spending the last few days searching for *me*?"

I stepped back and looked away from his blue and green hypnotic eyes. I didn't want to return to Dullsville's cemetery with him again.

"Luna claimed she saw you reflected in the Fun House's Hall of Mirrors," he said, walking closer.

I paused. I could barely breathe. I looked at the white-curtained window, planning to make my escape.

"But I knew better," he continued. "You might fool her with those circus mirrors, but not me. I saw Alexander bite you and transform you right in front of my eyes. I regretted the day I didn't get to you first."

I breathed again. But only for a moment as he inched toward me.

"Isn't Sterling fulfilling your darkest needs?" he whispered. "I thought you got what you wanted."

"I did."

"Then you wouldn't be here, now would you? Sterling's not cut out for what you really desire, is he? That's why you are trying to find me."

I paused. I stepped past him, but he grabbed my hand.

He lifted it. "You have very long love veins," he said, running his finger along a skinny horizontal blue vein, his black painted fingernail in sharp contrast to my pasty skin. "See here, how it splinters off? As if you were pursuing a path with one love, but then you chose another."

"I used to be crazy about Marilyn Manson. Now I love Alexander," I said sharply.

He held my hand tighter. "We are the same now, you and I."

"We never were, nor will we ever be, the same," I argued.

Jagger didn't seem convinced.

"How about we share a drink together?" he asked, lifting my wrist to his mouth. "Then we will be closer than ever."

I quickly jerked my arm away. "Alexander quenches any thirst I have."

"Is it everything you thought it would be? Being a princess of the night?"

"Why don't you ask Luna."

Then it hit me: If Jagger was here, where was his twin sister?

I raced past him, out to the deck of the treehouse, and looked out to the yard. Alexander was searching the poolside grounds.

A few yards from the treehouse, I thought I saw some long white hair poking out from behind one of the trees.

I turned around, expecting to find Jagger mischievously grinning. But he was no longer standing behind me.

Instead I saw Jagger and Luna darting from underneath the treehouse, through the backyard, toward my unsuspecting boyfriend.

"Alexander!" I called.

I was too far away to reach Alexander before they did. And what could I do against two real vampires, anyway? How could a mortal goth stop them?

Then I remembered. "Alexander—cover yourself! With a towel! Now!" I shouted.

He looked confused but snatched a folded beach towel from a lounge chair, crouched down, and enveloped himself with it.

I pulled my hoodie over my head and drew the strings tightly shut.

I grabbed the garage door opener from my pocket and pointed it at Henry's house.

I took a deep breath and pressed my finger on the silver button as hard as I could.

The lights burst on, illuminating the entire backyard, including Jagger and Luna.

The two vampires stopped dead in their tracks. The sudden burst of bright light was like kryptonite. They shielded their pale faces with their skinny bleach white arms. They each hissed and fled into the darkness.

I flew down the ladder and raced to the pool deck. Breathless, I finally reached Alexander, still covered, on a lounge chair.

I aimed the garage door opener at the house again, pressed the silver button, and the once-illuminated backyard turned black.

It took a moment for my eyes to adjust to the darkness. I could see Alexander, his hair tousled, a towel by his side.

"Quick thinking," he complimented, and gave me a long kiss.

"We better get out of here—," I said.

"Jagger will be more determined than ever to get Trevor now that he knows we've found his hideout. They won't wait much longer."

I f there ever was a morning I didn't want to get out of bed, this was it. After pressing the snooze bar repeatedly, I unplugged my *Nightmare Before Christmas* alarm clock and stashed it under my bed.

What I couldn't unplug was my mother's voice.

"Raven!" she called for the millionth time from downstairs. "You've overslept. Again."

After a quick shower, I threw on a black-on-black ensemble. I dragged myself into the kitchen to gulp down some of the leftover morning sludge that Dad called "coffee."

I found Billy Boy already commandeering the chair by the TV with our new house guest, Henry. The nerd-mates were glued to the screen, watching historic footage of battleships blasting their cannons and devouring Pop-Tarts and Crunch Berries.

With every crunch of the captain and boom of a

cannon, I felt like my head was behind enemy lines.

"Turn that off!" I whined, and switched the channel to the Home Shopping Network.

A petite blond with a perfect french manicure was modeling bedazzling silver bracelets.

"Hurry, there's only fifty seconds left!" I warned Billy Boy. "You could own one in just five easy payments. The blue topaz matches your eyes."

Billy Boy raced to the TV and wrangled the control out of my hand. "Get off!" he said, switching it back to the History Channel. "If you'd watch, maybe you'd learn something. Then your report card could be framed in Dad's office, instead of ending up in his paper shredder."

I stirred cream and a pound of sugar into a java-filled Dullsville Country Club mug and poured myself a small bowl of Count Chocula. The gun battle and excessive crunching continued. I could barely open my charcoal eye-lids wide enough to see the chocolate vampires floating in the milk among the marshmallow ghosts and bats.

My mom burst into the kitchen in her Corporate Cathy gear—a crisp gray DKNY pantsuit and Kate Spade mules—and opened the fridge door. "Morning," she said gleefully. "I thought you'd never get up."

"I didn't either," I grumbled.

"I saw Mrs. Mitchell at the pharmacy last night buying Trevor some cough syrup," she said, placing her Tupperware bowl filled with low-fat, low-taste premade salad in her Bloomingdale's tote bag. "Trevor must have the same cold you had."

"Yeah, he's been out of school. It's been the first time

I only detested school instead of hating it."

"Well, I think he's on the mend. His mother told me a girl has been bringing him protein shakes and he's feeling better."

"You mean one of the cheerleaders, right?" I queried.

"No. Mrs. Mitchell made it very clear this girl is new to town and dresses—well, not very conservatively," my mom said, grabbing a bottled water and closing the fridge door.

"You mean, like me?"

My mother paused.

It was Luna.

"Is it the white-haired girl Trevor was with at the Spring Carnival?" Billy Boy asked.

"It may be," my mom answered. "I didn't see them together."

"I just saw her from a distance," my brother said. "But a kid at Math Club swears she has a twin. They were spotted coming out of the cemetery. Her brother was dressed like he just stepped off a pirate ship.

"Kids are saying they sleep in sewers," Billy Boy continued.

"It's not nice to gossip," my mother warned.

"I heard they're ghosts. One dude claims you can see right through them," Henry said.

"And talk about tattoos and piercing," Billy Boy added, "I heard he has more holes in his head than you," Billy Boy said to me.

"I have tattoos," I said, rolling up my sleeve and showing him a bat tattoo.

"Your dad told you to wash that off," my mother advised.

"And he has pierced kneecaps," my brother went on.

"Well, I'll pierce your kneecaps if you don't stop gossiping like two old ladies."

"All right. Boys, you are going to miss your bus if you don't finish soon," my mother ordered.

Henry and Billy Boy placed their empty bowls in the dishwasher.

"Mom, did Mrs. Mitchell say this girl brought Trevor protein shakes?" I asked.

"Supposedly they are special shakes from Romania. I asked Mrs. Mitchell to get the recipe for me."

Delicious drink, I thought. *Ingredients: One cup crushed ice. One banana. One vial vampire's blood.*

"I don't think you'd like this particular Romanian drink."

Finally we got a reprieve from the gunfire, and a commercial for Garlic One gelcaps came on the TV. Billy Boy aimed the remote to switch it off.

"No, wait," I said.

"You're suddenly interested in history?" Billy Boy asked proudly. "Maybe I'm rubbing off on you after all."

"Shh . . ."

My mom followed Billy Boy and Henry as they headed for the front door.

"Garlic One," the commercial continued. "Natural and odorless. Helps promote cardiovascular health with just one capsule a day."

Their slogan should say, "An odor-free way to keep the vampires away."

I was struck with an idea. Why hadn't I thought of it sooner? There was nothing I loved more than a brand-new plan!

Hey, Beck, do you mind stopping at Paxx Pharmacy?" I asked my best friend when I hopped into her pickup. "I just have to buy a few things on the way to school."

"But Matt will be waiting by the bleachers for us. I don't want to be late."

"It'll only take a sec," I pleaded.

The old girl was as hot-glued to her soccer sweetheart as I was to my vampire boyfriend. I would have been sickened if I didn't understand her amorous devotion.

"Okay," she finally agreed. "I could get Matt some candy. He loves red licorice."

I remember when Becky and I would hang outside Paxx's and eat twines of red licorice until we felt ill. Now, instead of creating new memories with me, she was creating them with Matt.

I turned to my best friend, who was wearing khakis and a pale blue button-down shirt. As long as I'd known Becky, she'd worn jeans and an oversized sweater. How long had I not noticed the change?

"Besides, it will give us a chance to hang out," she added kindly.

Becky was right. I'd been so wrapped up in diverting the union between Trevor and Luna that I hadn't any time left to talk, or even open my eyes!

Now that we had beaus, we didn't cling to each other like we had before. Did that mean we didn't need each other at all?

"It's been forever since we've had girl time," I agreed.

"I know, it's great we have boyfriends, but I'm missing our friendship."

"Me too!" I said. "We have to make time for us."

"It's a pact," she said, extending her pinky finger.

"A pact," I said, entwining my own in hers.

More than spending time apart, I felt like I was in the dark alone, not being able to share with my best friend the fact that our town was crawling with vampires.

"If I tell you something, can you promise not to tell anyone? Not even Matt?" I asked.

"Is it about sex?"

"No. It's even more top secret."

"What's more top secret than sex?"

I was ready to spill my guts. To tell my best friend why my boyfriend was never seen in daylight. To explain to her why Jagger drove a hearse. Why the ghostlike Luna had suddenly come to Dullsville.

But Becky's cherub face looked so happy, her biggest concern being what new outfit to wear to school, what brand of candy treat to buy for Matt. I couldn't spoil her perfect world.

"We're having a pop quiz in Shank's class tomorrow."

"Duh," she said, rolling her eyes. "Everyone knows that."

"Really?" I asked, almost horrified. "Maybe I'm losing my touch."

I was hunkered down in the vitamin-and-herb aisle, studying Mother Nature's remedies and filling my red plastic shopping basket with vitamin C and boxes of Garlic One gelcaps, when Becky finally caught up to me.

"I thought you were feeling better," she said, holding several packages of red licorice.

"I am, but I want to stock up."

"Garlic tablets?" she asked, confused. "I thought you were over your vampire obsession now that you are dating Alexander."

"I am. I just saw this commercial—"

"Speaking of Alexander," she interrupted excitedly, "would you two want to meet up at Hatsy's Diner after the soccer game tonight?"

How could I tell my best friend no after we'd just made a pinky-swear pact to hang out more? As long as I was with Alexander and Trevor was home sick, I reasoned, we were all safe.

"Yes, that's a great idea. I don't think Alexander's ever been to Hatsy's."

Becky and I brought our purchases to the counter. We stood, unnoticed, as an elderly clerk hid behind a tabloid mag and her teenage clerk-mate filed packets of developed prints.

"Those two kids I was telling you about were in here last night," the elderly clerk gossiped. "I think they are cousins of that weird mansion family on Benson Hill."

"I heard they look like walking corpses," the younger one chimed back.

"They do. I just don't get why kids today think it's cool to look like they've just come out of a coffin."

"I've heard one of them drives a hearse."

Just then the elderly clerk put down her paper and spotted me. Her eyes bugged out like she'd seen a ghost.

"I'm sorry," she apologized. "Have you been waiting long?"

"An eternity!" I said.

So Jagger and Luna were beginning to make their presence known throughout Dullsville. Were they bored, careless, or marking their territory?

Even though Trevor and I'd spent our lives at each other's throats, I didn't want Luna and Jagger after his. Besides they were looking to do far more damage than wringing his neck. A mixture of emotions flooded through me—protecting a fellow Dullsvillian from a deadly duo, thwarting a plan to have a nefarious soccer snob wreaking havoc, and diverting a plot to have my nemesis turned into a vampire before I was.

I'd have to get these tablets to Trevor. At any moment, Jagger or Luna could strike—or in their case, bite.

Though keeping up my new vampire identity was exhausting, I was really beginning to enjoy it. Everything I felt before as a vampire-obsessed goth I now had to live out—my distaste for the light and passion for darkness, having a secret identity, and being an insider instead of an outsider. I imagined the rest—flying high in Dullsville's sky, living in a spooky dungeon, Alexander and I cuddling the day away in a king-size coffin.

As the sun began to set, I rode my bike to Trevor's, with my Paxx Pharmacy bag safely inside my Olivia Outcast backpack. I'd already called Jameson and told him I'd be a few minutes late to meet Alexander. It was crucial that I keep up my vampire charade and wait until darkness until I visited Trevor, just in case Trevor spilled my visit to Luna. If he shared with her that I'd visited him after school the first day he was sick, Luna could assume Trevor was delirious from his cold medicine. But now that my nemesis was on the mend, I had to cover my tracks. I couldn't give them any reason to suspect I was still a mortal.

"I've been waiting all day for you," Trevor said as he opened the front door. He was wearing plaid flannel pajama pants and a long-sleeve Big Ten surf shirt and was sporting a much healthier glow—a bad sign he'd be coming back to school, but a good sign he hadn't been bitten.

"You missed me?" I asked with a saccharine grin.

"I thought you were Luna," he said, disappointed. "We're not buying Ghoul Scout cookies today," he said, closing the door.

I quickly blocked the door with my boot.

"I'm putting the final touches on my health project," I said, opening the door and stepping inside.

"Do you want me to feel better or put me in the morgue?"

"Do I have a choice?"

"Why don't you write down in your report the reason for Trevor Mitchell's illness. Two words: Raven Madison. I'm sure the Infectious Disease Institute has heard of you," Trevor said.

I ignored his rude comments and walked into his newly painted sunflower yellow kitchen, which still smelled like fresh paint.

"I've heard you've been getting visits from a ghostly candy stripper. I mean, striper," I said with a grin.

"Sounds like someone is jealous."

I pulled out my Paxx Pharmacy bag and placed it on the granite-top kitchen island.

"My mom already got me medicine."

"It's just a few things so I can get extra credit. Vitamin C, a bag of cough drops, and Garlic One capsules."

"Garlic capsules? I'll smell like an Italian restaurant."

"They're good for cardiovascular health. Should help you on the soccer field."

"Didn't you see all my trophies? I can play in my

sleep," he said arrogantly.

I was running out of options, and time. I had to go for the jugular.

"Word on the street is, these are a major aphrodisiac. Gives off a scent that girls find irresistible. Something about pheromones. Anyway, someone like you shouldn't need it," I said, heading for the front door with the capsules.

"Hey, wait," he said, catching up to me in the entranceway. "Leave those here." He grabbed the package from my hand. "Not for me, of course. For the guys on the team."

One block north of Dullsville's downtown square sat Hatsy's Diner——a quaint fifties restaurant complete with teal blue and white vinyl booths, a black-and-white-checked tile floor, neon Coke signs, and a menu of cheese-burgers, atomic fries, and the thickest chocolate shakes in town. The waitresses donned red diner uniforms while the waiters dressed as soda jerks. Occasionally Becky and I would frequent Hatsy's after school when we managed to scrounge enough change to cover an order of onion rings and a mediocre tip.

Alexander and I arrived at Hatsy's. A few families and young couples were scattered around the diner. The soccer players were already gulping down malts and fries at two large tables. All eyes turned to us as we walked through the clean, crisp, bright diner in our usual blackness.

A surge of excitement shot through me—I felt like a gothic princess on the arm of her handsome gothic prince, although I knew the stares were from ridicule rather than envy.

Alexander studied the framed Bobby Darrin, Ricky Nelson, and Sandra Dee records, too engrossed in his new surroundings to feel self-conscious.

Matt and Becky were sitting alone in a corner booth.

"Hey, guys, we're over here," Becky called.

Alexander and I nestled into the booth.

"I thought you'd be sitting with the rest of the soccer team," I remarked as we grabbed the menus resting behind the chrome napkin holder.

"We thought it might be cozier if it were just us," Becky said.

A tall waitress with an hourglass figure, a brunette beehive, and white cat's-eye glasses approached our table, chomping on a wad of pink bubble gum.

"Hi, my name is Dixie," she said, cracking her gum. She pulled out an order pad from her white apron. "What can I get you?"

"Two vanilla shakes and an order of atomic fries," Matt said.

"And we'd like the same, but make the shakes chocolate, please," Alexander said.

Dixie blew a big bubble and popped it with her front teeth.

Then she sashayed off toward the kitchen. All the guys in the diner gawked at her, even Alexander and Matt.

"When I grow up, I want to look just like that," I said to Alexander.

"You already do," he said, putting his arm around me and giving me a squeeze.

Alexander's eyes lit up as he spotted the vintage tabletop jukebox. "This is cool," he said, flipping through the menu of fifties tunes. "I've only seen these in movies."

I'd forgotten that my boyfriend spent so much of his life hidden away in his attic room, far from the mundane musings of mortals. I got goose bumps seeing him so fascinated in his new surroundings as he examined the list of titles and artists.

"Elvis rocks," he said, elated.

I dug my hand into my purse and placed a quarter in the jukebox.

A moment later, "Love Me Tender" played over the speakers.

Alexander smiled a sweet smile and squeezed my hand. His leg was touching mine, and I could feel him tapping his combat boots to the beat of the song underneath the table.

"So what have you guys been up to lately?" Matt asked.

"Hunting for coffins," Alexander said.

Becky and Matt looked at us oddly.

"The usual," I said smiling.

Matt and Becky laughed.

"So how was your game?" Alexander asked Matt as he put his napkin on his lap.

"We kicked butt. But only because Trevor played."

"No," Becky defended. "You scored, too."

"I thought he was sick," I said.

"Well, he managed to show up and score a few goals.

As much as I hate to say it, we're not a winning team without him."

"Did he go home?" I asked.

"No, he's over there," Matt said, pointing behind me.

I turned around. Trevor was in the far end of the diner, playing pinball.

"He shouldn't be out at night," I declared.

Becky looked perplexed.

"I'm using him as my project for health class. The night air isn't good for a cold. Excuse me, I'll be back in a sec," I said, awkwardly scooting out of the booth.

I could feel eyeballs on me as I walked across the diner, but not for the same reason they had been looking at Dixie.

I tapped on Trevor's shoulder. "What are you doing here?"

My nemesis glanced at me and rolled his eyes. "Looks like I'm playing pinball."

"You're sick. You shouldn't be out where you can pick up more germs."

"Believe me, with you standing next to me, I've already picked up several diseases," he said, pressing the flippers with gusto.

"You should be at home," I ordered.

The ball hit a bumper, causing the game board to light up. "You left Monster Boy to talk to me?" he asked. "You've been to my house twice. I'm beginning to think—"

"It's best you don't think. Did you take your garlic?"

"I had a game, not a date," he said, tilting the machine.

"You should be resting."

"You sound like my mother," he said, banging on the flippers.

"Well, maybe you should listen to her."

"Why, so she càn tell me not to see Luna? Has my mom been talking to you?"

"She doesn't approve?" I asked, curious.

"What do you think?"

"Your mother is right this time. Luna isn't your type. You need a girl with a tiara, not a tattoo."

"But do I really? Luna dresses like you and you've been trying to convince me for years that you are not a mutant. Did you ever think it wasn't your clothes that led people to think you were a freak?"

"So what do you see in her?" I interrogated.

"She's the new girl, beautiful and mysterious. Kind of what you liked in Alexander."

"That's completely different. I like Alexander because he is unlike anyone I've ever met and exactly like me. But Luna isn't your type. She's too goth."

"Just like someone we know . . ."

"You'd risk your popularity for her?" I whispered with a twinge of jealousy.

I hated to admit it, but deep down I did wonder what Trevor saw in Luna that he didn't see in me.

"Are you kidding? I'll be even more popular for scoring the *new* goth girl rather than the *old* one."

It was as if he had just driven a stake into my heart.

"She and Jagger now hang out with me all the time,"

he continued in my face. "They watch me at practice and games. I'm more popular than ever—a king of both the insiders *and* the outsiders."

"I'm telling you, your mother is right this time," I tried to warn.

"Well, was my mother right about Alexander and his family?" he asked, referring to the rampant rumors spread throughout Dullsville that the Sterlings were vampires. "She thought they were weird just because they were different."

"So did you," I argued.

"She said they were vampires," he continued, hitting the ball again. "Had the whole town believing they were. Especially you."

"You were the one who made up and spread those rumors. But in this case, maybe you should believe it."

"That Luna is a vampire?"

I paused.

The restaurant went quiet.

Trevor let the pinball bounce against the bumpers and drop through the flippers.

Just then I felt someone behind me. I turned around.

Jagger, in a ripped white Bauhaus T-shirt and black jeans, and Luna in a black and pink minidress and pink fishnets, stood before me, glaring. She was beautiful. She looked like a gothic pixie fairy girl, with skinny pale arms dangling black rubber bracelets, her long cotton white hair flowing over her shoulders and bright blue eyes sparkling. Both stood in front of me like they were ready to extract me from the diner.

"What are you doing here?" she charged.

Suddenly, like a gothic Superman, Alexander appeared by my side. As Luna leaned in to me, Alexander bravely stepped between us.

"Good-bye, Monster Girl," Trevor said, taking Luna's hand. "C'mon, Jagger."

Jagger gave Alexander a deathly stare, then followed the odd couple toward the tables where the soccer snobs were eating.

I leaned against the pinball machine as Trevor sat at the head of the table with Luna and Jagger on either side. The soccer snobs inched away as if the Romanian siblings had rabies. The players continued to avoid eye contact and kept the conversation to themselves.

"We have to get to the treehouse," Alexander whispered. "While Jagger and Luna are still here."

Alexander and I quickly returned to our table to find our order had just arrived.

"What was that about?" Matt asked.

"We have to go," I said, grabbing my purse.

"But we just got our food!" my best friend argued.

"Becky and I can't drink four shakes," Matt said.

I glanced back at Trevor. The star player was shining in his spotlight, back from a cold to save the team. A girl on one side, his new friend on the other. It disgusted me.

"We really have to go—," I repeated.

"Just because Trevor and those guys are over there?" Becky asked.

"Yes," I said, "but not for the reason you think. I'll

have to explain it later. Trust me."

Alexander placed a twenty and a ten on the table. "Please, it's on me."

"Our lucky night—we can order burgers now," Becky joked.

I laughed and gave my best friend a quick hug.

While all eyes were glued to Dixie as she took Jagger and Luna's order, Alexander and I snuck out of the diner, past Jagger's hearse, and into the Mercedes.

"We better hurry," I said as we bolted through Henry's backyard.

Alexander and I didn't know how much time we had to remove the coffins before Jagger and Luna returned.

I scaled up the treehouse ladder and Alexander met me inside. When I pulled back the black curtain, the coffins remained as we'd seen them before.

Alexander stood behind Jagger's casket. Then he pushed the coffin with all his might.

Jagger's bed wouldn't budge.

"What's going on?" I asked.

"It's stuck."

"Is something in it? Maybe a dead body?"

"It would have to be several dead bodies. This thing weighs a ton."

Alexander opened the lid. All that remained inside was a rumpled black blanket and white pillow.

He closed the lid and tried to move it again.

"Maybe it's caught on something."

I bent over the opposite end, and together we pushed and pulled as hard as we could.

But the coffin wouldn't move.

"Let's try Luna's," Alexander said, brushing his dark locks away from his face.

I grabbed one end of the pale pink coffin and Alexander held the other. We couldn't lift Luna's coffin off the ground.

Alexander and I searched the hideout for anything we could use as leverage.

"Check this out," I said, pointing to a few nails lying next to Jagger's duffel bag.

"When I think we've thought of everything, so has Jagger," Alexander said, frustrated.

"I don't have any tools with me," I said.

"I think he counted on that," Alexander remarked, gently touching my shoulder.

Just then we heard the sound of a car driving up the road.

Alexander and I quickly escaped from the treehouse as headlights from Jagger's hearse shined on the driveway.

"I've heard about nailing a coffin lid shut, but never the whole coffin!" I said as we made a fast getaway.

The following evening, when I headed out the front door to meet Alexander at the Mansion, I found a red envelope lying on the porch. In black letters it read: RAVEN.

Inside, a red note with black typed letters read:

MEET ME AT OAKLEY PARK, Love, Alexander.

How sweet, I thought. A spontaneous romantic interlude in the park. Alexander Sterling was king of planning the most mysterious, meaningful, marvelous dates—a picnic at the Dullsville cemetery; a goth rock dance at Dullsville's Country Club golf course; picking out my kitty, Nightmare, at an abandoned barn.

I imagined arriving at the park, votives surrounding the Oakley Park fountain, bubbles floating from the steaming water, Alexander and I wading in our bare feet, our lips tenderly touching.

Then I wondered, was this note truly from my vampire

mate? Unfortunately, since I'd encountered Jagger at the Coffin Club, I had grown suspicious. After all, Jagger had met me in an alley in Hipsterville, appeared in my back-yard, and hid in the Mansion's gazebo. Then again, if it was Jagger, he could just show up at my house.

I hopped on my bike in my lacy black knee-length dress and pedaled my heart out to Oakley Park. I raced over the bumpy grass toward the swings. When I reached the fountain, my dream guy wasn't there. I walked my bike over to the picnic benches.

"Alexander?" I called.

All I saw were the flashing lights of lightning bugs.

Then I heard the music of the Wicked Wiccas being piped in from the outdoor amphitheater.

I walked my bike over to the domed stage where my parents dragged Billy Boy and me to see Dullsville's sym-phony orchestra play on Sunday nights during the summer. I had preferred sitting alone on the wet grass, lis-tening to the screeching violins in a rainstorm while my parents sought shelter underneath a tree, to watching them canoodle and dance to "The Stars and Stripes."

I coasted down the aisle of the theater. A lit cande-labra and a picnic basket were sitting on a black lace blan-ket, spread out center stage.

I leaned my bike against a cement bench. I raced around the orchestra pit and climbed onstage.

"Alexander?"

I heard nothing.

I searched the wings. I found only chairs and music stands.

I went to center stage and sat on the blanket. I opened the picnic basket. Maybe there was another note telling me to go to a different romantic location. But the basket was empty.

Something felt strange. The crickets turned silent. I stood up and looked around. Still no Alexander.

Then, right in front of me, stood Luna, in a tight black dress with mesh sleeves and pink fingerless gloves, a pastel pink amulet hanging from her neck.

I gasped and stepped back.

"What are you doing here?" I asked her. "I'm supposed to meet Alexander."

"He got a note, too," she said with a wicked grin. "'Meet me at the cemetery. Raven.'"

I glanced around, peering into the wings of the stage, squinting out at the empty seats. Jagger could have been anywhere.

"I'm here alone," she assured me as if she were reading my thoughts.

"I've got to go—," I said.

Luna stepped in front of me, her chunky black boot almost hitting my own. "I think Alexander can wait. After all, he's made me wait for him since I was born."

"I didn't have anything to do with that," I said, referring to the covenant ceremony in Romania where Alexander was supposed to turn her into a vampire. "And Alexander didn't either. He never made that promise."

"Don't defend him," she argued. "Besides, that's not why I'm here."

"Then why are you?"

"I want you to stop seeing Trevor," she said.

"I don't know what you're talking about."

"Don't play dumb with me. I know you visit him at night. And I overheard you at the diner. You told him to beware of me, like I'm some freak!"

"He has the right to know who you really are."

"I was a freak *before* I turned. Now I am normal."

"But you don't even know the real Trevor. Believe me, *he's* the freak."

"I don't remember asking you for your opinion."

"Jagger is not looking out for you. He's not concerned with finding you a soul mate. He's still looking to get back at Alexander."

"Don't talk about my brother like that. You don't know anything about him—or me. You don't even know me."

"I do know Trevor."

Luna's eyes widened. She stuck her hands in their pink fingerless gloves on her almost nonexistent hips.

"Trevor's right. You are jealous!" she accused. "He thinks you are in love with him. And I do, too."

"Then you are as loony as he is! You deserve each other."

"You won Alexander. I have a right to find my own fun."

"This isn't a contest. These are people, not prizes."

Her blue eyes turned red. She stepped so close to me, I could smell her Cotton Candy lip gloss.

"I want you to back off!" she said in my face.

"I want *you* to back off!" I said in her face.

If she was going to push, I was going to push back harder.

"I'm not afraid of you," Luna said.

"I'm not afraid of *anyone*," I replied.

I thought at any minute we were going to have a cat fight—or in our case, a bat fight.

"If you tell Trevor about me," she threatened, "then I'm going to tell him about you!"

"What about me?"

"That you are a vampire. That we are vampires."

She stepped back and folded her arms, as if triumphant. I didn't know what to say.

"Then tell him," I said finally. "He'll never believe you."

Luna stepped back and gazed at the moon.

"You are probably right," she relented. "I thought I saw you reflected in the Hall of Mirrors. Jagger convinced me it was part of the illusion. I guess I didn't want to accept that Alexander had turned you. It's odd really, not being like everyone else, isn't it?"

I'd never met a girl, or anyone besides Alexander, who acknowledged feeling the same way I did, vampire or not.

"Yes," I agreed.

Luna's dark mood changed. Her stiff shoulders relaxed. Her angry blue eyes softened, looking almost lost, and lonely.

"It's funny," she continued, "how much we have in common. We're not all that different, you and me. I've always been surrounded by real vampires. Ones that were born to the Underworld. I'm the only one I know who was turned. Until I met you."

I could see in Luna's soulful eyes that she was hungering for a connection. She reminded me of someone who was alone, living on the outside of life instead of thriving on the inside. She reminded me of myself.

"It's not fun being an outcast," I said.

Luna smiled a pale pink smile, like a warm hug was melting her darkened spirit.

She grabbed my hand as she sat down by the basket. "Sit for a moment."

"I really should go—," I said, resisting her.

"Just for a minute," she pleaded.

I reluctantly sat down on the blanket.

"Tell me, how did you feel when you turned?" She scooted closer and eagerly leaned in to me, like we were gossiping at a slumber party.

"How did I feel?" I asked, confused.

"When Alexander bit you."

I paused. If I answered wrong, I could blow my whole vampire cover. I was alone, onstage with a vampiress, without my garlic, a stake, or sunlight to hide behind, and Alexander was waiting for me miles away at the Dullsville cemetery.

"Please . . . tell me, how did it make you feel?" she repeated.

"Like magic," I whispered.

"Yes," she nodded eagerly.

"Like a life force I'd never known coursed through my veins and pulsed straight to my heart."

"Go on."

"I felt my heart stop, as if it had exploded with love, then beat again like it never had before," I said, getting caught up in my own imagination, almost believing it myself.

"Me too. . . . But you were in love."

"Yes. I've loved Alexander since the first moment I saw him," I said truthfully.

"He is gorgeous." Then she whispered, as if she were sharing a secret, "I had a fling."

"Who was he?"

"An acquaintance of Jagger's. I barely knew him. But he had a chiseled chin and a ripped chest. Deep blue eyes and spiky red hair like fire. He took me to a warehouse. We made out for a while, his lips were like velvet. And before I knew it, he had bitten me."

"Wow," I said, hanging on her every word.

"We were on unsacred ground, so we were not bonded for eternity. I never saw him again."

"That's so sad," I lamented, honestly feeling sorry for her.

"You were lucky; you found Alexander. So you see how important Trevor is to me. When Jagger introduced us and I stared into his heavenly green eyes, I immediately felt a connection. Not only is he handsome and athletic, but as I got to know him, I sensed that he had everything he could ever want but true love. This is what drew me to him. I'm looking for someone to quench my thirst—for all eternity." She fingered the pink amulet. "Jagger has different needs than I do. He hungers for the hunt, lusts for new prey. Finds ecstasy in the transformation of an innocent mortal into a bloodthirsty vampire. But for me, these bottles are growing quite tiresome. The hunt isn't sustaining me. It's flowing blood that I really crave. The sweet taste of red succulent liquid mixing with the salt of my beloved as it drips and dances on his flesh. To know that someone will ache for me as much as I hunger for him and eternally satiate each other. I want someone to satisfy my hunger forever."

"But Trevor's not good enough. You deserve better," I said earnestly.

She looked at me skeptically.

"You need someone who is intelligent. Sensitive. Mature. Courageous."

"He is those things. You don't know him the way I know him."

I knew I should go, that Alexander must be waiting at the cemetery wondering why I hadn't shown. At the same time, there was so much I wanted to know about Luna, about being turned, about becoming a modern-day vampiress. There was so much I wanted to know for myself. And I didn't know when I'd get another chance.

"Do you like being a vampire?" I asked, now the one riveted.

"I've waited for it all my life. Everyone in my immediate family is a vampire. When my younger brother, Valentine, was born, I dreamed that he would be mortal, like me. But when he wasn't, I cursed the day he was born. The last mortal in my family tree was my great-great grandmother, and I never even knew her. I spent my whole life living in the daylight while the rest of my family slept. I was never part of their world."

"How did you cope all alone?" I wondered.

"I tried to mask it by being a bubbly straight-A student, becoming popular with the kids at school. It put a strain on Jagger's and my relationship. I was jealous of Jagger and he was of me."

"Really? I can't imagine Jagger being jealous of anyone."

"I could see it in his face every time he awoke from his coffin. We had only a few hours together before I had to get to sleep. We'd sit in my bright pink room and I'd share every detail of my events that day at school."

"Who would want to go to school?" I asked.

"Jagger was especially interested in sports. In Europe, soccer is huge. He dreamed of being what he couldn't be—a soccer star. He would show up at night games, hungry to be a player instead of a spectator. But to the students he was odd—a kid who never went to school, was pale and skinny, and dressed like a freak. He was never included. Now he watches Trevor play soccer, wishing he had that life. I think that's why he wants Trevor for me."

For a moment Jagger and Luna weren't vampires but just teens like me who were tired of being outsiders.

"How do you like being a vampire?" she asked.

"Uh . . . I love it," I fibbed.

"But now you're different from your entire family."

"If you'd ever seen my family, you'd know I always was," I said with a laugh.

Luna laughed, too. It was like we'd known each other for years instead of only a few minutes.

"My little brother is a total nerd," I said, desperate to share my life with her.

"How old is he?"

"Eleven."

"So is Valentine! It's so refreshing to meet someone like you. You understand what it means to live in both worlds but beg for the darker one."

Luna pulled out a Pinky Paranoid clutch purse from behind the basket. "Want some candy?" she asked, handing me a Dynamite Mint.

I nodded and unwrapped the candy as she took out a hair brush. "Tell me about Alexander," she said, inching next to me. She began to brush my hair, as if we'd been soul sisters for years. I felt uncomfortable, as this girly behavior seemed straight out of a Gidget movie. Teens around Dullsville were never seen brushing one another's hair. Luna, however, was much more fairylike than any girl I'd ever met. I felt almost hypnotized and relaxed as she smoothed out my hair, opposite of the way I felt when I was a child and my mom ran a fine-toothed comb through my tangles.

"Alexander's so dreamy. His eyes are like milk chocolates. His attic room is filled with portraits he's painted of me and his family," I rattled on like a drippy girl, then changed my tone. "But it's hard sometimes," I confessed.

"I want to share our reflections. I want to have a photo of us on my night stand."

"Yes, it does have its drawbacks. But it's a small price to pay for an eternity together."

Luna pulled my hair off my shoulder and began to braid it.

"Where is the wound from Alexander's bite?" she asked curiously.

I quickly covered my neck with my hand.

She released my hair and raised her white, luxurious locks, exposing two round purple marks on her skinny pale neck.

"They say it takes a year to go away," she said. "I hope it stays there forever."

"Uh . . . it's not on my neck," I teased.

"You are wicked!" she said with a smile, but then turned serious. "I could have sworn Jagger said he saw Alexander bite you on your neck."

"I really have to go," I said, getting up. "Alexander will be worried."

I climbed offstage.

"Wanna hang out again tomorrow?" she asked, following me. "We can meet at sunset."

"I have plans with Alexander," I said, walking up the aisle.

"Then the next night?"

"I'll see," I said, grabbing my bike.

"Why do you need to ride here when you could fly?"

"I have to keep up appearances."

"Good thinking," she said with a wink. "I'll see you later."

I hopped on my bike. "Later!"

I pedaled off. When I turned back to wave, the amphitheater was empty.

I had to admit—I loved being a vampire. Luna not only believed I was part of the Underworld but wanted me as a friend. I felt like I was flying as I raced my bike through downtown and toward my house. I wondered where I would live. Perhaps my understanding parents could remodel our finished basement—board up the windows, remove the white carpeting, and dirty the cement floors with a few bugs and cobwebs. I could sleep in a black coffin with purple seams and silver studs. Or better yet, Alexander and I could live together in the factory with a super-deluxe two-person gothedelic coffin. Plenty of pillows and comfy blankets, with a built-in flat-screen TV in the lid and stereo speakers on the sides.

I pulled into my driveway and found Alexander waiting for me on the front steps, looking as dreamy as ever in black vinyl pants and a ripped black long-sleeve shirt.

"Where were you?" he asked, concerned. "I got your note about meeting you at the cemetery, but you never showed."

"I got a note, too," I said, showing him the red envelope. "To meet you at the park."

"But I didn't write a note."

"I know. Neither did I."

"Then who did?" he asked.

"Your spurned lover."

"Luna? She was never my lover."

"I know. I was just teasing."

"How did you know it was her?"

"She told me. When I showed up at the park."

"Did she hurt you?" he asked.

"She wanted to. It was all a plan to confront me about Trevor. She wants me to stay away from him."

"This is getting out of hand," he said. "I'll talk to her."

"No, she thinks I'm a vampire," I said proudly, placing my hand on his. "Can you believe it? We chatted forever. Like we were best friends."

"Jagger and Luna don't have best friends. We really have to be careful. There's no predicting what they'll do."

"But she really liked me," I insisted.

"I'm sure she did," he said with a smile. "We still can't trust them."

"Well, she trusts me."

"Because you are trustworthy. I know their family, Raven. They're not like you. They are vampires, remember. Real ones."

"She accepts me as a vampire. And Jagger is convinced I am one, too." I paused and looked up at my vampire boyfriend. "And I like it. Why can't *you* accept me as one?"

Alexander's smile turned into a frown. "I accept you as you are. I always have."

He turned away from me.

"I didn't mean to upset you," I said, reaching out to him. I gave him a squeeze with all my might. "I'm getting so caught up in this, I can't even think straight. You must think I'm so immature."

Alexander softened and caressed my hair.

"You know how I think of you," he said, his chocolate eyes staring into my own. He lifted my chin and kissed me tenderly.

"I don't know how much longer I can go on like this. When will we be together—just us? And not have to worry about Jagger, Luna, and Trevor?"

"How about now?" he said, suddenly bright. "I wanted you to have this." He handed me a wooden heart-shaped box that had been sitting on the window ledge.

My eyes lit up. "You are so sweet! And here I am being selfish."

I opened the box. Hanging from a silver chain was a pendant—black lips with a small vampire fang.

"It's a vampire's kiss," he said proudly.

"Alexander, it's beautiful. I'll wear it forever."

Alexander unclasped my onyx necklace and replaced it with the priceless one he had made just for me.

He gave me a long, lingering good-night kiss.

"Tell me. Would it be easier if I were a vampire?"

Just then my dad pulled into the driveway.

Alexander quickly stepped back into the shadows.

I waited for my dad to come up the front stairs. "Where did Alexander go? He was just here. I wanted to say hi."

"He had to get home before he turns into a pumpkin."

Exhausted, I walked into my darkened bedroom and switched on my *Edward Scissorhands* lamp.

I almost jumped out of my skin. Sitting on my bed, appearing more sinister than ever, was Jagger.

I let out a scream.

That only made the creepy teen smile.

"Raven? What's wrong?" my mom yelled up from downstairs.

"Nothing," I yelled down to her. "Just stubbed my toe." Then I whispered to Jagger, "What are you doing here?"

"Bats can sneak in anywhere. You should know that by now."

"I want you out of here!" I demanded.

"I won't be long. Luna had a lovely chat with you. She's very excited. She thinks she's found a new best friend."

"Well, maybe she has."

"She said you girls talked about all sorts of girly things. Boys. Hair. Vampire bites."

I caught myself in my dresser mirror's reflection and stepped back.

Jagger played with the nightstand light switch. On. Off. On. Off.

"Stop that!" I warned. Something was missing. "Where's Nightmare?"

I heard scratching coming from my computer desk file drawer.

I raced over and opened it up. "Nightmare!" I said, picking up my black kitten. "You poor girl."

"Odd," he said, leering at me. "She doesn't hiss at you."

"She doesn't hiss at Alexander either," I said, gently stroking her fur. "She has taste."

Jagger lay back on my bed, placing his red Doc Martens on my bedspread. "This is a cozy bed."

"Get your feet off of there!" I scolded, pushing his shoes off.

Jagger leaned across the bed and pulled up the comforter from the floor.

"Where is your coffin?" he asked. "Not under here."

He rose and slithered over to my closet. He slowly opened my closet door. "Not in here," he remarked. "Maybe you're hiding it under *your dress*," he said with a wicked grin.

"It's in the basement."

"Funny. I didn't see it down there."

My blood boiled. I felt enraged. Jagger had been slinking around my house with my family inside.

"It's hidden. Now get out—"

"Sure, but can you show me something?"

"The door? Or the window?" I opened the curtain and lifted the window.

Jagger remained still.

"Some of Trevor's friends said you showed up at

school. Curious, really. A vampire risking the sunlight."

"You'd believe a bunch of soccer snobs? They spread more rumors than the *National Enquirer*."

"Well, then," he said, sizing me up with his mismatched eyes, "I have noticed their penchant for gossip."

I felt a sense of relief, but only for a moment.

"At the drive-in I distinctly remember Alexander bit you on the neck. Blood dripping down your neck like a wild river, the sweet smell permeating the air. But Luna said she didn't see a wound. Maybe I could take a peek."

"You can leave. Now."

He stepped closer, his ice blue and green eyes piercing my soul.

"Show me your fangs and I'll show you mine."

"I only show Alexander," I said, inching back.

"What a waste, really." He took another step, pinning me against my computer desk. "So how do you like living this lie?"

"Lie?"

"Yes, it is a lie," he said, staring straight into my eyes. As if he were going to read my soul. "Pretending to be something you're not."

I gasped and looked away. My heart stopped. I bit my black lip.

I reached behind me, stretching my fingers across my computer desk in hopes of grabbing something to use as a weapon. At any moment Jagger was going to look into my eyes and hypnotize me and drag me back to Dullsville's cemetery. I fingered Billy Boy's two-ton encyclopedia.

"I think you enjoy being deceitful," he said, gently touching the vampire's kiss necklace. "Making believe to your family that you are still mortal."

I breathed again and released the book.

There was a knock at the door.

"I need my encyclopedia."

"Billy—go away."

"You borrowed it two months ago!"

"Billy. Billy—go away," I said sternly.

Jagger stepped back and I raced around him.

Billy Boy opened the door.

I turned around. The curtains were gently blowing. Jagger was gone.

"Is something wrong? You never call me Billy."

I closed the window, rushed over to my brother, and gave him a quick hug. "I never thought I needed to."

13

Gothic Fairy

The next evening, as I turned the corner to walk up Benson Hill, I saw a shadowy figure standing by the gate. Never one to retreat, I crept up the broken sidewalk slowly. I didn't want to be startled by Trevor or Jagger.

As I got closer, I saw a gothic fairy girl with long white-and-pink-streaked hair leaning against a tree.

"Luna—what are you doing?"

"Raven," she said, bouncing over and giving me a huge squeeze. "I thought I'd find you here."

"But I'm meeting Alexander," I said, almost apologetically.

"I know, but I thought we could chat for a few."

"I don't want to keep him . . ."

I looked up toward the Mansion. The attic window was dark.

"Well . . . maybe just a sec."

We sat on a few rocks outside the Mansion's gate.

"Trevor has a history test. I won't see him until this weekend. Jagger told me he saw you last night," she confessed.

"Did he tell you where he saw me?" I charged.

"In your bedroom."

"He can't do that again. He could scare my family."

"You did that to Trevor. You snuck into his room."

Luna had a good point. "That was different. I have a reputation."

"Jagger is a tricky one," she said with a hint of pride. "He's been teaching me so many things since I've been turned."

"Well, I hope they are good tricks," I warned.

"I love your purse," she said, touching the handle of my *Corpse Bride* clutch. "Can I see?"

"Sure." No one, not even Becky, ever got excited about my clothes or fashion accessories. I was proud to share it with her.

She placed it on her arm and modeled it. "So gloom! I love it."

"Thanks. I ordered it online. Maybe I can get you one."

"I'd kill for one," she said eagerly. "Got any candy? I gave my last piece to you yesterday."

"I should have some gum."

Luna unzipped the purse.

"Be careful, it's a mess in there," I warned.

"Wouldn't be cool any other way," she said with a smile.

I leaned back and watched the stars twinkling overhead.

Luna pulled out a pack of Gabe's Grape Gross-Out Gum.

She removed two sticks and returned the pack to my purse.

I didn't mind her rooting around. I didn't have anything to hide in there. Or did I?

"What's this?" she asked, pulling out Ruby's compact. My heart stopped.

"What do you need a compact for?" Luna asked skeptically, holding the white plastic compact and stroking the red ruby *R*.

"It's an heirloom," I said, trying to reach for it.

"An heirloom?" she wondered aloud. "It doesn't look that old."

Just then a Mustang drove up the road and stopped in front of the Mansion.

I grabbed the compact and purse and ran to the car.

"Matt! Becky! How are you guys doing?"

"Hey, Raven, what's up?" Matt asked.

"Hi, Beck," I said, smiling.

Luna inched up next to me. "Hi, Beck," she said, also grinning.

Becky's smile was strained. My normally amiable best friend looked at me with disdain.

"I thought you were hanging out with Alexander," Becky said.

"I am; I'm just on my way in."

"We just had to have a girl chat before," Luna chimed in.

I was annoyed. There was no need for Luna to try to make Becky jealous.

"I better go see Alexander now," I finally said. "I'll see you tomorrow, Becky."

"Yeah," she said.

I stepped away from the car. Luna put her arm around me and waved at Becky.

Becky politely waved back.

The Mustang headed down the windy road. Alexander had warned me about the motives of Jagger and Luna.

"Bye, Luna," I said, heading for the Mansion as she waited by the street.

This time I was the one to disappear.

14

The Invitation

The next day the usually early-bird Becky was late. I had showered, eaten, dressed, redressed, and was sitting on the front steps, my hoodie tied around my waist, writing Alexander love notes. I was ready to call the school day off when she finally drove up my driveway.

I got into her pickup, and she barely said hello.

"Where were you?" I asked. "Did you oversleep? Or get halfway to school and realize you didn't pick me up?"

Becky didn't answer but continued to drive toward school.

After a polite conversation with her responses being "uh-huhs," "sures," and head nods, I'd had enough.

"So what's up with the silent treatment?" I finally asked.

"Nothing," she said as she turned the truck onto the road that led to school.

"Aren't you feeling well?"

"I'm feeling fine."

"Then why are you mad?"

"I'm not mad," she said, and turned up the radio.

I turned the radio off. "Okay. Let me have it. What's up?"

Becky pulled into an empty spot next to the senior parking lot and turned off the engine.

"It just seems odd," she began softly. "You left Hatsy's as soon as our order arrived. Then shortly afterward Jagger and Luna left too. I heard you hung out with Luna at the park. And it was like you were best buds last night outside the Mansion."

"She's not my best bud."

"I know you have way much more in common with her," she continued. "The gothic clothes. The dark music. She probably loves vampires, too."

"Is that what this is about?"

If there was anything worse than the jealousy between sweethearts, it was the threat of a new best friend.

"You've found someone more like you," she said as she got out of the truck.

"I don't want someone more like me," I said as we walked toward school. "I want someone just like you."

In all the years Becky and I'd been friends, she never judged the clothes I wore or the music I listened to. Becky never asked me to be anything but myself.

"You want to know the truth?" I asked.

"Of course."

"You are right, I owe you that." Becky and I went into the side entrance and snuck underneath the staircase. "All right, here goes."

Becky looked anxious, as if I were going to hit her with "Yes, I've found a new best friend. Good riddance."

"This is top secret stuff," I began.

"Go on."

"All right." I took a deep breath. "Here goes. Luna and Jagger are vampires," I began in a whisper, "and they are trying to turn Trevor into one. We left Hatsy's because Alexander and I were trying to remove their coffins from Henry's treehouse, forcing them back to Romania." I sighed, feeling a sense of relief at finally being able to share my darkest secrets with my best friend.

Becky studied me. Then she burst out laughing. "You expect me to believe that?"

"Well—"

"I guess it was better than saying Luna and Jagger are friends of Alexander's from Romania," she said, "and you felt obligated to help out."

"Yeah," I lied. "Sweet, but anticlimactic."

The two of us laughed.

"I'm sorry. I just got a little jealous," she said.

"I'm sorry I made you feel that way. We'll always be best friends."

"Forever," she confirmed.

"For eternity," I added with a smile.

I was shoving my notebooks in my locker, which was filled with pictures of Marilyn Manson, Slipknot, and HIM, and stickers of black roses, spiders, and coffins, when I noticed Trevor passing out red flyers to the soccer snobs and cheerleaders. He was also taking pictures of them with his camera phone.

I wasn't aware Trevor had returned to school. I stepped back into a doorway so Trevor wouldn't spot me.

The bell rang and the crowds began to disperse.

A red flyer fell out of the goalie's notebook as he stepped into a biology classroom. Curious, I grabbed it. In black letters the flyer read:

Graveyard Gala
Covenant Ceremony
-Dare to dance among the dead-

Date: This Saturday
Time: Sunset
Attire: Nightmarish costume

Be there or be dead

I'd spent a whole lifetime partying alone at Dullsville's cemetery. Now all of Dullsville High was going to be at my hideout. And I wasn't even invited?

"Sticking your nose where it doesn't belong, Monster Girl?" I heard Trevor say from behind me.

"What's this?" I asked, shoving the flyer in his face.

"Jagger's hosting a party. It'll be the blowout of the year! I'm coming as the Grim Reaper. You're lucky. If you were invited, you could just come as yourself."

I gave Trevor a snarled look.

"Who is going to have a covenant ceremony?"

"Luna and I will be king and queen of the covenant. Like a medieval prom, in ominous costumes. It's a sexy Romanian ceremony I'm sure you've never heard of. When I accept the honor, Luna's going to kiss me in front of the whole school. It's going to be a total freakfest. But since you're not on the guest list," he continued, "you'll have to read about it in the school newspaper."

He grabbed the flyer out of my hand as a cheerleader and a soccer snob stepped in front of me.

Just then Trevor aimed his cell phone at them and a flash illuminated the hallway, momentarily blinding me.

When my eyes finally adjusted, Trevor and his cohorts disappeared into the crowd of students.

I stood in the hallway, motionless, surrounded by the sounds of closing lockers and classroom doors.

This had been Jagger's plan all along! The only way he could lure someone as conservative as Trevor to the sacred ground of a cemetery was the promise of a monster-size party and a never-ending lip-lock. The already pompous soccer snob would be sealing the deal with the gorgeous "new hottie" in front of the whole school. Trevor just didn't realize the deal would last an eternity.

"Raven," I heard Becky call from behind.

Becky and Matt pushed through the crowd of students and caught up to me.

"Did you hear about the Graveyard Gala?" she asked. "Seems like you would be the one handing out invites, not Trevor."

"I know. And to top it off, I'm not even invited. Not like I've ever been on the A-list before, but this is at a cemetery. My dream party!"

"I thought you would freak out!"

"Since you told Trevor to hit the road, the three of us are probably the only ones not invited."

Then I spotted a red flyer poking out of Matt's algebra textbook.

"You were on the guest list?" I asked, horrified.

"The whole soccer team is invited," Matt said.

"But you're not going, are you?" I asked.

"I have to," Matt confessed. "I don't want to be the only one in the locker room who wimped out."

"And you?" I said, turning to my best friend.

"Matt needs a date," she said apologetically.

I felt betrayed. Everyone at Dullsville High was going but me. Even Becky. More important, though, I was worried about Becky—I didn't want my best friend on sacred ground with vampires.

"Well, Becky, you can't go," I said, sounding like her parent. "Cemeteries make you nervous."

"I'll be there to protect her from any wayward ghosts," Matt said, putting his arm around my smiling friend.

Then I remembered the cemetery's caretaker and his dog. "Old Jim will be there with his Great Dane, Luke," I warned Becky.

"There won't be trouble," Matt said. "Trevor has assured everyone that on Saturday nights Old Jim has a barstool with his name on it at Lefty's Tavern."

"Promise me you'll come," Becky pleaded. "I'd feel better if you were there, too."

"You thought I wouldn't be there? And miss the chance to crash a party?" I said, opening a classroom door. "Only in my nightmares!"

I waited impatiently at the Mansion's front door as the sun fell into the horizon. Hues of lilac, lavender, fuchsia, and pink brushed across the sky. I wished I could share it with Alexander.

Soon I heard the Mansion locks opening and saw the iron doorknob turn. Alexander, handsomely dressed in a black-and-gray pinstripe silk shirt, black dress pants, and silver-flamed Gibsons greeted me.

"You look gorgeous," I complimented, stepping inside. "I've got major news!"

"So do I," Alexander said quickly. He gave me a sweet kiss on the cheek and closed the door behind me.

A delicious smell of grilled steak permeated the entranceway.

"Me first," I began, excited.

Jameson hurried out from the kitchen carrying a serving

tray of seasoned red potatoes. He placed it on the dining-room table, which was set for four.

"Hello, Miss Raven," Jameson said brightly, greeting me. "Allow me to take your jacket."

Confused, I reluctantly unzipped my black Emily the Strange sweatshirt hoodie.

"Everything is ready," Creepy Man said, taking my hoodie and hanging it in the hallway closet. "All we need is the guest of honor."

"What's going on?" I asked. "We need to talk—"

"Jameson invited Ruby to join us for dinner."

"Us?"

Alexander nodded.

"What a nice surprise," I said with a cheesy grin.

Normally I would have been ecstatic to be included in a dinner party at the Mansion with Alexander, the creepy butler, and the fabulous Ruby White. But we didn't have time for pleasantries and pastries when we had to think of a new plan to foil Jagger and Luna.

"I want everything to be perfect," Jameson said, straightening the black lace tablecloth. "I thought it would be easier if Miss Raven were here too. Miss Ruby might feel more comfortable in the Mansion."

"I don't mean to be rude," I whispered to Alexander as Jameson headed back to the kitchen.

"I know, it's a surprise to me, too. I barely had enough time to get you these," he interrupted.

Alexander picked up a pewter vase with three black roses and handed it to me.

I melted. I looked into his caring midnight eyes. For a moment I forgot about any other vampires except for mine.

"We have to talk," I said. "Jagger is—"

Just then there was a knock at the Mansion door.

Jameson burst out of the kitchen holding an elegantly wrapped white orchid and headed for the door. "I'll get it; you two settle in. . . ."

I couldn't settle anything. My heart was racing. My mind was restless. My stomach was doing flip-flops.

Jameson opened the front door. Ruby stepped inside, dressed in white pleated dress pants, a tailored cotton-colored blazer with a white lingerie top, and cream Prada pumps. She was clutching a Coach bag and a bottle of white wine.

Ruby's eyes lit up when she saw Jameson holding the flower. She nervously giggled as the odd couple exchanged the orchid and the aging Chardonnay.

"A white orchid!" she exclaimed. "Jameson, you didn't have to go to all the trouble," she said, her voice melting.

"A rare flower for someone as rare as you . . . ," the skinny butler complimented.

Ruby's eyes lit up and she gave him a kiss on the cheek. Creepy Man's deadly complexion turned bright cherry red.

"Hello, Raven," she said, giving me a quick hug. "I'm glad I get to see you again so soon."

"I know, isn't this wonderful?" I agreed with a Cheshire cat grin.

"Thank you, Alexander, for having me over," Ruby

continued. "I've always wanted to see the Mansion from the inside."

"Jameson can give you the grand tour," Alexander hinted so we could get a chance to talk.

"After dessert," Jameson said.

"I left something upstairs, Raven—," Alexander began.

"It will have to wait," Jameson ordered. "Dinner is served."

Alexander and I had no choice but to follow Ruby and Jameson into the dining room. Several candelabrum and silver candlesticks gently lit the darkened room, revealing a long oak table covered with a black lace tablecloth. Antique china, pewter goblets, and ancient silver utensils were set in front of each chair. Crystal glasses were filled with water. A few cobwebs still hung from the corners of the gigantic ceiling. The heavy red velvet drapes seemed to have been hanging there since the Mansion was built.

Ruby must have felt as if she were going to have dinner with the Munsters.

Jameson stood at the head of the table and offered an antique chair for Ruby while Alexander pulled out the adjacent chair for me.

I could get used to this. I felt like I was at a five-star restaurant. Normally at home, Billy Boy and I were on top of each other, fighting for the chair by the TV.

Alexander sat across from me. With the Frankenstein-size oak table and a huge white flowered centerpiece between us, it would be impossible to whisper my findings to him now.

Jameson uncorked Ruby's bottle and began to fill her goblet. I could see his hands shake as he tried not to spill any wine on her perfectly pressed ultraswank white outfit.

Alexander grabbed a red bottle sitting on a serving cart next to him and poured red liquid into his glass.

Ruby signaled Jameson to stop pouring her wine. "I didn't know you were serving steak. You can save this bottle for another time," she offered. "I'll just have what Alexander's drinking."

Alexander and Jameson paused, gravely glancing at each other.

"Uh . . . I think you'd prefer your Chardonnay," Alexander suggested.

Jameson grinned a toothy grin. "Alexander's on a strict vitamin regimen. That's his special drink."

"It's like drinking blood," I whispered, rolling my eyes.

Ruby wrinkled her forehead. "Then I'll stick with what I have," Ruby said.

We began to drink our various libations while Jameson kindly placed well-done steaks in front of Ruby and me. Jameson then set a plate before Alexander—an almost rare filet, the meat oozing blood-red juice.

As Alexander, Jameson, and I began to eat our dinners, Ruby intently watched Alexander eat his juicy steak like she was watching a juggler swallow fire.

"That's how they eat steak in Romania," I whispered.

"I've been to Romania," she quietly responded. "I guess I must have visited a different region."

I glanced at Alexander, who was eating quickly. A

nervous Jameson barely touched his food. Ruby ate slowly, savoring her dinner.

We made unbearable small talk and complimented our chef on the meal.

The candles flickered. Shadows danced about the room. The wind howled through the trees. With the four of us sitting around the table, I felt at any moment we were going to hold hands and perform a seance. All that was missing was the Ouija board.

The wax slowly dripped from the candlesticks. *Drip. Drip. Drip.* Like the ticking of a grandfather clock. This evening could go on forever.

"This Mansion is very . . . historic," Ruby said, trying to find a polite word. "Have you seen any ghosts?"

"Just my grandmother," Alexander said.

Ruby choked on her wine. "Excuse me?"

"This house used to belong to Alexander's grandmother," Jameson tried to explain. "But we never—"

"So you've really seen her?" I asked eagerly.

"She wanders through the halls at night," Alexander said in a low voice. "In fact . . . she's standing right behind you!"

I laughed, but Ruby jumped up from her seat as if she'd just seen the ghost herself.

Alexander and Jameson immediately rose from their chairs.

"I didn't mean to frighten you," Alexander apologized.

"Are you all right?" Jameson asked, offering her water. "Alexander gets these ideas. . . ."

Ruby was embarrassed. "I'm just not used to being in a house that's—"

"Haunted?" I asked.

"Large," she corrected. "And dark; I usually have all the lights on," she said with a forced laugh.

"We can light more candles," Alexander offered.

"Please. Sit, sit. And not another word," she said.

Jameson slowly returned to his seat and we continued eating our dinners. "So, Miss Raven, anything unusual happen at school?" he asked, politely trying to redirect the conversation.

"Other than that I showed up?"

My dinner mates laughed as if grateful for some comic relief.

"Well, a guy at school was talking about sneaking into the cemetery."

"The cemetery? That sounds like something you'd do," Ruby said with a laugh.

"He's not just sneaking in," I said, and then turned to Alexander. "He's going there on a date."

"Who would take a date to the cemetery?" Ruby asked, horrified.

Then Ruby eyeballed me and the other gloom-and-doom diners dressed in black around her.

We all stared back.

"Not me," I burst out.

"I wouldn't be caught dead," Alexander admitted.

"Poor taste!" Jameson proclaimed.

We quickly returned to our meals.

"Miss Raven, maybe I should have asked if you discussed anything *usual*," Jameson said nervously.

I politely laughed. But I had more info I had to share.

"Did I mention he's planning to kiss his girlfriend next to a coffin?" I said to Alexander.

Ruby cleared her throat.

"More water?" Jameson asked, clearly worried we were upsetting his guest of honor.

"I'm fine," she answered.

Alexander stared off behind Ruby and started pointing.

"Now are you going to tell me you see a ghost behind me?" she asked.

Alexander shook his head. "It's worse."

"I'm not falling for your tricks again," she said with a grin.

"Don't move," Alexander said, putting his napkin on the table.

Ruby slowly turned around. Hanging from the red velvet curtain right above her was a bat.

She wasn't even fazed. "I bet it's made out of rubber," she said, and got up.

Jameson called out, "Miss Ruby!"

My eyes bulged. Alexander rose.

"I'll show you," she said confidently.

Just then Ruby reached for the bat. All at once, it spread its wings wide and took off.

Ruby let out a bloodcurdling scream so loud I had to cover my ears.

The disgruntled bat flew around the room as Ruby hid

behind me, continuing to shriek.

"Does it have blue and green eyes?" I asked, shielding her.

"Who cares about its eye color!" she yelled.

Alexander tried to grab the bat, but it only flew higher.

"I'm going to faint!" she hollered. "I'm really going to faint."

Jameson and I helped a trembling Ruby away from the dining room and into the sitting room.

"Is it in my hair?" she asked, now sitting in a green Victorian chair.

"No," I reassured her.

"Where did it go?"

"It's in the other room. Alexander is going to catch him."

"Are there more?" she asked, her shaking hands covering her head.

"No, they live in the attic tower, far away from this room." Jameson tried to comfort his date with a glass of water. "I wonder how he got down here."

"I almost touched it!" she exclaimed. "I almost touched a rat with wings!"

Alexander came into the room holding a balled up linen napkin.

"He's completely harmless, see?" Alexander asked, innocently opening the napkin. Two beady black eyes stared back at us.

Ruby let out another bloodcurdling scream.

"Please take it away!" a haggard Jameson pleaded.

"Aww, he's cute," I said as Alexander walked out to the kitchen to set it free.

"I guess this means you're not staying for dessert," Jameson said.

"I'm stuffed, really," Ruby said, still in shock. "Besides, I have to open the office tomorrow." She rose from her seat.

"I understand," Jameson responded, his head hung low. He retrieved Ruby's purse and the flower from the hallway table and handed them to her.

"Thank you," she said quickly. "The orchid is beautiful. The dinner was delicious." Still shaken, Ruby headed for the door.

"The evening didn't go as I had planned," Jameson confessed sorrowfully, following her. "You are used to the finer things, Miss Ruby. I was wrong to think—"

"That's okay," she said softly. "I understand."

I knew Jameson had invited Alexander and me to dinner to make Ruby more comfortable. Instead we spent the whole evening talking about cemeteries and coffins. I felt awful.

"Please don't blame Jameson," I begged. "It's my fault Alexander and I talked about creepy things and spooked you. Jameson is a perfect gentleman."

"It's nobody's fault," she reassured. "I guess we were all a bit nervous."

"Then how about dinner tomorrow night?" I suggested.

"Well . . . ," Ruby began hesitantly.

"At a bright, trendy restaurant with upbeat music?" I continued.

"That might be nice," she relented.

"Just the two of you," I said.

"Just the two of us," Jameson eagerly agreed.

"And no mention of coffins, ghosts, or flying bats," I added.

"Well . . . it's a date," Ruby concurred with a smile.

Jameson opened the door for Ruby. He turned back to me and smiled a skinny-toothed smile and winked.

"From now on," I overheard him say to Ruby as he walked her to her car, "the only bats you'll see is when I invite you to a baseball game."

The Grim Plan

Alexander and I grabbed the savory desserts Jameson had made—placinta, fried sweet dough filled with chocolate—and headed up to the privacy of his attic room. "Trevor is taking Luna to the cemetery?" Alexander immediately asked, shutting the door.

"Jagger is planning a Graveyard Gala on Saturday night," I blurted out as we sat with our placintas on his mattress. "It's a gothic costume party with the highlight of the evening being a covenant ceremony. Instead of luring Trevor to sacred ground alone," I started, too excited to dive into my treat, "Jagger is inviting Dullsville High. Luna is going to bite Trevor in front of everyone—only no one will know what's going to happen, not even Trevor himself."

"How will he not know what's going on?"

"Trevor thinks he's going to be kissed by Luna, not bitten."

"They are going to be wearing costumes, right?" Alexander asked.

"Yes, Trevor is going as the Grim Reaper. It will be dark and all the partygoers will be wearing masks. While they drink, dance, and make out, Luna will finally have her long-awaited covenant ceremony. No one will know what is really happening."

"Then we have to stop Trevor from going," Alexander said, picking at his dessert.

"He wouldn't miss this for the world. He will be the star of the show."

"Then we have to tell him what the ceremony really is."

"He'll never believe me. Besides, they've already passed out flyers. With all of Dullsville High on sacred ground, Luna could easily take someone else."

"Then she'll have to believe she is with Trevor."

"Believe? Who will she really be with?"

"Me. I'll be dressed as the Grim Reaper, too. I'll be covered from head to toe. Luna won't know the difference."

"But you told me if a vampire takes another on sacred ground, then they are theirs for eternity. I don't want her to bite you and then I lose you forever."

"I don't either," he said, and squeezed my hand. "But when I take off my hood, she'll know Trevor has gone."

"Where will he be?"

"Safe, off sacred ground. At some point you'll have to distract him and lead him out of the cemetery," Alexander explained.

"I'm used to distracting people, just not on purpose. I hope everything goes smoothly. The whole school will be on sacred ground with two vengeful vampires."

"Bring some garlic just in case, and I'll take my antidote."

"I don't want to give you another shot," I said.

"Hopefully, you won't have to."

Shortly after sunset Alexander and I walked up the lonely road that led to Dullsville's cemetery. Although I wasn't actually a vampire, I felt like I was. I'd convinced twin vampires I was as undead as they were, I was on the arm of the most handsome of vampires, and I was going to party with a bunch of other ghouls. I was happy to be me—vampire or not.

I was dolled up as Elvira, in a long black dress with shredded spidery sleeves and a slit racing up my leg, exposing black mesh tights. Long black plastic fingernails flashed from my pale fingertips. My jet black hair was teased up like a fountain, the ends falling down over my shoulders. I revealed as much cleavage as I could manage to squeeze out in a recently purchased push-up bra. I'd also bought Alexander the last Grim Reaper costume left over from Halloween merch at Jack's department store. It was a black hooded costume with a skeleton mask and a plastic scythe.

"You look stellar," Alexander said, his midnight eyes sparkling as we walked together. "I can't believe I'm with you."

It was a dream come true for me to be strolling down the street holding the bony skeleton hand of the Grim Reaper—and even doubly dreamy that it was really my vampire boyfriend.

Cars lined the street leading up to the cemetery. At the far end of the road, parked alongside a Dumpster, I saw Jagger's hearse.

I was as excited as I was nervous to implement our plan.

When we turned the corner to the cemetery, Alexander said, "I brought my antidote. Did you bring your garlic?"

I stopped dead in my tracks. "I knew I forgot something!" I exclaimed. "It's in my night stand. We have to go home," I pleaded.

"We don't have time," Alexander warned. "The ceremony could be over by the time we'd return."

We reached the iron gate and climbed over the fence. When we were safely on the cemetery ground, I saw a sight I'd never seen before—and one thing we hadn't planned on. The graveyard was filled with Grim Reapers.

"How will we ever find Trevor now?" I asked. "It will take forever!"

My heart sank as I stepped over cans of soda littering

the graveyard. I bent down to pick up an empty can.

"We don't have time for that now," Alexander said again. "If we don't get to Trevor in time, the caretaker and the rest of Dullsville will have to worry about more than empty cans and bottles."

We passed a Grim Reaper who was talking to a werewolf. "Trevor?" I asked, but the Angel of Death shook his head.

We passed ghosts and ghouls dancing and drinking among the tombstones.

Sitting on a wooden bench was a familiar witch holding hands with Michael Myers.

"You are quite the spooky pair," I said.

"Raven," the witch said as the two rose. "I'm so glad you came."

"Wow, that is some dress," Matt said from underneath his hockey mask. "Maybe you could get a costume like that for Becky."

My best friend turned devil red.

"This party is great," Matt continued. "The whole school is here."

"We're looking for Trevor. Have you seen him?" I asked.

"No. Word has it that he's going to be in some medieval ceremony by the tombs in just a few minutes."

Then I noticed Luna a few yards ahead, placing a flower at the base of Alexander's grandmother's monument.

"Do me a favor; if things get weird, will you go

home?" I whispered to Becky.

"We are partying in a cemetery," she said. "Things are *already* weird."

I gave Becky a quick hug, and Alexander and I headed for the monument.

Luna stood up. She was beautiful—like a gothic prom fairy. She glowed in a ghostly white tattered prom dress, with a pink wrist carnation and combat boots. Her soft hair flowed over her shoulders like a waterfall; her frost white complexion, highlighted by heavy indigo eye shadow and pale pink lip gloss, glistened softly.

"Trevor said you weren't coming," Luna exclaimed, bouncing over to us like a butterfly. "But I knew you'd come."

"We weren't invited," I said, "but I wouldn't let that stop me. I wouldn't want to miss your covenant ceremony for the world."

"Look at what you missed in Romania," she said proudly to Alexander. She was beautiful as she giggled and did a flirty spin, modeling her tattered dress for him.

Alexander wasn't amused.

"Where's Trevor?" he asked. "Is he getting cold feet?"

"No, but he thinks I have his cold. When we met here tonight, I started to feel ill. Sweet, really. A vampire with a cold," she said with a grin. "So he went to his car to get me cough drops. He's dressed as the Grim Reaper," she remarked in a spooky voice.

"I know," I said. "So is everyone else."

"Stay here with me," Luna begged, taking my hand.

"We'd better find Trevor," I told her. "We need to start the ceremony before the cops get wind of this party."

She relaxed her grip. "You're right," she said. "Please hurry."

"Alexander, would you stay with me?" she asked sweetly.

I grabbed my boyfriend's arm. "Alexander has to come with me. I'll need him to help me find Trevor."

"Man, she really must still like you," I said as we walked past the tombs. "I had to pry her bony fingers off of you."

Alexander and I headed for Trevor, but we didn't know where to begin. The graveyard was full of Angels of Death.

We saw two Grim Reapers playing spin the bottle with a few cheerleaders dressed as red devils.

"Trevor?"

"Over there," one said, pointing her pitchfork toward the front of the cemetery.

"I'll wait a few minutes and double back as Trevor," Alexander said. "Make sure he gets out of the cemetery grounds. And I want you to stay away, too."

"So you can stand up there on sacred ground alone with two vampires?"

"I can't protect both me *and* you." Alexander lifted his skeleton mask from his face.

His charcoal eyes sparkled. He leaned in and kissed me.

"I'm going to double back now," he said, replacing his mask.

I waited for a moment and watched as the man of my dreams confidently, and selflessly, set forth on our mission.

"Trevor!" I called as I ran through the cemetery.

I caught up with one reaper.

"Trevor?"

"No, but I'm sure he's around," a girl's voice mumbled.

I raced toward the front gate. I looked for any Grim Reaper carrying cough drops.

Then I wondered, maybe Luna was making up the story. Maybe Trevor had been at the ceremony the whole time.

"Trevor?" I asked desperately to a Grim Reaper heading straight for me.

"Yes, Monster Girl?" He crossed his arms, his heavy, billowy sleeves hanging down.

My eyes lit up. Now that I had Trevor, I had to get him off sacred ground.

"I finally found you!"

A stone-cold skeleton mask stared back at me.

"Uh . . . Luna is still not feeling well," I rambled. "Allow me to escort you to get her cough drops."

I took his white skeleton hand and tried to lead him toward the gate.

The Angel of Death didn't follow.

Instead he held up a pack of vitamin C with his bony hand. He turned away from me and headed for the ceremony.

I raced after him.

"I've been trying to tell you," I began. "Luna isn't the girl you think she is. She's not some nice straight-A cheerleader. She's going to double-cross you."

He shook his head and walked on.

"Trevor. You can't!"

When I caught up to him, I grabbed the sleeve of his costume. With a quick jerk, he pulled his arm away.

I was on a mission, impossible as it might be. I grabbed his plastic scythe, but he continued to walk on.

I raced ahead, blocking his way with the scythe.

"Wait," I whispered, out of breath. "Please, before you go any further. You were the one who tried to convince the town about the Sterlings. Why don't you see Alexander in the daylight? Why did Luna and Jagger invite you to a cemetery? You were right all along. They weren't rumors. It was all because they *are* vampires."

I stared at his fixed skeleton face. He waved his skeleton hand and pushed his way past me. I followed him back to the site of the covenant ceremony.

A crowd of aliens had already gathered in front of the tomb. Ghosts and witches were everywhere, standing, sitting, leaning.

In front of the tombs was a coffin with a lit candelabra. Alexander, passing as Trevor in his Grim Reaper costume, was waiting on one side with a pewter goblet.

With all my might, I grabbed the arm of the Angel of Death standing next to me. "Don't go," I begged. "Please. Alexander is up there, trying to divert their vicious plan. Watch what happens, and if I'm wrong then *I'll* kiss you right here in front of the whole school!" I blurted out.

He stopped and looked at me for a few long seconds.

My heart ceased. I realized what I had just committed

to. Our plan had better work. I held all our lives *and* my mouth at stake here.

We hid behind some partygoers, standing a few feet from Alexander.

Then I saw Luna walking up the cemetery aisle, gravestones on either side of her, a dead bouquet in her hand.

Becky and Matt snuck in next to me.

"This is cool. It's like a creepy gothic wedding," the friendly witch said. "Maybe we can be next," she teased Matt.

I yanked the Angel of Death back. "I've tried to tell you all along," I said in a whisper. "You were right about the Sterlings. They are vampires. And so are Luna and Jagger. Please believe me. Before it's too late."

Alexander drank from the goblet.

Luna reached my Grim Reaper and drank from the goblet too. Then she said something inaudible.

"What did she say?" Becky asked.

"'To the king and queen of the graveyard,'" Matt repeated.

Luna turned to Alexander. She leaned in to him.

I gasped. The crowd cheered.

"No!" I shouted, lunging forward, but a cadaverous hand stopped me.

I turned to see the Angel of Death behind me.

Just then Alexander grabbed Luna's shoulders and held her at arm's length.

"What are you doing? Don't push me away!"

"Kiss her! Kiss her!" the crowd chanted.

But Alexander kept the vampiress at bay with one hand. He pulled off his reaper's hood.

"I'm not Trevor!" Alexander exclaimed. "Now you can stop your games."

"Why is Alexander there?" Matt said to Becky. "What's going on?"

Luna glared at my true love. She started to laugh. "It was never Trevor I wanted here. It was you!"

Alexander stepped back, confused. Luna grabbed his oversized sleeve. "Now I don't have to wait for you to take me. I can take *you*!"

I lunged forward, but the Angel of Death squeezed my shoulder.

"Get off!" I ordered.

Thank goodness Alexander was stronger than the waifish Luna. He held his scythe in one hand and the writhing vampiress at bay with the other.

On the far side of Luna a Grim Reaper pushed through the crowd toward the struggling vampires.

"Luna, what are you doing?" he yelled. "This wasn't the plan. You are not supposed to be with Alexander!"

The crowd cheered, "Fight! Fight!"

Alexander began to cough, letting go of Luna.

"This is who I've always wanted," Luna defended. "Alexander is who I've waited my life for." She coughed, too, and clung to the side of the coffin.

The hooded reaper yanked off his shroud. Blond hair flung down over his face. It wasn't Jagger. Standing in between Luna and Alexander was Trevor Mitchell.

I stepped back, shocked. If Trevor, Luna, and Alexander were struggling by the coffin, whose hand was on me?

I inched away and tried to release my hand. The Angel of Death only squeezed harder. Then he pulled me a few feet away from the ceremony.

I turned and tore off the reaper's black hood. Blue and green eyes stared back at me. It was Jagger.

"You aren't going anywhere, Monster Girl," he said with a seductive, menacing voice.

My vampire boyfriend grew red with rage as he saw Jagger by my side on sacred ground. "Raven!" Alexander called. He started to wheeze and began to stagger toward us.

Trevor glanced over, shocked and confused.

I tried to pull my hand away, but Jagger tightened his grip and started to cough.

Alexander was doubling over but was determined to reach me. "Jagger, let her go!" he warned.

With every step Alexander took forward, Jagger took one back.

The confused crowd started cheering. Some shouted, "Kiss! Kiss!" while others yelled, "Fight! Fight!"

Luna recoiled from the confused and rejected Trevor, her pasty complexion turning even paler.

Jagger's eyes began to tear. His breathing became labored.

What could be making all the vampires ill?

Then it hit me. The vampires began to get sick when Trevor showed up.

"What's wrong with Alexander?" I heard Becky ask Matt.

"Trevor's taken garlic pills!" I shouted to Alexander. "Take your antidote," I said, pointing to my leg.

Alexander wheezed but reached underneath his cloak and pulled out his serum. Becky and Matt ran to his side while Alexander jammed the shot into his leg.

Jagger backed up, pulling me farther away from the crowd.

"Get off of me," I said wedging my boot between us.

"Not so fast," he said with hypnotic eyes. "Alexander made a fool of our family in Romania, and you were planning to do it again tonight?"

"Let me go—"

"Where's your vampire bite, Raven?" he whispered.

"I told you, I can't show you."

"You were very convincing. Until Luna discovered a compact mirror in your purse. You led her on; you led us both on."

"I did not!"

"Then why aren't you wheezing now? And most important, what's this?" He reached underneath his cloak and pulled out a cell phone. He flipped the phone open and held it before me—a picture of a cheerleader and a soccer snob at school, taken by Trevor. And standing in back of them was a mortal Raven, reflecting back for all vampires to see.

"You have a cunning and crafty nature. You turned out to be more of a vampire than Alexander," Jagger said flatly.

Alexander pushed through the crowd toward us. Trevor followed close behind.

"What is Jagger doing with Raven?" Trevor asked.

"Back off!" Jagger shouted. "You will not make a fool of my family anymore."

"What's he talking about?" Trevor said, now standing by Alexander.

"Get back!" Jagger shouted to Trevor, coughing as he spoke. "You think you have it all with your sports and your pretty girls. But you were never like us and could never be good enough for my sister."

"You planned this all along?" Trevor asked Jagger. "Raven was right, trying to warn me about you for days. Why? Just because I was different?"

Trevor had picked on me all my life because I was the outsider. Now he faced the same ridicule.

"Go back to your soccer field," Jagger said. "This game is way out of your league."

I stared at my mortal nemesis, whose face was growing red with rage. For the first time in sixteen years, Trevor Mitchell had finally met a bigger bully than himself.

Trevor looked at Jagger as if he were a soccer ball that needed to be kicked into the opponent's goal.

"Get off," I said to Jagger. "You're hurting me!"

Alexander's eyes turned red. "Jagger. You have one second to let her go! Otherwise, it's all over!"

Jagger's grip was so hard around my wrist I couldn't move.

"It'll feel like a pin prick," he said to me in a seductive

voice. He gently stroked my hair away from my shoulders. He leaned toward me and flashed his fangs.

"No!" I cried.

And the world went black.

18

Cryptic Kryptonite

I awoke, lying flat on my back on the grass, the stars twinkling above me.

"Raven?" Becky asked, her hand outstretched. "Are you okay?

My world was dizzy. I grabbed my neck. "Am I a . . . ?" I asked.

Becky helped me up. "I thought you were kidding when you said they were vampires. I think that Jagger guy really believed he was. He tried to bite you."

I felt my neck for wounds.

Suddenly the memory started to come back. I never thought it would happen. My nemesis and the love of my life, enraged for different reasons, both staring straight at me.

I had spent the last few days trying to save Trevor from the clutches of a vampire and now he, alongside

Alexander, unknowingly saved me.

The impact of their tackling Jagger had sent me flying to the ground.

Becky and I now raced the few yards to the tombs, where a huge crowd had gathered. Alexander was standing over Jagger, who was coughing and wheezing. Luna was leaning against the covenant coffin.

Trevor had no idea that the garlic tablet was making them vulnerable. He thought it was his bravado.

The soccer snobs encircled Jagger and Luna.

Matt and Becky stayed by my side. "Alexander's deathly allergic to garlic," I said.

"It looks like Jagger and Luna are, too," Becky remarked. "That and being pummeled by Alexander and Trevor."

"I told Trevor the gelcap was an aphrodisiac," I proudly whispered when I reached Alexander.

"Apparently he told his friends, too," he said softly with a smile. "The entire soccer team must have taken them."

Alexander turned to Jagger and Luna. "It's time you return to Romania. For good."

"Yeah, go back to Romania, you freaks!" Trevor said, balling up his fists.

I put my arm around Alexander's waist and held him close.

Then I turned to Trevor.

"I guess you are the school bully again," I complimented.

Just then a dog started barking, distracting everyone. We all turned around.

"What's going on here?" Old Jim, the caretaker, called, holding a flashlight toward us.

Ghosts and goblins started to jump the fence. Werewolves and witches hid behind tombstones. The soccer snobs took off around the shed. Becky and Matt raced up the cemetery aisle.

"What's with all these cans?" Old Jim scolded. "I'm going to call the police!"

Alexander, Trevor, and I turned back to the coffin.

All that remained was the flickering candelabra.

Jagger and Luna were gone.

19

B ack at Alexander's attic room, after weeks of adventures with the twin vampires behind us, Alexander and I finally had a chance to be alone and chill.

I had a lot of time to make up for in the lip-action department. We cuddled and kissed in his comfy chair until I thought my heart would explode out of my chest. He nibbled playfully on my neck, and I wondered if it was hard to resist my mortal self.

"Anytime you are ready," I offered. "The cemetery is only a few miles away."

"I like you just the way you are," he said, and brushed a few strands of hair from my face. "You know that."

"But you may like me better," I teased.

He began tickling me, and I cried out in laughter. I leaned back and accidentally kicked something hard against the wall.

It was the door handle to his hidden attic room.

I was immediately brought back into the reality of the situation.

"Just for a minute?" I pleaded.

Alexander hesitated.

"After all I've been through. All we've been through. It would mean the world to me," I added.

Alexander paused. His midnight eyes could not mask the dark conflict that he was trying to conquer in his soul. After a moment he rose from the chair and offered me his hand.

Exhilaration rushed through me like I was Veruca Salt about to step into Willy Wonka's chocolate factory.

Alexander pulled out a skeleton key from his pocket, pushed away the comfy chair, and unlocked the secret door.

He slowly opened the entranceway into his cryptic world.

There, as I'd seen a few days earlier, a secret in the shape of a casket—a simple black open coffin with dirt haphazardly sprinkled around it. Next to it there was a wooden table with an unlit half-melted candle and a small, softly painted portrait of me.

I walked inside the room. Alexander followed me and lit the candelabra. The room was sparse—void of a decorative soccer headboard like Trevor's or hanging posters of sports teams like Billy Boy's.

I peered into his coffin: black sheets, a black pillow, and a rumpled blanket.

"I love it. You don't even make your coffin. Just like any teen."

I looked into his lonely eyes, which now sparkled.

Then I noticed something silver lying on the pillow, catching the candlelight. I leaned over and picked it up. It was my black onyx necklace that Alexander had replaced with the vampire's kiss one he'd made for me.

My heart melted as I held it in my hand.

"I sleep better knowing I have a part of you close to me."

No one had ever meant so much to me as Alexander. For my whole life, I'd suffered as an outsider. The fact that because of me he, too, felt less alone in his world was almost too much for this dreamy goth girl to bear.

Tears welled up in my eyes.

"May I?" I asked, motioning to the coffin.

Alexander's forehead wrinkled, then a smile overcame his face as if he were relieved to finally share a piece of him he had to keep private from the world.

I unlaced my boots and held on to the attic door as Alexander helped me yank them off. He held my hand as I stepped into his coffin. The mattress was soft against my socks. I lay back, and pulled the cozy black duvet over me.

The candelabra gently lit the room and shadows danced around like tiny vampire bats. I smelled the sweet scent of Drakar on the pillow.

The casket was small and claustrophobic. The sides of the coffin entombed me. I felt like one of the undead.

"This is so cool!" I shrieked.

I smiled up at my boyfriend as he gazed down at me with pride.

"I'm ready."

"I don't think—"

"But I have to . . . I need to know what it's like."

A small handle had been nailed inside the lid with a dangling chain.

I reached up and grabbed the chain.

I took a deep breath. I gently pulled the chain toward me. The heavy lid began to lower slowly. Alexander's smiling face began to disappear from view. Then his shoulders, his AFI T-shirt. Finally all I saw was his handcuff belt buckle. Light in the coffin gradually turned to thick black darkness until I couldn't even see the chain I was pulling; then my own hand disappeared.

I felt as if I were being buried alive.

The coffin lid lifted open and a blast of light hit me.

"Alexander—" I could hear a faint voice call from the other room.

I squinted and tried to adjust to the candlelight as I sat up.

Alexander held out his hand and pulled me out.

"But I didn't get to—," I began, like a disappointed child.

"We've got to go—"

"Alexander," Jameson called as he rapped against the bedroom door. "I'm going to retire for the evening and I'd like to say good night to Miss Raven," the butler said.

Alexander grabbed my shoes, blew out the candles, and locked the closet.

"We'll be right there," Alexander called back as I pulled on my boots and laced them.

If Jameson had arrived a few minutes later, I would have known what it was like to retire for eternity.

That night, as I rested in my own bed—a spacious double bed, with no walls or lids—I wondered what it would have been like to have lain in Alexander's closed coffin. Total darkness, without so much as a faint streetlight shining in.

I imagined how hard it must have been for Alexander to let someone, anyone—even me—into his darkened world behind the secret attic door. I smiled, knowing what I must mean to him to be the one he shared it with.

As I closed my eyes, I imagined my true love spending his sunlit hours alone in his coffin, inside the confines of a hidden closet, buried away from any sources of life—the sounds of birds, rainfall, or people. The world that Alexander thought was so cold, dark, and lonely was just that. My heart broke and began to shatter into a million tiny pieces. Tears began to well up in my eyes, thinking while I was at school, surrounded by students and teachers, that the love of my life was locked away, alone in the dark. There was no one to touch, say sweet dreams to, kiss or squeeze. I wondered if the world I'd been romanticizing for so long—his world—as Alexander had often told me, wasn't so romantic after all.

The town of Dullsville returned to normal. Students at Dullsville High gossiped about the Graveyard Gala and the sickly siblings from Romania—"Were they really ghosts, vampires, or just goths like Raven?" There were no more sightings of Dullsville's motley twins at soccer games, Hatsy's Diner, or graveyards. School talk quickly turned to upcoming exams and proms.

Trevor, with his renewed popularity, was back to scoring on and off the soccer field. My stomach knotted, knowing he was even more popular than he had been before.

However, I did notice a slight change in my nemesis's behavior toward me. He didn't invite me to parties, drive me to school, or offer to carry my books, but I'd occasionally catch him staring at me. Once he signaled for Becky and me to cut ahead of him in the lunch line. When I dropped my English folder in the hallway, I was amazed when he said, "You dropped your notebook, Raven," instead of referring to me as "Monster Girl."

I was most surprised, though, when he cornered me at the drinking fountain one day and said, "I wonder what would have happened if it had been my family who moved into the Mansion instead of the Sterlings."

"Then Alexander would be talking to me right now instead of you," I said, and walked away.

I couldn't resist egging on my flirty nemesis. I guess the soccer snob had gotten a taste of his own medicine—he knew what it was like not to be accepted. I'd let him soak it in a little longer.

Becky and I made a point of hanging out more—including a weekly after-school "girls only" shake snack at Hatsy's—while she and Matt continued dating.

The spring sun baked my pale skin and I was only comforted when the sun set and I could see Alexander again. During the evenings, Alexander and I snuck back into Dullsville's cemetery with garbage bags and picked up cans and bottles until we were exhausted. We discovered the coffins and nails and other gothic memorabilia were mysteriously removed from Henry's treehouse, presumably by Jagger as he and Luna fled Dullsville.

The following weekend Henry and his parents showed their appreciation for taking care of Henry. They planned a small backyard barbecue party for the Madison family and asked us to invite a few of our friends.

The backyard smelled of grilled hot dogs and hamburgers, fresh baked buns, and all the dill pickles one could eat. The sky was clear, showcasing a million twinkling stars overhead. Henry and Billy Boy were attempting dives in the heated pool. Henry's mother was giving my mom a grand tour of their five-bedroom house. His father and my dad were practicing golf swings in the backyard. Nina, the housekeeper, was serving refreshments to Ruby and Jameson at a picnic table. The butler seemed grateful to have someone else wait on him for a change. Matt and Becky were eating s'mores and hanging by the flower garden.

Alexander and I sat together on a backyard swing. "This is like a dream come true," Alexander said as we gently swung back and forth. "We can finally just focus on us now. Continue the traditional 'Boy meets girl, girl falls for boy, boy turns out to be a vampire' story."

I laughed, and Alexander squeezed my hand. I could tell he was as relieved as I was to finally have Jagger and Luna gone from Dullsville.

"I'm going to miss my life as a vampire," I confessed softly. "I was really getting used to it. Hiding from the daylight, finding adventure in the moonlight. Hanging out with a vampiress. I have to admit that there is a tiny part of me that is going to miss Luna, maybe because she has a life I'd always dreamed of, or maybe because she accepted me. And there's a slight part of me that will think fondly of Jagger—not his vengeful side, but his passion for who he is—a vampire."

"It's okay to have mixed feelings for them," Alexander assured me. "They were unlike anyone you'd ever known before. That's how I feel about you."

"I felt like I had found a group where I finally fit in—mortal or not."

"That's how I feel when I'm with you. We really do belong together," Alexander said, his lonely eyes a little less lonely. "No matter where we are."

Then I remembered how isolated I felt when we were apart. Even though his darkened world may not have been as romantic as I'd imagined, how bad could it be if we were in it, together?

"Maybe sometime soon we can make my dream more permanent . . . ," I suggested. It was fun to have vampires believe I was one of them. Now I just have to convince a third. But then I wondered if Jagger was right when he said I was more like a vampire than Alexander was. If I were turned into a vampire, would I be the kind of vampire Alexander was—or the kind that Jagger and Luna were?

I looked at Alexander, waiting for his response.

Billy Boy climbed out of the pool. He ran over to me and shook his wet hair at me like a soaked dog.

"Get off, you creep!" I shouted, covering myself from the spray.

My brother laughed, and I noticed even Alexander chuckling as he wiped water off his pale arm. Billy Boy ran over to the lounge chair where his stuff lay before I could wring his neck.

"Maybe we can sleep out in the treehouse now that your parents are back," Billy Boy said to Henry as he grabbed his towel.

"Yeah," he said, climbing out of the pool. "I have to get it cleaned up before that dude comes over to look at it."

"Is someone planning to buy your treehouse?" I teased.

"Just doing a report on it," Billy Boy said proudly. "Henry and I overheard this dude at the library asking the librarian for info on area treehouses. Naturally Henry has the coolest one, so I had to tell him about it."

"Well, you should be careful inviting strangers over," I warned, sounding like my mother.

"He's not dangerous," Billy said. "He's only eleven and skinnier than I am."

"But he is kind of strange," Henry admitted.

Billy Boy laughed as he toweled off his hair. "He is

major strange—looks like he should be your brother instead of me," Billy Boy teased. "Pale skin, pierced ears, black fingernails."

I stopped the swing. "Does this kid have a name?"

Billy Boy nodded.

"What is it?" I demanded in his face.

"It'll cost you," he said.

"It will cost you more if you don't tell me," I said, taking his towel, threatening to snap it at his feet.

"Fine," he said through gritted teeth. "It's Valentine." He yanked back his towel. "His name is Valentine Maxwell."

Valentine? That was the name of Luna's younger brother. An eleven-year-old vampire.

I looked at Alexander, who gave me a knowing glance.

I froze. My blood raced. My heart stopped.

Oh. My. Goth. It was one thing to have met a nefarious vengeful teen vampire, then to encounter the wrath of his newly turned twin sister, and have them turn my world upside down. It was quite another to have a preteen vampire now lurking and hanging out in the same library and treehouse as my younger sibling.

I couldn't even fathom an eleven-year-old vampire— his motives, what he hungered for, what powers he might possess.

If Jagger and Luna had disappeared on the night of the Graveyard Gala, what was their younger vampire brother, Valentine, doing in Dullsville?

I knew one thing—I'd have to find out.

Acknowledgments

With my utmost gratitude I would like to thank the following fabulous people:

Katherine Tegen, my phenomenal editor, for making the *Vampire Kisses* series possible. Your expertise, friendship, humor, and always insightful direction have enhanced my life and my work. Thanks for making my dreams come true!

Ellen Levine, my extraordinary agent, for your amazing advice and talent and for being an inspiration in guiding my career.

Julie Hittman at HarperCollins, for your wonderful suggestions, help, and friendship.

My brother, Mark Schreiber, for being my mentor and for helping me become the writer I am today.

My brother, Ben Schreiber, for your endless enthusiasm and support.

And Eddie Lerer, for being my Alexander and taking me out of Dullsville.

READ ON FOR A PEEK AT THE FOURTH BOOK IN THE VAMPIRE KISSES SERIES:

Dance with a Vampire

I awoke from a deadly slumber entombed in Alexander's coffin.

Since arriving at the Mansion shortly before Sunday morning's sunrise, I'd been lying next to my vampire boyfriend, Alexander Sterling, as he slept the weekend sunlit hours away, hidden in the closet of his attic room.

This was a dream come true. My first real taste—or in this case, bite—of the vampire lifestyle.

We nestled in my true love's bed—a claustrophobic black wooden casket. I was as blind as any bat; we could have been buried in the deepest recesses of a long-forgotten cemetery. Encased in our compacted quarters, I could easily touch the closed lid above me and brush my elbow against the side wall. The sweet scents of pine and cedar floated around me like incense. I couldn't see anything, not even my own black-fingernailed hand. No sounds were audible from outside the coffin. Not a siren, a bird,

1

or the howling wind. I even lost track of time. I felt like we were the only two people in the world—that nothing existed outside these confining coffin walls.

Blanketed by darkness and a soft-as-a-spider's-web goose-feathered duvet, I was enveloped in Alexander's arctic white arms, my head gently resting against his chest. I felt his warm breath against my cheek. I imagined his deadly pale lids covering his chocolate brown eyes. I playfully fingered his velvet lips and brushed my fingertips over his perfect teeth until I felt one as sharp as a knife.

I tasted my finger for blood. Unfortunately, there was none.

I was so close to being part of Alexander's world— forever.

Or was I?

Though it was Sunday and I was exhausted from having spent the past few weeks protecting my nemesis, Trevor Mitchell, from the fangs of twin vampires, Jagger and Luna Maxwell, I was restless. I couldn't change my sleeping pattern from night to day.

Cuddling close to Alexander and sharing his world, I wanted nothing more than to spend our time kissing, playing, and talking.

But as he slept tranquilly, I could only think of one thing: A preteen vampire had descended upon Dullsville. And his name was Valentine.

The younger brother of the nefarious Nosferatu twins had arisen from his own petite coffin a few days before from somewhere in the vampire world and had been spotted in Dullsville by my brother and his nerd-mate, Henry.

I could only presume what Valentine looked like based on my brother's description: pale skin, pierced ears, black fingernails. I imagined a smaller version of Jagger—cryptic, gaunt, ghastly. How cruel it was that Jagger's sibling was just like him, and mine the polar opposite of me. If only I had been blessed with a ghoulish little brother. We'd have spent our childhood chasing ghosts in Dullsville's cemetery, searching Oakley Woods for creepy spiders, and playing hide-and-shriek in our basement. Instead, I grew up with a brother who'd prefer to dissect square roots alone rather than dissect gummi worms together.

I wondered why Valentine suddenly showed up in the conservative town of Dullsville, far away from his Romanian homeland. Now that Alexander and I were free from the older Maxwell siblings, I'd set forth on a new mission—finding out the eleven-year-old Valentine's whereabouts and motives and keeping him from Billy Boy before it was too late. But during the sunlight hours, my brother and Dullsville were in no danger, so my mind strayed back to the only vampire I felt secure with.

As Alexander and I lay in the dark, entombed and entwined, I stroked his silky black hair.

There was no place for me in the daylight without him. I had accepted the dangers Alexander had so warned me about, but I couldn't spend an eternity in the scorching sun minus my true love. Didn't Alexander know how easily I could adapt to his world, sleeping together in our cozy casket, flying together in the night sky, living in the dusty old Mansion? I wondered what type of vampire I'd be: A gentle dreamer like Alexander or a bloodthirsty

3

menace like Jagger? Either way, since Jagger and Luna had departed from Dullsville, Alexander and I finally had a chance to share our mortal and immortal worlds. However, there could be an obstacle in my way, now that Valentine was in town.

Alexander stirred. He, too, couldn't sleep.

"You're awake," he whispered sweetly. "I'm sure it must be hard for you to adjust your sleep schedule."

I didn't want to admit that I couldn't be the perfect vampiress.

"I can't rest with you so close to me. I feel more alive than ever," I said.

My fingers felt around his smooth face and found his soft lips. I leaned in to kiss him, but my nose accidentally bumped into his.

"I'm sorry," I said with a giggle.

"One of the drawbacks of dating a mortal," he teased, a smile in his voice. "But it's worth it."